To Michael and

THANKS So much Roc Coming,

Best Wishes,

Kip Vander Hyde

MY FATHER'S KEEPER

MY FATHER'S KEEPER

A NOVEL

KIP VANDER HYDE

SEA LARK PRESS
GRAND RAPIDS, MICHIGAN

My Father's Keeper

Maps by Stephanie Milanowski

ISBN 0-9772451-0-1

MANUFACTURED IN THE UNITED STATES OF AMERICA

Book design by Stephanie Milanowski

I dedicate this book to my dear children, Taylor, Tripp, Isabel, and Olivia. Without you, it would have been impossible to write of the inherent love between a father and his child.

I especially wish to acknowledge Cathy, my wife, who has undyingly supported my dream even as our bank accounts dwindled and I made a nuisance of myself around the house.

Acknowledgments

I humbly and gratefully acknowledge the assistance rendered by various individuals during my research. Though it is fiction, significant parts of the story are based on fact and many characters that appear are historically known. I would like to thank former C Company Marines, Wilbur Bewley, Bill Finnegan and last, but certainly not least, my friend, John Joseph, of Street, Maryland. John graciously welcomed me into his home on two occasions to discuss what it was like to be a young Marine during the campaign on Guadalcanal. Our first session went six full hours without so much as a potty break. John is a remarkable man. His memory is nearly flawless—a treasure, of course, for any writer. His insights were invaluable and, above all, he is simply a good guy. I would also like to thank two other World War II vets, who though they did not fight in the Pacific theatre, gave me remarkable insights into the lives of those of their generation both prior to, and during the war. My pals, Babe Heffron and Bill Guarnere, both from south Philly and former 101st Airborne, 506th PIR troopers and members of the legendary defenders of Bastonge during the Battle of the Bulge. Thank you for your time and friendship, and above all, your service to our country.

I would like to also acknowledge the important contributions from Peter Flahavin of Melbourne, Australia, Nino Ricci of Toronto and Robert W. Harrison, M.D. of Grand Rapids, a former Navy corpsman. Peter has an abiding passion for the campaign on Guadalcanal and his skills as an historian have been of great assistance. Nino is

Acknowledgments

a successfully published novelist and was a great adviser in the intricacies of crafting a novel. Dr. Harrison's remarkable memory of World War II medical procedures and equipment was extremely helpful whilst writing passages involving care of the ill or wounded.

Lastly, I would like to thank my mother for her relentless encouragement and support during this project. As well, though he has been gone for many years, I am still grateful for, and inspired by, the example my father embodied as a good and honorable man.

*"We make a living by what we get,
we make a life by what we give"*.

Sir Winston Churchill
(1875–1964)

Prologue

The old man sat with his middle-aged son at a table in the smoky bar, sipping papaya juice, clutching a battered cardboard bound book in one hand and fingering a gold band in his coat pocket with the other. His simple brown linen suit was colored by a bright pinkish-white hibiscus carnation pinned to his lapel. The thin loose curls of his hair were a dull shade of silver. His time worn skin was leathery, a light shade of caramel. His hands, so deft and steady in earlier years, now nervously tinkled the ice in his glass. The bar at the Point Cruz Yacht Club in Honiara, on the island of Guadalcanal, was simple and largely unadorned. Every portal—the doors and large windows—was screened but open to the elements, allowing the unique, slightly unpleasant aromas of the southwest Pacific island to permeate the room. Nevertheless, the large American contingent in the bar was loudly celebrating; telling old stories and occasionally clapping each other on the back. Others, seated at tables, were more reserved, talking quietly about old memories; old wounds that still festered. The old man curiously observed the boisterous group in the bar. However, there was one American in particular who held him in thrall. He was younger than most. His slightly thinning hair was wavy and brown, the lower portions graying. He was at least six feet tall and his eyes were pale green. He looked on the older men in the group with something close to adoration. The young American was energetically engaged with the rest of the group, buying round after round and talking earnestly with the older gentlemen. The old man smiled warmly as he watched this American interact with the group. The young man was the reason he had journeyed to the island; the reason he was clutching the old battered book. He and his son were facing a very long, tiring journey in the morning. The trip would be made more difficult by a brief stop-over in Manila. So, with his son's urging, he took one last long look at the American before retiring. With the help of his son he slowly rose to his feet. As he shuffled out of the bar, tears spilled from his eyes.

1

Hill 73 on Skyline Ridge, Guadalcanal. It was early morning, August 7, 2002. A grizzled old Marine, slightly stooped and sporting a thick mane of silver hair, was speaking to the crowd gathered for the 60th anniversary of the U.S. Marine Corps landings on the island during the early days of World War II. The man's name was Anthony Scozzolari, 'Scooz' he said his old Marine buddies called him. The crowd, gathered around the podium positioned in front of a large granite memorial, was a mixture of elderly veterans, younger family members and local islanders. As Scooz regaled the crowd with warm, often humorous tales of Marine buddies, a lone American was struggling to concentrate on the man's words.

The air of the Southwest Pacific, already hot and wet, exaggerated the misery of Jack Macmillan's throbbing hangover. The heat sucked the sweat from his pores and gauzed his mouth as he worked to inhale air into his lungs. The previous night, he'd waited until the last veteran had left the bar before leaving it himself. Now he was regretting it. The greasy eggs and black coffee he'd had for breakfast in hopes of settling his stomach, had done the opposite. Still, Jack tried his hardest to respectfully listen to the man, for to him World War II combat veterans were larger-than-life figures, historical giants. They had been since he was a young boy and had immersed himself in the history of the war. The war was still his abiding passion. His visit to Guadalcanal to tour the old battle sites and honor those who had fought there had an added meaning for him. His deceased father, Tom, had served with the Navy on the island at some point during the war. As his father had never talked about his experiences, Jack had assumed there wasn't much to tell, so he was curious to see what his father had seen; perhaps even in some way find a clue as to when he'd been on the island and what he'd experienced there. To his disappointment, but not to his surprise, none of the old revelers in the bar could recall a Tom Macmillan. This only increased his skepticism regarding the timing of his father's service on the island.

Jack's attention was drawn back to Mr. Scozzolari as he related another amusing, affectionately delivered story about one of his former comrades. As he spoke, his head was in constant motion, his eyes scanning the audience. "You see, the war wasn't all fun and games and much of the time we were bored silly. So one day one of the fellas gets the bright idea that to pass some time, 'cause unlike the movies would have you believe, we were bored stiff most of the time, he's going to ride a croc down on the bank of the Tenaru!" As a titter of laughter arose from the crowd, Scozzolari's eyes suddenly came to rest on Jack. When they did he hesitated, then stammered, "Well . . . this . . . uh . . . this . . . uh . . . I . . . uh." Strangely, as he stumbled on his words he squinted hard at Jack. For several moments he quit talking altogether and just stared at him.

Then, he slowly turned away and continued his remarks. He kept glancing back at Jack as he spoke, a quizzical look on his face. Mr. Scozzolari's stare unnerved Jack and he was perplexed by the old Marine's strange reaction upon laying eyes on him. He decided he'd introduce himself when the ceremony was over and try to find out what the old man thought he saw. Jack looked down briefly, feeling dizzy from the hangover and heat. His head snapped back toward the old man when he heard him say, "So anyhow, our corpsman, Macmillan was his name . . ." This time both stared intensely at each other and Mr. Scozzolari once again stumbled on his words. Moments later he regained his composure and finished the story. "Uh . . . anyhow, as Macmillan patched the Marines' hand up, he

4

told him that it's not a good idea to try and ride a croc on account they don't seem to have a sense of humor such as horses and camels and the like." In a more somber tone he said, "I'm sorry to say that the croc cowboy was killed later in the war on Peleliu." Jack pondered the story for a moment, then decided the corpsman's name was likely a coincidence. It was not an uncommon name. After all, he thought, if his father had been a combat corpsman, he would have at least told him this fact. All there really was as testimony to his presence on the island was a small, jagged rock he carried with him everywhere. He had mumbled once that it was a souvenir he picked up on Guadalcanal, but that was it. When Jack was young and would ask his father about his service, he would only say that 'it was boring' and 'he couldn't remember much.' That was all Jack knew.

After several more speakers, the Royal Solomon's Band played a slow rendition of "Taps." As they did so, five veterans, all sporting World War II veteran caps stuck randomly with unit pendants, unfurled a large American flag. The solemn flag raising marked the end of the ceremony. As the flag crept up the pole, the crowd rose and followed its ascent, craning their necks skyward. The sudden move out of his chair, combined with the bending of his neck, caused a gag reflex to trigger in Jack's throat. He swallowed quickly several times, as saliva flooded the back of his mouth. Pale, with sweat streaming down his face and matting his hair, a sense of dread and near panic swept over him. Finally, after struggling against the swell, he shuffled quickly to the back of the crowd, leaned over a stone wall and just as the flag reached its apex, loudly vomited up his coffee stained breakfast. As he continued to wretch, several local people approached cautiously, inquiring whether Jack needed help. Jack, his head still down, urgently waved them away. He swore he could hear his violent wretches echoing off the walls of the memorial. When he was finished he rose, wiped his mouth and chin, and glanced ashamedly at the disassembling crowd. Some of the younger family members of the veterans, particularly the females, looked at him in disgust. He saw several of the old Marines from the bar smirking at him. One, a man from Maryland whom he'd shared several martinis with shouted, "Hey, young fella! I told you not to mix bourbon and gin . . . gets you every time!" This brought forth a burst of laughter from the other veterans.

Jack's humiliation was utter and complete. He managed a sheepish smile. His singular focus though was to make as quick and discreet a getaway as possible. Instead of seeking out Mr. Scozzolari, Jack hurried toward his rented jeep and sped off Hill 73. He was not only embarrassed but felt he'd almost emasculated himself in front of his heroes. He could not face them, not for a while at least. Instead of heading back to the hotel, he drove straight to a point on the beach between Pt. Cruz and the Matanikau River to explore an old battle site. All the way to the site he encouraged himself, "Forget about it, buddy, it could've happened to anybody. Hell, the old coots probably got such a kick out of it you'll be some sort of hero to them." After much of this self-encouragement he decided he'd recovered enough of his dignity to introduce himself to Mr. Scozzolari upon his return to the hotel.

He pulled up at the old battle site, or more accurately, massacre site. Several days after the landings in 1942, an ill conceived patrol headed by Lt. Colonel Frank Goettge, had been slaughtered here by Japanese Naval troops. Jack was anxious to see the spot where the young Marines died; a spot that had haunted his imagination for years. He was disappointed to find the once desolate beach now heavily populated with homes and people. It was hard to imagine the doomed patrol coming ashore at nightfall and meeting their fate from rifles and machine guns hidden in the dense, deserted jungle. Nevertheless, he knelt on the beach and reflected for a moment as he often had at other WWII battle sites and cemeteries; silently thanking the long-dead youngsters for their sacrifice and lamenting that he could not have been there to help or to have prevented their untimely deaths. Before he'd sold the family business and retired, his job had often taken him to Europe and Asia, where in his spare time he'd visit World War II battle sites and cemeteries. He'd toured more than a dozen battlefields and numerous American cemeteries throughout the European and Pacific theatres. At each location, it had been his practice to give thanks along with his traditional lament. After scanning the length of the beach one last time, he walked slowly to his jeep and drove back to the hotel.

He parked the jeep and took a deep breath as he prepared to face those who had witnessed his wretched performance on the hill. Upon entering the lobby, he was greatly relieved to see it was deserted. He suddenly recalled that the veterans and their families were taking a tour of Gifu and would not be back until dinnertime. By then Jack would be gone for the night. He was disappointed that the mystery Mr. Scozzolari presented would have to wait until the next morning, but there was nothing to be done for it.

After two stomach-settling gin and tonics and a club sandwich for lunch, he prepared for the adventure he'd been planning since he first decided to travel to the island. He intended to camp out that night on the banks of the Tenaru River. It was actually Alligator Creek, but the early Marine Corps crude reconnaissance maps had misidentified it as the Tenaru, a steadily flowing river farther to the east. For several decades after the war, historians had also identified the stagnant tidal stream by the Marine's designation, until closer investigation uncovered its true identity. Jack though, having read about the stream so often as a youth, refused to think of it as anything other than the Tenaru. It was the name of the first major land action on the island, a decisive American victory, and it was the name that the Marine veterans of the violent struggle would forever remember. Alligator Creek seemed too conventional, too contrived to do justice to the fight he had fought in his imagination for so many years. In his mind it was the Battle of the Tenaru, regardless of what historians had, in his opinion, annoyingly uncovered years after the conflict. On his way to the Tenaru, he planned to make a brief detour to Bloody Ridge as the drama-obsessed press referred to it, or more appropriately, Edson's Ridge, the Marine Corps' preferred designation, named after the larger than life commander during the ferocious fight. It had been a horrific two-night battle, fought between the Japanese and the Marine Raiders and parachutists five weeks after the Marines had landed.

His ultimate destination was very near the mouth of the Tenaru. For years, Jack had fantasized what it must have been like for the young American Marines as they waited in the dark, terrifying jungle for the Japanese to attack. Initially he'd planned to dig a trench and live much as the Marines had. However, as the time for his departure to the island drew nearer, the idea seemed less appealing. He worried about the rats and lizards that infested parts of the island. He also worried about coping with the possibility of the oft tropical downpours. So, he'd purchased a state of the art Gore-Tex pup tent from an upscale outfitter in Grand Rapids and hauled it with him. After lunch, he went to the marina at Point Cruz and procured a Coleman lantern and a dark green can of Deep Woods Off. For sustenance, two tins of tuna, a sleeve of crackers, and a quart of Jim Beam. The tuna and crackers, he believed, would best replicate the meager and simple rations the Marines endured during the campaign. They had no access to bourbon to smooth the terrifying, miserable jungle nights. But for Jack, it was a comfort he simply couldn't be without. It was his sleeping pill in the most comfortable of settings, and had been for the last three years, commencing shortly after his father had died.

Back at his hotel, Jack packed the foodstuffs and liquor in his large, aluminum braced backpack. Then, he reverentially picked up a dog-eared, tattered copy of a book he'd purchased when he was eight years old. It was the first book he'd read about the Guadalcanal campaign, in fact the first book he'd read regarding World War II. Richard Tregaskis, the author, had been with the Marines from the moment they landed. His wartime account of the early days of the campaign had been widely read at the time of its publication, as the book presented the Marine's bravery, competence, and tenuous position in the best possible light, giving hope to an American public desperate for proof that their forces could handle the seemingly invincible Japanese military. The book told a glorious tale of his fellow countrymen, bravely battling a barely human enemy . . . they, given to extreme treachery and brutality, with little, if any mercy. This was the book Jack wanted with him as he explored the site of the first battle. A book written in real time as the writer experienced the events. He smiled as he gently folded the book into a pouch on the back of his pack, stuffing newspaper on each side of it. As jingoistic and rose-colored as the book may have been, Jack decided Tregaskis was the best man to give him his tour of the Tenaru.

Leaving the rest of his belongings at the hotel, he took his daily doses of Prozac and Nexium, then loaded the jeep and set off for Edson's Ridge. Wearing an Orvis fishing vest over a white T-shirt, L.L. Bean boondockers, and cargo pants, and a blue Rancho San Marcos Golf Club baseball cap, he sped out of Honiara, skirting the south end of the runway at Henderson International Airport. He turned southeast toward the ridge, nearly a mile from the airport. Not knowing what challenges may arise in the night jungle, before he left Grand Rapids, he'd purchased a wicked looking, Cordura sheathed, Buck Alpha Hunter hunting knife off the internet. It was strapped securely to his Bean cargos and prodded his thigh reassuringly each time he braked. He quickly crested the north slope of the ridge and was immediately disappointed to see the locals had built a village on its summit. The shacks and tangles of long, thick grass conspired to hide any traces that might be left of the horrible battle. He drove to the areas where he estimated General Archer Vandegrift and Colonel Merritt Edson had located their command posts. Near a small, rocky outcropping roughly in the center of the ridge, he got out of the jeep and looked south into the jungle from whence the screaming, massed Japanese attacks had come. The Marines held the ridge until the Japanese force had spent itself, but just barely. Jack tried to imagine the horror, the sounds of battle and the specter of dying or dismembered young men. He couldn't of course. Nothing in his life could have remotely given him an idea of the hell it was on the ridge those two nights so long ago. He walked to a point twenty yards from the outcropping and knelt in a rocky clearing. One large rock protruded from the center of the clearing and Jack noted that its shape bore a remarkable likeness to the rock of Gibraltar. He picked up a small stone that looked much like the one his father had carried with him all his life. "Were you up on this ridge old man?" he said out loud. After a pause he muttered, "I don't think so." He threw the rock against the Gibraltar look-a-like, and watched it explode in pieces. After surveying the area for another few minutes, he gave his traditional closing and drove off the ridge. He reached into his backpack propped on the seat next to him and pulled out the bottle of bourbon. Holding the wheel and the bottle at the same time, he managed to twist off the ribbed, plastic cap and took a deep swig.

He drove north, roughly paralleling the airport runway. The last two hundred yards were cross country. The sensation of grinding the stripped down jeep through the underbrush was very satisfying and gave him a sense of living rugged and free. "Just wait 'til I get back to the club and tell the boys about this!" he said out loud. The rough track ended one hundred yards from the mouth of the river. To his right he caught his first glimpse of the Tenaru. He sat staring at the fetid water in awe. After several minutes he prudently began to set up camp 15 yards from the waterline. Before starting his tour of the battlefield, he doused himself with mosquito repellant, then struggled to set up his tent.

Never having been particularly handy, he cursed loudly while trying to erect the small shelter. "Fucking goddamn sons-of-bitches! Why can't they ever just make something simple? You gotta be fucking Einstein to figure out how to put this sort of shit together!" Finally, he was able to get the better of the tent. He then set out for the sandbar at the mouth of the Tenaru. In one hand he held the lantern, in the other, the quart of Jim Beam. As he walked toward the sandbar he noted that the area surrounding the creek was very different than it had been described by Tregaskis. The Lever Brothers groves and their orderly rows of coconut trees were gone. The landscape was dominated by tall grass, clumps of jungle undergrowth, flat, bushy trees, and the occasional palm. The river itself was much as it had been described, still and foul. The sand-

10

bar at its mouth prevented any real flow, except during the rainy season and very high tides, and the river was, in reality, a sort of natural, putrid reservoir.

He attempted to estimate where an abandoned amphibian tractor had been located in the creek during the battle. A Japanese machine gun crew had snuck into the tractor and had played havoc with the Marines on the opposite creek bank. After contemplating, and unsuccessfully trying to conjure up the sights and sounds of the battle, he trudged to the mouth of the river and looked out over Ironbottom Sound, so named for the dozens of warships lying on its bottom. He could see Florida Island on the southern horizon, sheltering the smaller islands of Tulagi, Gavutu, and Tanambogo, the sites of bitter battles fought by Marine raiders and parachutists before the Marines were fully engaged on Guadalcanal. To the southwest he saw Savo Island, its name made famous for a deadly naval engagement fought in its waters early in the morning of August 9, 1942. It was the worst defeat in open waters that the U.S. Navy would ever suffer. He stood mesmerized, looking at the island and its surrounding waters, semi-consciously reciting the names of some of the lost ships, "*Vincennes, Astoria, Quincy, Canberra . . .* over a thousand dead . . . I'm sorry guys."

He turned away from the sea after a few minutes. Searching the scrub just off the beach he found the weathered, overgrown obelisk that marked the spot where Private Al Schmid from Philadelphia continued to fire his machine gun at the attacking mass of Japanese troops, even though he'd been permanently blinded by grenade fragments. Jack knelt by the obelisk and remembered that there were two other members of the gun crew. One was killed instantly and the other wounded badly. It was then that Schmid took control of the gun and suffered the permanently blinding wounds to his eyes, yet continued to fire under the direction of his wounded buddy. Jack stroked the obelisk, trying hard to get a sense of the macabre violence that had occurred right where he was kneeling, and to somehow give comfort to those who had died. He poured a few drops of liquor from his bottle onto the ground, symbolically mixing it with the blood of the dead and wounded Marines, then took a swig from the bottle. He whispered his traditional thanks and lament, then rose and walked toward the jungle from whence the Japanese attacked.

He walked slowly out onto the sandbar. It didn't look at all sinister, and in fact, bright green plants, looking like land based lily pads, adorned the sandbar where hundreds of young Japanese soldiers were ripped apart by American rifle and machine gun fire, and 37 millimeter canister shot. He scratched a booted toe into the gray sand, recalling the appalling pictures of the dead Japanese the morning after the battle, half buried by the shifting tidal sands. He stared into the jungle on the other side of the creek where the Japanese survivors were cornered, then annihilated, the day after the attack. He issued none of his normal regrets for the dead Japanese, but did feel a brief stab of sympathy for them when pondering the stupefying idiocy displayed by the Japanese leaders who sent them to their violent and completely wasted deaths. The thoughts passed quickly though and he casually walked off the sandbar without a second thought. He strolled east toward Red Beach where the Marines had landed on August 7, 1942. Halfway to the landing beach, he noticed it was growing dark rapidly. The sand and heavy air had conspired to quickly fatigue him as well. He kneeled, lit the lantern and walked wearily back to his campsite. Somewhat to his chagrin, he felt very relieved when he arrived back at camp; the island was darker, more eerie than he'd imagined. The last thing he wanted was to be lost in the jungle at night. "This sure ain't St. Kitts, buddy," he said to himself.

After dialing the lantern to high and giving himself another coat of mosquito repellant, he decided to have his dinner on the riverbank. Knowing the jungle nights could be chilly, and as a further guard against mosquitoes, he pulled a gray sweatshirt over his fishing vest. The word MICHIGAN was stenciled in dark blue on the front. He sat down and took a deep, burning gulp of bourbon. After several more swigs, the warm, comforting feeling the alcohol gave him began to settle in. Still though, when he looked to the other side of the creek, a shiver went up his spine as he imagined the Japanese in the pitch black, massing for attack just yards away. He couldn't conceive the terror the young Marines must have felt. He tried hard to imagine the sounds and smells of the battle, but couldn't conjure them up. It was too quiet, too devoid of obvious human presence. His mind drifted from the battle to his immediate surroundings. The lantern cast an eerie golden glow on the surrounding vegetation and waters of the creek. Instead of trying to hear the jungle noises of the past, he listened in the present. Native birds screeched and small creatures rustled the tall grass around him. His head jerked in the direction of each sound. He gulped several mouthfuls of bourbon, steeling himself. Then a splash several yards upstream, unnerved him. He retreated to his tent, zipping it tightly; the bright light of the lantern created a soothing blue cocoon. There he ate his tuna and crackers, pretending they were C-rations, the meager, but chemical laced and calorie-loaded canned meals the Marines consumed during the war. He lit a cigarette from the pack of Marlboros he'd picked up at the marina. He only smoked when he was drinking; he couldn't abide the taste at any other time. With his knees pulled up and bound by his arms, he slowly puffed on his cigarette and took frequent pulls off the bottle of whiskey. He wondered what Laura and his kids, Joey 8, and Grace, almost 5, were doing back in Grand Rapids. He adored his children; loved them more than he ever thought possible. He ached thinking of them, but after he'd retired he'd grown accustomed to being away from them for periods of time: nighttime society functions, Vegas junkets and weeklong trips with his pals to exotic golfing meccas. So, safe in his tent now and increasingly drunk, it was easy to divert his mind back to 1942 and the battle of the Tenaru. He thought about Mr. Scozzolari and their strange long distance encounter at that morning's ceremony. "Gotta track him down in the morning," he drunkenly mumbled. "Gotta find out what the fuck all that was about."

Only a third of the whiskey was left. "You gotta get out there, buddy," he exhorted himself. "What would the goddamn Marines think of you, you dummy? Nothin' to hurt you out there, bud." He struggled with the zipper of the tent, finally opening it. Warily, he stuck his head out and looked toward the mouth of the creek. A quarter-moon provided enough light for him to just make out the sandbar. Emboldened by the whiskey, he slurred, "Damn it, I'm gonna go see what it looked like from Schmid's position in the dark." He rose to his feet with difficulty and staggered toward the mouth of the creek, drinking from the bottle as he went. When he reached the area of Schmid's position, he clumsily dropped to his knees and started to search for the obelisk.

After several minutes of scrabbling about, his forehead collided with the monument. "Christ!" he blurted. Rubbing his head, he rolled over and looked across the sandbar, picturing screaming hordes of Japanese charging toward him. "Banzai! Banzai!" he imagined them screaming. After a pause, he pulled his golf cap low over his eyes, pretending it to be a GI steel pot. Like a child playing war in his back yard, he thrust his arms straight out and clenched both fists as though he were holding the grips of a .30 caliber, water-cooled machine gun. "Motherfuckers!" he screeched. He depressed his thumbs on imaginary triggers and mimicked gunfire in a rapid staccato, "di,di,di,di,di,di,di,di,di,di,di,di,di!" He'd pause, then fire the fantasy weapon again. In his drunkenness, he could almost see the hordes of khaki-clad, bill capped Japanese soldiers attacking, but he felt little. After several minutes of fighting the imaginary battle, he rolled, exhausted, onto his back. He lit a cigarette and swigged the last few ounces of whiskey remaining in the bottle. The stars above him were brilliant and seemed to cover the sky completely as he sucked deeply for air. The twinkling kaleidoscope suddenly began to spin and tumble and Jack knew he had to get to his feet if he were to make it back to camp. There was one more thing he wanted to do though. He got up, flung the empty bottle into Ironbottom Sound, and staggered the short distance to the other side of the sandbar.

He did not hate the Japanese, the Japanese then or now, but was completely ambivalent toward them and their fate that August night in 1942. He simply wanted to see what it must have been like for them, charging across the sandbar into the deadly fire of the Marines. After stumbling about for several moments, trying to secure his balance, he flicked his Marlboro high into the air. The tiny ember emitted dim orange sparks; Jack imagined them to be products of a Marine flair, anticipating the charge. Digging his boots in the sand, he screamed, "Totsugeki!" Then, after moving several yards, yelled, "Banzai! You die Marines!" He staggered halfway across the sandbar, than started to lose his balance. Like most drunks, his body was slowly being pulled in a direction of which he had no real sense. Only slightly aware that he had lost directional control, he continued to stumble off course, directly toward the headwaters of the Tenaru. The down slope of the sandbar leading to the water acted as a spring board, and he was flung headlong into the foul, wet darkness. After a brief pause, a vague panic set in, and he began flailing violently. His mock battle from Schmid's position and his charge across the sandbar had left him weary as it was. His fight against the creek and water soaked garments and boots, further sapped his reserves of energy. The darkness and his terror made him unsure of his proximity to the shore. Slowly, he began to sink into the murky water.

In spite of his panic, Jack realized his clothes were weighing him down, dragging him toward the bottom of the creek. He tore off his sweatshirt first, then his fishing vest. Sinking still, he moved to his trousers, unbuckled his belt and ripped away the button that bound the fabric to his waist. As he peeled the pants downward, his sense of winning the fight with the river was shattered by a sudden realization. "The boots, the fucking boots!" his mind screamed. His lungs ached, desperate for air. Curling into the fetal position, he pulled violently on his boots. The first wrenched off as he settled into the silky slime of the creek bed. He went to work on the second as his energy and will began to dissolve.

Jack's eyes bulged. The wearying struggle and his oxygen-starved bloodstream combined to create a drugged, slow motion effect on his senses and movements. As a result, removing the final boot seemed an impossibility. Rapid, panic stricken thoughts grad-

15

ually gave way to slower, less desperate ones. Jack's hands, leaden with fatigue, continued to paw weakly at the intractable boot. Then, the last of his panic was suddenly replaced by a deep, aching sadness as snapshots of Laura and his children rolled through his mind. After a last feeble swipe at the boot didn't even find its target, Jack resigned himself to his fate. While waiting for the moment when he could no longer resist the urge of his lungs to inhale, he felt a slight sense of relief. He took a strange sort of comfort in the fact that his terrifying struggle against the creek, against life itself, was almost over . . . even though he had lost.

Wide-eyed, he peered through the black water to see what he could of his death spot. All was pitch black. Suddenly a bright shimmering light pierced the dark water. The light quickly expanded and illuminated all fields of Jack's vision, with one exception. Perfectly situated in the center of the light was a small, sky blue hole. He gazed through the opening, just in front of him, and saw a canal of sorts, rectangular in shape, its angles rounded off, softened. The sides of the canal contained gently undulating cilia that seemed to beckon him forward. Having given up on his earthly life, he assumed the canal was his final path to death, toward heaven or simply perhaps oblivion. He pitched forward through the opening with his final reserves of energy. He entered the canal and was pulled gently forward by the warm, swishing arms of its walls. His lungs were suddenly filled with air, though his crippling exhaustion still rendered him helpless. Borne slowly forward by the soothing, protective cilia, Jack peacefully awaited where the magical canal would carry him.

Slowly though, the caressing movement of the cilia became less dense, then completely faded away. Jack's deliberate, peaceful passage accelerated while the canal began to throb with steady contractions. His feelings of safety and warmth gradually receded, and renewed anxiety arose as the sides of the canal squeezed him, propelling him forward. A new wave of panic re-injected him with shots of adrenalin. A second portal, straight ahead, came into view. This portal, unlike the first, was unwelcoming, sinister somehow.

Dull hues of red and purple jerked and seethed at its entrance. The hole hissed and popped as Jack drew nearer. Sensing danger, he began to fight the swift current of the canal. Just as he did during his drowning, he thrashed wildly and thrust cupped hands toward the danger in a vain attempt to push it away. The canal and its pulsing contractions were too strong. It pushed Jack ever forward and finally, the hellish hole swallowed him. The hole, for all its fierceness, was shallow. It spit him out after a momentary, indifferent pause. A sense of falling through black space ended when he collided with something, causing a loud burst of air to be expelled from his lungs.

In shock, as well as utterly exhausted, he was unable and unwilling to care where he was. He was vaguely aware that his remaining boot, undershorts, and trousers were still hanging from his left leg, and that he was lying on gritty, cool ground. Beyond these slight observations, Jack was simply too tired and mind-fucked to care much about anything else. His eyelids batted up and down slowly, pausing longer at each closing. Finally, he passed into a deep sleep.

2

Moments later, or so it seemed, Jack's heavy slumber was penetrated by the dream-like sounds of men shouting urgently, and the dull sensation of someone poking at him, shaking him. Becoming more lucid, he heard a man, clearly American by his accent and verbiage, wonder, "What the fuck? Is the sorry bastard wounded? He ain't dead, I can tell that."

Jack opened his eyes slowly, painfully in the morning light, and saw a man squatting beside him, pawing and sniffing. The squatting man answered, "Naw, he ain't hurt." He continued in a heavy Texas drawl, "I reckon this fella's feelin' some pain though. He smells jest like he purfoomed himself up nice and purdy with some of my Unca' Ray's special mix. This boy's sleepin' a good 'un off . . . lucky bastard." Other men, shadowy ghosts surrounding him, laughed and hooted. Jack raised his head, straining to focus on the men.

Looking up he mumbled, "What the hell . . . what's going on? . . . who are you guys?"

"Geez, he's American!" one of the ghosts exclaimed. "I figured he was one of those limey plantation guys we heard about . . . holy shit!" Jack's vision steadily cleared, along with his senses. He saw a large man hovering over him. He was wearing a dark green, pot-like steel helmet and had a varnished wood stocked, bolt-action rifle slung over his shoulder.

"What the hell you thinks going on, you drunk son of a bitch?" the man thundered down at Jack. A sharp pain stabbed his ribcage.

18

"What the fuck you think you're doin' sleeping one off and lying naked in the goddamned dirt? And where the hell is your weapon and tags?" He punctuated his question with a disgusted, "Shit! Pull your fucking leggings up!" Jack struggled to pull his boxers and pants up as the man continued to fire confusing, incoherent questions at him along with spurts of saliva that flew from his sneering mouth. The man's spit was discolored and scented by chewing tobacco. Rubbing his aching ribs, Jack realized the man had kicked him with a heavy boot as the foul liquid rained down, staining his face and hair. His sense of confusion was joined by one of dread.

Finally spitting man fell silent, his anger apparently spent. Jack struggled to a sitting position in an attempt to restore a modicum of dignity. As he raised himself, the group of five or six men backed off a few feet and silently stared. He looked at each one individually as they formed a semi-circle around him. While taking in and briefly analyzing the appearance of the group, his tension and fear suddenly eased. Every man in the group was dressed alike. Each was adorned in the same olive drab helmet, fatigues and web gear. Their leather boondockers were identical, excepting only size. Like spitting man, every one was armed. Jack recognized a Springfield .03 bolt action rifle, a BAR, and a Thompson sub-machine gun. Knives with bayonet apertures rested in sheathes at each man's side. He felt foolish for being so terrified, not to mention extremely embarrassed, for the men were clearly kitted out in World War II era Marine Corps costumes and accessories. It was obvious that these men were members of one of the re-enactors groups; here for the anniversary.

He noticed too that behind them, the Tenaru lay still and foul, just as before, but somehow different. "Christ, was I that fucked up?" he wondered to himself. "I must've staggered upstream and crashed in the middle of these guys' campground. Jesus, this is humiliating."

Jack returned his gaze to the apparent leader of the gang. Spitting man was silent now, but still stared hard at Jack. "Shit guys," Jack said timidly. "Geez . . . this is really embarrassing. I came here for the ceremonies and camped out on the creek bank . . . you know . . . to see what it was like sort of . . . kinda like you guys. I . . . uh . . . drained a bottle of bourbon and ah . . . I guess I got really shit-faced."

The group of men stared at him in stunned silence. This only served to urge him to further explain his presence and condition. "I took a walk along the riverbank and stumbled and fell in," he continued with a nervous chuckle. "I guess I was messed up enough to think I was drowning . . . and . . . uh . . . I took most of my clothes off." Still the re-enactors only stared, slack-jawed.

"No, really . . . damn this is embarrassing. This is not a normal thing for me," he sighed. "I guess I was so fucked up that I walked upstream and fell asleep near you guys. So much for proper Boy Scout techniques, huh?"

Spitting man had heard enough. "Aw, Christ," he muttered. "Just great, a fuckin' looney bird and the war ain't hardly started yet." Spitting man's weary proclamation seemed to shake the other group members from their bafflement.

"Hey, gunny," the BAR man bellowed, "maybe this guy, like he says, is some sort of Boy Scout leader who takes his job just a bit too fuckin' seriously."

"Yeah," a Boston accented voice yipped. "This guy's supah scout. Fuck the state pahk this guy says. My boys ah gonna pitch they'ah goddamned tents and help little ole ladies across the street right here in the middle 'a fuckin' Japville."

The mocking tone of the World War II imitators brought Jack to a simmering anger. Spitting man interjected, "Awright you morons, knock it off!" In spite of his rebuke, Jack noticed a wry smile creasing his face.

The condescending grin of spitting man was the final indignity that overrode Jack's embarrassment and insecure need to explain his circumstance. "Okay, fuck you guys," he muttered. "I don't need this shit from a bunch of play actors." He took several steps downstream. His progress was terminated by a vise-like grip on his arm, roughly yanking him to a halt. It was the brawny BAR man.

"Whoa, bud," he said, "where you goin'?"

"I'm going downstream to find my campsite. I'm not part of your silly game."

"Not part of our *silly* game you say, your highness?" spitting man said incredulously. "Oh my . . . yes . . . let's all call foul and just go home. Let's dance around the campfire and throw fuckin' daisies at each other. Hell, maybe we should even hold hands and talk about how mean and nasty the goddamn Japs are!" As he talked, sprays of tobacco juice wet Jack's face.

Jack stammered in reply, "Christ, guys . . . whatever . . . just let me go pack up and get out of here."

"Let you go?" spitting man hissed. "Let you go where exactly? Listen, there ain't no *goin'* on this fuckin' island unless someone tells you to and I ain't told you! You're here for the duration, or when you get your sorry ass shot off, whatever comes first."

Spitting man turned his back disgustedly on Jack and addressed his men, "Okay, I gotta get the captain involved in this shit." Turning his head back toward Jack he said, "Tell me who you're with and your rank, the captain's gonna wanna know."

Jack sighed and said, "Jesus Christ. . . . my name is Jack Macmillan—I'm from Grand Rapids, Michigan, and I'm here alone on vacation for the ceremonies." Peals of laughter rose from the semi-circle as spitting man's face reddened, his eyes narrowing into tiny slits.

"I ain't got time for this shitbird! What unit you with . . . now!"

"Listen . . . I don't understand," Jack said haltingly, his apprehension returning. "I'm not with a unit or a group . . . uh . . . it's just me, like I told you."

"Holy Mother of Mary!" the Bostonian shrieked. "This fuckah's so mad he's gonna staht bahking any second."

"Zip it O'Leary," spitting man sighed. "I give up. I'm gonna go fetch the cap. You idiots keep an eye on party-boy here." He turned and trudged toward a small cluster of similarly adorned men 20 yards away.

"Hey, Cap!" spitting man yelled. "Sir . . . Hey, Captain!"

21

The captain looked up and shouted impatiently, "What do you need now, and why the hell aren't you and your guys moving west like I told you?"

"Sorry to bother you, sir, but Lt. Benson is busy casing those Jap stiffs over by the coconut dump, and I got a fucked-up situation here." The captain rolled his eyes and motioned spitting man toward him.

"Give it to me, Gunny, whatcha got?" Jack heard the captain call spitting man 'Gunny'. He realized that the vulgar man was playing the role of a Marine Gunnery Sergeant, the backbone of small Marine combat units.

Spitting man replied, "I don't really know." Pointing toward Jack, he said, "See that guy over there . . . that fucked-up looking guy in those funny lookin' boots and no shirt?" Following the direction of spitting man's finger, the captain's gaze settled on Jack, the semi-circle of men still framing him.

The captain muttered disgustedly, "Oh for God's sake, Gunny, what the hell is that?"

"Hell if I know, Cap," spitting man replied. "We found the son of a bitch sleepin' like a baby on the creek bank, smellin' like he just took a whiskey bath. Guy's American too, not one of those limey farmers like we first thought."

"You shittin' me, Gunny?" the captain asked.

"I ain't for sure, sir, and he looks kinda old, too," spitting man replied. "Sorry, sir, but this guy's a real case."

"Okay gunny, give me a few minutes and I'll come over," the captain sighed.

"Awright, sir."

As Jack was warily eyeing spitting man pointing toward him, a movement from the semi-circle shifted his attention. He saw one of the re-enactors moving toward him with a lit cigarette held in his fingers, poised like a dart. Aiming at Jack's midsection, the dart holder advanced steadily with a look of perverse pleasure on his face. Jack stifled a scream and shuffled backwards. Two men cut off his retreat as the fire-tipped dart stabbed at his stomach, just below

22

his navel. His flailing about and muffled shrieks caused the dart holder to pause and slowly rise up. The young man, an easy smile on his face, looked directly into Jack's eyes and said, "I'm just trying to help, bud."

Jack stuttered back, "Help . . . help with what? Goddamn it! You burning me . . . you burning me with a cigarette is help?" The young man stared at Jack, a look of sympathy and befuddlement in his droopy, kind eyes. The fair skinned boy's face was pocked with fiery red pimples, his matted hair dark brown.

Facing Jack squarely, the dart holder calmly reassured him, "I ain't gonna torch you, pops. I'm just trying to burn those fuckin' worms off your gut."

"What? What worms?" Jack asked, glancing down at his midsection. He saw half a dozen 2-inch-long leeches attached to his lower abdomen and stomach. The vile creatures were dark gray and fat, engorged with Jack's blood. He screamed in revulsion, "Get those goddamn things off me! Aw, Jesus . . . shit . . . ahh Christ!" This time he held still for the cigarette. His stomach churned at the sight of the monstrous leeches nursing on his skin. The parasites, burned by the cigarette, spasmed, shrank, then fell to the ground like black shit curds. In an instant, beads of sweat formed on his brow and a fever-like heat swept his body. He began to swallow deeply, rapidly, just as he had on Hill 73; bursts of saliva filled his mouth. As the last, singed leech tumbled to the sand; Jack turned his back to the young men and fell to the ground on all fours. The contents of his stomach rushed up and splashed loudly onto the sand. The convulsions continued, and after a few painful dry heaves, he was done. Jack staggered to his feet and turned to face his antagonists.

His wretched performance had in turn amused them, disgusted them, and finally engendered in them a reluctant feeling of sympathy. Jack, still apprehensive, yet embarrassed, said to the group, "I'm sorry for that . . . like I said I had a bit much to drink last night . . . and . . . uh . . . I really hate big bugs and leeches, you know?"

The boy who'd burned the leeches off said, "Its okay bud, I hate the creepy fuckers too." He casually tossed a green cloth to Jack. "Clean yourself up, guy. The puke and tobacco shit I mean." As Jack toweled off, the boy removed Jack's shiny new internet purchase from its sheath. He turned it in his hands, examining it closely. He let out a low whistle and said, "Damn, this is some blade. I've never seen one like this. This isn't issue is it?"

Jack was about to answer when the deep voice of spitting man barked, "What the hell's goin' on now? You boys givin' this hobo a bath or somethin'?"

The kind, pimple faced dart holder replied, "Naw, gunny, he puked after I burnt them worms off his belly. Then I almost puked watchin' him puke. So I gave him my rag and told him to wipe the shit off so we didn't have to look at it . . . and maybe puke . . . you know?"

Spitting man, clearly playing the part of a tough, wizened Marine Gunnery Sergeant, sneered and said, "What are you, Navy or Marine? We're here one day and you get drunk and puke on yourself. You're a fuckin' disgrace to either one of them!" Spitting man's countenance softened somewhat when he added, "Me and my boys though, would just love to know where you got your hooch. It must be some special shit to mess you up so bad."

Hoots and hollers rose from the semi-circle. "Yes, sir," the southerner drawled. "Ah would jest love to wet my whistle right about now on the stuff a' fucked this guy up so bad. Shit, we ain't had a taste uh the sweet stuff since New Zealand. So, where's your stash, pops? You'll share it with us sweet little things . . . won't you? Of course you will. We're your buddies aftah' all, ain't that right?"

"I don't know what you're talking about," Jack replied. "I bought my bottle at the marina in town. Go buy your own. And I'm not a Marine or Navy. You guys aren't either, so let's quit fucking around and go our separate ways."

Raucous laughter from spitting man and the others was cut off by a new voice. "Knock it off people," the voice said sternly. The

24

sharp command instantly quieted the men and they backed several steps away from Jack, allowing the voice a free path to him. Jack recognized him as the one spitting man referred to as Captain. He sidled up to Jack, their noses just a few inches apart. "Jesus Christ!" the captain blurted. Grimacing, he stepped backward. "You smell like shit . . . worse than this goddamn island! Where the hell you been?"

Delighted, the Boston boy cackled, "Cap, that lovely scent is a heavenly mixtuh' of the finest bourbon whiskey, Gunny's mella chewin' tobacco, and carefully aged puke."

"Shut up, O'Leary," the captain muttered. "For once in your life, just fucking shut up."

"Sorry, sir," O'Leary mumbled. The others in the group shot chilling looks at O'Leary while the BAR man thrust an elbow into his ribcage. Even spitting man was silent, completely deferential to the captain. It was obvious to Jack that the so-called captain held considerable sway over the group. Looking into the faces of the men he saw a hint of fear, but mostly respect. The captain, or whatever he was, was apparently a special man.

"Listen," Jack said. "As I told your friends here, I got drunk camping on the creek bank last night . . . and I guess got lost when I . . . um . . . went to explore the sand spit. I just want to go downstream, pack up my stuff and get back to the hotel."

"Your hotel, huh?" the captain calmly said. He paused, stroking his cheek, then said, "Listen, we're all friends here, bud, okay? First, tell me, you a Marine? What unit you with?"

Jack rolled his eyes and said, "Why do you guys keep asking me if I'm a Marine or a Navy guy? As I've explained, I'm here on vacation and to tour the battlefield a bit, so let's end this silly game . . . please?"

"Ahh . . . yah," the captain muttered. A look of bemused sympathy adorned his face. "So you're not a Marine then?"

"Of course I'm not. Do I look like a Marine?"

"Well no, I guess you don't, bud, and don't take this personally, but I'm pretty fuckin' relieved you're not." Muffled snickers rose from the group of men standing behind the captain. "Alright . . . shut up you guys," the captain said. Turning to his men, he murmured, "This guy's obviously a bit confused . . . nuts . . . or whatever. Have some sympathy. Jesus, look at the sorry fucker."

Turning back to Jack, he gently said, "I don't know if you're a plantation guy or some sort of lost traveler. But you're an American and we'll take care of you. You need to go see the doctors in sick bay and tell them your story. They'll look after you . . . keep you out of trouble. Okay?" Jack was struck by the captain's strong yet gentle bearing in relation to the others. Still his words were every bit as senseless. As Jack prepared a rejoinder to the captain's comments, a panicked yell split the air.

"Zero . . . Zero rolling in from the sea!"

The captain's head, followed by the others, whipped around, looking toward the beach. A second later the captain yelled, "Everybody down now! Down, down, down!" In an instant the men surrounding Jack collapsed and lay prone on the ground. Each and every one had his face buried in the dirt, their hands clutched up around their helmets. Violent, muffled curses rent the air.

Befuddled, Jack looked toward the beach and saw a white, single engine airplane flying straight toward him. With its fat black nose, radial engine and distinctive canopy, Jack immediately identified it as a Japanese, Mitsubishi Zero fighter plane, a remarkably accurate reproduction. His confusion was replaced by fascination. "Whoa," he thought to himself, "these guys are doing it up right; a perfect looking Zero making a strafing run on the Tenaru." Jack stood transfixed by the historic sight, wanting to hear the throaty rhythms of its engine and the rush of air as it passed overhead.

Jack's fascination was penetrated by the sound of the captain, lying on the ground just a few feet away, screaming at him. Jack reluctantly altered his gaze from the sky to the captain, and saw his head raised slightly, his face twisted in anger. "Get down you fuckin' idiot!" the captain shrieked. "Get down, now!" Jack ignored the screams of the captain and looked back at the Zero closing in. He squinted when pops of light began to dance on the leading edge of the plane's wings, followed seconds later by the sounds of loud, rapid cracks. His attention was drawn to a clump of palm trees between him and the plane, shivering and exploding, ejecting their coconuts and fronds in bursts of green and brown. The captain continued to scream at him as geysers of sand and undergrowth erupted in two straight lines, marching straight toward him. He watched as one geyser, unlike the others, exploded in red above a Marine hugging the ground. In a daze, Jack slowly sank to the ground. As he did he locked eyes with the captain, hoping to find some sort of explanation for the all-too-real re-enactment. Staring at him, Jack heard a hiss, then a dull crack. The noble captain's head disappeared in a spray of purple, red, and pale yellow. Simultaneously, particles slapped at Jack's face and chest, delivering uncountable, tiny stabs of pain. Stunned, he stared at the captain's headless torso, lying limp on reddened sand. Jack sucked deep breaths of air. His movements and thoughts slowed, as if he was stuck in a slow motion nightmare.

No longer having the captain's confident eyes to focus on, he staggered to his feet. A shrieking roar filled his ears. He screamed, "Oh, God . . . oh Jesus, help! I can't believe . . . I can't . . . I can't . . . this man is dead!" He wiped his burning face with the back of his hand. In shock, he slowly turned his palm over examining the thick, gooey mass his hand had removed from his face. He stifled a renewed urge to wretch.

Recovering somewhat, he turned to the men on the ground and yelled, "What the hell has happened? How could you fuck this thing up so bad? This man's head is gone! It's gone!" The other men remained prone, their faces burrowed deeply in the sand. Jack lurched toward one of them. He grabbed a shoulder and roughly flipped him over. He recognized the face of the sneering youngster from Boston. "What the hell is this?" Jack yelled.

"Let go of me you, you crazy bastahd!" the boy replied. "Leave me alone! That Jap ain't done yet, so fuck off!" In desperation and panic, Jack began to stagger downstream in a mad search for his campsite.

"Bastards running in again!" a voice shouted. "Take cover!"

Several men glanced up in an attempt to ascertain the plane's path of attack. One of them spotted Jack and croaked, "Fuckin' Jap's making another pass, you dumbshit . . . get down!" Without hesitation Jack hurled himself to the ground and buried his face in the dirt. This time he didn't watch the attack, but heard the same staccato cracks and zip of bullets entering the sand nearby.

The shooting stopped as the sound of the plane's engine faded out to sea. A minute or two passed while, in a daze, Jack kept his face tightly pressed to the ground. Then a voiced boomed, "Alright Marines. That son of a bitch is gone. On your feet and check your wounded! I want a full casualty report from each squad leader as soon as possible." Then in a gentler voice he said, "Captain Knowles is dead, so I'll take the company until we make a change." Jack looked toward the large, commanding voice and saw a small, stocky man. He continued to bark orders at individual Marines and exhorted those in shock to get moving and help their buddies. Desperate cries for corpsmen rang out. Jack staggered toward the man; the panicked roar in his ears slowly subsiding. As he made his way across the 30 yards separating him and the shouting man, a new and haunting sound assaulted him.

He heard a young voice moan, "Oh, God, help me . . . I'm hit bad! I don't wanna die . . . I don't wanna die . . . please! Please help me!"

Then another, "Oh, Jesus . . . I'm shot. I can't believe I'm shot!" Jack turned toward the voice and saw a young man writhing slowly in the sand, his arm missing at the shoulder. "I don't wanna be shot. I just wanna go home."

The sad, wretched moaning and grisly sights swirled maniacally in Jack's mind as he approached the shouting man. He stumbled up beside him, took a deep breath and gasped, "Excuse me. Uh, excuse me . . . I uh . . . I need some help. Can you help me for a second please?"

The man stopped shouting and turned toward Jack. In an instant he was on him. "Where the hell is your uniform and weapon, goddamnit?" he shouted. "We just lost some good Marines and you're standin' out here like it's a fuckin' beach party. What's your rank and unit, Marine?"

Taken aback by the sheer fury registered on the man's face, as well as his words, Jack stuttered back, "I uh . . . I'm not part of this mess. I don't know who you people are or what sort of game this is. I was just here for the ceremonies. Now with this fucked up . . . that guy over there dead . . . and . . . all these other hurt people and stuff, I just want to know what's going on." Jack noticed the man was wearing the insignia of a lieutenant colonel in the Marine Corps. Looking back at his face, Jack saw that his countenance had softened somewhat.

"If you're not a Marine then what the hell are you doing out here?" he demanded.

"I told you," Jack replied wearily. "I flew in from the states for a few days to attend the 60th anniversary ceremonies and I got lost last night when I was camping on the creek bank."

The stout man peered hard at him for a few seconds. He saw the bits of the captain's brain tissue and skull still clinging to Jack's face. With a deep sigh he said, "Listen, this is war and really bad shit happens. Captain Knowles was my best man, a good man, and I hate like hell to lose him. I know what you saw was pretty awful, but you need to hold it together. We gotta take care of each other; you can't be runnin' around out here scaring your buddies more than they already are. Now I'll ask you again, what unit you with and what's your rank?"

Sighing deeply, Jack replied, "I'm a retired businessman from Grand Rapids and I'm just on a short pleasure trip."

"Oh for chrissakes," the lieutenant colonel muttered. "Corporal Morales!" he shouted over his shoulder. "Get over here!"

Morales came running. "Yes, sir, Colonel."

Nodding toward Jack, the colonel told Morales, "Corporal, this man has had a bad shock and requires medical attention. Escort him back across the sandbar to the sick bay."

"Yes, sir," Morales replied. The private gently grabbed Jack's arm and began to lead him away.

29

"Wait," Jack said. "Would someone just please tell me what the hell is going on for god sakes? I just want to find my gear and leave . . . that is all I ask! I'm not going anywhere with this man, do you understand?"

The stocky man sprang toward Jack, his face red, veins bulging in his neck. He yelled, "Listen, you sorry bastard, I ain't got time to be wet nursin' your sort right now. You get your butt to the aid station! You move now or I swear I'll shoot you myself! Now get the fuck out my sight, you fuckin' son of a bitch!" Jack was stunned by the man's seething anger. He decided the best thing to do was play along. He allowed himself to be led downstream by the young man. As they approached the mouth of the Tenaru, Jack recognized the point where the creek bank suddenly veered east at a sharp angle to the seashore. It was here that he had set up camp the night before. He desperately looked around for his equipment. As he did so, he noticed slowly, as if his mind were resisting it, that the area looked very different than it had the night before.

"What the . . . what?" he stammered. He rubbed his eyes violently, but the scenery didn't change. As far as he could see, huge coconut palm groves grew on both sides of the river bank. The only features that remained familiar were the Tenaru itself and the sandbar at its mouth. He found no sign of his jeep or bright blue pup tent. When they reached the area where Pvt. Schmid's position had been, the obelisk was gone. Then, a mind-bending vista spread out before him as he and Morales breeched the palm grove and stepped onto the sandy beach. Jack abruptly stopped and slowly sank to his knees, Morales vainly trying to hold him upright. On the previous evening, during his walk on the beach he had enjoyed the tranquil, vacant waters of Ironbottom Sound and its waves rhythmically breaking on the sand. Now, the waters were teeming with ships of all shapes and sizes. Shark-like silhouettes of old three-stack destroyers and cruisers steamed back and forth several miles out to sea, parallel to the beach, shepherds to their flocks of nearer fat, rusty cargo ships. To the east, lighters and wooden landing boats buzzed back and forth between the supply ships and the beach. Jack could only stare in wonder at the frantic, water-borne ballet.

"Oh my Christ, this is impossible . . . completely impossible. These ships were cut up for scrap decades ago." Glassy eyed, he turned to Morales and said, "What's going on . . . how can this be?"

Morales looked at him sympathetically and replied, "Just calm down . . . those ships are here to take care of us. Let's move on now, bud."

"Okay," Jack said numbly, mesmerized by the ships. "Okay . . . yeah . . . let's move on . . . let's move on." Jack, however, couldn't will himself to move. Morales firmly, yet with a marked gentleness, wrapped his arm around Jack's back raised him to his feet and coaxed him across the same sand bar he had drunkenly charged across the night before. After crossing, they continued eastward down the beach. All the while Jack stared out at the ships in stunned silence. His fixation on the seaborne beehive was interrupted by jeeps and tracked vehicles passing in the opposite direction. Dumbfounded, he watched as diminutive M4 Stuart tanks and ancient one-ton International Harvester trucks ground past him. Behind them young soldiers, many yapping excitedly about the lack of a contested landing, streamed past in ordered lines of olive drab.

As they trudged through the sand, Jack quietly muttered questions to himself. "What in hell has happened?" He had given up the thought that this was some horrific nightmare as the sounds, smells, and the pain were all too real. As well, the natural rhythm of the events and dialogue were too chronologically correct, unlike the manic, warped movement of time in a dream. "I would have heard something about this group somewhere," he whispered to himself. "There are hundreds of them and they can't all be playing some game. Those dead guys were dead. Christ . . . what can this be?" Morales could clearly hear his ponderings, but said nothing. Jack thought back to the previous evening and the strange journey he'd dreamt he took while nearly drowning in the creek. For the first time, the possibility that something inexplicable and completely fantastic had occurred, briefly entered his mind. This couldn't be heaven, he thought. Just the fact that he'd had the thought brought forth a sardonic chuckle.

He shook his head and said, "Naw, buddy, there's an explanation for this . . . don't start losing your shit, bud." He thought of Laura and the kids back home, and a stab of grief and guilt pierced him. Perhaps Laura had been right and the trip to the island had been a dreadful idea.

His thoughts were interrupted when Morales directed him to a path leading into the coconut grove. They entered the grove and directly in front, 20 meters away, stood a rugged lean-to of sorts. Planks of wood forming a shape similar to a soccer goal were draped with a heavy green tarpaulin. A dirty cloth depicting a red cross was pinned to it. Morales guided him to the entrance of the lean-to. Once inside, Morales turned to him and said, "Sit there . . . on that crate right behind you. I gotta get you checked in with the docs." He turned, took a step, then stopped and looked back at Jack. "Oh . . . and don't even think of movin' . . . I got my eye on you."

In spite of his bewilderment and fear, Jack was able to take in the sights and sounds of the aid station. The station itself was utterly crude in comparison to what Jack knew of military medical facilities. There were no beds or cots, just blankets and ponchos spread in the dirt. A metal pole with a single light bulb stood in the center of the lean-to. A crude, chunky battery pack lying on the ground provided its energy. Wooden crates of bandages, syringes, and various medications lay strewn about. They had not been unpacked and organized; just broken into, their contents ripped out as needed. Jack heard the same groans he had back at the creek, though now they were softer, less panicked. Medical people were busily attending to the wounded men with a quiet urgency. Every now and then a terse command burst forth, bringing a frenzy of attention to one of the wounded. He heard one of the medical men in frustration curse, "Where in hell are the plasma bottles damn it! They were supposed to be priority! Goddamned supply idiots!"

Overall though, Jack was struck by the focused efficiency of the medical staff working in conditions he could not have previously imagined. He noted the gentle care they dispensed to the injured men. They talked softly to them, assuring the men that all would be well. The boys who were wounded beyond the capabilities of the station were quickly patched up, the holes in their flesh plugged, broken bones stabilized. Then a doctor would clear them for evacuation to the beach and a ride out to one of the ships standing offshore. On the ships, apparently, they could get relatively thorough, sanitary medical attention. The boys whose wounds were not so severe, flesh wounds, cuts and abrasions, were returned to their units after treatment. Due to the overflow caused by the strafing aircraft, some of the men were laid outside the protection of the lean-to. Ponchos and various canvas type fabrics, as well as mosquito netting, were used to shelter them. Jack's unwilling fascination with the crude, yet remarkably humane and efficient functioning of the aid station, was broken by the muffled weeping of an injured man lying on the ground a few feet away.

The young man was sobbing quietly and talking to himself. "Christ Cap . . . Christ! Why'd you have to die? Shit . . . we just got here. I don't know if I can do this without you, Cap." Jack looked at the young man's tear streaked, pimpled face and recognized the kind boy who'd burned the leeches off his groin and lent him his towel. It appeared he'd been lightly wounded in the leg. Jack glanced over at Morales having a discussion with what seemed to be a very impatient doctor. Morales pointed at Jack several times then threw up his arms in frustration.

Jack turned his attention back to the heartbroken boy. The boy's grief was so raw, so sad, that it momentarily overrode his own feelings of anger, confusion, and fear. He looked so young. Jack wondered how he'd gotten wrapped up in this mess. Without wanting to, he felt a deep sympathy for him, an emotion he'd rarely felt for anyone back in Grand Rapids, except his own family. The utter horror and misery Jack was witnessing had somehow softened him. He leaned forward and quietly stammered, "Hey . . . I saw what

33

happened . . . what happened to your captain. I'm uh . . . sorry. Can I . . . um . . . can I do anything?"

The boy turned to him, stared for a moment then said, "What the hell would you know, you crazy bastard? You ain't even a Marine!"

"I guess your right, I . . . I don't know what the hell I am right now . . . or what I'm doing here. But I'm not crazy . . . or at least I don't think I am . . . maybe I can help is all I'm saying."

"No," the boy sniffled. "You can't help . . . nobody can . . . nobody can understand. Cap was the best . . . you don't know . . . nobody knows. He's been looking out for me ever since I got outta boot camp. Now he's dead and I don't know . . . I just can't believe it."

Just then Morales returned with an irritated looking young man. Morales said to Jack, "This corpsman's gonna look after you. I gotta get back to my unit." Morales headed toward the door, then stopped. He turned and said to Jack, "Good luck, bud."

"Okay," Jack muttered, averting his eyes. He felt uneasy accepting comfort from these men, but the sights of the aid station had softened his view toward his tormentors.

The medical man knelt down beside Jack and rolled his eyes. "Listen, bub, Lieutenant Smith and Commander Goldman are too busy with the real wounded right now to deal with the likes o' you," he grunted. "Have a seat on them duffels outside and I'll be back." Jack hesitated, uncertain. "Go on, get your butt on them fuckin' bags." Jack had noticed the corpsman earlier. He spoke with an unmistakable south Philadelphia accent and his colleagues referred to him as Turk. He was at least six feet tall and sturdily built. His hair was thick, jet black, and a heavy stubble shadowed his face. His intense, dark brown eyes were topped with bushy black eyebrows. His lips were full and deep red, their edges defined as sharply as if they had been carved by a scalpel. Though he was handsome in a rugged way, his overall appearance was quite fearsome. However, Jack had noticed that the gruff young man had been very gentle and kind in dealing with the wounded men. He'd dealt with him differently though. Jack had gotten a sneer while the others received reassuring smiles.

"Alright . . . alright," Jack mumbled. He looked at the distraught young boy and said, "It'll be okay . . . hang in there." The boy just stared on at the canvas ceiling.

Jack walked outside the lean-to over to a large lump of canvas bags and sat down reclining on them. He still had a clear view of the activity inside the aid station. He abruptly noticed a tanned, curly haired doctor staring intently at him. Jack averted his eyes, strangely ashamed. After a moment he returned his gaze to the doctor and watched him work. Compared to the others in the station, he seemed unusually calm and gathered. He gave orders with a quiet confidence and respect, no matter the urgency of the situation. The bedside caring and professionalism of the others was touching and impressive to be sure. Though in comparison to this doctor, it was what one expected, conventional and learned. The curly haired doctor's nurturing and care of his patients was different . . . lending an almost spiritual aura to his conduct. He seemed more than a mere physician doing his best to apply his technical knowledge to the men's wounds. He *was* more, but exactly what, Jack could not place. He was different, that was all Jack knew. His fascination with the unusual doctor and the drama playing out in the filthy tent was suddenly interrupted by the return of Turk.

"What's your name?" he barked.

"Jack . . . Jack Macmillan," Jack replied.

"Listen, Macmillan, as I said, we really ain't got time for your type right now, so you jest rest your little self on them bags. As we speak, my boy Cudlipp is rustling you up some proper dungarees . . . didn't think you'd wanna dance around here in those paratrooper pants or whatever the fuck they are. And where the hell did you get them ugly fuckin' boots?"

"L.L. Bean catalog," Jack said flatly. "Thanks for arranging the clothes, but there's nothing wrong with me and as soon as I get them I'd just like to wander back to the Tenaru and figure out what's going on here."

"There's nothing wrong with you, huh?" Turk sneered. "You're trying to figure out what's going on here and you say there's nothing wrong with you? No, you need to be cleared by one of the doctors before you're going anywhere."

Just then, a wiry, boyish looking soldier, apparently Cudlipp, approached Turk with a bundle of clothes. "Got, 'em Turk," Cudlipp said.

"Excellent work, Cuntlip!" Turk said. The boy rolled his eyes, handed the clothes to Turk and shuffled off. "Look at these lovely fuckin' garments, General . . . a spiffy new uniform for you. We'll pin your medals to 'em later, okay?" He tossed the bundle at Jack and said, "Put 'em on!"

Turk's sarcastic demeanor pressed Jack's patience, but he was grateful for the clothes. "Thanks," he said to Turk. "When can I talk to your doctors though? I need to get out of here as soon as possible."

"Just sit there on them fuckin' bags goddamnit!" Turk barked. "If you haven't noticed we got some boys who are hurt pretty bad. The docs will see you as soon as they can, if that's okay with you."

"Alright," Jack muttered.

"I'll be back to check on you soon. Oh, and don't go nowhere, General," Turk growled.

It was just a few minutes after Turk left that Jack rose off the bags and slipped away. His escape went unnoticed as the medical people were feverishly attending to the wounded. The beach was still crammed full with vehicles and troops, so Jack turned and headed inland. He walked 100 yards then turned west toward the creek and the previous night's campsite in hopes of somehow finding his gear and jeep. The grove was empty and quiet. The linear layout of the palm grove allowed him to move quickly. He stopped though, when he came upon a tattered clump of khaki clothing lying directly in his path, 20 feet away. He slowly approached the bundle. As he moved closer he heard a mellow drone, not the buzz of a singular insect, but that of a chorus. After a few more cautious steps he saw that the clump was in fact a man, lying still on the

36

ground. He realized too that the symphonic buzz came from a cluster of flies circling above the man, intermittently alighting on him. Jack inquired quietly, nervously, "Hey . . . hey you okay?" There was no reply. The man appeared quite small. He was wearing sneakers. The tops of his shoes, as well as his thick calves, were wrapped in a swathe of beige cloth. Jack hunched down and nudged him. "You okay . . . you awake?"

The man's cap had fallen over his face. Jack picked at it, trying to dislodge it so he could look into his eyes. Finally, he flicked the cap off and recoiled in horror. "Shit! Oh Christ!" he gasped. He fell backwards off his haunches and scrabbled away from the dead man. A dark, perfectly round hole was centered on his forehead. Bustling yellow maggots were crawling in and around the hole. The man's mouth and nostrils were filled with the vile creatures. His face was grotesquely swollen, colored by death in a shade of bluish-gray. Jack stood up panting, his mouth once again filling with bursts of saliva. He forced himself to look at the corpse one more time before he bolted back toward the aid station. As he huffed and grunted through the palms, he kept picturing the dead man's unseeing eyes. They were dark and narrow . . . Asian.

He arrived back at the aid station, but stopped a few yards short and sat down on a coconut log. He dropped his head to his knees and cradled it in his arms. He talked to himself in agonized grunts and sobbed, "What the fuck . . . what's happening here? It can't be . . . it can't be! Oh, Jesus where . . . what's happened?"

With his head down, Jack hadn't noticed the mysterious tanned doctor walk behind the lean-to and light a cigarette. After his first puff the doctor heard Jack's sobs and jerked his head toward the sound. He found Jack perched on the log, flicked his cigarette away and walked toward him. He stood in front of him for a moment, then sunk slowly to his knees. "You okay, mate . . . something I can do for you?" the doctor asked. Startled, Jack jerked, then hastily wiped at his face.

"No problem . . . I'm okay," Jack said. "I'm fine." He glanced at the doctor, then shamefully averted his eyes. Jack noted that the doctor spoke with an Australian accent. His skin was darker than a white man's, but its color was not completely definable. It was of an almost golden cast. His mouth was wide and his pale green eyes were perfectly round. His close cropped, tightly curled hair was brown, not black. He was roughly Jack's height and build. Jack wondered at the origins of the man.

"I saw you in sick bay an hour ago. I'm sorry for the way Turk treated you . . . he's young and excitable and the Marines are his heroes. He's actually a pretty good bloke though, and a bloody fine corpsman."

"Whatever," Jack mumbled. "But, I'm fine and I just need to figure out . . . hell, I guess figure out what I'm doing here."

"What service are you with?" the doctor asked.

"I'm not in any service," he continued, less confidently this time than with the others. "Uh, like I've told them, I'm uh . . . ah, a retired businessman from Grand Rapids, Michigan. I'm simply here to tour a bit. Then, Christ, you people show up and everything goes to hell."

"I see," the doctor said slowly. He held out his hand and said, "My name is Ian . . . Ian Smith. I'm in the Australian Navy on exchange with the U.S. Navy. This," he said pointing to the ramshackle lean-to, "this is Medical Company E, 1st Battalion in all her bloody glory. We're attached to the First Marine Division as basically a small rear area aid and clearing station. What's your name?"

"Jack . . . Jack Macmillan," he replied, shaking hands with the doctor.

"Nice to meet you, Jack," Ian said. "You said everything went to hell when we landed. What did you mean by that?"

"Everything has changed since last night; the old ships and tanks . . . the dead guys . . . and the other crazy shit. Jesus, I just want to go home . . . my wife, my kids." Ian looked at Jack intently, digesting his words.

"What other crazy shit are you referring to?" he asked.

"The soldiers . . . the restored Zero, the dead Asian guy I saw just now back in the jungle . . . I don't know . . . I can't figure it out.

Christ, maybe I've lost my mind and none of this is happening outside my own head. Maybe none of this is real." Jack smiled thinly and said, "Hell, man, maybe you're not even real. But I was definitely on Hill 73 for the anniversary ceremonies yesterday, I know that for certain. That was real."

"Ceremonies?" Ian asked. "What ceremonies would those be?"

With head in hands, Jack responded, "What else on this shit hole? It's the anniversary marking the landing of U.S. forces here during World War II. Hell, it happened years before I was born and now I see all this shit? Christ."

Ian, still on his haunches, watched Jack rub his forehead for a few moments, then he put a hand on Jack's shoulder and said softly, "I see. Listen, I have to get back to the station. You come with me, mate, and as soon as I clear the last of the patients we'll talk and I'll try to help you get where you need to be, okay?"

Jack replied sullenly, "What the hell. I don't know what else I'm going to do." Ian rose and extended his hand toward Jack, easing him off the log. As they entered the lean-to, the sun was setting over Savo Island.

"You're going to have to sit on the bags again for a little bit while I finish up. Then we can walk down to the beach and talk some more, alrighty?"

"Okay."

"You must be hungry . . . can I get you something to eat?"

Jack hesitated, then said, "Yeah, actually I am pretty hungry . . . thanks."

"Okay, sit there and I'll have some food delivered. I'll only be about 45 minutes or so."

"Thanks," Jack mumbled. He looked around the tent and noticed that things had quieted down a bit. Still, the pathetic scenes of suffering, pain, and sadness remained. He watched as Turk gently spoon fed water to a twitching boy. Cudlipp was racing about, ensuring that each wounded man was as comfortable as possible. Ian alternated between conferring with corpsmen, and quietly conversing with the injured boys. Once again, Jack was struck by the gentle care those in the tent were receiving. It was completely incongruous to what was occurring outside. Turk finished with his patient and stood up. He stopped suddenly when he saw Jack parked again on the bags.

"Hey!" he shouted. "I hope you been out killin' Japs. Thought I told you to keep your butt on them fuckin' bags, General!"

"Quiet, Turk!" a stern voice interrupted. "Get back to work!" Jack looked up and saw Ian glaring furiously at Turk. With reddened face, Turk grunted and beat a hasty retreat to the other side of the lean-to. Jack and Ian's eyes met briefly. Jack nodded slightly in thanks. Ian returned to his rounds, while Jack scanned the lean-to. He searched for the young boy who had been so distraught over the loss of his captain. He found him lying on the ground just a few feet away, sound asleep. Fresh bandages wrapped his lower leg. He noticed that someone had washed the dirt and blood from his face and hands.

He then saw Turk removing a reddish-yellow dressing from a young man's shoulder. In the waning light, Turk's eyes darted back and forth between the man's eyes and the bandage. Each time he looked at him he softly said, "Okay . . . you okay?"

"Yeah, I'm fine," Jack heard the boy moan through clenched teeth.

Turk murmured, "Okay then, Marine . . . we're gonna go a little more and then I'll put a spankin' new field dressin' on you. Just a few more tugs, okay?"

"Okay, Doc, go ahead . . . just do it . . . I just wanna sleep."

Jack looked away, not caring to watch any more of the removal of the crusty bandage. When he did, he saw Cudlipp walking toward him. He kneeled and announced, "Got your chow for you, sir. No spoons or forks, sir . . . unless you got your own and I kind of guessed you probably don't . . . so I brought a tongue depressor . . . should work just fine, sir."

"Thanks," Jack said. "You don't need to call me sir though. Just call me Jack."

"Okay," the young man replied. "So you aren't an officer then?" Jack paused briefly, watching Cudlipp struggle with two small olive drab cans. The opener he used to de-lid the can was strange and crude.

"No," Jack said. "How about you Cudlipp? Geez, what's your first name?"

"Franklin," he replied. "Frank. I'm glad you aren't an officer. Most of them are idiots, if I may be honest. My parents warned me about them, said they were pseudo-intellectual hyper-egoists; mostly East Coast guys." Jack watched as the boy pried the can open. Cudlipp looked to be 16 at most. His uniform and helmet seemed to swallow him. His fragile size was accented by his fair skin and dainty, almost feminine hands. His hair was jet black. The contrast in colors was highlighted by fiery red lips. Jack understood why Turk had mocked the boy. He had seen it countless times on playgrounds, in locker rooms and fraternity houses. The boy's eyes though, deep brown . . . almost black, were hard and confident. Jack had first taken note of them when Turk had converted Frank's last name into a vulgarity. Cudlipp passed the opened can to Jack along with the small, wooden paddle. Jack stared into the can, then said, "Oh my, what is this?"

"Sorry to disappoint you," Frank said. "The C's and some Spam are all there is on this stinking island so far, and we don't have a lot of that stuff. They were in such a rush to load the ships in New Zealand that a lot of the most important stuff is still in the bottom of the holds out on the ships. Scuttlebutt has it that the Marines liberated a whole bunch of Jap food near the airfield, though. I heard they said it wasn't too bad . . . rice, canned beef, fish, crab, and the like. Maybe when we move up we can get some of that, but for now the C's are all we have and actually, from what I've heard from some of the old China Marines, the C's are quite an improvement over what we would've had just a few years ago. Jeepers, after the chow on the ships from San Francisco and Wellington, I must admit they're not all bad."

41

"What you call C's . . . do you mean C rations?" Jack asked.

"Yeah, of course," Frank replied. "They're loaded with calories and protein so you don't need much, which I suppose is a good thing."

The can was labeled 'MEAT STEW'. Both it and the labeling looked identical to the old C-rations he'd seen in pictures and in museums. They had been replaced years ago by pouched foods and later, MRE's. Jack stuck the paddle into the congealed lump. It heartily resisted his attempts to penetrate it. Finally though, he freed a glutinous lump of stew and put it in his mouth. After a few chews he closed his eyes and said, "Oh . . . my . . . God, this is bad, really nasty. It's greasy and kind of tastes like chemicals or something. These really are C-rations aren't they? Where'd you get them?"

Frank looked at Jack quizzically then answered, "Well, some of the orderlies picked them up from the supplies stacked near the beach. And that chemical taste is the preservatives . . . they give it its distinctive flavor. Would you care for a nice red Bordeaux, or perhaps a full-bodied Merlot to complete your dining experience?"

"Hell yes!" Jack said gratefully. Frank reached down and handed Jack a tin cup. Jack reached for it and took a deep drink. "Oh, Christ!" Jack choked. "What the hell is this?"

Confused, Frank stammered, "Why it . . . its powdered fruit drink from the C-ration box. You didn't think it was really red wine did you?" Jack paused and looked at Frank. He saw the young man's eyes were wide, his mouth agape. He wanted to ask the officious, yet kind young man, as he had the others, what was really happening, but the C-rations, the ships, the dead men, the authentic dress and weapons had his mind whirling with possibilities, one in particular which he wasn't yet ready to confront openly and completely.

"Naw, of course not," Jack finally replied. "I was just a bit surprised. I haven't had this before; stuff tastes like gasoline."

Frank, looking slightly relieved, laughed and said, "I've heard it described a lot of different ways, but yours is probably the most accurate of all. Gasoline . . . boy, that nails it!"

At that moment, Turk walked up and snipped, "Hey, Frank, ain't you got better things to do with your time than jawin' with this goldbricker?"

Frank's eyes fired and he said tersely, "What business is it of yours, Turk?"

"I'm just tellin' you, Frankie, that this guy don't need any fuckin' help. He ain't hurt."

"Listen, go peddle your own papers, will ya'?" Turk shook his head and stalked off.

"Christ, is he an asshole or what?" Jack said.

"Turk? Nah, he's actually a pretty good guy," Frank responded.

Jack studied the boy's face a moment and said, "He doesn't seem to treat you too well."

"His bark's a lot louder than his bite. He's a good fella," Frank insisted. "He wanted to be a Marine . . . he worships those guys. Just look at the way he cares for them. He wanted to join the Marines after Pearl Harbor, but they wouldn't let him on account of some problem with his feet. So Turk begged and begged to be a Navy Corpsman. I guess they got tired of his carping and ok'd it, but said he couldn't serve with a combat unit. That really burned him."

"Pearl Harbor . . . what do you mean?"

Cudlipp, looking perplexed, said haltingly, "Yeah, last December, right after it happened." Jack looked down, and tightly squeezed his eyes shut.

"You can go now, Frank . . . go please . . . look after the other men." Jack mumbled.

"You're right," Frank replied, "I do need to go but I'll be back in a few to see how you're doing."

"Yeah, fine . . . that's fine. Just go," Jack said while staring through the boy, staring at nothing. Frank stood up and moved away.

Suddenly snapping to, Jack said, "Wait . . . I want to ask you a question."

"Sure," Frank said.

"I'm curious. Compared to some of the others, you're an artic-

43

ulate, well spoken guy," Jack began. "As well you seem to know a lot about fine wine and food for a guy your age, and considering the era you represent. How is that?"

A broad smile creased Frank's face and he explained, "Well, my mom and dad are professors at Stanford. We have a cabin north of San Francisco in an area called the Napa Valley. They're growing lots of grapes for wine there and my folks are really interested in it. They're even messing around with wine making themselves, so I guess it's rubbed off on me . . . the French terminology and stuff."

"I see," Jack said slowly. "I've been to the Napa Valley several times . . . to Silverado and some other places. They produce some great wines."

"Wow," Frank said. "You're the first guy I've ever met who's heard of the valley and knows it makes wine." His dark eyes shone with delight. "The wines are good I guess, and we don't make much yet, but you just wait; once we get it right, and we will, California will produce the greatest wines in the world . . . better than the French even. It'll take some time, but mark my words!"

Jack gazed at Frank glassy eyed, and said, "Yeah . . . right, I will Frank. For now though, you need to take care of your other patients."

"Okay, talk to you later," Frank replied.

Frank returned to his duties while Jack contemplated their discussion in a daze. He slunk down into the bags, trying to make sense of it all. Trying most of all though, to ignore what may be the fantastic truth. After a few minutes, Ian appeared and asked, "Ready to take a walk?"

"Hell yeah," Jack wearily replied. They walked down the path toward the shore. The beach was quiet save for the sound of the surf lightly splashing on the sand. The stars and moon were shrouded by clouds, so they navigated their way along the beach by the phosphorescent sprays of blue-green sea water bursting as the waves broke on the shore. They walked along for a time in silence, occasionally answering the challenges of sentries with a password. When the horizon sucked the last light from the sky, Ian turned to Jack and said,

44

"We probably shouldn't go much farther, mate. The Marines have cleared the area, but you never know. The Jap is a sneaky bugger. Let's sit down here and enjoy the surf." They sat on the sand, arms resting on their knees. The clouds parted and the moon glistened off the waters of the sound and bathed Ian's face with a dull glow. Jack, remembering that Ian had told him he was from Australia, broke the silence with a question. "You're an Aborigine aren't you?"

"Very good," the doctor replied. "Most people outside Australia don't guess that, because I have quite a bit of European blood in me. That's why I'm here with your Navy. The Australian boys would figure me out right away and wouldn't care for an 'Abo' giving them medical treatment. But the Yanks, excepting you that is, can't quite figure me out, so it's okay . . . at least I hope. I'm from Adelaide. How did you guess I was Aborigine?"

"I traveled to Australia quite a lot in the '80s. The Aborigines kind of intrigued me, and I did some guided tours in the outback."

Jack's comments seemed to hang in the air for a moment. Jack turned toward Ian and saw him gazing at the luminescent surf. After a minute or so, Ian finally asked, "The '80s, Jack? What were you doing there in the '80s?"

"I was setting up distribution for the family business in Sydney, Melbourne, and Perth . . . beautiful country." Semi-consciously he added, "You guys did a hell of a job with the Summer Olympics a couple years ago."

Ian reclined on the sand and was silent for several moments. "Have you read much about our 'Dreamtime'?" he finally asked.

"I have a bit in fact."

"Did it make any sense to you?" Ian asked.

"Not really, to be honest," Jack replied. "It all seemed a bit confusing and fantastic. No offense, but I kind of saw it like really old religions that worshiped inanimate objects, trees, rocks, and mountains and stuff. It just didn't seem real to me."

"Hmm . . . not real," Ian said. "That's an interesting way to look at it." A minute of silence passed, then Ian said, "Tell me Jack, what you've experienced today . . . does it seem real to you?"

"No . . . well yes . . . um no. I mean . . . not real in a real sense," Jack stammered. "I know all this is really happening . . . I'm not crazy or hallucinating; I'm pretty sure of that. It's just that I am uncertain what the reality of this is, not whether what has happened today is real or not. You know what I mean?"

Ian chuckled and said, "I think I know what you mean, mate." Ian paused for a moment then said, "I disagree with your assessment of 'Dreamtime' though Jack . . . in fact, I must say you are quite wrong. You see . . . ."

"Hey," Jack interrupted, "with all due respect, I'm not in the mood to get into a deep philosophical debate concerning spiritual beliefs . . . believe me."

"No, of course not, and that is not my intention," Ian replied. "I am only interested in discovering the reality of your presence here. A reality that, to you it seems, is elusive and perplexing. Earlier you questioned your state of mind. Are you concerned you've gone mad?"

"Jesus . . . I don't feel like I've gone mad in any way," Jack said. "I can think clearly, and my memories of home and just a few days ago are crystal clear. I just can't figure it out."

Ian replied softly, "I don't believe you're mad, Jack. But this is a war. Bad things are happening . . . you've seen them. What don't you understand?"

It was apparent to Jack that Ian was approaching his situation very cautiously, almost as if he were trying to gently lead him in a direction, to a conclusion. Still he protested, "Damn it, I told you, Ian. I'm here for the ceremonies . . . there's no war here . . . there can't be! The war here ended 60 years ago . . . other than the minor tribal skirmishes and stuff."

Ian put his hand on Jack's shoulder and said slowly, "Jack, there is a war going on here. You saw it. You witnessed horrible things; that man's head exploding, the dead and wounded Marines. You saw the ships and planes. You saw the misery of the wounded boys back there. You saw those things . . . what else can they possibly mean?"

46

"Hell if I know," Jack muttered. "Hell if I know . . . you tell me, Ian. Christ . . . tell me! What is going on? Do you know?"

Ian hesitated a moment, then gently squeezed Jack's shoulder. He took a deep breath and said, "It's a war . . . a real war between the U.S., Australia, and Japan. That much I do know Jack . . . that is the reality right here, right now."

After a pause, Jack guffawed and semi-hysterically blurted, "What are you telling me? You telling me I'm in the middle of World War II?"

"Easy, mate . . . listen . . . listen to me for a moment, okay?"

"Yeah, okay . . . okay . . . I'll listen, Doc. I'll listen just as long as you make some sense of this."

Ian continued, "Jack, as I said, I honestly don't believe you're delusional, or despite the horrible things you witnessed today, are suffering from any sort of war neurosis. I studied these things during training and you show no signs of either. So, something else has occurred . . . let's try and figure it out together . . . okay, mate?"

"Okay," Jack murmured.

"Good . . . that's good," Ian replied. After a pause, he asked slowly, "Now don't get upset, but I want you to tell me what year it is."

Jack grunted bitterly, then said, "Last I checked it was 2002, but who the hell knows? Who the hell knows if I'm still on planet Earth?"

Ian laughed lightly and said, "I can assure you, mate, that like it or not, you're still on Earth." He paused for a moment then with a very gentle tone said, "Listen carefully Jack . . . listen and don't shut me out, okay?"

"I'll try."

"Jack what I am about to tell you may be a shock, but what I tell you is the truth . . . can you accept that?"

Jack closed his eyes, dropped his head and said barely above a whisper, "I can try; that I can promise."

"Good," Ian answered. "Here it is . . . if you ask any man on this island, or any sailor aboard the ships standing offshore what year it is, their answer will be very different than yours." He paused again then said, "As well, their answers will all be the same, each and every one of them."

Eyes still shut, Jack said, his voice quaking slightly, "So tell me what their answer would be?"

"All of them Jack, every single one, would say it's August 8, 1942."

Jack immediately pounded his fists on the sides of his head. "But it's not . . . it can't be! Hell, I flew here on a jet! I talked to my wife and kids last night before I left for the Tenaru! Not possible . . . fucking not possible!" Ian did not reply. His hand remained on Jack's shoulder. Jack drew his arms over his head and groaned, "Oh, Christ, oh, Jesus . . . what the hell has happened? I need to get home now! I need to be with Laura and my kids."

After a few minutes, he composed himself and Ian said, "Jack, let's talk about this a bit. Talk about last night and your camping trip, okay? Maybe we can make some sense of all this."

After a moment, Jack replied shakily, "Yeah, I guess we should. Maybe we can get me back where I belong."

"Yes, perhaps," Ian replied. He allowed Jack a few more moments to think, then said, "So if I'm not mistaken, you are willing to at least explore the fact that it may be, as I believe it is, 1942? That somehow you have arrived here from the future?"

"Oh, god . . . oh, Jesus, to hear it put that way . . . I don't know," Jack whispered. "I don't know . . . but I guess I need to consider everything, don't I?"

"Good . . . listen . . ."

"I mean, oh my Christ . . . I mean?" Jack interrupted. "I've read some of Stephen Hawking's stuff and Einstein's theories regarding quantum physics and parallel universes and stuff; but Jesus Christ . . . it can't be!" He paused a moment, rocking back and forth on his haunches, his head resting on his knees. Then he chanted in a quiet monotone, trying to accept something he couldn't yet completely believe, "Still, I'm here, I have to keep an open mind . . . I have to keep an open mind . . . right? They say it's possible . . . they say that. It could be." Then he raised his head, looked at Ian and said, "How in Christ's name are you so calm, and how can you so easily believe that I may have slipped back in time?"

"That's essentially why I asked you what you knew of our 'Dreamtime'?"

"How's that?" Jack asked.

"In my early years I was raised in a traditional Aboriginal community. We survived as hunter gatherers and lived, compared to the Europeans, quite rough. But this had always been our way, and we lived our lives under the guidance of our spirit ancestors or the 'Dreaming'. We had no need or concept of material possessions, land ownership or conquest, whether it be military or socio-economic. We don't even have words in our vocabulary that describe such things. We were a happy, flourishing people until the Europeans came and began building cities and taking the resources from the land. It all went to bloody hell when they decided to assimilate us into their society; guess they thought they were doing us a favor. I was taken away from my parents in 1927, when I was 11. You see, I had European blood in me from two generations back, and the bloody government decided that those of us who had fair skin and some precious Anglo-Saxon blood should be directly assimilated. They said they were taking me because the conditions we lived in weren't fit to raise a child. I was placed with a white couple in Adelaide. I was luckier than most, I guess. They're good people, and raised me well."

"Jesus Christ," Jack said quietly. "I'm sorry."

"It's alright, mate. I haven't seen my parents since. I don't even know where they are or if they're alive, but I'm doing okay. Anyhow, I'm telling you this for your sake not mine."

"How so?"

"You see I've experienced Western beliefs, philosophies, and culture as well as those of the Aborigines. Western culture has no spiritual belief system or capacity to accept what may have happened to you. You would insist on calling on science to either prove or disprove it. We Aborigines, on the other hand, are deeply spiritual; we believe everything that happens in the world, life, death, the sprouting of a seedling, the presence of a lake or stream, are all based on the subconscious . . . or the dreaming of our ancestors. You Europeans know religion, but you don't know true spirituality. This is essentially why it is easier for me to accept what may have happened to you, than it is for you. Our people don't even have a word for time or a true defined concept of it. There is no past, present, or future. Everything in life is a movement through space, or a dream turned into its physical manifestation. You have been dreamed here by some spirit, Jack. You have not traveled back in *time* as much as you have moved through *space* as a spirit's dream, and now in reality are here . . . here in this space . . . not time."

"I don't know, man," Jack said. "That sounds pretty creative and interesting but it doesn't go very far in explaining what happened."

Ian patted Jack on the back, laughed, and said, "See, mate. Spoken like a true European. What happened most probably can't be explained scientifically. But that doesn't mean it didn't happen. I believe that for some reason the spirits dreamed you here, that you are here for a purpose. The minute I saw you today, I felt you were different, that a unique spirit was within you. I can't explain it, Jack, and I don't feel a need to."

Jack recalled how Ian had stared intensely at him in the lean-to. He felt comfortable with the mysterious doctor and began to talk. He told him about falling into the creek the night before, and the strange, welcoming tunnel he'd been drawn into. Ian simply nodded his head. After hesitating, Jack finally asked Ian a question he himself had been avoiding. "Do you think I drowned in the creek? Do you think I'm dead?"

"I don't believe so," Ian replied. "You may have traveled to another place at the behest of the spirits, but you are not dead, at the very least not your soul. I am not imagining that I am sitting here talking to you after all, eh mate?"

"Tell me, if you were raised in both cultures how is it you have chosen to maintain your beliefs in the Dreaming. I mean, I com-

50

pletely understand the western world has fucked you and your people over pretty good, but it is pretty darn civilized and advanced."

"You have to know Jack, know who you are and what you believe before you could truly understand my choice. You must simply open your mind and actually see the world around you, understand its meanings and purpose. Second, when that captain's head exploded in your face this morning, would you call that a civilized, advanced act? Is hoarding great wealth and land civilized and advanced, or is it really rather pointless when one considers the true human needs, spiritual and otherwise?"

Jack rubbed his head wearily and said, "This is getting a little too philosophical for me. I can't take too much onboard right now. No offense, Ian, but I need time to think."

"Of course you do. I'm sorry for taking this a bit too bloody far. We can talk more about these sorts of things later. I have to get back to the station anyway. I'll probably be gone a couple of hours, so why don't you sit here and relax . . . think about things. Do you smoke?"

"Only at parties and such but, god, would I love a smoke now."

"I'll have Frank run you down a pack of Lucky Strikes, a lighter, and a poncho. You don't want to be caught with a lit cigarette out here; use the poncho to cover up. These jumpy sentries are liable to bloody shoot you."

"Hey . . . thanks, man," Jack said as the doctor strode off.

Minutes later, Frank delivered the pack. Jack covered himself with the poncho, pulled a cigarette out and lit it. He kept the lighter lit and examined the pack. On the back was printed an ad for the purchase of war bonds. He took a deep drag off the unfiltered cigarette; the strong tobacco burned his lungs. After he exhaled, he slowly shook his head and said, "Christ . . . Lucky Strikes." He thought about what Ian had told him regarding Aboriginal spirituality and how it may not explain time travel, but it would readily accept the possibility, or even perhaps the necessity, of it. Then he thought of Laura and his kids, Joey and Grace. He couldn't bear the thought of not seeing them again. When he sold the family business, he'd planned to spend a majority of time with his family. It hadn't really happened though, as much of his time was spent at the club, parties, or various community functions. As well, as his drinking increased, he stayed away from home. He didn't like the kids seeing him drunk. Now his heart ached for them; nothing else in his life, just them. He whispered to himself, "Stay cool, buddy. You'll get home."

He stubbed out his cigarette and spread the poncho out beside him. He laid back on the beach, arms behind his head. He thought back on spitting man, the Zero, the captain's headless torso, the dead Japanese man and the wounded boys in the tent. Again, the sites and sounds swirled maniacally in his head until he cupped both hands over his ears and began to softly cry, "Oh, Jesus . . . Oh, God, help me," he moaned. "Take me home, please take me home." He shook his head and said, "Get a grip, bud. Get a grip!" Suddenly, he felt very tired, his mind completely wasted. He couldn't sleep, but he strangely, yet comfortingly, fell into a sort of dormant state: unthinking, unfeeling.

3

It seemed only a few minutes had passed when Jack felt someone gently shaking him. "It's me . . . Ian."

He rubbed his eyes and muttered, "Oh, shit."

"What's wrong?" Ian asked.

"I'm still here, that's what's wrong."

Ian chuckled sympathetically and said, "Well, it's good you got some rest."

"Yeah, I guess," Jack replied. "Thanks for the smokes, Doc. They're very strong, but have a lot of flavor. I'm used to filtered lights."

"Don't know anything about your 'filter lights' but you Yanks do know how to make a fine cigarette. I went to medical school in London and the cigarettes there tasted like bloody horseshit. After the war started, and especially during the Blitz, you could only get one or two brands."

"The Blitz?" Jack asked.

"Oh yeah, sorry mate," Ian said. "The Blitz was when the Germans raided London and other . . ."

"I know what the damn Blitz was, Doc," Jack mumbled. "Tell me what year it is again."

"Same year it was earlier . . . 1942."

"1942 . . . shit . . . goddamnit!" Jack sputtered. Jack paused then said, "When Laura and I got married she gave me a gold band with the date of our wedding inscribed on the inside. I'll show it to you tomorrow in the light. It doesn't read 1930 something or 1940 something. It reads 2/8/1990."

"I believe you, mate, just as you need to believe me when I say right here and now, it's August 8, well actually now, August 9, 1942."

They were silent as Jack once again pondered Ian's suggestion. If it were true, Jack was not sure he could handle it. The thought of being separated from his family by over half a century was an unbearable prospect on its own. Also, the idea that he had somehow traveled back through time was enormously mind-bending. The two ideas combined, if he accepted them, could be overwhelming. So, like a child in denial, he continued to resist what was becoming increasingly obvious. Jack said quietly, "August 9, 1942 . . . Christ! I've read about this day and those that followed since I was a little kid!" Jack buried his head in his hands and softly moaned. Then, he suddenly jerked his head up and stared out over the black water of the sound. "Hey, Doc, what time is it?" Jack's breath came in short, tight bursts. Beads of sweat formed on his brow and his heart raced.

"I can't see my watch, but I'd guess it's about 0130 hours."

"Okay . . . okay," Jack whispered.

"What is it, Jack?" Ian asked.

"It's proof . . . or no . . . it will tell me what's going on. We'll know, Ian. We'll know at 1:55."

"We'll know what?" Ian asked.

"If it happens at 1:55 I'll know for sure. I'll know what's really happened to me. Take your watch off," Jack demanded, his voice pitched higher with stress. "We can read it with your lighter. I need to know what time it is to the minute until five of two."

"Okay, mate," Ian replied. He un-strapped his watch and asked, "What are we waiting for? What's going to happen at 0155?"

"I hope nothing," Jack said. "But if by some crazy black hole, Albert Einstein, Stephen Hawking type shit, it is 1942, a whole hell of a lot is going to happen. Give me your lighter, Ian." Ian handed over his lighter and Jack rolled the wheel against the flint with shaking hands. In his desperation Jack could only produce a spray of sparks. "Shit!" he exclaimed.

"Whoa there, mate," Ian said. "Slow down . . . you're jerking it too much when you roll the wheel; the bloody thing won't light."

"Okay . . . yeah okay," Jack replied. He forced himself to calm down and finally produced a yellow flame that stung his eyes in the darkness.

"Cup it!" Ian hissed. "Bloody hell, Jack, cup the damn flame! Remember what I told you about the sentries!"

"Then hold the goddamn watch, man!" Jack said shrilly, "I only have two fucking hands."

"Alright, stay calm, mate," Ian admonished. He took the watch and held it low near Jack's lap. Jack held the lighter in one hand and covered the flame with his other. The heat rising from the tiny fire burned the palm of Jack's protective hand, but he hardly noticed.

"1:38 . . . it's 1:38!" Jack said in a desperate tone that was at odds with a simple reportage of the time. He snuffed the flame and stared out to sea.

After a pause, Ian asked anxiously, "What is it? What is it you think might happen?"

"Oh not too much, Doc," Jack said flatly. "Just the biggest goddamn surface battle the U.S. Navy ever fought . . . biggest defeat too. If it is 1942, it will start at 1:55 out there around Savo Island. That's what the historians called it . . . The Battle of Savo Island."

"Crikey," Ian replied, a hint of anxiety creeping into his voice. "You say it was a defeat?"

"Hell, yes . . . a bad one."

"Bloody hell."

Jack went on. "The *Astoria*, the *Vincennes*, the *Quincy* and your *Canberra* . . . all sunk. Over a thousand dead, and hundreds others burned and mutilated. It was a complete one-sided slaughter." Ian was quiet, save for a handful of pebbles that rattled nervously in his hand.

"Jesus, this is crazy," Jack muttered. "No way . . . no goddamn way." Still though, Jack lit the lighter again and said, "1:43 now. Twelve minutes to go."

They sat silent in the sand, staring intently toward Savo Island. Both of them were too tense and deep in thought to carry on further conversation. Jack checked the watch several more times. The last time, he announced that it was 1:52. At that moment, the hiss of large waves very near shore broke the still night. The waves then fell upon the beach with a crash. There was a pause, then a new set of waves tumbled onto the sand. Ian whispered, "There must be some weather out there I reckon."

Jack stared glassy eyed at the blue-green luminescent waves. He gasped and mumbled, "Oh God . . . oh my God . . . oh, sweet Jesus, help me."

"What, what is it?" Ian asked urgently. Ian watched as Jack rose and stumbled into the crashing surf. Strangely, he sat down and let the waves wash around him. Ian quickly followed and knelt down next to him. "Tell me, Jack. Tell me what's happening!"

"Oh my god," Jack muttered. "I don't know if I can take it, Ian. It's too much . . . the whole thing is too fucking much for me. My family . . . and now I'm going to sit here and watch 1000 Americans get massacred. I can't handle this . . . I can't do this!"

"You'll be fine. Stay calm now," Ian soothed. Jack began to shake and tears filled his eyes. "What is it Jack?" Ian asked. "What is it about the waves?"

In a daze, he replied, "It's not the weather. See . . . see how a set comes in then it's calm again . . . then another set comes in. It's not weather, Doc."

"What is it then?"

"They're wakes . . . wakes from warships . . . big ones. I . . . I read about them."

"Jap warships?" Ian asked.

"No . . . ours, the southern group steaming toward Savo. Christ, they're . . . they're steaming straight into a Jap ambush. Oh, Jesus, oh god! We couldn't see them because of the dark. But they're there. Any minute now . . . any minute. Oh, Jesus, help me . . . please help me!" Jack cried. Then, forgetting about himself, he suddenly turned to Ian and yelled, "We've got to warn them, we've got to tell them to run! They're not ready to fight a night battle like this. We've got to warn them!"

"There's no way Jack . . . we don't have a radio, and even if we did what good would it do? Just stay calm, mate. There's nothing we can do."

Jack thought for a moment. The ships had steamed past, miles off shore, and the wakes they produced were just now reaching the beach. Jack knew Ian was right. It was too late. The Japanese warships would already be in amongst the Allied fleet. "Goddamn!" he groaned. A feeling of utter helplessness, unlike anything he'd ever felt before, enveloped him.

Kneeling in the surf, Ian put his arm around Jack's shoulders and they stared in silence toward Savo Island. Moments later they lurched in unison when the black sky over Savo suddenly turned bright green. Both of them stared at the dull, eerie light with an immediate sense of dread and horror. Jack drew his knees up, wrapping his arms around them. He rested his chin on them; tears filled his eyes. He rasped one word, "Flares." The green flares dropped by airplanes were quickly followed by flashes of white-yellow light that brightly lit the night sky . . . lit the world, it seemed. The heavy overcast would suddenly appear thick and menacing, then disappear in an instant when there was a lull in the flashing. "It's started," Jack said quietly. "In a minute or two we'll be able to hear it." The flashes illuminated their faces in a pale, ghostly light. Ian stared wide-eyed at the unfolding disaster, while Jack rocked slowly back and forth in the surf, moaning softly. Tears streaming down his cheeks glistened in the lightning bursts of the big guns and their exploding shells. They sat in the surf, two solitary people huddled together, watching the historic tragedy play out on the vast, natural stage. Then deep, vibrating rumbles, like thunder over Lake Michigan, Jack thought, rolled across the sound and joined them. The sounds of the guns booming and shells exploding on the hulls and decks of the American ships, lent a new horror to the scene. "Oh, god. No!" Jack screamed. He'd often read about the great sea battle, fantasizing what it must have been like to witness it. He would have given much to have the opportunity. Now though, he stood up and began to slog his way through the water toward the battle. "No, goddamnit, no!"

Jack knew for certain now it all was real, and the horror he felt put him on the verge of hysteria. "I can't just stand here and watch this!" he yelled, as a new flood of tears streamed down his face. "They're killing them; killing them all. I gotta get home. I want to go home!"

Jack's outburst broke Ian's trance, and he rose and moved quickly after him. "Steady, mate . . . calm down now . . . there's nothing we can do!" he shouted. He grabbed Jack by the collar and said, "Easy now, mate . . . take it easy!"

Jack stopped, but sobbed, "You take it easy, goddamnit! You take it fuckin' easy!" Jack swept his arm violently behind his head, broke Ian's grasp on his collar, and turned toward him. The flashing lights had reached such a frequency that they cast a constant glow, illuminating Jack's wild-eyed, desperate expression.

Ian raised a hand and said, "Okay, Jack . . . just calm down now. You have to stay calm . . . it won't do you any good to lose your head."

"Fuck you!" Jack yelled. He whirled around and looked out over the sound toward Savo. His sense of frustration and helplessness increased. It was a sense he felt not just for the young sailors, but for himself as well, trapped in a nightmare, decades from home. He balled his hands into fists and raised them to the level of his head, screaming like a wounded animal at the sounds and sights rising before him. "Go, goddamnit!" he yelled, shaking his fists. "Get the hell out of there! Run, goddamnit . . . run now!" After a pause, he continued more slowly, more softly, "Run boys . . . run . . . they're going to butcher you. You'll just die . . . that's all . . . nothing else . . . you'll all just die." Jack sank to his knees, the water up to his neck, and sobbed. Tears slid off his chin and mixed with the waters of the sound. Ian waited a few moments, then knelt down in the surf.

"What can I do for you, mate?" he asked.

Jack was quiet for a moment, then said, "Do for me, Doc? It's nineteen fucking forty-two and I'm watching a bunch of Americans get slaughtered. Christ, Doc . . . I was born in 1957! I don't think there's a hell of a lot you can do for me."

"Maybe not," Ian replied. "Maybe there is though. You need to calm down and give it a chance." Jack said nothing, so Ian continued, "Listen, the first thing we have to do is get back to the aid station. It doesn't do you, or me for that matter, any good to sit here and watch this."

As it did earlier, Ian's voice had a calming effect on Jack. "Yeah . . . yeah, okay," he said after a pause. He looked out at the death-dealing flashes, then quickly averted his eyes. It was just young men, real men like those in the aid station, not larger-than-life fantasies, dying in a hellish maelstrom, far from home. "I can't handle this . . . not now . . . it's too awful, the battle . . . everything." They slogged out of the surf and slowly trudged back to the aid station. Jack fought a sudden urge to sprint back to the head of the Tenaru, jump in, and drown himself in hopes of finding a way back home. Ian's comforting arm around his shoulder, as well as his earlier words, compelled him to stay, to wait and see what destiny had in store for him. His mind drifted back to the conversation he'd had with Laura shortly before he'd left home.

"You're the father of two young children, for godsakes!" she'd shouted. "You're drinking and depression has been hard enough on this family. Now you're gallivanting off to some godforsaken South Seas Island, leaving me alone with the kids for two weeks! Let alone the fact that you've picked an island where your own government recommends caution. What am I supposed to think Jack? Really . . . tell me."

"Listen, Laura," Jack had replied. "I told you this was my last hurrah. I'm going to cut down on my drinking when I get back and start a new business or something. Trust me. Besides, you know this is about my passion, so how wrong can it be? They say you should pursue your passions right? It's for my dad too, you know. It'll be fine, really."

"Don't give me that crap about your dad. I know how you felt about him so don't even go there. This has nothing to do with your dad. As for your passion, in what way are you really pursuing it, Jack? How much meaning does sitting at a hotel pool, partying between the occasional foray to an old battle site, hold? Are you going to write a book, or film a documentary? It's all about you, Jack, just like everything else these days. You need to figure out what you're looking for, or what it is you're running away from, before it's too late. I don't know what to think of you anymore, Jack. I just don't know."

He'd bristled and said, "Oh come on, Laura. You don't understand, and you never will. I'm going to Guadalcanal, so just accept it. End of discussion."

The discussion ended. Though Jack knew Laura had been right. World War II history was a passion of his, but the trip was selfish. He went because he could, and besides, he had nothing else to do. He had sold the family business and retired. His relationship with Laura had become distant, then strained, as he drifted along with the rest of the idle rich, her values not changing to keep pace with his new lifestyle. After various housing and car projects were complete, he found himself spending increasing amounts of time at the club and rarely having a normal conversation with Laura. Somehow, through it all, he'd tricked himself into believing that he was satisfied with the life his business acumen had provided; the pills the doctor prescribed were merely a shield against what he liked to believe was a genetic predisposition to melancholy.

When Ian and Jack reached the aid station, the wounded Marines in the lean-to were sleeping peacefully, as their countrymen were being slaughtered just miles away. In spite of the frightening cacophony and bursts of light, Frank was quietly moving amongst the soldiers, checking on them, gingerly tucking green woolen blankets up around their necks. Other corpsmen stood together in a group outside the lean-to, anxiously chattering away about the sounds and sights of the naval battle. Ian and Jack retreated behind the lean-to, putting it between them and the battle, and sat down. They each lit a cigarette. Jack puffed on his slowly, staring blankly at the ground. Minutes later the sky suddenly went black, as the flashes abruptly ceased. Only the faint glow of far off burning warships offered light. A short time afterward, the rumbling sounds of the battle died out.

"It's over," Jack said dully.

"How you doing, mate?" Ian asked.

Jack looked up, and slowly answered, "I'm okay I guess." He paused, then looked directly at Ian and said, "I'm sorry, Doc. I'm sorry for losing my shit on the beach. It's just too much . . . my being here . . . the battle and all. I'm sorry . . . you've been really good to me."

"Bloody hell, are you kidding, mate? You've had a horrible, fantastic shock. I'd say your reaction has been pretty sane."

Jack stubbed his cigarette out in the dirt and rubbed his hands through his hair. "I have to accept this, don't I? I have to accept fully that this has really happened, and that I really did just see a thousand of my countrymen die. Men who died before I was born."

"I believe you do," Ian replied. "It's all you really can do." Ian rubbed his hands together and nervously looked at Jack. He seemed to want to speak, but didn't. Jack had seen the look before. It was the same look a sales manager had on his face when he was trying to summon the courage to ask Jack if his performance had placed his ongoing employment in jeopardy. It was the same look a longtime, formerly faithful customer had on his face when he was about to tell Jack he was considering other options for supply. Jack almost laughed at the similes. They seemed so insignificant now; though just a day ago they represented the greatest conflicts Jack had ever faced.

Jack said, "What is it, Doc . . . what do you want to ask me?"

"Jack, I know your situation is awful and frightening and I feel great sympathy for you."

61

"Ask your question," Jack urged. "I'm doing okay now and I give you credit for that . . . so ask."

"Okay. You said the sea battle was a terrible defeat for our navies. Even my, or Australia's *Canberra* was sunk and many of your ships, yes?"

"Yeah, a real disaster," Jack said. "We gained nothing at all from it, in fact, because of it the Navy got spooked and hauled ass, or hauls ass tomorrow with half the supplies still in the holds of the supply ships." This latest information creased Ian's face with concern.

"Oh my, well that lovely bit of information makes my question all the more interesting." He paused, seeming to search for the right words. "What becomes of us? What's going to happen to us now that the fleet has been decimated as you describe and the supply ships leave?" He hesitantly added, "I hate to ask in a way . . . it seems bloody selfish considering your, shall I say, predicament?"

Jack smiled wearily and said, "Predicament? Yeah, that's what this is . . . a predicament. Just a little matter of slipping back six decades is all."

Ian grinned sheepishly and said, "Perhaps that is a bit of an understatement, mate. No offense intended."

"Don't worry, Doc. I take no offense, and everything will be okay. It's going to be a long, tough campaign and the Navy will come back. We'll win in the end. The Japs aren't strong enough. They constantly underestimate our strength and will to resist them, and their tactics are antiquated. It'll be tough though . . . real tough."

Ian looked at Jack for a moment then said, "Thanks for that. I hated to ask . . . but the sea battle scared me, I must admit. I guess we need each other, eh, mate?"

"No problem," Jack replied. "And you're right; we do need each other I guess. As I said, it'll be a long slog; half a year or thereabouts. A lot of guys are going to die and it's going to be particularly hard the first couple of months. Very little food, air cover, and supplies. We can talk about it later, but you'll probably spend more time treating disease cases than battle casualties."

"Okay, I can handle that," Ian said. He chuckled self-consciously and said, "I guess I was worrying that we'd all die or be taken prisoner or something, you know?"

"I understand."

"One more thing, Jack . . . a request."

"What is it?"

"Beyond what you just told me, I don't want to know anything else about the future, or your world's past; unless of course it would help in the care of my patients. I have no need to know anything else. The future is your Dreamspace. Not mine."

"I'm not sure what you mean by that, but I suppose I can understand why you don't want to know. No problem."

Suddenly Jack jolted upright, and stared glassy-eyed into the darkness. "What is it?" Ian asked nervously.

In a daze, Jack replied, "He might be here. He might be on this island somewhere . . . oh my god."

"Who's here, Jack?" Ian asked. "Who are you talking about?"

In a near whisper, he answered, "My father . . . my dad. He's dead, but he might be here."

"Bloody Christ!" Ian gasped. "Your father is on Guadalcanal?"

"It's possible . . . I don't know for certain, but he did serve on shore here with the Navy at some time. He never talked about it, so I'm not sure when he landed or what his job was."

"Bloody hell, mate," Ian muttered. He lit Jack another cigarette.

After a drag, Jack said in a monotone, "He's 19 . . . Christ, he's a teenager. He went in after Pearl Harbor."

"What are you going to do?" Ian asked.

"Do . . . do about what, Doc?" Jack said in a daze.

"Your father, what are you going to do about him? Are you going to try and find him?"

Jack rubbed his eyes wearily and said, "Oh Christ, I don't know. I need time to think about it. For god sake," he laughed bitterly. "My father?"

"Yeah, I reckon it's too bloody bizarre to take in all at once," Ian responded. "You're right; you need to sleep on it. We'll talk more tomorrow, okay?"

"Right, Doc." Jack emitted a chuckle and said, "Hell, maybe I'll wake up in the morning and this day will have been a nightmare to end all nightmares."

Ian smiled weakly, "Don't count on it, mate, in fact you need to be emotionally prepared for a stay here with us." Jack looked at Ian's kind face. He felt grateful that Ian was looking after him. The Australian doctor had an almost shamanistic quality about him. It was obvious he could see things that Jack couldn't, that he was better equipped to accept the unexplained and weave it into his life, and now Jacks. Jack instinctively knew that Ian would be a tremendous asset in his staying sane, or for that matter, simply surviving and finding a way home.

"Listen, mate," Ian said. "We're breaking camp at 0800 so we need to get some sleep."

"Okay," Jack said flatly.

"Right then . . . off to bed with us. I'll get you a blanket and you can curl up where you want. I'll let you decide which spot has the best view. I won't wake you until just before we break camp, okay? You need to get as much rest as possible, old man."

"Thanks . . . Jesus, thanks for everything today, Ian," Jack said wearily.

After Ian gave him a wool blanket, Jack laid down on the dirt floor of the aid station. He noticed Frank was up again, quietly making his rounds. He watched him for a moment, then for the first night in years, he fell hard asleep, completely sober.

4

The groan of diesel engines and shouted commands woke Jack from a deep slumber. The first thing he saw when he opened his eyes was the last thing he had seen before he fell asleep. Frank was busy again, this time spoon feeding the wounded their breakfasts of prunes and oatmeal. Jack rubbed his eyes and let out a low groan. Immediately his stomach tightened and a blackness settled over his senses. Nothing had changed during the night other than the fact that he felt rested. He was still here and so were all the others. "Oh, goddamn," he moaned. Frank heard Jack's lament and ambled over.

"Good morning, Jack," he said. "How you doing?"

After a pause, Jack muttered, "I'm fine, Frank . . . just fine." He didn't feel fine at all though. In fact he felt he was quickly sinking into a deep depression much like the one he had experienced the previous year in Grand Rapids. The thought terrified him as he recalled the effect it had wreaked on his psyche. For a week or two he was barely able to function. His deep melancholy made him feel weak and nauseous. He cared about nothing. The pain the emotional aberration had produced was in some ways physical and relentlessly present. It hammered at him day and night until he thought he was going mad. Sleep was only acquired after generous helpings of bourbon. Borrowing from his political hero, Winston Churchill, he called the debilitating emotional state his 'Black Dog'.

He'd gone to a psychiatrist he often played golf with, and tried to put the blame on Laura, representing her as a badgering housewife who was completely overreacting to a mere funk. The doctor though, after talking to Jack and running tests, told him he believed he was indeed suffering from a serious depression. He gave him two prescriptions: one a tranquilizer, the other, one of the new anti-depressants. He also told him to cut down on his drinking and to exercise every day. Reluctantly, he took the prescriptions, telling the doctor they would get Laura off his back. The tranquilizers, in fact, gave him immediate relief to the point that he could function again. After several weeks on the anti-depressant, he felt nearly normal. He did cut down on his drinking and made a stab at exercise on Laura's treadmill. His new lifestyle didn't last long though, and his medication was his primary method of coping. Now his pills were back in his hotel room in Honiara. If a similar depression set in, he wasn't certain if he could possibly cope with the intense emotional assault of the 'black dog'. The dread he felt nearly turned to panic. He hadn't noticed Ian watching him intently from across the aid station, 15 feet away.

"Hey, you sure you're okay?" Frank asked. "You don't look so hot." Jack rubbed his eyes, and just as he was about to answer a light kick thudded on his behind.

He slowly turned and looked up. Ian was standing over him with a slight frown on his face. "Alright, Macmillan," he said sternly. "I've been up for two hours and I think you've had enough beauty sleep for one night. It's time to get to work."

Jack sat up with a quizzical look on his face. "Jesus, Doc," he said. "Give me a chance to wake up will ya?"

"You've had enough time. We're moving up and you need get to work like the rest of us. I want fresh dressings on every one of these men before we move."

Jack rose slowly and stared at Ian. He was shocked by his demeanor; even his face seemed to have changed. Frank stood next to Jack with a look of surprise. "You're a corpsman?" he asked in wonder.

"Of course he is," Ian replied sharply. "He suffered a concussion during the Jap air attack yesterday but he's fine now. He needs

66

to get to work along with the rest of us. He's a retread from the first war, so he's a little rusty, Frank. You let him observe your work with the patients, then let him re-dress the last one."

Jack continued to stare at Ian, trying to make sense of his strange, new demeanor. After a pause Ian barked, "Alright then chaps, get on with it! We don't have all bloody day, do we?"

"C'mon, Jack, let's get started," Frank urged.

Ian turned crisply and walked away. He stopped suddenly, turned and said, "One more thing, Frank."

"Yes, sir?" Frank replied.

"Before we move out, scrounge up a canteen, mess kit, a bag and boondockers for Jack here. We have extras somewhere in our supplies." Ian looked at Jack's brushed leather Eddie Bauers and shook his head slightly, "You gotta get rid of those . . . the Marines might get the wrong idea about you. We can't have that, can we?" Even after the jibe, Jack noted that Ian remained stony-faced.

"Now get to work, lads," Ian ordered before walking away.

Jack stood for a moment, numb and bewildered. "Let's get to work," Frank urged once again.

Jack turned slowly toward Cudlipp and studied his pale, young face for a moment. He forced a wan smile and said softly, "Yeah, okay . . . let's get started."

Jack followed Frank to the nearest stretcher and they knelt down on either side of it. "Hey, Leonard," Frank said with a broad smile. "Bad news, buddy. I gotta change your dressing before we move out."

"Aww fuck, Frank!" the Marine groaned with a New England accent. "Why don't you guys quit messing with me and let me get back to my unit? I ain't even hurt that bad . . . hell you guys have hurt me worse than the damn Japs!"

Frank laughed and said, "You're right, Leonard, you aren't hurt too bad, but you don't want your leg to get infected do you? If it does, Doc Goldman just loves to saw off limbs . . . he lives for it you know . . . right Jack?" Frank said with a wink.

Jack smiled nervously and hesitated. Finally he stammered, "Hell yes . . . hell yes . . . he, ah, last night. Last night I woke up . . . just as the doc was laying a big fucking saw to my right arm."

Leonard's and Frank's grins boosted Jack's confidence and he continued, "I screamed and asked . . . 'what in hell are you doing, Doc?' He looked at me all disappointed and said, 'Oh, for chrissakes man, buck up! You're left handed, goddamn it, so you don't really need the right one, do you?" Frank hooted and Leonard's grin widened into a broad smile. "I said hell, yes I do, Doc! Now get the hell off of me!"

"What'd the doc say then?" Frank asked, egging Jack on.

"The son of a bitch said, oh all right goddamnit . . . you big baby. I'll just have to get my kicks from the stupid-ass Marines!"

Cudlipp winked again at Jack. Through a smile Leonard groaned, "Alright you fuckin' idiots. Go ahead . . . but make it fast. It hurts like a son of a bitch when you pull the old bandage out of the hole." Jack felt a burst of pride and energy when he saw the effect his story had had on the wounded boy. Though still in somewhat of a state of shock over what had transpired over the last two days, Jack was very aware that the boy was a combat wounded World War II Marine, one of his heroes. The very fact that he had affected the boy's morale created a feeling of exhilaration. The 'Black Dog' took a step back.

"Oh and one other thing, Frank," Leonard added. "Tell your boss I don't wanna stay here one more minute than I have to. I need to get back to my unit. Tell him that, okay, Frank?"

"I'll tell him, Lenny-boy," Cudlipp responded. He nodded toward Jack and made belated introductions. "Leonard, this is Jack. He's a corpsman like me and he's going to help out. Jack, meet Leonard, the orneriest Marine in the entire Corps."

"Nice to meet you, Leonard," Jack said.

"Same here, Doc," the boy replied. "I hope you aren't as fucking ham-handed as Frankie here. Son of a bitch causes me more pain than when the damn log went into my leg in the first place." At first, Jack was taken aback by the boy calling him 'Doc'; then for

68

some reason, he felt a surge of pride. The 'Black Dog' retreated further.

Frank laughed and said, "First of all, Len, it wasn't a log. It was more like a twig. Second, I take extra special care with you because I don't want to hear anymore of your bitching than I have to." Jack looked at each of the boys as they bantered back and forth. The looks on their faces contradicted their sarcastic chatter. Each wore a grin denoting the fact that they were clearly enjoying the exchange. Though they had known each other for only a day, they had developed a gruff affection toward one another that was unique to young men thrown together in a common and dangerous circumstance. Their relationship left Jack feeling old and envious. His life for the past 10 or 15 years, hell perhaps forever, he thought, had been completely devoid of the fraternal bonding the two boys enjoyed.

Frank began to unwrap the soiled dressing adorning Leonard's leg. Leonard, in mock agony, groaned, "Oh goddamn you, Frank! You fucking butcher, you sadistic bastard! You're killing me . . . everything's going black . . . oh god . . . bye Pa, love you Ma . . . you too little sis . . . it's all over . . . I'm gone."

"Shut up, Lenny, you big faker!" Frank laughed. "I haven't even gotten to the inner layers yet. You can't feel a thing."

Jack grinned and asked the young Marine, "How'd you get hurt?"

Frank let out a snort and said, "Tell him Leonard . . . tell him how you got shot by a palm tree."

"Fuck you, Frank, you rear area shit," Leonard spat, though Jack noticed the grin had not left his face. He turned to Jack and said, "I'll tell you the tragic tale if you promise to keep your mouth shut!"

"Cross my heart."

"A Jap plane strafed my unit on the other side of the river yesterday morning. I saw him coming and ran like hell into the groves. I crouched down at the base of a palm and damn it if that Jap pilot didn't see me there." Leonard looked up to make sure Jack was listening. Satisfied, he continued his tale.

"Sure as hell that damn Jap said, 'Why that's Leonard Chesnek from south Boston. I think I'll just jink over a bit and shoot his little ass off.' So the Jap pumps my fucking tree full of Jap bullets. I'm making myself as small as possible, but one bullet hit that tree just right and I swear half that damn tree splintered off and stabbed into my leg. Hurt like a son of a bitch."

Frank couldn't help himself and guffawed, "Half the tree, Lenny? I was there when Doc Goldman pulled that chunk of wood out of your leg, remember? With a scalpel, I may have been able to make a stout toothpick out of it, but nothing more."

Suddenly, Leonard turned serious. "Then why the hell can't I go back to my unit? Why the hell did I have to come here in the first place, Frank? Shit, a fucking piece of wood!"

"Leonard," Frank said gently. "Dr. Goldman and I have explained it to you a dozen times. You know how fast infection can set in, in an environment like this? You don't want to lose your leg do you? You'll be good to go soon enough. The Japs will wait for you, I promise."

Frank was down to the final layer of cotton gauze. Its snowy whiteness had turned to hues of red, black, brown, and yellow. As he very slowly worked on the last layer, Jack continually waved his hand above the wound to ward off the fat black flies that circled over the boy's injury. After the last layer was peeled away, Frank prepared to pull a plug of gauze out of the deep hole the palm splinter had gouged out. "This is the hard part," Frank said. "Pay attention, but also try to keep him as comfortable as possible." Jack looked down at the boy and nervously wondered what he could do to ease the boy's suffering. Frank pulled away the gauze that was stuffed in the open wound. Jack didn't look, but he could hear it. The gauze made a wet sucking sound as it separated from the wound, causing Jack to shiver in spite of the heat.

Frank worked slowly and carefully, trying to minimize the pain as best he could. He said, almost as if he was talking to himself, "The wound is jagged and deep. It wasn't clean enough for Doc Goldman to sew up, so we have to keep swabbing it and let it heal on its own. He'll be fine in a few days, but his leg will have a bit of a dent in it for the rest of his life." Leonard winced and sighed painfully. Beads of sweat formed on his brow as the bandage tore chunks of dried blood and pus from the wound. Jack cursed to himself silently as he struggled to find a way to comfort the boy.

Haltingly, he said, "So you're from Boston, huh, Leonard?"

In spite of his agony, the boy answered through clenched teeth, "I am . . . greatest place on Earth. You been there, Doc?" he asked hopefully.

Jack looked at Leonard and saw the pain in his eyes and the sweat rolling off the sides of his forehead. He reached across the boy and grabbed one of Frank's green cotton cloths. He gently dabbed the boy's head and neck and said, "Hell, yes I've been there, Leonard . . . the Harbor, Quincy Market, all the history. You're right; it's a hell of a place."

Cudlipp pulled the last of the bandage off and Leonard sighed. His body visibly relaxed as the pain-induced tension drifted away. He looked up at Jack and asked, "You been to Fenway for a ball-game, Doc?"

"No, I never made it there."

"Oh, then I'm sorry, Doc, but you haven't truly been to Boston 'til you've seen the Red Sox at Fenway." Leonard said seriously. "Nothing like it in the world, Doc. I shit you not."

Leonard reached into his shirt and pulled out a shiny silver pendant attached to a greasy leather rope. He proudly held it up for Jack to see. The pendant was in the shape of an English 'B'.

"Very nice," Jack said. "I'll make sure I get there next time I'm in Boston, okay?"

"You do that, Doc. Hey, look me up . . . I mean it. I'll take you to Fenway, you'll have more fun than you've ever had, I promise. It's Leonard Chesnek, 23 Shannon Street, South Boston. You be sure and look me up now, Doc."

Jack was just about to answer when a stern voice asked, "What are we having here boys . . . bloody tea and cakes? What in hell is taking so long, Frank?" Ian stood over them, glaring.

"Sorry, sir, it was really stuck and I guess . . . I guess we were talking a little." Frank replied. "I'm just getting ready to swab and rewrap . . . we'll be done in just a minute, sir."

Ian hesitated, then said, "Jack, you swab and Frank will finish up."

Startled, Jack looked up at Ian and asked, "You sure?"

"I'm sure. Now finish up here and move on. You still have four men who need fresh dressings and we're starting tear down. So get on with it; and Frank?"

"Yes, sir?"

"I've changed my mind. I want Jack to clean all the wounds and then wrap the last man like I said." He turned to Jack and said crisply, "Now pay attention!"

"Okay, I will." Jack was still perplexed by Ian's demeanor.

Ian left and Frank handed him a forceps, cotton swab, and a pan of clear liquid. So as not to alarm Leonard, Frank merely nodded and said, "Go ahead, Jack, swab the wound."

Jack placed the cotton swab in the forceps and dipped it in the solution. The solution sloshing around in the tin pan smelled strongly of alcohol. He slowly moved the cotton tipped forceps toward Leonard's wound. He held his breath as he touched the gory injury with the cotton swab. Leonard let out a small groan. Jack retracted the swab and cursed under his breath.

"Go on, Jack," Frank encouraged. "It's not you . . . it's the solution. It stings pretty good, but it's not as bad as old Leonard here makes it out to be. The best thing is to do it quick and get it over with." Jack dabbed at the wound while Frank gently wiped the boy's brow and told him it was just about done. Finally Frank said, "Okay, great job Jack . . . let's get you wrapped up, Leonard." Frank sprinkled some sulfa powder on the wound and quickly began to re-dress it. Jack watched closely and noted the tightness with which Frank bound the injury. He carefully counted the number of revolutions the bandage made around the leg, and then watched Frank fasten the gauze with pins.

"Sorry if that hurt, Leonard," Jack said as he wiped the last beads of sweat off the young man's face and neck.

"No problem, Doc," he said with a smile. "All joking aside, I know you're helping me get better and I appreciate it, no matter how fucking much it hurts."

Jack smiled broadly and said, "Thanks . . . thanks a lot. I'll see you in Boston and you can show an old man a good time."

"Hell yes I will, Doc; you can count on it."

Jack and Frank moved on to their next patient and worked quickly, this time keeping the banter to a minimum. At each stop Jack found the swabbing procedure came easier to him. Leonard's words had lifted his spirits considerably. 'I know you're helping me get better' he had said. The words had not only boosted Jack's confidence, but had also given him a slight sense of belonging, of contributing. By the time they reached the last patient he was completely immersed in the care he and Frank were providing for the injured men. He suddenly realized, with great relief, that his depression had completely vanished and that he actually felt good for the first time in twenty-four hours. In fact, he couldn't remember the last time he'd been so focused and energized. He couldn't know it at the time, but for the rest of his stay on the island, the 'Black Dog' would challenge, but never fully return.

5

The last patient was grievously wounded, much worse off than the others. The triceps on his right arm had been shot away. Due to the serious nature of his injury, he would not be moving up with the others. A Higgins boat was waiting to transfer him to a ship offshore as soon as Frank and Jack were done. The man had been given a heavy dose of morphine to deaden the pain. The strong narcotic left him groggy and barely conscious. Frank, therefore, quickly removed the dressing as the man felt little of anything.

The wound was hideous. It was deep red, and the flesh that remained was torn and chunky. Sinews of muscle tissue were visible as streaks intertwined with the pulpy flesh. The smell wafting up from the injury seemed strangely warm and only slightly unpleasant. Frank quickly swabbed the wound, sprinkled it with sulfa and handed a fresh dressing to Jack. "You ready?" he asked.

"Yeah, sure," Jack said. "I'm a bit clumsy with my hands, so you walk me through it . . . okay, Frank?" Ian quietly approached and stood over them, observing. Jack gingerly lifted the man's mangled arm and set it on his lap. He placed bandages, similar to Ace bandages, he thought, around the wound. Then he unfurled a four-inch wide swath of cotton dressing from the roll, and carefully placed it over the top half of the wound. He slowly rotated the roll around the arm half a dozen times. All the while, Frank quietly coached.

"Tighter Jack . . . pull it a little tighter . . . you won't hurt him. It's important you get a good tight wrap so the wound stays clean and discharge is minimized." Jack nodded and made the necessary corrections.

"You're doing great, pal," Frank said. "But make sure you keep your wraps lined up . . . you want one solid cover over the wound." Jack finished and Frank pinned the bandage describing to Jack all the while how he was doing it. Jack repeated the process on the bottom half of the wound, taking great care to properly overlap the dressings.

Sweat dripped off Jack's brow as he concentrated intently on his work. Finally, he was done with the wrap and carefully pinned the end of the dressing to its bulk. He sighed and looked at Frank, "How was that? Did I get it right?"

Before Frank could reply, Ian interrupted, surprising them. "Good work, Jack . . . very good. That Marine won't need to worry about infection or excess bleeding due to the quality of your wrap. If it happens it won't be your fault. It's the best we can do in the field. He'll get more advanced treatment out on the ship. He'll be fine . . . though he still could lose the arm." A hint of a smile crossed Ian's face and he repeated, "Good work."

Jack looked up at Ian and smiled. "Good . . . thanks, Doc."

"Okay now, get this man down to the beach, his boat's waiting. When you get back, load the other men on the hospital truck parked at the head of the trail . . . then report back to me."

Jack hadn't noticed until that moment that the lean-to was gone, loaded onto the waiting trucks. They had finished with their last patient in the open air of the coconut grove. He wondered how he could not have noticed the canvas covering coming down around him. He groaned when they lifted the stretcher off the ground. Frank asked, "You okay? Pretty darn heavy, huh? Normally four guys would carry this, but it's not far to the beach and this guy's pretty little."

"I'm okay . . . no problem," Jack grunted. "I'm just not in very good shape is all. Doesn't help being an old man either, I suppose."

Frank looked back at Jack for a moment and asked, "How old are you? No offense, I'm just curious."

"Old enough to be your daddy, let's just leave it at that, okay?"

"Okay." After a pause, Frank said, "Why'd you volunteer for this?" Jack only grunted, so Frank added, "I mean . . . the only guys here your age are the senior officers. It seems a bit unusual for a guy your age and rank to be out here. Heck, even the gunnery sergeants seem a lot younger . . ."

"It's a long story, Frank." Jack cut in curtly. "I'll tell you some day, but not now while I'm trying to breathe and remain upright."

"Okay sorry," Frank said. They staggered down the path toward the beach. Sweat soaked the back of Jack's shirt and stung his eyes. The joints of his elbows ached and stabs of pain shot through his lower back. He breathed in the heavy air in short gulps.

"Fucking golf," Jack muttered absently.

"Golf . . . what?" Frank asked.

"My back," Jack said. "I play a lot of golf back home and it's messed up my back some. Carrying the stretcher puts a bit of a strain on it."

Frank was silent for a moment and then asked, "Jack?"

"Yeah," he gasped.

"If golf is messing up your back so bad, why don't you just quit playing?"

Jack grunted, "Good question." He paused to catch his breath then said, "It's what I do . . . who I am I guess . . . it's like . . . what would I do if I didn't play golf? So being the tough son of a bitch I am, I simply play through the pain." He glanced down at the badly wounded boy on the stretcher and sarcastically added, "You see, Frank, it's my great sacrifice for society. I struggle on in pain, rising to the challenge of smiting the most trying of golf tracks. It's my duty."

Frank glanced back at Jack, a look of complete befuddlement on his face. "I don't get it," he said.

"A little advice, Frank," Jack rasped. "It's probably a waste of your time trying to figure out an old fart like me."

Frank turned back toward the beach and said, "There it is, down there to the right." Jack looked down the beach and saw a boat with a small Red Cross banner flying from its stern. As they struggled toward the boat, Jack looked in awe at the wooden, wedge-shaped boat. "Christ," he muttered to himself, "A goddamn Higgins boat." He recalled they'd been manufactured by the thousands, primarily in New Orleans. The shallow draft ramp boats had deposited American soldiers and Marines upon hostile beaches all over the South Pacific, Africa, and Europe. They were recognized most as the craft that had delivered thousands of young Americans to the Norman shores of France on D-Day. The boat was open to the elements, and its huge, bow door, the one component made of metal, yawned open vertically on the sand. Until now, the only Higgins boats Jack had ever seen were in movies and pictures in books. As they approached the craft, Jack's physical discomfort was forgotten as he stared in awe at one of the foremost symbols of America's role in freeing the world from the unspeakable tyranny it had faced in the last century.

Frank and Jack carried the wounded man up the bow door that also served as a ramp. They laid him gently on the deck next to badly burned sailors from the previous night's sea battle. After depositing the litter on the deck, Jack thought about the horrific battle, and realized the horror and pain these young men must have experienced and were still experiencing. He went from man to man, touching each gently on the shoulder; giving them quiet words of encouragement. Then he walked over to the starboard side of the boat and touched the boat's painted wood gunwale. He slowly rubbed his hand back and forth on the wood, lost in thoughts of what this awkward little vessel had contributed to the freedom of the world. He thought of the thousands of men who had huddled, cold and seasick, behind its wooden walls; their only protection against the hell lashing out at them from deadly shorelines. They rode the boats in, even though it was the last thing they wanted to do. For many, the little wooden boat would be the last thing they saw on earth. He thought back to his several visits to the cemetery at Omaha Beach in Normandy and the large, yet graceful statue in the center of the main memorial. The sculpture was named "American Youth Rising from the Sea." It depicted a young man reaching up out of the waves; not so much reaching for the shores of France it seemed, but for heaven itself. During his visits, the sculpture had impressed Jack, but left him feeling no real deep emotion. Now though, glancing down at the burned, torn boys lying in agony on the deck of the famous boat, a lump formed in his throat.

"Hey, Jack . . . what the heck you doing?" Frank said, interrupting his thoughts. "We have to get back and load up the other guys."

Jack whirled around, blinking away his tears and said, "Oh yeah, sorry . . . lets go."

The coxswain of the boat had also witnessed Jack's strange ritual. As they were heading down the ramp he yelled mockingly, "She's a beautiful little boat, mac, but she don't like to be petted."

Jack stutter-stepped, but did not look back. After a brief glance toward Jack, Frank turned his head and said, "Sorry, sailor, but we've gotta get back and fight the war . . . have a pleasant boat ride, you moron!" Frank's unexpected outburst left the snide seaman speechless and Jack surprised, even though he had witnessed the diminutive boy's aggressive handling of Turk the previous evening. They walked back to the path in silence, Jack occasionally glancing at Frank. Frank's pale face had turned bright red and a deep frown split his boyish face. After several moments, Jack spoke.

"Thanks for putting that guy in his place, Frank, but it wasn't a big deal." He chuckled and added, "I don't want you getting beat up defending my honor."

"Listen, don't flatter yourself; it's not just about you," Frank replied sternly. "I can't stand people who don't know when to be serious or when it's okay to mess around. There were wounded guys on that boat, hell dying guys, and he should have been keeping his eyes on them, not being a stupid wise-acre!" Jack looked at the young boy in amazement. For one so young, his intensity and principled senses were remarkable. Jack couldn't help but wonder where life would take the boy.

78

They arrived back at the former aid station and helped finish loading everything onto the trucks and Lt. Smith and Lt. Cdr. Goldman's jeep. When they were done, Jack was utterly exhausted. He felt slightly nauseous and the sharp ache in his back caused him to lean forward while standing. Sweat soaked him from head to toe, his hair greasy and matted flat. His soft bicep muscles contracted and the lower halves of his arms strangely rose on their own. Jack crumpled on the beach and sipped from a canteen Frank had handed him. Ian was supervising the loading of the last bits of medical gear nearby, so Frank had decided they should wait to report until he was done.

While they waited, Frank walked over to one of the trucks and, as Ian had instructed him to do earlier, gathered up some gear. He came back carrying a pristine World War II steel pot helmet, a beige musette bag, and web belt, as well as a canteen, along with a pair of brown, ankle high boots or boondockers, as the Marines called them, long before L.L. Bean borrowed the name. Frank tossed them in Jack's lap. He fingered the new boots and canteen, awed by them, their newness. Jack slowly, reverently put the steel helmet on, surprised by its weight. He removed his brushed leather boots and put on the boondockers, then clipped the canteen to his belt. With a weary grunt he rose and walked over to a jeep and looked at his reflection in the windscreen. For a moment he was dumbstruck, then slowly nodded, satisfied; a World War II G.I. was staring back at him.

His sublime, almost childish reverie was shattered moments later when Lt. Cdr. Goldman announced, "Alright, that's it! Load up . . . we're movin' out!" Ian turned and approached Jack and Frank.

"Frank you ride in the truck with Doctor Goldman; he wants to stay with the patients," Ian said. "It's going to be rough going when we cut up through the jungle, so keep a good eye on the men."

"Yes, sir," Frank said, and marched off to the ambulance. Jack began to follow Frank, but was stopped by Ian laying an arm across his chest.

"Not you, Jack . . . you ride with me in the jeep." Jack had assumed from Ian's previous demeanor that he would want him to continue to care for the wounded men. Jack was surprised at his feelings of disappointment. The ride in the jeep after all, would be much more pleasant than in the truck with the wounded.

"You sure, Doc?" he asked. "Frank may need a hand and I'm more than happy to help."

"No, you're riding with me," Ian replied. "Turk's riding with Frank . . . they'll be fine. We're not going very far."

"Okay," Jack said reluctantly. He climbed in the jeep and Ian pulled away to the front of the small convoy.

"Where are we going then, Doc?"

"The other side of the Tenaru, up the beach a ways and then inland to the airfield," he replied.

"Henderson Field?"

Ian looked at Jack for a moment, then grinned. "So that's what they're going to name it, eh mate?"

Jack closed his eyes for several seconds, shook his head lightly, then replied, "Yeah, that's right. They named it after a Major Lofton Henderson, a Marine pilot killed at Midway."

"I see."

After several moments of silence, Jack asked, "Why did you want me to ride with you?"

"I wanted to see how you're doing . . . to see if you're feeling better than you were when you woke up." Jack jerked his head toward the young doctor.

"You knew didn't you, Doc?" Jack said.

"It was pretty bloody obvious and I warn you, if I see you getting wobbly again, I'll kick your bloody bum even harder. You mustn't let what's happened destroy your spirit. Without it, your soul or even your physical being will slowly die, much as has happened to many of my people since the Europeans came and trampled their known, comfortable ways. It is only my opinion, but I believe there is a purpose for your fantastic journey, and that you have to do your best, whatever that may mean to you, regarding the events that have

80

occurred. As I said last night and as I believe so deeply, there is no time, only space. This is your reality now, your space."

Ian paused for a moment, looking at Jack to see if he was focusing on his words. Then he added, "When I looked at you this morning, I could see clearly that you didn't want to accept what has happened and make the best of it. I feared you were in danger of shattering your own true self; whatever that may be. You must believe Jack; you simply must believe that the spirits have placed you here for a reason. You must have faith that somehow, sometime you will come to learn what that reason is."

Jack pondered the doctor's words for several moments. He recalled how much better he'd felt after caring for the wounded. Then he said, "It took me a while to figure out why you were barking at me this morning and treating me like the others. You forced me to look beyond my own troubles and focus on the pain of other people, didn't you? Kind of keeping me busy in a way; well only God knows why, but it worked. Thanks, Doc."

"Don't mention it, mate. But it's not just to keep you busy, that's not enough. That simple thing is not why I believe you're here. Like you said, you already experienced it this morning while caring for those suffering and in need of help. Beyond that, I don't know, Jack. This is your journey. You must simply let the spirits guide you and fight hard against your instincts to measure your life by what was. I can only help you so much. Your incredible presence here may not be grand or overtly obvious; but it is as real as the water lapping on the beach just outside your window. That's enough voodoo from me, mate; most, if not all needs to come from you, from inside."

Jack remained silent for a minute, staring out at Ironbottom Sound. Then he looked forward out the windscreen; a slight frown creased his brow. "There was a war fought in Southeast Asia a couple decades after this one. The American soldiers fighting there referred to someone at home as being 'back in the world'. I think that fits for me when I'm referring to where I came from. Anyway, back in the world I was . . . well let's just say that I couldn't have done *there* what I did this morning. I would have left it to others, not worried about it and pursued my own agenda; if you know what I mean."

"I assume you are referring to your pursuit of status and possessions above all else. If this is true, your life would have little meaning to my people and questionable morality; but it would not mean you are inherently bad, just misguided . . . lost."

"Oh good," Jack said with an ironic light chuckle. "I feel so much better about myself."

"Sorry, mate, but I believe you are going to have to try to understand these things, understand yourself back in the world, as you say, if you are to find some sort of meaning in all this. Bloody hell you've kind of been stripped naked after all, don't you think?"

"I don't know, Doc. I don't know if any of this will ever make sense. And why me? Hell, I may not have been the greatest role model but I wasn't a complete prick."

"I can't answer that, mate. But I've already seen a goodness in you that you yourself may never have recognized or wanted to recognize. I saw that basic goodness this morning in the aid station, and yesterday when you tried to help the Marine who was crying for his captain. You, for some reason, are being given a chance to find something. What that is neither you nor I can know at this time. Christ, you may find that you are a hopeless son of a bitch . . . who knows? I can't answer that for you, but for now try and take some comfort in the fact that you've accepted what's happened and that you are dealing with it as bravely as any man could be expected to."

"Hell, Doc," Jack said. "I'd probably have blown my brains out by now if not for you. In fact, before you stuck your boot up my ass this morning I thought of running back to the Tenaru and drowning myself. It'd either take me home or I'd be dead, either of which I figured would be better than slowly going mad. After this morning though, I feel the only logical thing is to ride this out if I can; see where it takes me."

"Jack, even with my beliefs and easy acceptance of who and what you really are and where you came from, this is still the most incredible thing I've ever experienced. It's not just fascinating, and it is; but, to me it is a sign of hope that the spirits will ultimately guide us to a better place. I feel deeply in my soul that you are here for a purpose, not as some sort of amusement for the heavenly spirits or as a penance; but I am just a man like yourself. I cannot know for sure."

They carried on in silence; driving slowly so as not to jostle the patients and equipment in the trucks. Jack pondered the remarkable young man sitting next to him, and what he had said. He felt strongly compelled to place his trust in him. He wasn't sure if his beliefs and theories were mere rhetoric or spiritual insight. Nonetheless, Ian seemed a lifeline of sorts; a mentor in the preservation of his sanity.

His attention was diverted back to the move of the convoy as they turned south onto a bumpy jungle track and cleared the jungle after two-hundred yards. A large, mostly bare plain spread before them. Squinting, Jack could see the airfield shimmering in the distance, its contours distorted by the heat rising from its surface. A captured Japanese bulldozer lumbered along the length of the runway like a giant gray beetle. Jack gasped in amazement at the sight of Henderson Field. Unlike a few days ago, the runway was no longer a two-mile strip of black tarmac, but was surprisingly short and dusty. The modern air terminal was gone. Dilapidated, Japanese-built supply buildings dotted the area around the runway. Just to the west, a relatively tall, yet rickety Japanese style headquarters rose above the field. "Jesus, god" he whispered to himself, "The Pagoda." The Marines had christened the building as such due to its resemblance to that type of structure. It would become the air operations center, a beacon of hope for the beleaguered Marines. The sight of the airfield he'd been reading about since he was a child left him breathless. Seeing it now, there was almost something holy about it, a pathetic, desert-like strip of land that was destined to save thousands of lives. An unconscious smile creased his face, and he looked to the sides of the road and saw that intermittently, the ground on either side of the road was infested with growths of thick green, razor sharp, six-foot high stalks of grass. "*Kunai* grass," Jack said out loud.

"What's that, Jack . . . what did you say?" Ian asked.

"Oh . . . nothing . . . nothing," he said nonchalantly.

Ian glared at him. "It sounded like you said 'coon ass' . . . you calling me names?" First befuddlement, then horror clouded Jack's face. Ian, seeing the look on Jack's face, erupted in laughter.

Confused, Jack said desperately, "God no, Ian! Of course I didn't . . . I couldn't . . . I'd never say . . ." Ian only laughed harder as Jack sputtered. "Kunai grass . . . kunai grass . . . that's what I said, Doc. Jesus, I'm not the sort of guy that would say something like that."

Ian stopped laughing. "I know you wouldn't, mate . . . I'm not completely daft you know. I knew what you said. They told us about the *kunai* before we landed . . . how it'll cut you to bloody ribbons if it rubs against bare skin. I was just having a little fun with you is all. God knows, with the bloody heavy stuff we've talked about over the last day and what you're dealing with, we deserved a little relief."

Jack smiled, rolled his eyes, and feigning irritation said, "So, you're a goddamn shaman, soothsayer sort of shit, *and* a comedian." Jack, in fact, was delighted that Ian felt comfortable enough with him to tease him. "And just how the hell do you know that coon is a derogatory reference to a black man or African-American as we refer to them now back in the world?"

"I've read some books about the deep south in your country, books about negro and white culture and the history of the relationship between the two. Not a pretty story I must say . . . but one I have a natural interest in, of course."

"I'm sure you do, Doc," Jack said somberly. "Just how tough is it for your people in Australia? I mean besides your being assimilated and all."

Ian stared straight ahead for a moment, sighed, and answered, "First, you have to understand that it's a very different situation than your Negroes face, not necessarily better or worse, just different. A much better comparison is to your native Indians. In fact, I have read more about them than the negroes, and it is shocking how similar our cultures and our experiences with the Europeans have been. But hey-o, let's leave this discussion for later, mate. We're going to be at the site of the hospital in a bit and I want you to do some things for me."

"Sure, okay," Jack said immediately, secretly hoping he hadn't reached too deeply too early in their friendship, but grateful that Ian had some work in store for him.

In an officious tone, Ian said, "A Pioneer unit has supposedly delivered a hospital tent to the site. We are damn lucky to get one by the way. When we get there, Dr. Goldman has asked me to supervise construction with our guys helping the Pioneers. You were a businessman, so I want you to do an inventory of all the non-construction materials the Pioneers are supposed to have for us. Things like meds, drips, surgical equipment, dressings, and the like. Get it done as quickly as possible, and then bring the list to me for review, understand?"

"No problem, Doc," Jack said eagerly.

"When you're done, I'll check it over and make up my own list that fills in what the Pioneer battalion has not delivered. You take that to the supply boys . . . they're probably still on Red Beach, so you'll have to take the jeep or one of the trucks. Find whoever's in charge and get as much stuff on the list as you can. I hear some of these supply chaps are real pissers. Not all of them mind you, but be wary. You'll need to find a way to work with these guys and not let them get to you. It's all about our patients . . . nothing else." Excited at the prospect of his independent mission, Jack had barely heard, or for that matter cared, about the caution Ian had delivered. The warning therefore, and several to follow, went unheeded. He would have to learn on his own and pay a price while doing so.

As they entered the airfield perimeter, Jack gazed in wonder at hundreds of men busily constructing defenses and shelters and completing the partially built airfield itself. To a man with an abiding passion for the history of World War II, it was as if he had entered a military themed Disneyland-like fantasy, contrived only for himself. Jeeps, one-ton International Harvester trucks, and captured Japanese Chevys buzzed and rumbled around the airfield. Gazing to the south, Jack could make out clusters of 75mm and 105mm artillery batteries hidden in clumps of trees. The guns were laid out so they could mass their fire on any area of the perimeter. Most were anchored in shallow pits. Engineers, Pioneers and gun crews were laboring in the clawing heat, cutting down tall trees to clear lines of fire. The Japanese contingent on the island was made up mostly of Korean laborers, 'termites' the Marines called them, along with a small naval combat unit. Most of them had fled into the hills when the American fleet began shelling the field and its surroundings. The Japanese Army would not make an appearance for nearly two weeks.

He saw other men, most shirtless, others clad only in their skivvies driving graders and pulling heavy steel rollers up and down the airfield. All were in an urgent quest to prepare the field for the desperately needed American combat aircraft that would provide a protective umbrella over the toehold represented by the Marine perimeter. The aerial umbrella would hopefully fend off both air and sea borne attacks. As well, much needed supplies could be flown in on transport aircraft, which then, shed of their cargoes, could fly the more seriously wounded back to fully modern hospitals at the various islands designated as staging areas. It was clear to Jack that the urgency with which the men were carrying out their arduous tasks belied the fact that each understood just how vital the airfield was to the success of not just the campaign, but perhaps to their very survival. The clattering, creaking equipment appeared ancient to Jack, and at the very least, wholly unreliable. It almost seemed to him that the scene was simply a vast historical stage, a living museum of sorts. He shook his head and softly said, "My god."

"You sure seem to be enjoying yourself, mate," Ian said.

"I shouldn't admit it, but I am," Jack replied. "This is fantastic . . . unbelievable. Look up there." Jack said, pointing southwest toward a rise. "It's the Pagoda . . . the goddamn Pagoda, Doc. Look at it will you?"

Ian's eyes followed Jack's pointed finger and said, "Yeah, I see it . . . it does look like a pagoda. What in bloody hell is it?"

"The Japanese built it. It'll serve as our air operations center . . . unbelievable!" Jack exclaimed. "Oh and look over there, Doc. See those little tanks? They're Stuarts . . . agile but real vulnerable . . . and over there . . . see all those anti-aircraft guns? Some had crude radars attached . . . didn't work too well if I recall. Oh, and look at Henderson; goddamn Henderson Field . . . fantastic!"

"Fascinating. Glad you're enjoying yourself, mate, but I should remind you that all this stuff is real . . . you're not on some Hollywood movie set."

For several moments, Jack stared at the young men occupying a machine gun nest by the side of the road, then said, "You're right, Doc; guess I got caught up in it a bit. It's probably hard for you to understand, but I've been reading about this stuff for most of my life. Now to see it, it's amazing . . . hell it's marvelous!"

"Marvelous? Crikey, mate, just because you've arrived here in a rather unusual way doesn't mean you can't get your own bum shot off."

Since awakening on the riverbank the previous morning, Jack had felt many forms of fear and dread, but for the first time, Ian's comment awakened a new fear: not deeply felt, but clearly perceptible. It was a fear of a violent death, or a slow, miserable one from the myriad diseases that would soon assault all those on the island. He gazed again at Henderson and its surroundings. The sight still left him awed and curious. But suddenly, it seemed darker; it was less a grand display for his amusement and more a scene inviting a distinct sense of dread and uncertainty. He wondered what the other men must be thinking and feeling, as their senses were not tempered by any knowledge as to what was to unfold. The enormity of being the only man on the island who had that information suddenly seemed a terrible burden. He was immensely relieved when his thoughts were interrupted by Ian grinding the jeep to a halt at the edge of a stand of palms interspersed with short, scrubby trees and underbrush.

The stand lay 250 meters southwest of the runway, in sight of the Pagoda. Waiting, just as Ian had predicted, was a squad of Pioneers with a truckload of supplies. Ian was pleased to see that the detachment had already done a good deal of work. Twenty meters inside the tree line, with axes, saws, and shovels, they had cleared out a sizeable plot. The ground had been scraped clean. The scattered palms were left standing to provide visual cover for the aid station as well as cooling shade. A sweat-drenched man approached the jeep. He was shirtless, wearing what appeared to be a makeshift pair of shorts and non-issue boots. He was tall and lean; sinews of muscle glinted off his tanned body, the likely result of years of heavy labor. His hair was closely cropped and blonde. His small gray eyes were in remarkable proximity to one another. The odd effect was exaggerated by an elongated nose that divided them.

"You the sick bay boys?" the man asked gruffly.

"Yes indeed," Ian replied. "Lt. Ian Smith, M.D., Royal Australian Navy Medical Corps." He held out his hand to the man.

The pioneer ignored Ian's offer of a handshake. "An Aussie, huh?" Good guys, the Aussies. I have to admit I haven't run into many the likes of you though. What are you exactly? Can't tell if you're a half-nigger or just unlucky."

Jack stiffened. "I don't believe you've introduced yourself properly, Marine," Ian said icily, his jaw muscles tightening.

The pioneer glared at Ian and opened his mouth angrily, then closed it. He smiled stiffly and drawled, "No offense, Lieutenant. Ah'm jest a curious sort of fella is all."

"Okay, no offense taken," Ian replied. Ian's clipped tone said otherwise. "So who are you and what's your job?"

"Ah'm Sergeant Dunwoody, 1st Pioneer Battalion. Me and my boys is here to set up the sick bay. We's already off to a good start."

The sergeant's eyes narrowed slightly, and smirking he said, "You jest make sure your hospital boys stay out of our way an' my boys will have the tent up as quick as you can say, 'nigger cotton picker'."

"Hey!" Jack yelled. He was furious and took a step toward the younger man. He'd never considered himself a bigot or prejudiced in any way; yet he was largely ambivalent, even ignorant of the indignities minorities suffered from others. This event involved Ian though, and for the first time in his life, it was personal. Ian raised up his hand, stopping Jack's foolish advance. Ian's eyes remained locked on the sergeant's with the same chilling stare Jack had seen in the tent the night before. Ian slowly moved forward until his face was less than a foot from the end of the man's jutting nose. It seemed he held it there for an eternity, before he finally spoke. When he did, his voice was quiet, almost inaudible to Jack standing just a few feet away. Its hardness though was shocking and impressive. Jack hadn't noticed, but Turk had slipped up behind him and was carefully surveying the situation.

"No, Sergeant," Ian hissed, "You are very bloody wrong about procedure here. Lt. Cdr. Goldman is tending to the wounded and *I* will direct the hospital's construction. You may assist me in that task *or* labor with the others under my direction . . . your choice. As well, I have detailed my men to work side by side with yours, so you don't cock things up." The man stepped back slightly, a look of shock and confusion registering on his face. Ian filled the newly opened space between them and said, his voice raised, "You understand, mister?"

The sergeant looked at Ian uncertain, then glanced briefly at Jack. He looked back at Ian in fury, but was lost for words. Jack started when a hard, cool voice sounded out behind him. "The lieutenant asked you a question, Sergeant," Turk said. "I suggest you fuckin' answer it. The doctor don't like to be kept waiting, and neither do the wounded guys in need of the hospital." For a moment, Jack thought the man would burst into tears from frustration and anger. He chuckled out loud at the thought. The man whirled and

89

fixed a hateful glare on him. Turk moved up beside Ian and stared the sergeant down with a menacing scowl. The man fumed, hesitated, then spat in the dirt.

"I fuckin' understand, Lieutenant . . . sir!" the man said. "But we don't work side by side with niggers in the United States Marine Corps!"

Turk clenched his fists and moved threateningly toward the man, but was halted abruptly by Ian tugging at his shirt. "Easy, Turk," Ian said. "Good then." Ian replied calmly. "Grab a shovel and help your men clear the rest of that brush. I'll tell you what to do after that." Ian lifted his right hand to his forehead in salute. To Jack's and Turk's delight, they realized Ian's salute was not entirely proper. His hand was squashed up against his forehead and face, nearly closing his right eye, and was not horizontal, but a perfect 90 degrees to the ground. The look on the man's face made it appear as if his head would spontaneously combust. He spat again, then whirled and stalked off toward his men.

"A little advice, Sarge," Turk shouted after him. "If you catch a Jap bullet one of these days, you may want to make sure that the poor bastards who have to drag your shit-sorry ass in don't bring you to this station!" Turk's comment stopped the man in his tracks. After a brief, quaking pause, he continued on.

"That's enough, Turk," Ian said. "Alright, let's get to work. Jack, grab the inventory sheet from the jeep and get started. Turk, you and Frank move the men off the trucks and get them under some shade." Ian turned and headed toward the tenting materials in the Pioneer's truck. Turk and Jack headed back to the convoy together. They walked a ways in awkward silence. Turk spoke first.

"Um . . . I'm sorry I was a bit rough on you yesterday," Turk said. "I uh . . . Frank told me you're a retread from the first war or something, and I don't know what you was fucked up about yesterday. But I um . . . I been watching you today. You're doing pretty fuckin' good . . . and ah . . . Frankie also told me how you handled Lenny this morning, cheering him up and all. And hell, just now, for a guy your age to move on a guy like that asshole Pioneer took some balls . . . guess I misjudged you some. I look forward to working with you, okay?"

Jack smiled and said, "Hey, no problem." Jack had, in fact, surprised himself when he aggressively made a move toward the bigoted Pioneer. He had never been a violent man; having largely been discouraged of such behavior by his father. Ian though, in just twenty-four hours, had instilled a sense of loyalty and protectiveness he'd never felt for any other man.

"You did good back there, yourself," Jack said.

"Whaddya mean?" Turk asked.

"Looking after Ian like that; took some big balls considering the guy was a sergeant."

"It was no big deal. Now don't get me wrong, I ain't no nigger lover myself. Hell they're flooding into south Philly to work in the yards and all, and I guess the stupid bastards will fuck things up good. But Doc Smith is different. Nigger, chink, fuckin' Indian, or whatever he might be, Doc Smith is Doc Smith. He's the best . . . the greatest. I'd bust my ass for him. Nobody's gonna mess with him while I'm around." Jack winced a bit at the boy's comments, but he quickly reminded himself that 1942 was a long way from 2002, and besides, Jack thought, somewhat self-righteously, the boy was learning some tolerance. Instead of chastising Turk for his obvious bigotry, he simply said, "Well, I can certainly understand your feelings about the lieutenant. He is special." Jack patted Turk lightly on the back and turned toward the truck containing the medical supplies the pioneers were to have brought with them. Turk headed back to the truck carrying the wounded.

91

6

Jack hauled himself into the canvas covered bed of the truck and began his inventory. The heat was stifling, so he removed his shirt. To allow easier movement amongst the stacked boxes and crates, he took off his boots. Each wooden container was stenciled with the contents it held. SYRETTES-MORIPHINE-100 CT, COTTON GAUZE-25 ROLLS, SYRINGE-GLASS-200 CT, FIELD DRESSINGS-50 COUNT. Every box was stamped: US NAVY. Each time he uncovered a new type of supply he noted the category and put a slash beside it. When he uncovered the fifth case in a category, he drew a horizontal slash through the first four marks. He worked quickly though it was difficult reading some of the crates. He'd redistribute stacks to get at hidden containers. When he finished he was covered in sweat and utterly fatigued. He jumped from the back of the truck feeling dizzy and nauseous. He hadn't exerted himself to such a degree in years. He slumped to the ground and took a long pull off his canteen. As he did so, a shout, stuttered with laughter, rang out. "Bloody hell, mate, you look like you just went the distance with bloody Joe Louis!" It was Ian.

Jack looked up wearily and said, "Yeah, and that's about the way I feel too. Jesus, I'm out of shape."

"Trust me, you're doing great, mate. Crikey, with this bloody heat it's even tough on the boys." Ian knelt beside him and said, "I've changed my mind about your trip to the supply section. There's just too much that needs doing here."

Disappointed, Jack asked, "Are you sure, Doc?"

"It can wait 'til morning . . . you can go at daybreak."

"Okay," Jack said, relieved that he would still carry out the mission.

"Come with me . . . I want you to oversee the set-up of the lean-to," Ian said. "We're going to use it for our sleeping quarters. You'll also need to write up a bunking schedule. I'll give you the men's shift schedules so you can make sure each man is getting space under the shelter to sleep." Re-energized, Jack hopped up and followed Ian. Again he felt grateful that Ian was engaging his leadership and organizational skills. Back in the world they'd been utilized for one purpose only: profit generation. He was consciously struck by the irony that, for the first time, his learned skills would be used to produce something completely unknown to him in his previous life. In turn, he found that irony generating feelings of fulfillment he'd never known. Ian turned and pointed to a patch of forest that had been cleared thirty meters from where the hospital was already going up. "See that over there?" Ian asked. "That's where the lean-to goes. I'll send some men over and you get 'em started. Anchor as best you can so it doesn't bloody blow away."

"No problem," Jack said. Ian turned and began to walk away. Jack stopped him by saying, "Hey, Doc, sorry about that asshole Pioneer."

Ian turned again and took several steps back toward Jack and said, "I'm used to idiots, mate, believe me. And, while we're on the subject, you aren't a youngster anymore. You advance on a man like that again and he may tear you apart. There are some hard blokes on this island, Jack. This isn't your country club . . . be careful." Just days ago, Jack could hardly imagine thinking ill of any veteran of Guadalcanal. But his anger and revulsion toward the horrid man had opened his eyes somewhat.

"I guess I have a bit to learn . . . I'll be careful."

Ian smiled and as he sauntered off said, "Thanks for sticking up for me though, mate." Jack nodded. Still shirtless, he turned and walked toward Frank and Turk who were busy minding the wounded under the shade at the jungle's edge.

"How's it going, guys?" he asked.

Frank looked up and said, "Geez, how's it going for you? You don't look so good."

"Considering I nearly succumbed to heat stroke in the back of that goddamn truck, I'm doing okay." Turk peered up at Jack, stared for a moment, then snickered.

"What's so funny?" Frank asked.

"Oh nothin' really . . . I was just wonderin'."

"Wondering what?"

"Oh, I was just wonderin' if you and I will grow a set like that when we're Jack's age."

"What . . . grow what?" Frank asked, clearly confused.

"Tits."

Frank looked at the ground and muttered, "Oh geez, Turk!" Jack could see that Frank was enjoying the jab. He could not see his face, but his entire upper body convulsed with silent laughter.

Jack cocked his head and dryly replied, "Oh . . . very funny." His passive, collegial reply freed the two boys to laugh openly. He watched them for a moment, a wry smile on his face, then said, "I'm not sure about Frank, but you'll definitely grow a nice set Turk; real big and hairy."

Turk choked off his laughter and said, "Hey, no offense, Jack."

"None taken, asshole," Jack retorted. He walked back to the truck to wait for his charges. He fetched his shirt and put it on. Moments later, he saw Ian leading a group of sweat soaked men in his direction.

"Right then, chaps," Ian said to the assembled work detail. "Hospitalman Macmillan here is going to supervise the set-up of the company quarters . . . such as they are. As you can see, the hospitalman is no spring chicken, so don't expect too much heavy lifting from him, but he is the boss." Jack frowned at Ian, but in truth, he was enjoying the mocking banter between he and the others immensely.

Ian walked off without another word and Jack turned to the unit. The thought of ordering the men to work, these men of

94

Guadalcanal, unnerved him at first and momentarily stripped him of his natural self-confidence in directing others. He steeled himself by acknowledging the importance of the cause in which he was now a part. He cleared his voice, regained his confidence said, "Okay guys, let's get busy." Contrary to Ian's crack, Jack pitched in and helped carry the tenting supplies to the clearing. The men had erected many shelters during training, so there was not much Jack had to do in the way of supervision. He checked the quality of the lashings and moorings and urged the men on when their work slowed. After discovering an anchor stake that had been haphazardly plunged into the ground, he gently admonished the group. "Remember guys, tropical storms can get real nasty. This thing needs to hold up to heavy winds and rain. Make sure you get everything as tight and secure as possible."

The men looked at him dully, put-off it seemed, by the officious demeanor of a man of such low rank. He re-anchored the stake himself. As he did so, he thought back with considerable bemusement at his own bumbling, profane attempts to erect his fancy pup tent on the banks of the Tenaru, just a few nights before. At the time, the feeble attempt was merely a part of his make-up, his background.

The young men quickly assembled the lean-to. When it was done, he gazed at the structure for a moment. He was not satisfied. If the prevailing winds during rainfall were anything near westerly, the shelter would be useless. He told the men to collect thirty or so palm fronds along with a dozen bunches of the hemp-like vines that hung from nearby trees. Grumbling, they set off while Jack collected long, narrow branches that had fallen to the ground. When the men returned with the fronds he instructed them to lash the fronds together side-by-side, using the sticks for horizontal support. When they were finished, they set the wall up against the open side of the lean to, essentially forming a garage door made of jungle fauna. After sending the men back to Ian, Jack positioned two long sticks as props on each side of the wall. When it rained, they could simply remove the props thereby enclosing the shelter.

When, he finished, Jack took several steps back, smiled and said out loud, "Perfect."

As he walked back toward the trucks he noticed the hospital was nearly complete. Like the lean-to, it was crude and rough. Still he was impressed by its sturdiness. He went inside and saw Frank settling several Marines onto bedrolls on the dirt floor. Two stretchers balanced on saw horses comprised the operating theatre. He found an empty crate and laid the shift schedules out. He was immensely pleased to see that Ian had put him on the same rotation with him, Frank and Turk. Jack made sure they were all on the same sleep shift as well.

It was somewhat complicated getting things organized to ensure each man a free bedroll when it was his time for rest. However, years of budgets, resource allocation, and materials planning had trained his mind well for the task. The work came easy to him and he was finished in a half-hour. He looked at the finished schedule and shook his head. "Holy Christ," he thought to himself, "back in the world I would've done this on my PC and it would've taken twice as long getting it all tidy and lined up and shit." Looking upon his crude, yet perfectly sensible creation, he said out loud, chuckling, "Progress, huh?" He froze for a moment, realizing that he had just repeated, verbatim, something his father said to him each time Jack had suggested the latest bit of vague electronic wizardry that would supposedly take their business to the 'next level'. He quickly shook the thought from his mind.

He presented the schedule to Ian. "I think this will work out fine, Doc. What should I do now?"

"Bloody hell, Jack!" Ian exclaimed. "You're done with this already? Crikey, it would've taken one of the other men all bloody night."

"For christsakes, Doc, it's not exactly nuclear physics."

"No, I don't suppose so . . . nuclear physics, huh?"

Jack shook his head slightly and said, "So, what now, Doc?"

"Well the station is finished and you've got the quarters up, so now we just unpack the supplies and wait."

"Wait for what?" Jack asked.

Ian replied, "Wait for customers."

"Oh yeah," Jack said quietly. He turned serious and said, "It'll be at least a week 'til there's any real serious action or epidemics. But if you're able I'd suggest we meet privately tonight and I can shed some light on when we can expect them and in what numbers. I'll always respect your desire to not want to know what the future holds, but I think I can help with casualties and such."

"Okay, good," Ian replied. "That'll work well because I want to talk to you some more about your job. My bloody office is being re-decorated, so I'll come get you at 2000 hours and we'll find a log to recline on. I'll bring the fags."

"Deal," Jack replied. Exhausted from his labor, Jack walked up the road a ways, found a shady spot and sat with his chin resting on his knees. Occasionally, jeeps and trucks ground by, moving supplies from one point to another as the Marine perimeter slowly took shape. In between, columns of thin, sweat-drenched Marines marched past. Jack recalled that the voyage on the transports to the island had been very rough on the men. The food the Navy transports served was inadequate and barely edible. Most men had lost 10–15 pounds before they'd even hit the beach. The flesh around the eyes of many of the boys was puffy from insect bites. Some were badly sunburned, while those who had taken more care represented a pale, clammy contrast. Nevertheless, the Marines were in high spirits, bantering back and forth; some were loudly bellicose, reminding their mates what they would do to the Japs once they came to grips with them. Jack, fascinated at once by the historical sight, nonetheless noted somberly that the young men had not yet tasted battle. He wondered who of them would die, who would lose a limb, his penis, his mind. As he pondered the enormity of what he was witnessing, another company of Marines, roughly 150 men, hove into view. The company's HQ platoon led the column that was then divided into four platoons, a lieutenant leading each. As the column passed, Jack nodded and exchanged waves with several of the men.

As the third platoon in line approached, a Marine shouted, "Hey, Lieutenant Grimes! I think we should turn back. It's starting to smell like Brooklyn around here. That ain't good, sir."

A few boys hooted and protested as a slight smile cracked the lieutenant's lips. "That's just the Japs you're smelling, Lou. If you smell something really rotten, that means we took a wrong turn and we're in the goddamned Bronx." More protests and laughter followed as the Marine named Lou shook his head and sputtered to himself. Another voice called out.

"Macmillan! Yo, Mac!"

Jack straightened and reflexively answered, "Yes?"

"What now, Ski?" a Marine, apparently sharing Jack's last name, replied.

"My goddamned blister is killing me! It's as plump as a tit on a Rush Street hooker. If this fucker bursts, we're all gonna drown, I swear."

"Quit your moaning, Ski. I'll have a look at it when we stop for a rest." Jack squinted through the setting sun at the boy the Marine had referred to as Macmillan. He hadn't given much thought to the coincidence of their common names, but when he was finally able to focus on the young man, he gasped.

"Oh . . . Jesus!" He ducked to the ground, concealing himself in the thick brush, his breaths coming in short, panicked gulps. His mind spun wildly, but he kept his eyes glued on the young man. The boy's helmet was strapped to his backpack, exposing a head of thick, wavy brown hair. His brown eyes were narrow, but un-menacing. He strode along in easy, gliding steps, not the steps of an aggressive warrior. His handsome face was kind looking, but faintly taut; as if he carried some secret worry. His shoulders were slightly hunched. Jack watched aghast as his father walked past, just fifteen feet away. Moments later he lost him in the gaggle of Marines. He lay prone in the grass for several moments, trying to collect himself. He forced himself to slow his breathing. As he did, he noticed that the last platoon in line was passing by. Slowly, he staggered to his feet and jogged after the tail of the column. When he caught up to the last Marine in the column, he grabbed him by the shoulder and spun him around.

"Hey, what the hell, bud?" the man protested.

"Sorry . . . sorry," Jack replied breathlessly. "I uh . . . I just have a question."

"Well then fucking ask it! Grab me like that again and I'll crack you in the teeth!"

"Sorry. It's just . . . It's . . . um, what unit are you guys?"

"C Company, 1st of the 2nd."

"Okay . . . okay," Jack said, still gasping for air. "Uh, can you tell me where you guys are headed? I mean where you're digging in?"

"They told us somewhere on the eastern perimeter. The Tenro River or somethin' like that. Hey, you okay, pal?"

"Yes . . . yes I'm fine." Then muttering to himself he said, "Right, C company of the First Battalion . . . the Tenaru."

"Yeah, that's it," the boy said. "They told us we're to hold the east edge of the perimeter down near the beach. Why? What's it to you?"

"Uh . . . just curious; um . . . I'm a hospitalman and I guess it just makes me feel better knowing where you guys are establishing defenses," Jack lied. He forced a smile and said, "A bit jumpy I guess. Sorry for grabbing you."

"Don't sweat it," the boy replied. Jack stood in shock as the column marched on. The Marine he'd questioned turned to the man walking next to him. He jerked his head back toward Jack, and said something that started them both laughing. Jack didn't care. Dazed, he stumbled back to the hospital and found Ian organizing medical supplies and documents.

"Doc," he said, breathing heavily. "Can I talk to you for a minute . . . right now?" Ian took one look at Jack and immediately agreed. They stepped outside the hospital and found a place to sit. "I just saw him. Jesus Christ, I just saw him." He held his head in his hands and said, "Oh god, it was him!"

"Who, mate?"

"My father . . . he marched by . . . God help me . . . just a few feet away. They even called him by name." Jack sighed and added, "The column he was marching with was a combat unit. What the hell do I do?"

Ian put his hand on Jack's knee and replied, "First thing you do mate, is calm down. You knew it likely that your father was here . . . now you've seen him. I can understand how incredible, bloody hell, even unfathomable it must be, but you need to keep your head and decide what you want to do next. Do you want to meet him, avoid him, bloody Christ, tell him who you are . . . what?"

"Jesus . . . How should I know? How can I know? I mean there isn't a goddamn guide for this sort of thing, you know?"

Ian thought for a moment, then replied, "Of course there is; it's in you, mate. Give yourself some time to get this incredible thing in some sort of perspective and you'll find the answer in your soul. What you decide to do is very important as you don't know where it might lead you. Take some time."

"I don't know, Doc. I feel like I want to see him, observe him as much as possible, but talk to him?"

"Jack," Ian implored, "slow down. You're already being accepted into the group here and you've already contributed. You told me earlier that it helped keep you together; focus on that for now. You can be a great help to these boys. The spirits who have dreamed you here will guide you where your father is concerned, I'm quite sure of that."

Jack was silent for a moment, then said quietly, "Okay, Doc. I trust you; I guess I have no choice. I'll keep my shit together as best as I can and take some time concerning how, or if, I want to approach him . . . my father. One thing I know already though is that I want to see him again. Just watch him, see how he moves, how he talks."

"How about this? Why don't you try and find his location tomorrow after you visit the supply dump? Watch him and his mates. Then you go from there. Do you have a rough idea where he may be?"

"Yeah," Jack said laconically, "on the Tenaru close to its head."

"Good then. It's time for dinner, mate. Let's see what wonderful delights they have prepared for us this evening."

"Alright, Doc, but one more thing."

"Yeah, mate?"

"My dad was in the U.S. Navy, yet he was marching with a Marine combat force to the front lines. The only thing he can be is a Navy combat corpsman. The first big battle will be fought at the Tenaru in less than two weeks and his battalion will be in the thick of it." He laughed quietly, a laugh slightly tinged with disgust. "And all my life I thought the old man had been a clerk for god's sake."

7

Captured supplies of Japanese rice and tinned, oily fish were dinner that evening. Less delectable items from the Japanese stores, such as snails, fish heads, and octopus would be held in reserve until absolutely needed for sustenance. Jack, much more spoiled than the others, detested the generally acceptable C-rations and looked forward to the meal. As it was still light, the unit cooks built a fire to boil rice. A group of ten men, including Jack, sat on the ground in a circle near the fire.

The men groaned when they cut open the tins and saw and smelled the fish. Jack gamely followed Ian's advice. He focused solely on playing his part with E Company, his company. Good naturedly he said, "Aw c'mon guys, ignore the smell; you just have to know how to prepare it properly." Frank, Turk, and the others watched curiously as Jack took a few fillets and carefully laid them in a mess tin. He walked over to the fire and sautéed them lightly in their own oil. "Any soy sauce?" he asked no one in particular. A cook heard him and sneered, "No goddamned soy sauce, bud, but we got us a very fine lemon-butter sauce you might find to your likin'." Jack laughed with the others as he returned to his spot with the warm fillets. All eyes were on him as he carefully laid the small fillets over a bed of rice. The men watched in amazement as Jack expertly lopped off a piece of fish and filled the remainder of his spoon with rice; all in one smooth motion. Not a grain of rice was lost. He moaned and said, "Oh my yes . . . almost perfect. All that's missing is a little soy sauce, Japanese, not Chinese mind you. The Chinese stuff is too smoky for a heavily flavored fish dish like this. Tsunami's sauce is the best. Actually, a little Frank's Red Hot sauce would do nicely with this as well." The young boys were befuddled and fascinated at the same time. With each bite, Jack emitted a satisfied moan as the young men watched silently. Marines and Navy men, as a rule, complained about their food; it was a traditional pastime. To observe one of their own treating a meal as if it were a pleasurable, almost sexual encounter, was alien and slightly disturbing. It wasn't exactly unmanly, just odd in the extreme.

"Goddamn, pops," one boy said in astonishment. "I ain't never seen nobody eat like you . . . 'specially since I joined the Navy."

Jack smiled and said, "I enjoy a fine meal young man. It's one of life's simple pleasures. You'll learn when you get a little older."

The men continued to stare at Jack, more in amusement now than surprise. "Holy Christ." One youngster tittered. "You see him eat that Jap fish like God himself made it or somethin'? Hell, I bet ole' pops is in fucking heaven when he's eatin' pussy!" The men exploded in laughter at the crude joke, just as Jack would have when he was their age. Jack let out a pained groan, but retained his smile. He'd succeeded in forgetting about his father for the moment and reveled in the attention these grand warriors, as he'd considered them back in the world, were lavishing on him.

Finishing his meal, he put his arms behind his head, leaned back and said, "Yes, and just like after sex, all I need now is a good smoke." Several of the boys clawed at their shirt pockets, and in an instant four cigarettes were thrust in Jack's face. With a grin he took all four and accepted a lit match from Turk. Caught up in the moment, he mindlessly took his show too far.

"Ahh yes," he sighed. "Outstanding dinner . . . not as good as sushi, but good nonetheless."

"Shushi . . . what the hell is shushi?" Turk asked.

"*Su-shi,*" Jack corrected. "Raw pieces of fish laid over little mounds of sticky rice. Tuna's the best . . . especially 'toro' . . . the fatty kind. It tastes like really tender, mild prime rib . . . it's fantastic." The group's silence set off belated alarms. He looked at Turk and saw that his jaw had dropped. He slowly gazed upon the rest of the men. They were all staring at Jack, dumbfounded.

Turk cursed and said, "Raw fish? You eat raw fish? Jesus Christ! Was you raised by fuckin' bears or somethin'?"

Jack cursed himself silently as he fully realized his mistake. He recovered quickly though. "Before the war, I used to travel to California during summer break from my teaching job. I uh, through friends at home, uh . . . got to be friends with a Japanese family. They taught me to eat and enjoy sushi. I'm serious, it's pretty good. I like to try new things."

"Jesus H," Turk grumbled. "Leave it to them little monkeys to eat uncooked fish. They ain't human, I swear. But what's your excuse, Jack?"

Before Jack could reply, one of the boys chuckled and said, "I wonder how much raw fish the California Japs are getting in the internment camps!" Light laughter rose from the cluster of men. Jack believed the resettling of people of Japanese ancestry during the war to desolate internment camps had been a mistake driven not so much by xenophobia as ignorance. Jack had become friends with several Japanese-Americans during his business career, some whose parents or grandparents had been resettled to the camps. But, he reminded himself, it was 1942 and these young men—and the nation as a whole—had been traumatized and driven to paranoia by the Japanese surprise attacks in the Pacific. He kept his mouth shut.

8

To Jack's surprise, after chow, Ian decided that all five of the remaining wounded were fit to return to their units. Indeed, the men were not gravely injured, however, they were not being sent home for bed rest, but back to the putrid, rotting jungle and inevitable combat. Jack looked on sadly as the Marines were given hand written medical instructions to pass on to their unit's corpsmen, who would now be their sole caregivers. He overheard Ian expressing concern that the field medics would have trouble deciphering the scrawled instructions. Ian lamented, "What I'd give for just one bloody typewriter."

Several of the men were given medicines and swabbing solutions, also to be handed over to their corpsmen. The corpsmen assigned to combat units were mostly young and of limited medical experience. They had been trained over very short spans of time in basic trauma care, hygiene methods and disease prevention. Still, for the combat Marine, they were the first barrier between them and the loss of limb or life. For that, they were revered and very welcome members of their units.

Jack watched Leonard Chesnek, the kid wounded by the palm tree, limp off to a waiting open bedded truck, his rifle slung over his shoulder. The instructions for his medic were stuffed into a breast pocket. Chesnek wore a wide smile and was joking loudly with the other wounded Marines. Jack walked up to the truck just as the driver started the engine. He thrust his hand out to his first patient and said, "You take good care now, Leonard . . . best of luck to you."

The boy grabbed Jack's hand and let out a whoop. "Hey, Doc!" he said enthusiastically, "They're finally letting me out of this goddamn butcher shop." The truck slowly began to pull away and the boy yelled, "Thanks for taking care of me, Doc. And don't forget; 23 Galway Street, South Boston! Fenway fuckin' pahk, Doc!"

"I won't forget!" Jack shouted back. He waved as the truck sped away toward the Tenaru. Jack smiled as he watched the boy reach into his shirt and pull out his Red Sox pendant. He waved it excitedly at Jack just before the truck disappeared around a bend. Jack had trouble understanding why the young men were so excited to be returning to their units, bivouacked out in the open rotting jungle, completely exposed to the elements and eventually the enemy. Still standing in the road, Jack decided to talk to Ian about his decisions regarding the wounded Marines. It made no sense to him. The men would be of little use to their comrades, and the first real battle was days off. It seemed cruel to send them back while they were still healing. Jack though, believing completely that Ian was a caring and intelligent man, wondered how he could so callously send the boys back to the line.

Jack found Ian in the hospital. "Could I talk to you for a sec, Doc?"

"Sure, what's on your mind?" Ian replied.

"No offense, but I don't understand why those boys had to go back to their units so quickly. They're still pretty roughed up, and as I told you, there won't be any significant action for days."

Ian's eyes narrowed slightly. "They and their leaders don't know that do they? Remember, this isn't some friendly neighborhood hospital back stateside."

"I know, but Jesus . . ."

Ian cut him off with a wave of his hand and said, "Jack, you observe and learn; that's all you need to concern yourself with. That's for your own good as well as that of the sick and wounded. As much as you admire and care for these men, this is a war . . . a

106

real one; not one picked up off the pages of a book you read or a movie you took in at the local bloody cinema."

Jack winced at Ian's rebuke, thought for a moment then said, "Sorry, Ian, you're the boss. I guess I have to get used to a guy nearly half my age being in that position. But it just seems so harsh, so . . . I don't know . . . so goddamn sad or something." Stroking his forehead, he said, "Jesus, it's hard; I mean they really are just kids. But I'll do my best to stay out of your way, I promise. Apology accepted?"

"Yeah sure, mate," Ian replied. Jack nodded and walked outside. He leaned against a palm and smoked one of the cigarettes he'd collected after his meal. Just as he took his last drag, a jeep roared up and stopped. The driver shouted for help. Jack stood frozen as several corpsmen ran past him toward the vehicle. A corpsman was sitting on the back edge holding a stretcher in place. A Marine, moaning loudly, was lying on it. Taking a deep breath, Jack tentatively approached.

"Sniper near the Matanikau!" the corpsman perched on the jeep yelled.

A voice behind Jack calmly, yet firmly, said, "Where is he hit?" It was Ian.

"In the gut . . . just once," the corpsman replied.

"Once is enough," Ian said dryly. After giving the wounded man a quick look over Ian said, "Okay chaps, move him inside." Ian removed the field dressing that had been applied and wiped blood away from the wound. A small hole, perfectly round, lay an inch above the man's navel and Jack noticed that small lumps of congealed sulfa powder lay in and around the wound. The Marine's moans grew louder as Ian probed the hole with a pair of forceps. Frank wrapped a blood pressure cuff around the boy's arm and soon announced that the reading was good.

When Ian finished, the young man's moans died away. Ashen faced, he looked up at Ian and said with a strange calm, "I can't move my legs, Doc. I can't feel nothing in 'em either." Ian cursed quietly and frowned. Noticing the reaction, the boy asked, "Am I dying, Doc?"

Ian, quickly masking his concern, smiled and said, "No, you're not dying, lad. The bullet didn't hit a major organ and I don't detect any serious internal bleeding. But we do need to get you out to a ship for surgery right away." He turned to Frank and ordered, "Frank, one dose of morphine, no more. I want him to be able to talk to the docs on the ship. Zellner, take the jeep to the radio shack and tell them to call the Navy. They need to send a boat immediately to Lunga Point. Tell them this man needs immediate surgery . . . go!"

Frank, stoic and non-verbal, jabbed a morphine syrette into the man's leg, and in what seemed to Jack a remarkably short time, the boy visibly relaxed, his breathing less panicked. Turk dabbed the Marine's forehead with a wet cloth. "You'll be okay, mac." he said. "The docs will patch you up and you'll be home in no time." Frank redressed the wound and they waited for Zellner to return. A minute later a vehicle pulled up outside the tent, grinding its gears and skidding to a halt. By the sound, it was a truck. Again, an urgent shout for help. This time, Jack ran with the others.

"What's up?" Turk yelled.

"Busted leg . . . real busted. Dumb shit walked in front of our truck," the driver said. "With these fuckin' blackout lights, it was like he just appeared in front of me like a fucking ghost. There was nothin' I could do." The man was gently lifted out of the truck. He was quiet and his eyes were glassy. Deep shock had set in. Someone turned on a penlight, illuminating the man's injury. Jack involuntarily gasped and recoiled in horror. Two jagged bones, snowy white, protruded from the lower half of his left leg. The bones appeared as strange stalks growing out of a pulpy mass of pink/red soil. Jack quickly recovered, hoping no one had noticed his reaction, but he could not bring himself to look directly upon the injury. While watching a football game in the '80s he had looked on in shivering horror as the leg of the Redskins quarterback was snapped like a twig. Ever since then he'd had to turn away from the TV when other such leg, knee, or ankle injuries were replayed constantly by the broadcasters. This was much, much worse than the stomach churning injuries he'd seen on television.

It turned out the men who delivered the injured Marine were cooks out gathering supplies, so nothing had been done to treat the man's injury. He was rushed inside and Ian, with the help of Frank, sanitized the wound and then, with a ghastly scraping sound, set the leg. The boy's screams sent Jack stumbling backwards to the edge of the tent. Ian and Frank applied a splint crafted from Japanese lumber. Moments later Zellner came hurtling back up the road and skidded to a halt outside the tent. "Landing craft is on its way from Red Beach . . . should be at Lunga in fifteen," he shouted.

Without looking up from his work, Ian said, "Turk, make sure that Marine's tagged properly for the shipboard docs, then ride with Zellner to the beach. I'll be done with this chap in just a minute, so you can take him with you as well."

"Okay, Doc," Turk replied.

In just minutes the tranquility of the aid station had been replaced by an atmosphere charged with chaos, urgency, and gore. The sense of relief Jack felt upon the departure of the terribly injured young men left him feeling guilty, helpless and confused, as if he were an undeserving interloper on the historic, yet horrible, events. He was able to finally cognate that what was occurring was the fundamental and most crucial business of the hospital: urgent, critical care of badly injured young men, some who would, inevitably, die. He could not conceive how he could be of any real help in this undertaking; he couldn't even bring himself to look upon a broken leg. To bolster himself he whispered, "You'll figure something out, bud. Talk to Ian about it tonight, he'll know what to do." Jack shook his head, realizing that for the first time in his life he was accepting the mentorship of another human being, in this case, one nearly half his age. He felt a hand on his shoulder.

"You ready to grab a few smokes out back and have a bit of a chat, mate?" Ian asked.

"Sure," Jack said.

"Hey, Frank. Jack and I are going out back to have a fag or two. You be sure to yell for me if we get more wounded. Dr. Goldman is sleeping and I don't want him disturbed unless absolutely necessary, understand?"

"Yes, sir," Frank replied.

Ian and Jack exited the tent and walked into the forest. It was pitch black so they walked slowly with their arms extended in front of them, feeling their way forward. "A bloke could get fucked up good just trying to find a little privacy on this bloody island," Ian muttered.

"Yeah, well at least the Japs can't see us . . . or at least they can't see you," Jack teased, trying to push out of his mind the horrors he'd just seen at the aid station.

"Bloody right you are," Ian said with a chuckle. "Perhaps I missed my true calling. I should've been a night fighter in the Aussie commandos. Go out at night and carve the Japs up with a bloody great knife and such."

"Sounds exciting, Doc," Jack said. "But somehow I think we're all better off if you stick to carving on Marines with a scalpel." Moments later they bumped into a fallen tree that formed a perfect bench. They sat down and lit cigarettes. Jack heard a burst of laughter float above the quiet forest, and looked back in the direction of the hospital. He could just barely discern a dull, golden glow coming from the tent. After what he had just witnessed in the hospital, the sounds of merriment seemed out of place. They combined to give a surreal, almost ghostly quality to the night.

Ian sighed and said, "Bloody hell, I suspect the gut-shot lad's spine stopped the slug. Maybe the doctors offshore can do something, but I doubt it. Christ, think of it, a few miserable days on this bloody rat hole and then they send you home in a wheelchair for the rest of your life." He chuckled bitterly and added, "But, as I've heard your blokes say, whoever said life was fair?"

"Yeah uh, yeah, that was pretty awful." Jack hesitated for a moment, then stammered, "That, uh . . . that was pretty wild just now, huh, Doc? Pretty, gory and all."

"Listen, mate," Ian said, sensing Jack's discomfort. "Don't worry about your reaction when you first saw the boy's broken leg.

It's always tough the first time, but trust me, you'll get used to it."
Jack was disappointed that Ian had noticed his performance, but
was relieved to hear him express confidence that he would learn to
cope with it. "I'm not going to sugarcoat it for you, you're going to
have to prepare yourself, mate," Ian continued. "Just think what it
will be like when the Marines actually engage. Take what you saw
and multiply it by a factor of ten . . . and we won't be saving them
all you know. We'll be dealing with not just wounded, but the dead
and dying as well."

Jack hadn't given these facts much consideration. He not only
knew for a fact that the wounded would come pouring in, but he
also knew when. After what he had just seen, the prospect of what
lay ahead made him anxious and doubtful. He thought back to the
day before when he had entered the crude lean-to; it seemed like
weeks ago. Though he was numb and disoriented, he still remembered the chaos and misery; this, after only two passes by a solitary
aircraft. Jack wondered if he really could deal with it; if he could
care for his heroes and not dishonor himself before them. Never
before in his life had he really considered failure. Now however, the
thought of failing here, amongst the men he admired the most, was
almost unbearable. He shook his head rapidly, purging the prospect
from his mind.

"So, think you can handle it, mate?" Ian asked in a tone Jack
found unnervingly nonchalant.

Jack sighed, then replied, "Depends, I guess."

"Depends on what?"

"I felt really helpless when those two men came in just now,
hell, not just helpless, I nearly goddamn fainted. If I can only stand
there and watch until they're ready to be swabbed or wrapped or
something, I don't know if I can hack it."

Ian laughed quietly and said, "Jack, you aren't a surgeon or a
trained medic. It'll take some time and exposure, but don't you
think for a second that you won't be busy as hell when business is
good. You'll be running your bloody bum off. And Jack?"

"Yeah?"

"You can hack it," Ian said firmly. "Like I said earlier, you're tougher than you think. God knows you've never really been tested, except for those bloody three-foot putts at your golf club . . . crikey, no offense, mate."

"None taken," Jack said with a chuckle. "What will I do when things get rough?"

"Lots," Ian said. "You'll be called on to do lots. When a heavy volume of wounded comes in over a short period of time, you'll be running around like a bloody dervish. You'll learn to triage, assist in surgeries, change bedpans, move stretchers, redress the wounds that the field chaps didn't have time to do properly, administer meds, those sorts of things." The prospect of him taking on duties such as these intimidated Jack somewhat, but also left him with a never before felt sense of satisfaction. An ironic smile creased his face as he realized that back in the world he'd be angling to run the hospital, not actually engage in the dirty work.

Ian interrupted his thoughts, his tone more somber, "There'll be other things to do too, when things are really rough."

"Yes?"

"Administrative details mostly. Retrieving and recording men's personal information; cataloging and inventorying their belongings . . . that sort of thing."

"No problem," Jack said casually.

"Not for the wounded, Jack," Ian said slowly, "for the dead." Jack's sense of satisfaction was suddenly tainted with dread; his stomach and jaw muscles tightened. He'd never so much as touched a dead man, not even his own father. "You, along with the rest of us, will have to remove dog tags and any personal items from the body and clothing. They have to be documented and inventoried for shipment to next of kin. Graves registration will have to be contacted for pick up, and the body will need to be prepared for burial."

Jack had no way of knowing if he could perform this duty, but he would have to try. "You'll have to do it, bud . . . you'll just have to gut it out," he silently admonished himself. Ian puffed on the last dregs of his cigarette and said nothing more. Jack decided he should respond bravely, so Ian's confidence in him remained strong. What he said though, did not come out quite as he had wished.

"Uh . . . yeah . . . okay, Doc," he stammered. He coughed nervously and said, "I, uh, I've never touched a dead body . . . ah, but I think I'll do okay with it."

"It's a war, Jack . . . the real thing. We're all going to have to do things we never imagined. Like we talked about earlier, this is no bloody masculine fantasy. We're going to be tested for real, you included. I understand it might be tougher on you than the others because of your age, lack of training and the sheltered life you had back in the world. I truly feel sorry for you, but you can do it, mate; you have to. Not just for the lads, but for yourself as well."

Jack quickly lit another cigarette and thought about the countless hours he'd spent reading about and studying the battles of World War II. He had often wondered how he would have handled the stress, misery, deprivation and horror of frontline combat. He knew all along the likelihood of him ever having to perform in these conditions was remote. Yet he wondered all the same. As well, he had always suspected most other men pondered the same thing to varying degrees and depths. Now the thought of actually living the nightmare fantasy, after a life of comfort and shelter, left him doubtful and scared . . . scared to death. Frightened somewhat for his safety, but mostly frightened that he would fail, that he would let them down. As he had just minutes before, he once again shook the unbearable thought out of his mind.

Ian, thankfully, changed subjects by informing him that he had dummied up papers and that Jack was now a real live U.S. Navy Hospitalman, Third Class. He had also ordered a set of dog tags containing a fictitious serial number, and created a personnel file for Jack with the battalion. Ian apologetically told him that since no records of him existed back in the States, he, unfortunately, would not receive a pay packet. Jack burst out laughing at Ian's last comment, particularly in light of the sincerely remorseful way he'd delivered it. At first Ian was taken aback, but then he too realized the absurdity and joined in the laughter. Soon both men were wiping away tears as the irony of the comment settled deeper.

After their amusement subsided they sat quietly for several minutes, lost in their own thoughts. Save for an occasional burst of laughter from the aid station and sleeping tent, the only sounds were those of the jungle. Tropical birds, perched high in the palms, screeched in loud, grating tones. Rats and lizards slithered and scampered about, rustling the underbrush. Back in the world just the sight of one of the vile creatures would have filled Jack with revulsion. Now though, after everything that had happened, he hardly gave them a second thought. Every few moments a hand slapping skin and a low curse punctuated the nocturnal ministrations as Jack and Ian mashed huge mosquitoes against their faces and necks. In the distance, clusters of muffled shots rang out from time to time. The green, jittery Marines were firing at shadows or the sounds made by the jungle's inhabitants.

Ian broke the silence asking, "You haven't told me about your journey here. Can you remember what you were doing before you ended up in the middle of the bloody war?"

Jack was quiet for several moments then, said, "As best as I can recall I made my journey, as you call it, from the bottom of the Tenaru."

He told Ian the story of his childish drunken charge across the sand spit at the head of the creek and his unintended plunge into the black water. He described his struggle with his boots and the tunnel he entered just as he was preparing to die. He told him how the tunnel was welcoming at first, then turned menacing, before ejecting him out onto the riverbank. He told him about the soldiers waking him up, spitting man and the leeches. The Zero raining death and the captain's head exploding. When Jack finished, they lit new cigarettes and listened again to the sounds of the jungle. Once again, Ian broke the silence.

"Tell me, mate, have you thought about going back to the creek to try and find that portal back to your world?"

"Of course I have. I was too fucked up yesterday to really give

114

it a try . . . that dead Jap soldier freaked me out. I thought about it too this morning before you kicked me in the ass. Now today, after seeing everything, after the stuff in the hospital and trying to help out and all . . ." Jack paused for a moment, then quietly continued, "After seeing my dad and all . . . shit, I don't know."

"I see," Ian murmured. "Not to push you too hard mate, but any more insight on how you want to handle your father?"

"I'm doing my best to try not to think of that," Jack muttered.

"Okay," Ian replied softly.

"No. I mean . . . uh . . . I uh, I don't know. It's too mind-blowing, too bizarre." Jack went on to describe the distant relationship he and his father had from his teen years on, and how the chasm grew when he joined the family business. How it completely fractured when Jack, having taken legal control of the business after his father suffered a stroke, immediately sold it, creating great wealth for both of them. He described his father's moroseness and detachment when away from work, and his idiosyncrasies, such as putting people into neat categories. He told him about his father's poor business instincts and waste of profits due to his overt focus on the well-being of his employees. He told him about, in his words, the silly rock his father carried around, a souvenir of his time in the service. He told him how frustrated he was that his father refused to talk about his wartime experiences, only saying that it was a long time ago and he couldn't remember much.

"Christ, who am I to say, but there may be some bloody good reasons for you two to get together," Ian said.

Jack emitted a soft groan and said, "It's creepy; he's just a kid for chrissakes. Anyhow, what good would it do me or him if we were to meet and talk? We're from different worlds now."

Ian was silent for several moments, then replied, "Maybe it wouldn't do any good at all. But it's hard for me to see what harm could come of it."

"Hmm," was Jack's grunted reply.

"I'm curious," Ian continued. "You say you admire and deeply respect the men fighting here. You even said they're your heroes.

But your father's here too. I am curious as to why he's different, even if he didn't talk about his wartime service."

Jack thought for a moment, then replied, "I don't know. I was too close to him, I guess. I could see all his faults . . . never considering that he could have done something out of the ordinary. The other veterans I didn't know, of course, so they seemed larger than life to me. And remember, before today when I saw him march past, I only ever thought him to be vaguely connected with the war; not a real player in it somehow."

"Hmm, interesting, mate," Ian said, almost sounding sarcastic, Jack thought. "Even that bloody baboon with the Pioneers this morning; he's still larger than life to you?" Jack began to explain that that experience, combined with seeing his father, had not perhaps changed his basic beliefs about the war, but at least his perception of it. Before he could continue, Ian suddenly gripped Jack's arm, threw his cigarette to the ground and whispered urgently, "Quiet . . . listen!"

Jack sat still and silent, straining to hear what Ian had. They held their breaths and listened. After a moment, the suspense was too much for Jack and he whispered, "What'd you hear?" Before Ian could reply, Jack heard several rhythmic crunch-like sounds directly behind. The pace of the sounds was clearly not the footsteps of a rat or lizard. These footsteps were human. A bright, white curtain of light seemed to flash before his eyes and his heart raced; the onset of terror was instantaneous. The thumping stopped for a moment, then started again, except now the sounds came from the side and were closer. His terror and panic increased, and he felt a strong urge to jump up and run back to the hospital. He knew if he did they may die, but the urge was remarkably strong. Ian seemed to sense this as he put his hand on Jack's shoulder and lightly squeezed. The thumps were in front now; the man seemed to be heading in the direction of the tent. Ian leaned over and whispered in Jack's ear.

"It's a Jap . . . he didn't smell like one of our boys. He's wounded . . . pretty badly I think. My guess is he's looking for food

116

and water . . . maybe even some medical supplies." Jack remembered reading about starving Japanese sailors and Korean laborers sneaking into the American perimeter at night in search of food and water. Ian was probably right, but Jack couldn't understand how he knew the infiltrator was hurt.

"How do you know he's wounded?" Jack whispered back.

"I smelled it . . . there's lots of blood and a festering wound." Ian thought for a moment, then said, "I doubt he poses much of a threat and he can't see us anyway. We'll circle around the station and alert the sentries. Maybe we can get him to the station, patch him up and give him over to the intelligence chaps." Jack's panic had abated, but he still would have preferred to stay put until the enemy soldier had finished his business. Besides, he thought, they couldn't be certain the man was alone, and the thought of running into one of them was terrifying. Ian was right though, it would be wrong to simply sit the situation out.

"Okay," Jack said weakly. "I'm game."

They stood up and Ian whispered, "I'll navigate. You grab my belt." They turned right and slowly and as quietly as possible walked 30 meters, then turned 90 degrees left toward the road that led to the station. When they reached the road Jack was nearly overcome with relief and exhilaration; they had successfully eluded the ghostly intruder and he hadn't let his panic get the best of him. They ran the 30 meters to the tent. When they arrived, Ian calmly informed the armed naval sentries who provided security for the hospital as well as having the responsibility of Shore Patrolmen. He told them where he roughly judged the man to be. Candles burning in the hospital shed just enough light for Jack to make out the shadowy features on each sentry's face. They were wide-eyed, not with fear he noted, but with excitement.

"You're shittin' me!" one of the boys whispered excitedly. "This is my first Jap hunt. Let's get in there before the son of a bitch gets away!"

"Whoa there, lad," Ian whispered back. "You need to try to capture the infiltrator first and kill him only if necessary. He's badly

117

wounded and is likely just scrounging for food and supplies. Also, the intelligence chaps would give their bollocks for a prisoner to interrogate, so take it easy, understand?"

"Yes, sir," the five men said in unison.

"Good, uh . . . what's your plan then, chaps?" Ian asked. The young, navy sentries looked at each other nervously, then whispered excitedly back and forth. Finally, one of them spoke up.

"Um, sir . . . we'd kind of be more comfortable if you'd come up with the plan." Jack heard Turk quietly guffaw in the background.

Ian hesitated then hissed, "Oh bloody hell, this is great, lads . . . just great! I've never fired a gun in my entire life, much less trained in field tactics!"

Snickers from unseen hospitalmen, increased both Ian's and the sentry's frustration. "You can do it, sir, just use some of your aboorig'nal bush trackin' skills," Turk whispered loudly.

"Shut up, Turk. You bloody wanker!" Ian hissed.

After several moments of awkward silence, a short, stocky sentry stepped forward and said, "I think I know what to do, sir." In the dull, distorting light, the man seemed almost perfectly square.

Ian turned to the sentry and said, "Thank God. So what's your plan then, lad?"

"I've been trained to speak Japanese, not the whole language or anything, but just enough to talk 'em into surrendering and stuff," he said. "We can't just go charging into the bush in the dark and all. If he's armed, one of us is dead for sure and so is the Jap . . . kinda defeats the purpose. We can't use illumination for one lousy Jap either . . . too risky."

"Go on," Ian said.

"Well, we'll surround the area where you think the Jap is and I'll try to talk him out. You know, offer him food and medicine and stuff. If he runs or makes any aggressive moves, we'll open fire on him."

Ian immediately replied, "Makes bloody sense . . . do it." The sentries quietly took up their positions. Moments later the negotiator's voice boomed through the jungle. The deep bass coming from

such a small man surprised Jack. Ian had accompanied the negotiator while others of the hospital staff, Jack included, had crossed
the road and lay on the ground, watching the show.

After a few uncertain moments, a weak, high pitched voice
wafted from the tree line. "No soldier . . . no soldier please. U.S.
okay . . . U.S. good."

"He wants to surrender," Ian said to the negotiator. "Tell him to
come out so we can treat his injuries." In halting, clumsy Japanese,
the Marine passed on the message. They heard the brush rustling,
then a stooped figure stepped out of the trees and sank to the
ground. The sentries rushed up and pointed their rifles at the man.
"No Japanese me . . . no Japanese me please, thank you," the man
said desperately.

Ian walked quickly to the captive, knelt down, and cupping a
penlight in his hands, examined him. His clothes were tattered and
his skin was covered with abrasions and sores. A jagged wound lay
just beneath his shoulder; pus-filled and squirming with maggots.
The unarmed man looked up at Ian with pleading eyes. "This isn't
a Jap soldier," Ian declared. "He's one of the Korean laborers we
heard about."

"A fuckin' termite? What's the difference?" one of the sentries
asked. "Ain't all them slanty eyed bastards the same?"

"Quiet," Ian said icily. At that moment the skies opened and
torrents of rain fell. Jack had never felt, or for that matter heard,
rain quite like it. The drops were so large and densely packed it
seemed as if their force would slowly drive him to the ground. The
hissing, slapping noise they created as they flew through the air
and slammed to the ground was almost deafening. To be heard, Ian
yelled, "Get him inside!" Two sentries leaned over, each looping an
arm under the laborer's armpits. They dragged him into the tent,
followed excitedly by the entire hospital staff. Once inside, he was
given water and a C-ration. Jack smiled as he realized it was probably the first time the man had eaten anything remotely similar to
franks and beans. He didn't seem to mind though, as he ravenously
slurped his meal. While he ate, Ian examined his wound. When he

had finished eating, Frank put an ether soaked cloth over the man's mouth and nose and he quickly went to sleep.

"Shrapnel wound . . . probably got hit by naval gunfire before we landed," Ian announced. "Bloody nasty, but he'll be okay." Ian then deftly trimmed the pus and dead flesh from the wound while Turk removed the maggots with small forceps. After sterilizing the injury, Ian sewed it up and applied a bandage. "Zellner!" Ian shouted, "Go to the radio shack up the road and call the intelligence chaps. Ask them what they want us to do with this bloke. Oh, and don't forget your 'brelly' lad." The men all smiled at Ian's last comment, but Jack noticed that they all remained transfixed by the diminutive Asian man lying on the stretcher. He was not a Jap, but to them he was close enough. It was the first time any one of them had laid eyes on a live enemy, and they were curious and fascinated. Jack knew it likely that many, if not most of the staff, didn't even know where Korea was or the fact that it was essentially occupied by Japan. To them, he was the enemy, plain and simple, and they were sizing him up. Jack felt obligated to speak up and enlighten his comrades.

"This guy . . . this Korean, is basically a slave and that's why he surrendered so easily, poor bastard. It would've been a lot different if he were a Jap."

"What do you mean he's a slave?" one boy asked.

Jack reminded himself to be careful not to give away too much, then replied, "Japan occupies Korea. They basically indenture guys like him and attach them as heavy laborers to their army. Some are fairly loyal to the Japs but most hate their guts."

Turk snorted and said, "I ain't never read about no Ko-reans in the sports page . . . you sure 'bout all this?" Jack laughed along with the others and was reminded once again that his lifelong heroes weren't wise old men now, but just boys, most of whom knew little of the world beyond their own villages, towns, and cities.

"I'm sure, Turk," Jack said. "The Japs are nasty pieces of work. We should feel sorry for this guy."

120

"I say bullshit to that," another boy said. "You sure seem dang smart and all Jack, but I think all the bastards are evil little monkeys." Other boys nodded their heads in agreement. Jack decided he had gone far enough and therefore did not rebut. He merely grabbed a cloth, doused it in a bucket of water and began to carefully clean the blood, grime, and pus off the prisoner, then dabbed at the man's wounds with alcohol and iodine, finally sprinkling them with sulfa powder. Jack shook his head at the irony, held by the fact that just seventy-two hours ago he wouldn't have voluntarily ventured within twenty yards of a creature in such condition.

When Jack and Ian had finished with the Korean, Ian suggested they retire to their quarters and catch some much needed sleep. Doc Goldman was due on duty any moment. The rain had let up briefly, and they slogged their way slowly through the deep, sticky mud to the lean-to.

Just before they arrived, Jack suggested, "Hey, Doc, how's about one more smoke?"

"You betcha' . . . as you Yanks say."

"Hey, you're catching on, Doc," Jack said laughing. "A few weeks with me and I'll have all the Aborigine and Euro-contamination out of you; fully Americanized you'll be."

"God help my bloody soul then," Ian grunted. In silence, they stood in the mud, sucking on their cigarettes while the mud sucked on their boondockers, causing them to noisily shift their feet every so often. Jack sighed and blew a conical smoke-plume up into the black sky. "That was good, mate," Ian said suddenly. "It was good the way you explained that poor blighter's situation to the boys."

"Yeah?" Jack replied. "Don't know how much good it did though."

"How much good it did? Oh, I think it did some good. It's like anything else, some of the boys will take it to heart and others won't, or perhaps more accurately, can't. Hell, isn't that human phenomena the reason we're on this bloody godforsaken island in the first place?"

Jack smiled wanly and said, "Yeah, I guess that's exactly why we're here. When the goddamn paranoid, self-hating, insecure idiots get some power, things get fucked up real quick. I hate to tell you, Doc, and without giving any details, it's still going on back in the world. In fact, in some ways, it's worse. And it's not just geopolitical stuff; it's crept deeper into our society, altering the older, simpler values." Jack's last statement, created an involuntary and uncomfortable sensation within him, a feeling that seemed to crawl up his spine. He'd felt the gnawing, unexplained feeling before, but never this strongly.

"I'm not surprised about new wars or the change in values. The first seems to be a constant, while the other seems to be the natural progression in many so called, 'developed societies'."

They threw their cigarettes in the mud and Ian moved toward the entrance of the tent. "Doc," Jack said, stopping him, "back there in the jungle, thanks to the Korean, we never really finished talking about my being here and my dad and all. Well, I've got a question that's bothering me."

"What is it, mate?"

"Wouldn't a normal fellow, without any equivocation whatsoever, want to get back to his family and out of this hell? I mean, Jesus Christ, I can't believe I'm saying this, but if I had a choice, I'm not sure what it would be. Christ, in the last two days I've felt things, both good and bad, that I've never felt in my life. Believe me; I love my family more than life. But I'm feeling more and more like I belong here, like being here is . . . is, Jesus, I don't know. It's changing things somehow, that's all. It's hard to explain, but possibly to want to be here instead of with my family? What does that say about me?"

"Listen, mate," Ian said. "You didn't ask for this and I don't know much about your life back in the world, Jack, but you've already told me enough to make me wonder if this journey of yours may not be for the best for all of you, your wife and kids too. You're here helping others, with no payback, no ego boost, nothing perhaps but misery. Any feelings of guilt over your uncertainty is a senseless waste of energy, energy you're going to need."

Jack rubbed his eyes and yawned. Suddenly the long day was a heavy weight on his mind and body. "Enough of my neuroses, Doc, let's get some sleep."

"Right-o," Ian replied. "Remember your trip to supply in the morning."

"Can't wait," Jack said earnestly.

The palm door to the lean-to had been closed during the downpour and Jack opened it so they could enter. "Pretty nifty, eh, Doc?"

"A beaut for sure," Ian said. When the wall shut behind them, Ian lit his penlight and slowly shone it around the interior of the pitch-black dugout. Men laid sprawled about on bedrolls. Ian chuckled and said, "This reminds me of the bloody caves we used to have play-abouts in back home when I was a nipper. In fact, that's exactly what we'll call this marvel of engineering you've created . . . the 'Cave'.

"I'm honored, Doc," Jack said with mock solemnity. They laid down on their assigned bedrolls. Each surrounded himself with mosquito netting and closed his eyes. Besides the low rumble of snoring young men, the only sound was Turk mumbling and cursing in his sleep. The netting was only partially effective, and it wasn't too long before the first mosquito stabbed Jack's neck. He slapped at it and thought for a moment. Then whispered to himself, "Nine to ten days until they start coming in." He thought of the thousands of men sleeping nearby, or at least trying to sleep. In ten days time many will have contracted the mosquito-borne disease malaria, dangerously weakening the strength and fighting ability of the Marine force. He imagined hordes of mosquitoes, at that very moment, descending through the blackness to alight on their targets, planting the seed of the disease with their tiny, yet poisonous daggers. He made a mental note to warn Ian about the timing and severity of the disease that was soon to engulf the medical units on the island. He also noted that the malaria boys would start coming in about the same time the fighting picked up. "Christ," he murmured to himself. "You've got a lot to learn in 10 days, bud."

He promised himself he would faithfully take the atabrine tablets they were to begin distributing in the morning and follow all other precautions. He couldn't get malaria he thought . . . he simply couldn't; there was too much to do and he worried he would be too weak to continue through the fever, chills, delirium, and extreme fatigue the disease could bring. Perhaps, he thought wishfully, it's impossible for me to contract the disease due to some quirk of metaphysics . . . who knows? This led to another thought; one Ian had referred to earlier. "Could I really be killed?" he wondered. Not in the sense of statistical probability or other conventional possibilities. The question was, could a man born in 1956 be killed in 1942? Did he physically die in the creek? And could he die again? The paradoxes sent his mind spinning, but his exhaustion overwhelmed him and he fell asleep.

At 3:00 AM Jack was wakened by the sound of a sputtering, coughing airplane engine, the clang of an air raid warning bell, and urgent shouts inside the Cave, as Ian had christened it. After clearing his head, Jack realized 'Washing Machine Charley' or 'Louis the Louse' as the Marines would come to know him, was making his first nightly visit. The small, dilapidated plane carried one bomb, and its purpose was more to steal sleep from the Marines rather than to do any real damage. It was an effective strategy. He noted it was raining again, yet in spite of that, the palm door flew open and the lean-to emptied quickly as men scrambled into foxholes they had dug earlier. Jack merely turned over and listened to the plane pass by. He wondered if the ragged rhythm of the engine really did sound like a 1940s washing machine. He knew the plane would never hit anything, at least not on his side of the airfield. Later, the Japanese would attack the field with organized flights of multiple medium bombers and fighters, strafing, and bombing. When these occurred he would have reason to join the others.

In a few minutes Jack heard the dull crump of the plane's payload explode harmlessly on the ridges surrounding the airfield. Its mission complete, it chugged away and the all clear sounded. When the men returned to the tent, there was Jack, eyes closed, but still awake. "Holy shit." one boy said. "That son of a bitch is one strange bird. First he's eatin' raw fish, now he's snoozin' through a damn air raid."

"Yeah," another added. "I think either he's got huge balls or he's just plain nuts." A satisfied smile creased Jack's lips as he slowly drifted off once again.

9

He woke with a start the next morning to a blood-curdling scream inside the Cave. The screech was immediately followed by loud cursing. "Snake . . . fucking snake! Oh fuck . . . Jesus, God!" Jack sat up just in time to see Turk, clad only in his Marine issue underpants, run from the Cave, his eyes bulging and jaw clenched, in a state of complete panic. As soon as he departed, the lean-to rocked with raucous laughter and catcalls.

"He's followin' you, Turk!" one boy hooted. "You don't run faster he's gonna' sink his fangs into your big hairy ass!" As the laughter settled and the boys rose from their bedrolls, Jack heard Frank chortle, "Good old Turk. He'd take on King Kong all by himself but he sees a little snake and completely loses his mind."

"Yeah," another boy said, "remember that time at New River? That snake crawled across his boondockers when he was on the shit pot and he went runnin' through the company area with his trousers down around his ankles, screamin' the whole way. Goddamn, that was funny!" Jack smiled as he put his boots on. Even the tough boy from South Philly had his fears. Several of the boys were poking at the offending reptile with a stick as Jack hurried out of the Cave, anxious to start his day. He consumed his breakfast of boiled Japanese oats and raisins. The other men carefully picked out the weevils that populated the Japanese oats, before they ate. Jack, on the other hand, dug right in. He recalled reading that the weevils were full of protein, something that was already in short supply.

"You guys shouldn't pick the weevils out of the oats," Jack said cheerily. "They're full of protein and you really can't taste 'em."

"They look like fuckin' rabbit turds," Turk said.

"Well they're not . . . they're full of good stuff. You really should leave them in . . . you're going to need all your energy, boys, and these little buggers can help." Jack insisted. The less squeamish among them stopped picking and started eating; the others groaned and continued to harvest the weevils. Jack again made a mental note to talk to Ian about it, so he could educate the men with greater credibility. He nearly inhaled the rest of his breakfast and went looking for Ian. He found him in the aid station tending to the wounded Korean laborer, who looked much better than the previous evening. His eyes were more alert, rested. He lay on his bedroll smiling slightly as Ian checked his dressing.

"Good morning, Doc," Jack said.

"Morning, mate; just getting this poor blighter ready for the intelligence chaps. They should be here anytime now to take him away."

"Uh-huh," Jack said dully. "I'm ready to go to supply, Doc, but if I can I'd like to take a truck, not the jeep."

"A truck?" Ian asked. "You can easily fit everything on the list into the back of the jeep, and it's a hell of a lot easier to drive on these bloody roads."

"I'm going to try and scrounge up some cots for the hospital while I'm there, so I need a truck."

Ian smiled and said, "I'm not sure how much luck you're going to have with that, but let me finish here and I'll get you set up." Jack waited impatiently. It wasn't just the fact that he was anxious to use his talents to contribute to the unit. It was also the thought of driving around the Marine perimeter, free and unfettered. Perhaps he would drive to the Pagoda, or to Kukum, the Matanikau and Pt. Cruz; locations he had studied and fantasized about for decades. It was a feeling not unlike the first time he soloed in his dad's Cadillac on his 16th birthday. Tempering it somewhat was the thought of finding his father along the banks of the Tenaru. He wanted desperately to see him again, to observe him; but this urge was still accompanied by a sense of uneasiness, as if he were violating some sort of natural code. Ian finished with the prisoner and Jack followed him outside. They walked toward a scruffy looking man standing by a truck. "Logjam, is this lorry available?" Ian asked. Jack felt slightly sorry for the man as he assumed the moniker referred to his stained and horribly crooked teeth.

The man looked at Ian quizzically and replied, "What in damnation is a lorry, sir?"

"Oh right . . . this truck, is this truck available?"

"Yeah sure. You want me to pick something up?"

"No," Ian said. "Macmillan here needs to pick up some supplies down at the beach; he won't be long."

The man eyed Jack warily and asked, "He know how to drive one of these?"

"Of course," Jack replied. "I drove a stick for years before going automatic. It's like riding a bicycle; you never forget." Logjam and Ian stared at Jack blankly. He quickly realized his historical faux pas and decided there was nothing to do but simply carry on. "Okay, I need to get going," he said.

Jack climbed in the cab and surveyed the dash board. He grabbed the shifting mechanism on the steering wheel shaft and depressed the clutch. He first searched the steering column then the dashboard for the ignition, unsuccessfully. Smiling nervously at Logjam, Jack suddenly remembered many World War II trucks were started by depressing a large button situated on the floor board. He sighed with relief when he found the button. He depressed it with his foot and the engine roared to life. Jack smiled, waved down to Ian and let the clutch up with one foot while slowly depressing the gas pedal with the other. The clutch was balky and more resistant than what he was accustomed to. Still smiling, he looked ahead and shouted, "Tally-ho!" Then, to Jack's consternation, the truck's gears ground together with a horrible metallic crunch; the vehicle lurched violently once, then again, and stalled

128

out. Logjam groaned loudly and shouted, "Goddamnit, Lieutenant, that idiot's gonna wreck my truck!"

Ian ignored the man as Jack shot him a sheepish glance. "No problem," he said. "It'll just take me a bit to get used to this gearbox." He started the engine again, shifted into first, and this time very slowly released the clutch. The truck again jerked, but this time he managed to keep the vehicle moving forward. When he felt he'd gained enough speed, he attempted to shift into second, as he passed the group he had eaten breakfast with, still sitting in a circle. Once again the metal gears screeched and rattled as they ground together. The heads of the men shot toward the grating sound. Just as they did, the truck jerked and stalled again.

"What the hell?" Turk yelled. "What kind of fuckin' moron is drivin' that thing?"

Jack saw the group out of the corner of his eye, but pretended they were not there.

Suddenly one of the men recognized him. He whooped and hollered, "It's pops . . . it's Macmillan!"

"Jesus Christ, you're right . . . it's ol' Jack!" Turk cackled. One of the boys jumped up and ran excitedly toward the truck. The others followed, howling with laughter. As they approached, Jack cursed under his breath and re-started the engine. The men crowded around and fired loud, boisterous catcalls up at Jack.

"What ya doin', pops?" one boy shouted. "You trying to make the Japs think we got a whole tank division revving up?"

Turk yelled in mock concern, "Stand back boys, that motor's gonna start throwin' off shrapnel any second. Wouldn't be right somehow to be killed all the way out here by a goddamn Chevy would it?" Jack smiled uneasily at the men. He was embarrassed, but not greatly. After all, he'd never driven a beast quite like this, and he took satisfaction from the fact that the company was getting some amusement from his clumsy, yet honorable travails. Finally, he gathered up enough steam to leave the hopping, delirious group of men behind.

Jack could hear Turk laughing uproariously as the truck lurched and ground away. "Go, Jack . . . go!" he yelled.

Another boy shouted, "Drive, pops, drive that fucker all the way to Tokyo! They'll hear you comin' and beg to surrender."

The other boys waved their arms wildly; urging Jack on. "Go, pops, go!" Jack looked straight ahead and extended his left arm out the window. He cocked his elbow vertically at a perfect 90 degrees. Then, he clenched his fist and pointed his middle finger toward the sky. He held the pose until he rounded the bend, and knew the rollicking group of boys could no longer see him. He retracted his arm and smiled. "Shitheads," he muttered, a wry smile creasing his face.

He backtracked on the road the convoy traveled the previous morning. The rutted track forced him to repeatedly change gears so it wasn't too long before he became relatively practiced on the awkward gearbox. He passed newly dug machine gun pits and foxholes, some already covered with coconut logs, grass, and mud. Various tents and lean-tos had sprung up like olive-drab anthills in the last 24 hours. The Marines were digging in to stay, even though the Navy had largely abandoned them after the Savo sea battle.

Jack had always considered Admiral Ghormley's decision to retreat, with half of the desperately needed supplies still onboard, to be over-cautious if nothing else. Now however, seeing with his own eyes what the Marines were up against, that they were young and human, not numbers or anonymous subjects in grainy black and white photos in history books, he was incredulous and outraged. The Savo battle had indeed been savage, leading to a horrifying loss of men and equipment. Still, Jack thought, "How can you simply leave 10,000 young men in desperate straits, in unimaginable conditions, against an enemy of, as yet unknown strength?" He shook his head and cursed. "Thank God they finally relieved Ghormley and put Halsey in charge," he said out loud.

The road turned extremely muddy when the truck entered the jungle bordering the beach very near Lunga Pt. He drove as fast as he could without losing control in the slime. As he traversed the cut

130

that led to the beach, he observed an obstacle of sorts ahead. Stretching across the road 30 meters in front of him was a depression three meters wide and full of water. It lay right at the end of the road. "Alright, you pig," Jack said. "Let's see what you got!" He jammed the accelerator to the floor and let out a whoop. The engine roared, its tires spinning in the muck, then slowly gaining traction. The truck picked up speed quicker than Jack anticipated and before he could adjust he was on top of the hole. The truck slammed into it, jostling Jack violently about the cab; his hands torn from the wheel. "Shit!" he yelled. The truck clattered and banged, rocking from side to side. To his horror it shot out onto the beach, straight at a cluster of Marines. "Look out!" Jack screamed. He slammed on the brakes as the men scattered. The brakes and soft sand brought the truck to a rapid halt and Jack's nose impacted sharply on the top of the steering wheel. Dazed, a throbbing, heavy pain spread from his nose throughout his entire head. He was blinded by tears and felt a warm, sticky substance ooze from his nose. He quickly forgot the pain though, when the horror of what had occurred sunk in.

"What in the hell are you doing, you stupid shit?" a man screamed. Jack heard someone jump on the running board beneath his door. He wiped his eyes and looked at the man. He grabbed Jack's shirt collar and shouted, "You trying to kill us, you goddamn idiot? Isn't it enough that the Japs and jungle are trying to get us? Now we've got numb-fucking-skulls like you takin' a shot?"

Appalled, Jack raised his hands and said, "I am really sorry, man. Jesus, I'm sorry . . . I was trying to get through the mud and it got away from me. Everyone's okay, aren't they?"

The man loosened his grip on Jack's collar and replied, "Well, other than Tonelli over there, who I think crapped his pants, we got lucky. Jesus Christ, you gotta be more careful, mac. What is this, the first time you've drove one of these fuckers or something?"

"No," Jack lied. "I just lost it I guess . . . I'm real sorry." He looked past the man and shouted to the others, "Sorry guys, I screwed up." The men concurred with profane mutters. "As long as you guys are okay, I need to go and pick up some hospital supplies."

"We're fine. You a doctor?" the Marine asked.

"A hospitalman," Jack said.

"You guys bored and trying to drum up a little business or something?" Jack heard laughter rise from the group and noticed that a slight smile had appeared on the man's face.

"Naw," Jack said, forcing a smile. "Like I said, I just screwed up . . . sorry again."

"Well, I guess we all do from time to time . . . but try to be more careful, okay?"

"Okay . . . yeah . . . I will."

The man jumped off the running board and looked back up at Jack. "Good thing you work in a hospital, bud."

"Why's that?"

"Looks to me like you got a busted nose," he said with what Jack thought was a satisfied grin.

They exchanged a wave and Jack turned up the beach and drove very slowly, much as one does after receiving a traffic violation. He pounded his fist on the steering wheel and hissed, "You dumb shit, Jack . . . use your goddamn head!" Unlike his grinding departure, this incident was more than embarrassing; it had nearly been a disaster. He felt deep anger at himself for his careless mistake. He was genuinely excited, and felt fortunate for the opportunity to help care for the men on the island. Then, on his first mission, he nearly squashes a group of them underneath a one-ton truck.

"Christ, this isn't a goddamn game, you idiot!" His self-castigation complete, he then reassured himself, "You'll be okay, buddy, you'll be fine. Just use your head." He calmed himself enough to refocus on his mission. He wasn't sure exactly where the depot was; only that it was still at the site of the initial landings, Red Beach. Ian had told him to simply drive east until he found it. He passed various stockpiles of supplies. After several minutes he spotted a mound of crates filled with medical supplies. He stopped the truck just short of the depot and jumped to the ground. A navy stevedore with a clipboard was marking off crates nearby. Jack walked over

132

and said, "I need to pick up some supplies for the 1st Battalion, Company E aid station. Can you tell me what I need to do to get them?"

"Sure," the man replied eagerly. He turned toward Jack and said, "First you need . . . holy shit! What happened to you, mac? Looks like Dimaggio mistook your schnoze for a curveball." Jack, having forgotten his injury, grimaced as he remembered the near catastrophe, his hand reflexively moving up to his nose. He could feel that it had swollen and was tender. "Goddamn. I hope the monster isn't broken," he thought. He felt rivulets of blood that were slowly drying in the humid air. When he touched them his fingers stuck slightly.

"Oh, not a big deal." Jack finally replied. "Just a little collision with my steering wheel on the way here . . . speed kills, you know."

The man stared at Jack for a moment, then said, "Ouch. So you need some supplies?"

"Yeah . . . for the 1st Battalion, E company sick bay," Jack replied. While the man detailed the procedure for requisitioning supplies, Jack opened his canteen and soaked one of his sleeves with water. Like a little boy outdoors in winter, he gently wiped the sleeve back and forth beneath his nose. The man winced slightly, then finished with his instructions.

"Thanks a lot," Jack said. "You say the supply tent is in the trees over there?" he asked pointing behind him.

"Yeah, start there and when you get your slip come back and I'll give you a hand."

"Thanks."

"Oh, and a little advice, friend . . ." the Man said. "Biggs is a first rate asshole. Don't piss him off or you may not get your supplies."

"Who is Biggs?" Jack asked.

"Captain Earnest J. Biggs, U.S.M.C." the sailor replied. "He's the boss and every supply requisition has to be approved by him. He's crooked as Capone and just about as mean . . . so be careful."

"Thanks for the advice," Jack said. He remembered what Ian had told him about some of the supply people. He wasn't too concerned though, he'd dealt with all kinds during his career. Jack found the tent containing the supply administration group and walked inside. A pudgy boy sat at a simple rectangular desk, the first Jack had seen on the island, tabulating figures from small slips of paper. "Excuse me," Jack said. "Where can I find a guy named Biggs?"

The boy looked surprised, then said warily, "What do you need him for?"

"I need to pick up some supplies for the hospital and I under-stand that he's the guy who needs to approve the requisition."

"That's right," the boy said. "Wait here. I'll go get him. Oh, and if I were you I wouldn't go around here referring to him as Biggs. He'll have your ass, I promise you. It's 'sir' or 'Captain', bub."

"Yeah okay," Jack said impatiently. He surveyed the dark tent. The shade lent by the jungle canopy kept the heat within it bear-able. Several men were busily scribbling on, transposing and reviewing various documents. Jack saw a man clacking away on a typewriter. It reminded Jack of the types he and Laura had seen while antiquing in Northern Michigan. Jack recalled hearing Ian complain about the lack of a typewriter when they were writing out medical care directives for the five Marines being sent back to their units the previous evening. He'd been concerned that the unit corpsmen would have difficulty deciphering their handwriting. After a minute or two, the pudgy boy returned and sat down. With-out looking up he said, "He'll be here in a minute."

Having been alerted by the man outside, Jack stared down at the boy and asked, "Why is it a captain has to sign a release for every requisition? Hell, it's just medical supplies, not airplanes or tanks."

This time the boy looked up at Jack before he spoke. He looked Jack over uneasily, as if he perceived some sort of danger. "I don't know," the boy replied, "I ain't fuckin' Admiral Nimitz, and besides, I ain't figured out an officer yet. All I know is the captain likes to know who's taking what, where . . . day and night."

A damned control-freak martinet, Jack thought to himself. He had dealt with that sort often during his business career. When you had authority over such men, it was easy to deal with them and get from them what you needed. However, when they had authority over you, it was often impossible to accomplish anything beyond the man's own selfish whims and needs.

Suddenly, a voice barked, "What do you need?" Jack turned and saw a man who must surely be Biggs. He was standing with hands on hips, looking slightly annoyed. Biggs was of medium height and build. He appeared quite fit and youthful. He locked his gaze on Jack with bright blue eyes. He was handsome, Jack thought, but not in a rugged all-American way; his look was soft, one might even say, feminine. This look was exaggerated by the fact that his uniform was spotless and his thick brown hair was meticulously combed and gelled.

"Well, sailor?" Biggs barked, "I haven't got all goddamn day!"

Jack checked his temper and replied, "I need to pick up some medical supplies for the Company E, 1st Battalion Field Hospital at the airfield . . . uh, sir. It's all on this list that one of our officers signed." Jack silently congratulated himself for remembering to use the proper salutation.

"Let's see," Biggs grunted. Jack held out the list and Biggs snapped it from his hands. Jack watched him closely as he rubbed his chin. Finally, he looked up and said, "Yeah, I suppose we have everything on this list and there's nothing on it that means shit to me."

He signed the document and handed it back to Jack. Jack looked at the typewriter and said, "Oh, and there are a couple more items I need that are not on the list . . . the Doc just wrote down the medical stuff . . . maybe you guys can help me."

Biggs' eyes narrowed and he took a step toward Jack. "Guys?" he hissed. "Did you say 'guys', mister?" For a moment Jack was shocked by the man's pettiness in the midst of an active campaign, but then he remembered reading countless examples of the chicken-shit ways of many members of the officer class in all the services. It certainly wasn't the rule, but every man had experienced it and often found it to be the most unpleasant aspect of their military service.

135

Jack again cursed himself for his carelessness and stammered, "Sorry, sir. I didn't mean any disrespect."

"I am a goddamn captain in the Marine Corps. I'm not a *guy*, you understand, sailor? Now get the hell out of here before I change my mind about those supplies!" With men like Biggs, Jack had committed one of the gravest sins. Under no circumstances would these men tolerate any show of disrespect or lack of subservience, no matter how unintentional or trivial. Jack knew it would be difficult, but he had to try to make amends. He hadn't even completed his request for the extra supplies. He stood up straight and carefully avoided direct eye contact with Biggs.

"I am very sorry sir . . . it won't happen again, I assure you. I'm the supply clerk for my unit and I'll be coming here a lot, so I don't want to do anything to offend the captain, sir." Jack felt slightly foolish as he carried out his act, an act he had learned from viewing countless war films back in the world. He was a little surprised, but pleased in a way, at how easily he had referred to himself as a clerk.

"Oh, is that right?" Biggs dripped. Jack glanced at Biggs and noticed that in spite of his sarcasm, he had relaxed and seemed somewhat pleased. He was putting on quite a show for his subordinates Jack thought. "I am just so pleased to hear of your intentions regarding me, old man. I'll sleep so much better tonight." Biggs paused, glared at Jack then continued, "What's an old bastard like you doing with a job like this anyway?"

Jack thought for a moment, and on a hunch replied, "I have a business background so one of our officers thought this would be a good job for me."

Biggs snorted and said, "A business background! Now that's a good one. What kind of business . . . a newspaper stand?"

Jack's temper flared, his face flushed with anger. "No sir," he replied barely above a whisper. He had never dealt well with men like Biggs when he was not holding the cards, and it had gotten him in trouble on several occasions. He remembered Ian's prescient warning about his handling of the supply people and forced himself

136

to calm down by reminding himself that the consequences of losing his temper could hold much graver circumstances than merely a lost customer or a disgruntled employee.

"Jesus Christ, you can't know the first thing about business," Biggs said. Like most men of his ilk, particularly young ones, his warped ego drove him on. Jack knew, for he'd been a young hotshot himself once. "I have a degree in finance from Dartmouth University, and up until a few months ago, I was kicking ass at one of the largest investment banks on Wall Street. Does that mean anything to you . . . Wall Street.?" Jack's hunch about the man being a business type was right, though his strategy of connecting with him on the subject had failed miserably. Biggs was simply too arrogant. "I'd still be there too," Biggs continued, "if it weren't for this goddamn war. Instead I'm stuck here with screw heads like you and Wimpy here," he said, nodding at the doughy clerk. Jack's alarm rose as Biggs became highly agitated, his face red and his voice shrill. "My boss at the firm was a first war Marine vet and the asshole told me to volunteer for the Corps to avoid the draft. He said he'd see to it I get a nice job at the Pentagon and ride the goddamn thing out. But no, it turns out that son of a bitch has no pull and the Corps, who can't tell talent from turds, assign me to supply. That was bad enough, but then the geniuses send me to this goddamn shit hole!"

Biggs tirade wasn't only disgusting, but caused Jack even greater concern. His extreme bitterness at the perceived injustices dealt him would make him all the more difficult. As well, Jack felt let down by the arrogant, selfish man. Intellectually he knew that there were evil, greedy men in the services during the war. Emotionally though, he had always wanted to believe that the men were special; above most human failings, excepting his own father. He sighed, disappointed with the reality of what Biggs and the loutish pioneer of the previous day represented. However, the good men, the majority he hoped, deserved admiration. He was determined to find a way to work with Biggs or, if need be, work around him. He re-opened negotiations. "I'm sorry," he said. "I hope your career isn't affected, sir." Jack thought about the 400,000 American careers that would never start, or restart, after the war. He struggled to contain his emotions.

"Affected . . . that's a good one!" Biggs laughed bitterly. "I made more money in a week back home than I'll make in this crap outfit in a year. It already is affected, you dumb shit."

Jack was determined to acquire the extra supplies, so he took a breath and said, "About the supplies not on the list, sir."

"What about them?" Biggs sputtered. His tirade complete, he'd calmed down considerably.

"I just need some cots and a typewriter for the hospital is all . . . we really need the stuff badly."

"No cots, no typewriters," Biggs growled. Jack thought for a moment. He realized there was no way to engage Biggs in any sort of thoughtful conversation. His earlier missteps made it too late to exploit the captain's massive ego. He knew there was no way to really gain the empathy of a man like him, so he decided his only course was to keep pressing and perhaps annoy Biggs into giving him what he needed. He nodded toward the typewriter and said, "You have a typewriter there, sir, we could really use one at the hospital . . . it could actually save lives. The men have trouble. . . . ."

"Listen, old timer, I don't give a shit about your problems," Biggs interrupted. "That typewriter is mine and the only cots on this whole goddamn island are mine. In fact, we're putting them up in our quarters this very afternoon. Now take your goddamn requisition to one of the men outside and quit wasting my time." Biggs turned and walked rapidly toward the back of the tent.

"But sir," Jack called after him. Biggs kept walking and Jack knew he'd been defeated . . . at least for now.

"Goddamn," he whispered, "the bastard has cots and he won't give them to me . . . won't give them to a field hospital for chrissakes." The pudgy clerk had heard his comment and coughed, shifting uncomfortably in his chair. As Jack walked back to the truck, he pondered other ways to acquire the goods. He was utterly determined to succeed in this small transaction. But to him, at that moment, it was the most important one he'd ever engaged in.

As he sat on the running board of the truck thinking, he recalled the coiffed and impressively degreed young men he'd dealt with in New York when he sold his family's company. They were bright, slick, and highly paid, the elite of the capitalistic money game. Jack had always resented them, perhaps was even a little jealous of them. The work they performed, and its resulting benefits to the economy and their clients, seemed grossly out of proportion with their pay or stature. Men like him, or at least he liked to believe, created true systemic wealth and jobs. He was uncomfortably jabbed for a brief moment though, with the memory that over a hundred jobs his father created were vaporized within weeks of him selling the company. That was different though, he thought to himself; it was his company to do with as he pleased. Nevertheless, he quickly shook the thought from his mind. The men and women on Wall Street, he believed, simply moved money and infrastructure from one point to another. They of course were not all bad, and some were very good and giving people. Biggs, however, was the worst of them, greedy beyond all reason and utterly blinded by his own ego. Jack was absolutely determined, more determined than perhaps ever in life, to win. There was something else he meant to defeat; he could feel it, but couldn't, or wouldn't identify it. "Fuck you, Biggs!" he said under his breath. "You goddamn punk!"

Jack pulled himself into the truck's cab. He removed a pencil from his breast pocket and glanced around to make sure no one was watching; then pressed the requisition against the dashboard. Just below the last item on the list, he carefully wrote, 'Cots—15 + bug nets'. Then, using his fingers, he aged all the items on the list equally by smudging the paper. Finished, he returned to the stevedore and handed him the requisition. The boy read down the list and looked at Jack quizzically when he had finished. "He's giving you the cots? He told us they were for him and his staff and weren't to be touched."

"Hey, those cots are for wounded Marines; Mr. Biggs isn't a complete asshole you know," Jack lied. "He said the wounded fellas should have them."

The man eyed Jack suspiciously and said, "I ain't known him to be anything other than a complete asshole all the time . . . are you sure?"

"Look there," Jack said pointing to Biggs signature, "he signed it didn't he?"

"Yeah . . . I guess he did." The boy paused, thinking. Then he said weakly, "Okay . . . I better not catch shit for this though."

"How can you get in trouble? I'm the one who gave you the requisition. You're just following written orders, right?" Jack asked.

The man shrugged. "Okay . . . I guess it's alright." Jack felt a pang of guilt for deceiving the decent young man. However, it passed quickly as he reminded himself of the worthiness of his cause. Ian, Frank, Turk, the wounded . . . they were all counting on him. They headed into the dump and Jack suggested they gather the cots last so they wouldn't get broken by the wooden crates holding the medical supplies. He wanted to make a quick getaway after the cots were loaded. They promptly found the crates they needed, then Jack pulled the truck to the other side of the dump where the boy said the cots were located. He looked around anxiously as they threw the cots and mosquito netting into the back of the truck. They finished quickly and Jack thanked the boy for his help. He jumped into the cab and pulled back around the dump. The pile of cots, thankfully, did not rise above the truck's gate, so he knew he was home free. He whistled to himself as he passed between the tent and the dump. He was feeling quite heady and daring. He had never 'stolen' a thing in his life, or in fact taken any real liberties with societies laws and rules. This though, he thought to himself, was very different. He was not some petty thief, but a man trying to do right for those carrying the burden of the war; simply put, it was justice being done. He recalled as a boy reading tales of the master 'scroungers', not thieves, who were unusually active on the supply starved island. He had reveled in the stories and saw the men as audacious and clever heroes.

As he ground past the tent, he noticed a group of men cooling off in the surf, smoking cigarettes. He recognized them as the men

140

who had been working in the tent. Amongst them was the man who had been pecking at the typewriter. He drove on briefly, then slammed on the brakes. He put the truck in reverse and jumped out when it reached the entrance to the supply tent. Not knowing when the men's break would be over, he moved quickly. Upon entering he was disappointed to see Wimpy still at his post. Jack stutter stepped, but the boy remained glued to his work, so he continued walking toward the typewriter perched on an empty crate. He quickly snatched it up and tucked it tightly to his lower chest like a halfback in the open field. As he headed toward the door, Wimpy looked up and saw Jack making his break with the typewriter. The boy's eyes widened and he stammered, "Hey . . . what . . . where are you going with that?"

Jack froze, knowing the boy would raise the alarm if he carried on. He would not only lose the typewriter, but the cots as well. He thought hard for a moment then leaned over and placed his face inches from the boy's. "Listen," he whispered, "this will help us care for combat wounded Marines back at the hospital. If you say one word about this, I'm going to tell their buddies what you did. I sure as hell wouldn't want to be you when they come to have a little chat about it."

The boy hesitated and stared at Jack with a look of fear and indecision. Jack knew he was weighing the lesser of evils, so he fixed him with an icy glare and said, "Just tell your asshole boss you didn't see anything and you'll be fine, understand?"

The boy thought for a moment then said anxiously, "Okay, okay . . . just go; get the hell out of here before someone sees us." Jack headed for the door, then stopped, and like some overly dramatic Hollywood Robin Hood, turned and winked cockily at the boy. Once back in the truck, he set the machine on the bench next to him and turned west toward the Tenaru. Although he was very anxious to deliver the goods to the hospital, he did not want to miss the opportunity to try and find his father's position. The unnerving thought of seeing him again was overridden by the joy and pride Jack felt regarding his adventure at the supply dump.

141

After he was out of earshot, he pounded the steering wheel and yelled, "Yehaaa! Oh yes . . . yes you brilliant bastard!" He laughed wildly as he pounded the steering wheel over and over again. "Take that, you fucking asshole, coward, son of a bitching, Wall Street piece of shit!" he screamed. "Captain Ernest Biggs of Dartmouth fucking University . . . goddamn bean counter! Don't fuck with Jack Macmillan the newspaper vendor, you asshole!" In a brief moment of clarity Jack noted that he couldn't remember the last time he felt so happy and proud. A quarter of a mile from the Tenaru, he boyishly broke out in song.

> *737 comin' outta the sky'*
> *Oh won't you take me down Memphis on a midnight ride,*
> *I wanna move.*
> *Playin' in a travelin' band, yeah!*
> *Well I'm flyin' cross the land, tryin' to get hand,*
> *Playin' in a travelin' band.*

He jerked his head up and down as he sang, keeping beat with the guitar riffs playing in his mind. Using his fingers, he recreated the staccato drumbeats of the early '70s Creedence Clearwater Revival hit. It was a song he often sang either out loud or to himself when he was excited. He noticed a group of Marines, occupying a machine gun nest on the edge of the jungle, staring at him slack-jawed. He leaned out the window shouting, "Hey boys, how's it going?" They didn't return his greeting but only stared at him quizzically. Jack laughed loudly, then continued singing.

> *Take me to the hotel, baggage gone, oh, well.*
> *Come on, come on, won't you get me to my room,*
> *I wanna move.*

Singing the tune reminded him of the time he tried to teach it to his son, Joey, who was six at the time. "Okay, Joe," Jack had said, "I'm going to teach you one of the greatest up-rhythm rock songs of all time."

Joey's eyes lit up and he squealed, "Okay, Dad! What song?"

Jack leaned forward in his leather easy chair and proudly replied, "*Travelin' Band;* you've heard me sing it before!"

With a frown dimpling his forehead and his big blue eyes looking sympathetically at his father, Joe slowly, sadly said, "Dad, there's just one problem."

Surprised, Jack asked, "Problem, what problem, buddy?"

"Dad," his son said, pausing dramatically, "Well the problem is . . . I hate that song."

Jack recalled achingly how he'd immediately swept his son up in his arms and kissed the top of his head. He'd laughed and said, "That's okay, bud. You don't need to learn the song if you don't want, okay?" As Jack recalled the feel of his son's soft hair on his lips, his singing slowed and became quieter, then stopped completely. He said out loud, "Oh Joey . . . buddy-man, my sweet little guy."

His euphoria suddenly evaporated and he slouched in his seat. He thought of the times Joe, or his five-year-old sister, Grace, would crawl into bed and nestle in between he and Laura. He remembered the feel of their soft, warm, little bodies as they cuddled him closely. He smiled as he thought of how Grace would place her hand on his cheek as she drifted off, a little anchor keeping her close. "Oh god," he said quietly. The ache he felt for his kids was more than just an emotion, it was a physical pain; like withdrawal from an addiction. He moaned softly, seeing clearly now that they were the only things he'd found true joy in over the last several years, or for that matter, his entire life. The 'Black Dog' snapped at his heels.

Suddenly, he sat bolt upright and said firmly, "No, no, no, no, no, no! Don't go there, buddy! Focus . . . focus bud! Fight it, buddy," he said. "Fight it . . . focus on what you're doing at the hospital. The kids are fine . . . they're fine. Focus!" Jack successfully purged the loving, but painful thoughts from his mind. He had dodged another assault on his spirit, but the incident had completely vaporized his euphoria. As he slowly crossed the sand spit at the head of the Tenaru, he gazed at the spot where his drunken

143

charge had ended two nights ago. He squinted hard, looking for something in there that would give him a clue to his journey. The water was only black though, still and foul, giving up nothing. He shook his head slowly, rubbed his eyes, and refocused on his next task.

10

Immediately upon crossing the sand embankment, Jack found a dirt track running between the river and the palm grove. It was the same track that the Marine had led him up on the way to the aid station shortly after the Zero had blown the captain's head off. The river represented the extreme western edge of the Marine perimeter. Machine gun bunkers and foxholes dotted the area around the sand spit. He turned onto the road and stopped near a small group of Marines digging a fighting hole. "Hey guys," he shouted, "can you tell me where C Company, 1ˢᵗ Battalion is dug in?"

"Sure, mac," one of the shirtless Marines answered. He jerked a dirty thumb up the road and said, "Go about a hundred yards or so upstream; you'll find 'em dug in there." Jack slowly pulled forward, scanning both sides of the road for signs of his father's company. Finally, he saw a crude wooden sign stuck in the ground on the side of the road. Written clumsily with chalk, it read:

C COMPANY, 1ST OF THE 2ND
WIPE FEET BEFORE ENTERING AREA

Jack pulled the truck into the tree line alongside the road and dismounted. He stayed in the grove for cover and walked forward parallel to the company's positions. C Company's positions included freshly dug two-man foxholes and machine gun nests twenty meters or so from the creek bank. Observation and listening posts had been dug at the edge of the creek. Slightly behind the main line of resistance, dual mortar squads had been set up. Their crews were busy building dirt and log berms around them. Jack walked slowly, looking carefully at each man. After advancing for several minutes, he noticed a Marine lying on his back in a foxhole. One of his bare feet jabbed out of the top of the hole, the leg resting on the edge. Another man was applying some sort of salve to the Marine's foot. Jack inhaled sharply, stopped, and dropped quickly to the ground when he recognized the man. It was Tom, his father, not more than twenty meters away. He scrabbled forward several feet and hid behind the trunk of a palm; all the while keeping his eyes glued on his teenage father. He couldn't hear what his dad and barefoot man were saying, but their conversation seemed lively and his father was smiling. Jack watched as Tom finished by taping a square bandage to the man's foot and then helped him put his sock and boot back on. As his father walked away from the hole the Marine called out, "Thanks, Doc!" Tom waved a hand without turning around.

Jack watched his father move amongst the platoon. He was handing large white tablets to each man; each time insisting they take the pill while he watched. Jack guessed they were salt tablets, staple necessities in the stifling heat. He closely inspected his father's every move, every mannerism for familiarity; in some ways hoping he would find none. It wasn't to be, for this man was most definitely his father; the friendly, yet slightly tight smile, the stooped shoulders, the easy gait and above all, the slight, almost imperceptible distance with which the man held himself in relation to his fellows. It was a trait, hell, a flaw that Jack knew and had felt many times. After a time he glanced at his watch and was shocked to see forty-five minutes had passed since he'd arrived at his dad's position. He knew he had to get the truck back, and besides, he'd started to feel strange, as if somehow he was stalking his own father. As he climbed in the truck, his feelings about being on the island with his young father, as well as what he should do about it, were more confused than ever. He felt a strong urge to meet his father, perhaps even befriend him. At the same time, the prospect

146

frightened him and evoked a sort of sadness. He hadn't a clue why it made him feel sad; it just did. He decided he would talk to Ian that night and get his take on it. For now though he did his best to rid the visage and thoughts of his father from his mind. "It'll be okay, bud," he said out loud. "You'll figure it out."

To keep his mind occupied he began to think about how he should prioritize the rest of his day. By the time he pulled up in front of the hospital he'd decided he would present the typewriter to Ian first; then unload the medical supplies. After that, he'd set up the cots and mosquito nets. He grabbed the typewriter and walked inside the hospital. Upon entering, he saw that a number of new patients had arrived. Strangely, he couldn't detect any obvious injuries to the men. Jack winced as a strong, fetid odor drilled into his nostrils. He noticed Frank crossing the tent with a bedpan tucked under each arm. Still holding the typewriter, Jack said, "Hey Frank, what's going on? What happened to these guys?"

Frank turned and said, "These poor guys . . . Hey . . . a typewriter! Where'd you get that thing? They said there weren't any on the island."

Jack set the machine on a crate. "Just took a little creativity and planning is all," he said.

"Great job, Jacko. This will be a big help," Frank said as he casually clacked the typewriter keys. Frank's reaction elevated Jack's dulled spirits, but he deemed it unwise, under the circumstances, to overplay his triumph and said nothing more. He saw Ian talking to one of the new patients and approached him.

"Hey, Doc," Jack said. "What's with all the new patients?"

Ian smiled at him and, ignoring his question, said, "A typewriter huh? I don't know where you found that thing and maybe I don't want to know, but well done . . . well done, mate. That's going to make a bloody big difference in writing out charts, orders and the like. Thanks a lot, mate."

"No problem, Doc," Jack airily replied. It was the sort of response, the tone of which, if delivered properly, was humble and conceited all at once.

Ian eyed him more closely and said, "What happened to your nose? It looks a tad puffy and there's some dried blood in your nostrils." Jack told him how he'd collided with the steering wheel when he was forced to brake quickly, but did not tell him he'd nearly taken out a squad of Marines in the process. Ian, using both forefingers, gently moved Jack's nose from side to side. "You received a mighty blow, but she ain't broken, mate; just bruised up real good."

"Ah great," Jack said. He quickly forgot about his nose, screwed up his face and said, "Jesus Christ, Doc, it stinks like shit in here. What's going on?"

"It stinks like shit in here because it is shit . . . shit tainted with vomit," Ian replied. "These poor geezers were on patrol last night and picked the wrong pond to take a drink. Nasty cases of gastroenteritis, or dysentery, whatever you please; all of them. Vomiting, cramps, the shits . . . the whole lovely package. All we can do is empty their bedpans, clean their vomit, and try to keep them hydrated until it passes. We also received a minor burn case and a broken wrist."

"Gross," Jack muttered. He was relieved he had a job to do outside the tent as the prospect of full bedpans and vomit did not appeal to him.

"You have any problems at the supply dump?" Ian asked.

"Nah," Jack lied, "they were better organized than I expected and it went like clockwork."

"Good . . . good work."

Jack proudly added, "I managed to pick up some cots as well."

"Bloody brilliant, mate. You're going to be a hero with the lads." Once again, Jack underplayed his caper with nothing more than a shrug.

"Well, I've got to get busy unloading the supplies and setting up the cots," Jack said. He turned toward the door but Ian stopped him.

"Not so fast, mate. These boys are shitting and puking like fountains. I'm sending a shift on break so we need all available hands on deck."

Jack frowned and said, "I'm not too good with smells, Doc. You sure you want me to help?"

"Remember our talk last night in the jungle? You'll get used to this and everything else you'll be doing." Jack detected a slight smirk on Ian's face. "Just think of them as one of your own little nippers. I'm sure you managed okay when they were sick."

Jack remembered how badly he'd felt when Joey or Grace had been sick. The miserable young boys were pasty and soaked with sweat. Intermittently they would moan when a wave of cramps seared their insides. He felt slightly ashamed that he'd wished to avoid helping them, but was concerned that he'd embarrass himself in front of the Marines by gagging or, God forbid, vomiting. He steeled himself as best he could and said, "Alright, Doc. What do you want me to do?"

"Frank will show you the ropes," Ian replied.

Jack found Frank and said, "Doc wants me to help out. He said you'd show me what to do."

"Sure," Frank said. "Not much to it though once you get past the smell."

Jack suddenly had an idea and asked, "Hey, where are the surgical masks?"

"Somewhere out on the ships I'd guess," Frank replied.

"Damn," Jack muttered. He thought for a moment about what else he could use. He spotted a gauze roll nearby, held it up to Frank and said, "Voila."

"What are you going to do with that?" Frank asked. "These guys don't need bandaging."

"No," Jack replied, "but I sure as hell do." He unfurled a section of bandage and clumsily began to wrap it around the lower portion of his face.

Frank looked on for a moment in confusion then realized what Jack was doing. He chuckled and said, "Not a bad idea . . . but you really do get used to it, you know."

"Maybe you do, but I'm not so sure about myself," Jack replied. Frank reached up and took the bandage out of his struggling hands and wrapped it quickly several times around Jack's nose and mouth.

"A cull mur turnsh," Jack said, his voice muffled.

"What?" Frank asked. "I can't understand what you're saying."

"A cull more turnsh . . . ish shtill shtints!" Jack yelled through the gauze. The muffled cry drew the attention of several hospital-men working nearby. They turned and watched the strange pan-tomime; at first bewildered.

Frank nodded and said, "Oh, okay, I got you now." He finished the job by pinning up the cloth. Those watching had figured out what Jack and Frank were trying to accomplish and their confusion turned to hilarity. The men whooped and hollered which shifted the attention of the others to Jack and Frank standing forlornly in the middle of the tent. Soon the entire tent, with the exception of the patients, was rocking with laughter and catcalls.

"Hey, Jack," a hospitalman yelled, "Great scarf! You might wanna go with something a little brighter next time though. Dull white don't suit you exactly."

Another man said, "I ain't sure he's breathing, Frankie! Kick him in the nuts to make sure."

Once again Jack found himself enjoying the attention and col-legial acceptance of the boys. The bandage hid a broad smile and he clasped his hands together and raised them above his head like a victorious politician. He was also pleased to note that the jerry-rigged filter was quite effective, though hot. Frank was bowing to the crowd when Jack turned to look at him. Over his shoulder he saw Ian approaching. He did not look happy.

"What in bloody hell is going on?" Ian hissed. "You may recall that this is a hospital and that we have some very sick people here. And what they don't need is a bunch of bloody childish fool-abouts from the very people who are supposed to be caring for them."

Frank crestfallen, replied, "I'm sorry sir, I wasn't thinking. I was helping Jack cover his nose and mouth and I guess the guys thought it was pretty funny."

"Well stop this bloody schoolboy shit and start taking care of these men, both of you!" Ian whispered violently. He hovered for a moment, glaring at them in such a way that Jack felt as if he was actually shrinking. Finally he said, "And get that bloody bandage off your face, Jack, it's an insult to these Marines. It's for mending wounds, not plugging your bloody nose!"

Jack quickly and shamefully replied, "Okay. Sorry, Doc." But by the time his words made their way out of the mask, he ashamedly realized they were only a mush of unintelligible sounds. He stood in the middle of the room feeling abashed and stupid. Frank quickly reached up and unfurled Jack's wrapping as Ian stalked off. Jack and Frank said nothing to each other; their chagrin rendering them speechless. Frank, frowning muttered, "C'mon, I'll show you what to do." Jack felt dreadful. Ian was absolutely right to upbraid him in front of the other men. He had callously donned the wrapping, then proceeded to put on a show while the sick Marines from the combat patrol were in agony just feet away. He'd done the thing that he dreaded the most; let the young Marines down, just as he had on the beach that morning in the runaway truck. To most people it would have been a minor, relatively routine upbraiding by an officer. To Jack though, it was a major transgression; an unacceptable failure. In the past, his reaction to a mistake would have been largely to deny accountability or simply feel sorry for himself. Now though, he acknowledged his mistake, shoved aside his feelings, and eagerly listened to Frank's instructions so he could quickly get to work helping with the young Marines.

Frank showed him where and how to clean dirty bedpans and how to position them beneath the patients. Rags were scattered about to clean up vomit and glops of watery feces that had escaped bedpans. He struggled as he cleaned his first pan in the large tub of water just outside the tent. The water was already the color and texture of the pan's contents; its stench overpowering. On several occasions Jack gagged and choked back vomit, but after a half-hour or so, it became easier, just as Frank had said it would. Besides, Jack felt the work to be a welcome penance.

151

After a couple of hours, the boys had nothing left to shit out or throw-up. Jack and the other hospitalmen focused on hydrating the men and cleaning them up. As he tended to each man, he apologized for his earlier antics. By mid-afternoon the pace in the tent had slowed considerably. Ian approached Jack and said, "There's not much left to do so you can go unload the truck and get the cots set up now."

"Yes, sir," Jack replied. He surprised himself by using the formal title. Just 24 hours ago, it wouldn't have happened. Jack worked on setting the cots up for the rest of the day. He carefully aligned them in neat rows and attached mosquito netting to each one. Jack enjoyed the work, but was still quite bothered by the incident earlier that day. He was anxious to meet with Ian. As he was admiring his work, Turk entered the hospital and clapped Jack on the shoulder.

"Good work, Jack-o," he said. "This is fuckin' great! No more kneelin' in the goddamn dirt." Turk's words lightened his mood. It wasn't too long before Turk had spread the word about the new trappings in the hospital. In spite of his improved spirits, Jack was still apprehensive that he had lost some of Ian's respect; time traveler or not.

Dinner that night was rice and prunes. After the Navy transports retreated, General Vandegrift, the Marine commander on the island, had ordered the men down to two meals a day; enough certainly to subsist on, but not enough to maintain weight or energy levels. Jack watched in frustration as most of the boys painstakingly picked the weevils out of the rice, despite his urgings. Just as Jack started eating, Ian ambled over with his mess tin and sat down next to him.

"How you doing, mate?" Ian asked.

"I'm fine, Doc," Jack said. "Listen, I'm really sorry for my stupidity in the hospital today. I don't know what I was thinking. I promise you, it won't happen again."

Ian looked at Jack and smiled. "No worries, mate," he said. "Crikey, everyone throws a clanger from time to time. No hard feelings, okay?"

"Okay, thanks," Jack said. He was enormously relieved and the subject was dropped. He told Ian about stalking his father and invited him for a smoke and a chat about it later in the evening. "Sure," Ian replied. "I scored a bloody great huge bottle of Jap *sake*. I'll bring it along. Let's find a different place to meet this evening though. That lovely spot in the jungle last night was a little dodgy for my tastes."

Jack laughed and said, "Good idea, come find me when you're ready." Jack hadn't had alcohol in nearly three days. It was the longest dry spell for him in years. Strangely, with all that had happened he hadn't felt the least bit of need for a drink.

As they were finishing their last bites of rice, a jeep came hurtling up the road and slammed to a halt in front of them. Jack looked at the driver and reflexively ducked behind some of the other men. It was Captain Biggs from the supply dump. Biggs leapt from the jeep, strode angrily toward them and yelled, "Who's the commanding officer of this unit?"

Ian stood up and said, "I'm acting in command . . . Lieutenant Smith. Lt. Commander Goldman is at a meeting at one of the other sick bays. What can I do for you?" Biggs peered at Ian for a moment with a look of distaste then said, "One of your men collected some supplies from a medical supply dump on Red Beach this morning, correct?"

"Correct," Ian said, "why, what's the problem?"

"The problem," Biggs hissed, "is the little matter of fifteen cots and a typewriter that went missing not long after your man left . . . *my* cots and *my* typewriter goddamnit!"

Out of the corner of his eye Jack saw Turk jump up and head for the hospital. He ducked inside and came out a few moments later carrying a crate covered by a blanket. He walked behind the tent into the jungle. A minute later he rejoined the group empty handed. Jack caught his eye and winked. Turk smiled and gave a short nod. There wasn't much they could do about the cots though.

"What makes you think my chap pinched your goods?" Ian asked.

153

"Because the son of a bitch asked me if he could have our type-writer and cots, that's why!"

"I see," Ian said. "And I take it your answer was no."

"Of course it was no! They were mine goddamnit!"

"And who are you, if I may ask?" Ian asked ever so politely.

"Captain Earnest J. Biggs, CO of the medical supply depot your man robbed." Biggs' eyes left Ian's as he surveyed the group, looking for the thief. Jack knew there was no point in hiding and waited to be uncovered by the enraged officer. It didn't take Biggs long. His arm jerked up and he pointed it at Jack as if it were a cutlass. "That's him . . . that's the shitty old bastard!" Biggs screamed. Biggs stepped toward Jack, but Ian shuffled over and stopped him.

"Easy there, mate," Ian said. "Calm down and we'll get this straightened out."

Ian turned toward Jack and said, "Did you take this man's cots and typewriter?" Ian had posed the question slowly, in a voice like that of a mother interrogating her mischievous two-year-old, but exaggerated. Jack detected a hint of a smile on his face.

"No, sir," Jack said innocently. "I didn't take his stuff, sir."

"You goddamn liar! You're headed for the brig, mister!" Biggs spat. "Where's the sick bay?" Over his shoulder, Ian lazily pointed his thumb like a hitchhiker flagging down a ride. Biggs stormed off toward the tent, tore open the door and went inside. It was silent for several moments than an angry, animal like scream sounded. "Goddamnit! Son of a bitch!" They heard Biggs yell. The tent door flew open and Biggs furiously strode toward Jack. Even though the man out ranked everyone there, most of them were having difficulty suppressing laughter and they looked down, covering mouths with hands.

"Those are my fucking cots, goddamnit!" Biggs shrieked. "I want them loaded on a truck right now!" Biggs' eyes were bulging, his face red with fury.

Ian turned to Jack and said with a barely detectable smirk, "Where'd you get those cots, sailor?"

154

"I found them at an ammo dump on the other side of the air-field," Jack replied. "They were good guys. When I told them they were for an aid station they told me to go ahead and take 'em. They even helped me load 'em up." The subtle jabs at Biggs' selfish, dis-gusting behavior were noticed by everyone but Biggs himself.

"Bullshit!" Biggs grunted. "The typewriter had my unit mark-ings on it. I'll prove that this man is a thief!" He strode off once again toward the hospital.

As they followed Biggs to the tent, Jack whispered to Ian that the typewriter had been taken care of by Turk. Upon entering, they saw Biggs on his hands and knees looking beneath the cots and crates, all the while cursing furiously. Finally, Ian could control himself no longer and laughed out loud. Biggs rose and hissed, "What's so damn funny, Lieutenant?"

"Captain, you're making a fool of yourself. There's no type-writer here. You need to get in your jeep and leave before I get tired of this silliness and get Lt. Cdr. Goldman, our CO, involved."

Biggs clenched his fists and stomped a boot that clanged inad-vertently on a bedpan. He pointed at Jack and said, "Listen, your man . . ."

Biggs' stomp on the bedpan had made a loud crash and Ian sprang forward cat-quick, thrusting his face inches from Biggs. "No! You listen you bloody parasite!" Ian barked. "I don't give a shit what your rank is! You get the hell out of my hospital right now and never come back, or I'm going to tell these Marines here that you were the one who threw a bloody tantrum over a bunch of stuff you can more easily do without than them, the one's who are actu-ally doing the fighting and the dying! And that's *after* I let my own boys teach you some fucking manners!"

Biggs visibly deflated and retreated several steps. He realized he couldn't win against a medical officer in his own aid station, regard-less of hierarchy, particularly one who was so determined and didn't seem concerned with doing things by the book. He shot Jack a hateful glare, then composed himself and said, "My beef isn't with you or your men, Lieutenant. But, I think it's obvious to everyone that that old son of a bitch took my gear, and I only want it back and him punished."

Ian glared at Biggs for several seconds then said, "Get the fuck out of here and never come back, or my boys and these Marines might not be so patient next time! On second thought, if you set foot in this hospital again, I'll break your bloody face myself and you can tell your CO I said so!"

Turk, standing behind Biggs, said icily, "This is a hospital and we've got plenty a cute little gadgets to cut a man's fuckin' balls off just as clean as you like."

Biggs seethed, but didn't turn to see who'd made the threat. With a hint of trepidation showing in his eyes, Biggs turned and walked quickly out the door. He trotted to his jeep and roared off. Jack and Ian looked at one another and grinned. "What a bloody asshole," Ian said.

"Tell me about it," Jack replied. "You should have been there this morning. I've dealt with his type before and there's no winning with them unless you have more power . . . or you cheat."

Ian grinned and said, "So I'm the power guy and you're the cheater, huh, mate?"

Jack smiled and replied, "Yeah, I'm the cheater, Doc. It's my only real war-fighting skill. Problem is I'm going to have to deal with that prick again. I'll have to figure out a way to ratchet up my techniques."

"After what I've seen today, I'm confident you'll figure out something, mate." In a more serious tone, Ian said, "No more lying to me though. I understand why you lied and I suppose I would've done the same, but no more; I won't accept it, understand?"

"Yes, sir," Jack said in as sincere a tone as he could muster.

"Still I must say I'm proud of you mate; good work." Jack nodded eagerly. He felt he was now officially back in good graces with Ian, and was surprised how happy it made him. He marveled again at the young doctor: smart, fearless, prescient, highly honorable, and honest. In Jack's mind, the almost mystical aura about him grew. He knew for certain now that he would happily follow him, follow him loyally. The first time in his life he deigned to follow any-one.

With Biggs' departure everyone returned to the chow station. Jack finished his meal listening to the boys talk of home. Mostly it was baseball, food, and girls. Jack enjoyed the lively chatter and their youthful exuberance regarding things that long ago had lost their magic for him. He could still effortlessly name the starting line up of the 1968 World Series Champion Detroit Tigers by position: Horton and Freehan from Detroit, Cash, McAuliffe, Wert. Stanley from Grand Rapids and Northrup from Alma. And of course the great Al Kaline. Sparma, Lolich, Mclain and Wilson made up the rotation with John Hiller as the brilliant closer. Gates Brown, the "Gator", was the team's exceptional pinch hitter and was from Michigan as well. The fact that so many of the players were natives of the state made them all the more beloved.

As he listened to the boys talk about their Yankees, Dodgers, Red Sox, Indians, and Cubs he remembered the time his father took him to his first game at Tiger Stadium in 1966. When they'd entered the stadium's dark, cramped concourse, Jack, wearing his battered glove, was giddy with excitement. When he caught his first glimpse of the field through an opening in the concourse, his eyes widened and his mouth fell open. The grass glittered with a seem-ingly supernatural shade of brilliant emerald. The infield dirt was unlike any ball field dirt he'd ever seen; glowing orange/brown and pristine as though it had been mined in some enchanted quarry. The Tiger players, though far away, appeared to be giants; their home uniforms were whiter than snow. He remembered his father's smile when he hugged him tightly around the waist and said, "Thanks for bringing me, Daddy . . . this is like a dream or some-thin'!" It was a joyous day. One of the few days that Jack had his father all to himself.

He leaned back and listened to the boys hilariously debate over which team had the best radio broadcaster. He recalled how he used to go to sleep with a transistor radio balanced on his ear . . . the deep, soothing voice of Ernie Harwell lulling him to sleep.

The Tigers . . . he thought, just a ball team, but they had brought him so much joy. As an adult he'd lost the feelings of cozy excitement the team had given him; nothing had stepped in to take its place. He couldn't name a single member of the current team. Sure, he'd taken Joey to a Tigers game, mainly to say he'd done it. Though more like a rock concert than he remembered, it still had seemed too simple, too common for him to waste his time on. There were flashier, more exciting things to do, things those in his socio-economic class had seemingly been conditioned to do. A weekend carousing in Las Vegas, or a few days skiing the powder at Vail or enjoying the sands of a Caribbean island. These certainly had to be more fulfilling than a mere ballgame or a weekend trip to Chicago with just he and Joey to see the museums and the Cubs at Wrigley. Now though, as the boys switched their simple debate to girls and the shapes and size of their various physical attributes— and how these made one more attractive than the other—he reflected on his essentially scripted life back in the world. He shook his head and sighed, acknowledging the simple secret that he hated skiing, the cold, the crowds and the plain fact that to him, the sport itself was quite tedious.

The trips to the Caribbean with Laura and the kids were less relaxation than hard work. The stress of flying, praying that you would make each connection and that your bags would be on the other end when you arrived, was nearly enough in itself. Then, the kids, not having a clue whether they were in Kentucky or the Caymans, or caring for that matter, required a great deal of attention considering their ages, just to keep them entertained and not drifting from the crowded beaches out to sea. Back in the world he'd considered his junkets to Vegas with something akin to ambivalence, a place where one could drink unabashedly and do a myriad of stupid things. Now, sitting in the steaming heat of Guadalcanal with a group of young men who knew little of the world, the place seemed vile, horrid. He'd been there several times, but couldn't remember much, as he'd remained drunk throughout most of his visits. He only remembered feeling a distinct sense of loneliness. But he'd done these things and kept on doing them.

The stinking island seemed to be opening his eyes ever wider, like nothing else in his life. Listening to the boys' simple discussions, for the first time in his life, he questioned, or perhaps was able to question, his approach to life back in the world. Thinking back to his youth, it was as if he'd lost something, or simply never found it . . . never even bothered to look for it.

A voice suddenly interrupted his thoughts, "Come with me, Jack," Ian said. "Let's go check on the lads in the hospital."

Jack took a moment to shake away his thoughts, then slowly looked up at Ian and said, "Uh . . . oh sure, Doc." They ambled off toward the tent and went inside. Ian inspected the injured and instructed Jack to check on each of the boys who had come in with the intestinal problems. He went from cot to cot checking on their patients, making sure the men were keeping hydrated. They were feeling better, but still very fatigued. Jack did his best to cheer them up, but it was hard work considering their conditions. He was wiping a soldier's brow when the door to the tent flung open and someone entered. Jack didn't look up, assuming it was another member of the staff. Then a voice bellowed, "How're these goldbrickers doing?"

Jack looked up, but the man had his back turned to him. Figuring he was from the sick men's unit Jack answered, "They're one hell of a lot better than they were this afternoon. They need lots of liquid though, before they can be moved." The man turned and looked at him. Jack looked casually back at him for a moment, then started and stumbled back a step. His throat contracted, making it difficult to take a breath. He reached out to a stack of crates to steady himself, and his gaze fell from the man to the dirt floor of the hospital.

"Hey," Jack's young father asked, "you okay? You don't look so good."

11

Without lifting his eyes and still leaning on the crates, Jack stammered, I . . . I uh . . . I'm . . ."

Before Jack could find his words, their exchange was interrupted by the sound of shouting, screaming men, and a jeep sliding to a rapid halt outside the tent. A panicked voice shouted, "Help . . . goddamnit . . . help! I've got two fucked up real bad!" Another man's agonized screams, piercing and animal-like, indicated to Jack an incomprehensible level of fear and agony. In an instant, his father, along with Ian and another corpsman, darted out of the tent leaving Jack alone with the sick Marines. His mind spun and he was momentarily disoriented by the fantastic verbal encounter with his father. Yet the urgent shouts and horrible screams from outside cut through the shock. He wanted badly to help, but couldn't move.

Squeezing his eyes tightly shut, he rubbed a hand across them and muttered, "Get a grip, bud. You've got to help! Forget about it . . . get out there . . . now!" The manic pep talk continued for several moments until he felt strong enough to move. He took a deep breath, steadied himself, then shuffled toward the entrance. Upon exiting the tent, he saw a jeep with two litters perched on its rear walls. A nervous, cursing Marine shone a flashlight on two injured men. Ian was assessing the men's injuries as quickly as possible before moving them. Jack stutter-stepped when he saw his father standing next to the jeep. Moving forward, he exhorted himself under his breath to ignore his father's presence and to focus on the injured. When he was close enough to see the injured Marines, he cursed. "Jesus!" he choked. After reflexively turning his back for a moment, he forced himself to turn and look at the men. "You'll get used to it, buddy," he whispered through clenched teeth. "Do your job . . . just do your job." He moved to the side of the jeep opposite Ian and his father. The flashlight glared brightly, clearly exposing the men's horrific injuries.

The screaming boy's body was covered with blood and gore of varying shades: red, purple, and snow white bone. His face was a pulpy mash of pink, its features nearly obliterated. What was left of his tattered, shredded garments clung to his body, glued there by his blood. The man's screams birthed in his brain as words, but came out of his mouth in unintelligible howls, spraying all of them with foamy blood. Jack noticed that his boots seemed to be the only part of his body that hadn't been touched by whatever maelstrom had engulfed him. In a daze he droned, "His boots are in good shape so his feet should be okay." The mindless comment, caused him to wince, but mercifully no one seemed to have heard. He turned to the other injured man, the quiet one, and surveyed his wounds. Unlike his friend, his boots were not okay. In fact, they had gone missing along with the lower halves of his legs. In the swirling haze of his mind, Jack for some reason wondered if the boy's boots were still attached to his severed legs. He hadn't noticed that Tom had moved to his side.

Over the screams, Ian asked the distraught Marine holding the flashlight, "What happened to these men?"

"Oh Christ, sir!" the Marine sobbed. "It was fucked . . . oh Jesus!

"Calm down, Marine," Ian said softly. "Just tell me what happened."

I don't know for sure, sir. They're best pals, both from Detroit. Really good guys . . ."

"What happened, Marine?" Ian asked again more firmly.

The young Marine stammered, "Like I said, I don't know for sure. They were digging a foxhole together and then . . . then they just blew up . . . oh God . . . I can't believe this shit . . . I can't believe this is happening!"

"Probably hit an unexploded naval shell or mortar. There'd be nothing at all left of them if whatever it was hadn't been buried." Ian muttered. "Okay, I'm ready to have these men moved inside. Bloody Christ! What I'd give for a bloody proper operating theatre . . . bloody damned Navy!" Jack hadn't seen Ian this agitated before; he knew the two boys were in deep trouble.

"Hospitalman, up front!" Ian shouted.

Jack replied meekly, though immediately, "I'm here sir, what do you need?"

Without looking up, Ian said, "Inside now and make sure the braces are ready for these men's litters. I want sterile water, bandages, grease, sulfa, tourniquets, blood pressure cuffs, morphine, and a scalpel set up by each litter and I want it done bloody quick! Go!"

Jack heard Dr. Goldman yell, "Turk, Cudlipp, Turner, Abramowicz . . . scrub!" Goldman, upon hearing the screams, had scrambled out of the Cave to assist.

Jack turned and raced toward the tent. He was vaguely aware of someone following him. "I'll give you a hand," said a voice from behind.

"Okay thanks," Jack said hurriedly.

As they entered the tent, Jack turned toward the man who had offered to help, and saw that it was his father. He quickly averted his eyes and hesitated for a moment, collecting himself. He urged himself to focus on his job, remembering the two torn bodies outside. Finally, Jack mumbled, "Um . . . uh, why don't you get one station ready and I'll do the other."

"You got it," his father replied. In spite of his fright and addled emotions, Jack's nervous directive and his father's eager reply made the situation almost mind-numbingly surreal. The unprecedented reversal in roles was alien, even wrong, Jack thought. As his father began to prepare a cot, one of his sick buddies asked, "What in hell is going on, Tom?"

"Two guys got real fucked up digging a foxhole. It looks like their shovels must have struck an unexploded shell of some sort. It ain't pretty boys, so brace yourselves," Tom warned. Jack figured that what the Marines in the tent were about to see would be a first for them. Besides broken limbs, superficial cuts, and abrasions on the playground and training fields, they were uninitiated when it came to the butchery modern weapons produced; he wondered how they'd react.

"Bringing 'em in!" Dr. Goldman shouted. Jack rushed to the door and held it open for the two litters. The two mutilated Marines were promptly set on top of the saw horses. Ian and Dr. Goldman hurriedly scrubbed their hands and lower arms in a pan of water and soap, then donned rubber gloves. Goldman ordered Frank to administer morphine to the men and Turk and Abramowicz to start plasma drips for both. Ian barked, "Move the gastro's to the Cave!" Under his breath he added, "No need for them to lay here and watch this." Hospitalmen, along with Tom, began to quickly escort the sick Marines out the door and onto bedrolls in the Cave. Ian took the screaming boy and Dr.Goldman the legless boy. They quickly went to work clamping off arteries while the corpsmen assisting them cleaned the wounds, applying sulfa powder and dressings anywhere they could. To Jack, what seemed like antique-looking blood pressure cuffs were wrapped around an arm of each boy. It was a frantic, bloody race against the life flowing out of the men's bodies. Jack backed up ten feet from the operating stations and watched; feeling completely helpless. He heard Turk's voice cut through the fog that the sounds and scenes had created in his senses. "These are our only two bottles of plasma, sirs. We gotta make 'em count."

"Bloody Christ!" Ian hissed. "You can't be serious, Turk! These men don't have a chance without more plasma!"

"Sorry sir, this is it," Turk said nervously. "Some Marine colonel from Division requisitioned the other six bottles we had. He said there's a shortage and he wanted some stored closer to the lines."

This time the normally mild mannered Dr. Goldman spoke, "No shit there's a shortage, but why in hell didn't someone tell Dr. Smith or me, goddamn it! And a Marine for godsake? I don't care if goddamn General Vandegrift himself comes sniffing around here. This is a Navy hospital and only we decide what is best. From now on no outside influence that could affect the function of this hospital is to be agreed upon without my or Lt. Smith's approval."

Dr. Goldman's unusual tirade impressed the men in the tent. He took his job of saving lives very seriously. Turk, crestfallen, looked down and said, "I'm sorry, sirs. I just didn't think we'd need more than this tonight if any at all and I figured Jack would pick more up tomorrow. I'm . . . Jesus . . . I'm sorry. I really fucked up."

"Well, there's nothing to be done for it now. We just have to do the best with what we have," Dr. Goldman said with determination. They worked furiously for the next twenty minutes, trying to save the young men.

The screaming boy died first. Frank had reported that his blood pressure was dropping quickly and his pulse was weakening. Then, with his middle and index fingers pressed up against the boy's pulpy neck, Frank said calmly, "No pulse, sir." Ian ignored him and kept working. Frank kept his fingers on the boy's neck. A minute later Frank, still cool and professional, reported, "Still no pulse, sir. I'm afraid he's gone, sir." Ian leaned up toward the boy's dead face searching for his eyes. If they were still there, they were impossible to find. Ian's head dropped and he cursed softly.

"Find what you can of his effects, lads, and call the graves chaps," Ian ordered somberly. "Clean him up and take him outside."

He walked over and stood beside Dr. Goldman, "Anything I can do Bill?" he asked.

"The legs were severed so damn coarsely, that I'm having trouble locating the flow points. He's losing blood twice as fast as we're getting the plasma into him, what little we have left. Why don't you

164

take the right leg?" Ian moved to the other side of the litter and began searching for the severed veins and arteries from whence the boy's life spilled. His face was just an inch or two from the stump, and blood spattered his face and surgical cap. Moments later, once again, a severe drop in blood pressure was reported; then a weak pulse. The boy, glassy eyed and gray, expelled a last raspy grunt, then died. Jack leaned up against a crate, stunned and horrified by the bloody deaths of the young men. He didn't know who they were; didn't know their names—only that they were good buddies from Detroit. There was nothing resembling glory, noble sacrifice, or even some sort of justification regarding their youthful deaths. They were far from home and they were dead, that was it . . . that was all. After the second body had been removed, Jack saw Ian standing directly in front of Turk, his arms outstretched, his hands grasping the boy's shoulders, gently shaking him. The tough young man was weeping. Jack couldn't hear Ian's words, but he could tell he was aggressively reassuring the boy. It was too much, he thought to himself; it was all too much. The room spun before his eyes and he dazedly stumbled toward the hospital door.

12

Shocked by the carnage and the rapidity with which the lives drained out of the two boys, Jack staggered out of the hospital. In the moonlight he saw blood staining his hands and he felt it drying on his face. He knelt down by a puddle of muddy water and washed himself. The dirty water painted the gray pallor of his face with a light coating of reddish-brown. He rose and walked toward the Cave. As he drew near he suddenly stopped and slumped to the ground; his father's voice was emanating clearly from the lean-to. He rested his forehead on his knees and for a moment felt he may vomit. The urge passed but it seemed, as it had on the first morning, that he was again waging a war with insanity. Coming face to face with his teenage father, and actually speaking to him, had weakened his grip on reality and reason. With the horrible deaths of the two young Marines, it suddenly seemed too much for him to bear. He was again tempted to run back to the fetid river and drown himself, in hopes of finding the portal back to his natural life. He implored himself in desperate whispers to breathe slowly and calm down. Trying to erase the smell of blood and excrement, he chain-smoked until his lungs burned. Slowly, he regained his composure and his grip on reality. He raised his head when he heard his father talking again.

Jack recognized the tone of his father's voice. He was talking to the sick men slowly and affably. His words were sincere and caring, bereft of any ego or condescension. It was just like at work, he

166

thought. His father would stroll the various departments of his company once a day, every day, greeting workers and inquiring about various details or events in their lives and whether they had everything they needed. When asked for input about personal issues or other daily challenges his employees faced, he'd deliver it in a calm, reassuring manner, taking great care to ensure he was not giving guidance that had any chance of causing harm. If he felt he was unqualified to give valued advice to an employee, he was honest with them and suggested they seek assistance elsewhere. Jack had always found it rather odd though, that he never socialized with his employees, even those in high positions, outside of work, or became truly close to any of them. He was simply their protector; a guardian in a way, of their well-being. Jack had always felt the daily walk-about was somewhat silly and a waste of time. Now though, coated in dirt and blood and emotionally drained by the deaths of the two Marines, he wondered. It seemed his father saw his employees just as he had his unit mates. Their care was his abiding responsibility, his purpose, even though he maintained an emotional distance from them all. Resting his head in his hands he whispered, "You never really stopped being a corpsman, did you, you old bastard?" For the first time since he was a child, the thought evoked feelings of pride in his father. Then suddenly, a picture of a withered, elderly man, lying dead in his coffin, snapped to his mind. He shook his head in short, rapid jerks, trying to dislodge the picture as the old gnawing sense of unease rose in his spine. At that moment, Ian trudged up and knelt next to him.

"You okay, Jack?" he asked.

"Uh . . . yeah, I'm okay."

"Give me a bloody fag will you, mate?" Ian's intrusion had thankfully purged the picture of his dead father from his mind.

"Sure," Jack replied. He took out a cigarette, handed it to Ian, then spun the wheel on his lighter. The light from the flame illuminated the young doctor's face. His appearance was dreadful, and to Jack, alarming. For the first time, he appeared vulnerable; utterly human. His smock was soaked in blood, as were his hands. Here and there little daubs of red smudged his face. He looked exhausted and sad; his hands shaking as he held his cigarette up to the flame.

"How's Turk doing?" Jack asked, setting aside his own tortured feelings.

"He'll be fine. He knows he messed up, but he also knows, as I told him, it wouldn't have made any difference for those two boys. Turk is a sensitive lad, but he's smart and tough. He'll get on with his job."

A thin smile appeared on Jack's lips. Surely, in spite of his own disappointment and frustration, Ian had worked his magic on the distraught young man and Turk would indeed be just fine. Jack watched him for a moment puffing rapidly on his cigarette, then asked quietly, "How're you doing, Doc?"

Ian wiped a bloody hand across his eyes and sighed, "Not too bloody good . . . We lost both of them . . . both of them. Bloody Christ, I can't believe it . . . I can't bloody believe it."

Jack paused for a moment, not sure of what to say, "I uh, I'm really sorry, Ian. You did everything you could . . . they just didn't have a chance."

Ian sighed deeply, "They may not have had a chance, but who knows, if we'd had the right equipment . . . bloody Navy!"

"That may be, Doc, and I'm no expert, but from the look of those boys, I don't think the best equipped hospital in the world could have saved them."

"Yeah, well at least they would have had a shot . . . at least I could've tried to do something other than sprinkle bloody sulfa on them and search for invisible arteries."

Ian was clearly upset, if not grief stricken, Jack thought. "Were those your first two, Doc . . . the first that died?" he asked.

"Yeah, they were the first. I mean I was on teams during residency when we lost people on the table, but I felt like I was just one of the worker bees then. This is different, more personal I reckon. I knew it would come someday, and with all my training I was prepared well for it, but it's bloody tough. I hate feeling helpless; I hate that feeling more than any other."

"You're hardly helpless, and like I said, you did the best you could with what you had to work with." Jack paused, then added, "Besides, with the injuries those boys had perhaps it was God's mercy that took them." As soon as the words left Jack's mouth he knew it had been a stupid thing to say to anybody in similar circumstances. It was doubly stupid to say it to Ian, for he, of course, didn't believe in God, at least not God as most of the world knew him.

Ian took a deep drag off his cigarette, than bitterly exhaled the smoke. "No offense, but that's a load of crap, mate. Where was your God's bloody mercy when they were digging that foxhole in the first place? Where was your God when the Navy ran away and where was He when this whole bloody disaster started in the first place! For me mate, your God or Allah, or Buddha, or whoever they all are, are just bloody convenient icons for men to hide behind when they fuck things up! That's all." Ian paused, flicking his cigarette away angrily. "Besides, Jack, my job is to heal as best I can . . . period; not judge the future quality of a patient's life."

Jack realized he wasn't doing Ian much good, and felt badly that he could not comfort him as Ian had him many times since his arrival on the island. He mumbled an apology and shut up. Several minutes passed in silence. Finally, Ian stood saying, "I'm going to check on the Marines inside the Cave. If you'd like, I'll grab my bottle of *sake* afterwards and we can have a drink. I could really use one myself."

"Sounds good," Jack replied. "I'll wait right here." Ian took several steps toward the Cave before Jack stopped him. "Wait, Doc. You may want to take off your smock and wash up a bit before you go in there."

"Oh, right," Ian replied dully. "Thanks, mate." Jack started to tell him about his father, then stopped. He was afraid of what Ian might say or do, that he may force him to somehow engage with his father. Ian turned in the direction of the hospital and wearily trudged off. A few minutes later he reappeared, cleaned up and clutching a book. He handed the book to Jack saying, "A gift from me to you, mate. This is a pretty good Brit primer on basic critical care. Read a chapter a day and go to Frank or Turk with any questions. Every other page is blank for taking notes. It should help you get up to speed pretty quickly."

Jack looked at the dark green, cardboard covered book. The title read *RMC Field Medical Manual: 1939*. He rubbed his hand over the cover and felt a distinct sense of honor in receiving the book. He looked up at Ian smiling, and said, "Thanks, Ian. Thanks a lot. I'll get started on this right away." Ian nodded, and walked into the tent. Almost immediately, Jack heard him engage his father in a discussion regarding the condition of the Marines. It went silent for several minutes as Ian moved from cot to cot, checking on each man. Jack knew this was unnecessary as the boys were nearly recovered. He realized that Ian was doing it for himself more than anything. He then heard Ian and his father in another discussion. He strained to hear what they were saying, but couldn't.

Ian exited the tent and sat down next to Jack. As on the previous two nights, Jack had strangely felt no urge to drink for the first time in years and after this day, it was stranger still. But he was anxious to spend some time alone with Ian, so he said, "You ready to go get that drink, Doc?" He began to rise but Ian grabbed him by the sleeve and pulled him back down.

Ian said quietly, "Jack, I know who that corpsman in the Cave is. I couldn't shake the feeling that I had seen him before, then, all of a sudden it hit me and I asked him his name."

Jack hung his head and said slowly, "Unbelievable eh, Doc? I buried that man three years ago. I talked to him briefly when they brought the casualties in you know. The voice is stronger, but it's the old man's voice for sure." Ian remained quiet, allowing Jack to continue. Jack laughed bitterly and said, "I'm old enough to be my father's father Ian, what the hell is that? What am I supposed to do? Introduce myself and tell him I'm his unborn son here from the future?"

"Listen there's no way I can understand what you're feeling right now so I certainly can't tell you what you should do," Ian

170

replied softly. "But he's bunking with us tonight so he can escort his buddies back to their unit in the morning. You need to decide if this is an opportunity for you, or something you'd rather not face."

"An opportunity?"

"An opportunity a lot of blokes would kill for, I'd reckon," Ian replied. "An opportunity to know their fathers when they were young and innocent; before they were fathers."

"What the hell good would that do me?" Jack said, a hint of nervousness in his voice.

"It might not do you any good at all, but there's only one way to find out, mate." They sat in silence as Jack considered Ian's comments. An occasional burst of laughter sounded from the Cave as the Marines razzed and cajoled each other. At one point Tom's voice rang out loud and strong, teasing one of his mates.

A boy shouted in reply, "Christ, Macmillan, I just might have to knock you flat on your ass!" The threat was followed by loud guffaws.

His father replied, "With what, a fiery stream of shit?" The sick men laughed loudly and new insults spilled forth. He was surprised by a new emotion invading his senses. He wasn't angry or confused; he was jealous; jealous of the young men and their easy camaraderie with his dad—something he'd never had. He'd only seen it with the company employees during working hours, but as the profit-focused general manager, he'd viewed it with derision, not envy.

Ian brought his attention back by saying, "I'm going to fetch my bottle and we'll have a drink or three and see where things lead us." Ian stepped inside the Cave and reappeared just moments later, carrying a large green bottle. They set off toward one of the new bomb shelters. The men had been working on them the last two days and they were crude, but impressive nonetheless. The Marines had dug several caves into the side of a hillock that abutted the northern side of the Cave. The walls and ceilings were braced with logs and slats of wood the men had purloined from abandoned Japanese supplies. The dirt floors of the shelters were sunken so that any shrapnel entering the openings in the dugout sprayed harmlessly over the men's heads. Jack stood outside the shelter Ian had chosen, and wondered at the stamina of the young men. They must have shifted several tons of dirt in the heat for this one shelter, he thought. It made him feel old and tired.

He crouched and stepped inside. In the dark, he couldn't see that the floor was several feet below him. For an instant he felt he was freefalling down a dark shaft. He landed with a thud on the floor of the shelter. His head bounced off the packed dirt and for a moment he was stunned. When his senses returned, he did a strange thing, a thing that surprised and confused him. He started to cry, softly at first, than harder until his entire body convulsed with heavy sobs and his tears rained onto the dirt floor. Back in the world he'd occasionally tear up at a movie, but never in his life had he cried like this, not even when his father died. He sensed Ian quietly kneeling beside him, but heavy, uncontrollable sobs continued to wrack his body. After what seemed to him an eternity, he slowly regained his composure. He sat up and dragged his sleeved arm across his face, smearing the red/brown mud he'd used to wash up into tribal-like swirls and streaks. Ian placed a hand on his shoulder.

"You okay, mate?" he asked.

"Jesus," Jack muttered. "I'm sorry, Doc, I don't know what the hell came over me." Jack's sobbing had subsided, but tears continued to flow from his eyes. He continued to wipe at the streams, sniffling like a heartbroken little boy. "I guess I'm just tired and the fall pissed me off . . . hell, I don't know." Ian lit a candle, exposing Jack's war-painted face now streaked by tears.

"Listen, mate," Ian said softly, "no need to apologize. "Christ, you've probably intensely experienced every emotion known to man today. My God man, you aren't crying because you're tired or you bumped your bloody noggin on the floor. You're crying for those two boys back at the hospital; you're crying for your father too, I reckon. Don't ever apologize to me for being human, mate; a caring human."

172

In the past, Jack had always immediately classified any sort of sympathy or comfort offered to him, as a sort of patronization, an attempt by the giver to gain favor, or feel better about himself. It was one of the traits he'd assumed he'd inherited from his father. This time though, Jack took the words of comfort to heart. After a minute or so, he wiped away the last of his tears and said, "Let's just be bloody thankful I wasn't carrying the bottle." Ian chuckled, though to Jack it seemed somewhat forced and sad. Jack sniffed loudly one last time and said, "Let's open the bottle for god's sake."

Ian lit a candle, opened the bottle, and took a deep swig. He immediately groaned and rasped, "Bloody hell, this grog tastes like flippin' dingo piss!"

Jack smiled and said, "It's an acquired taste. You'll get used to it. Just like you told me I would this afternoon with the bedpans and puke. I prefer it cold, the *sake* I mean, but beggars can't be choosers, particularly not on this godforsaken shit pile."

"You've had this swill before? Why in hell would you drink this if you had other choices?" Ian asked.

"It goes well with Japanese food . . . it really does."

"Oh yeah, I heard about that. Some of the boys told me about the raw fish you said you ate; is that for real?"

"Sure, back in my day it's real popular. People all over the world eat it. The world was a hell of a lot smaller then, than it is now. No, I mean . . . uh . . ."

Ian grinned and said, "I know what you mean, mate."

They first talked shop. Ian told Jack he wanted him to return to the supply dump the next morning and scrounge for any supplies that needed replacing, particularly plasma. He asked him, if possible, to one way or another find an electrical generator for the hospital. After the past few hours, the thought of returning to Biggs' little kingdom was not in any way daunting. In fact, he relished the thought as it seemed it would give him a much needed infusion of control and purpose. He told Ian he would head out at first light, and assured him that if a generator were available on the island, he would find it. They returned to trivial chatter, Jack describing his kids, and Ian talking about life in Australia, while they lit cigarettes and passed the bottle back and forth. It helped distract them from the awful memories and confused thoughts the day had produced, long enough that is, until the fiery wine could take over. The *sake* was fast-acting, so it wasn't long before they both felt a warm, relaxing fog blanket their senses.

Ian stubbed out a cigarette and said, "You want to talk about your father?"

Jack paused, then replied, "Maybe, in a bit." Jack took another deep pull on the out-sized bottle and felt the warm, heavy tasting wine fill his mouth. It was stronger than the type he'd tasted back home and burned as it slid down his throat. "Besides, Doc," Jack added, "you've had a tough night; you don't need to be worrying about me."

"You're wrong Jack, I do. No offense, but it's bloody fascinating to say the least; and it'll help me get those two lads off my mind."

Jack just nodded and changed the subject saying, "There are a few things I've been meaning to talk to you about."

"Go ahead."

"The atabrine pills issued this morning work fairly well against malaria; one hell of a lot better than quinine."

"Yes, I'm aware of that."

"The problem is a lot of the boys aren't going to take them. That and the fact that a lot of them won't take proper precautions against getting bit in the first place is going to lead to a goddamn epidemic on the island, starting in roughly two weeks."

"Why won't they take the pills?"

"They don't like the taste, and man after I took mine this morning I can see why. As well, somehow a rumor starts that the pills will make you impotent."

"Oh bloody Christ!" Ian spat. "That's ridiculous." He paused, then continued, "Thanks for telling me. I don't suppose we can stop the rumor from spreading, but there are some things I can do to get the message out . . . anything else?"

"Yeah, one more thing, I told the boys they shouldn't pick the weevils out of the rice or oats. They are a little gross, but they're a great source of protein . . . I read that, too. Most of 'em ignored me and I thought they might listen to you if you gave 'em a talk."

"Good idea, I'll do it first thing in the morning," Ian replied. "Is that all?"

"Yeah, for now."

"Well, anytime you remember something else that may be of use, you let me know, okay? Just remember I don't want to know anything beyond what I can do to make the medical care here better; don't tell me anything I don't need to know."

"Sure," Jack replied. Jack lit another cigarette and several more minutes passed in silence. Jack felt the old familiar feelings of numbness and time slowing as he passed from a state of mild intoxication to drunkenness. He wondered what his father was doing back in the Cave and, less inhibited from the effects of the wine, felt an urge to go and see. Not really an urge to interact with him, but as earlier in the day, simply an urge to see him . . . to just look at him. He was too frightened though, too mind-fucked by it all.

Ian, equally intoxicated and seeming to have read Jack's mind, finally broke the silence. "Why don't you go meet your Dad? It's a tad risky I suppose, but I think on balance, it could be a good thing for you mate."

Jack replied, "I knew the guy for over forty years, Doc. I don't think I need to go 'meet' him."

"You know what I mean," Ian replied impatiently. Of course Jack had understood his meaning. Jack sighed and ran his hands through his hair. He knew that Ian was probably right, but the thought unnerved him. How would he introduce himself? What would he say?

"My father and I never really got along," Jack suddenly said. "He was real distant and it seemed all he really cared about was the goddamn company. Then when he can't run it anymore, and I sell it for a shit load of money, he tells me I betrayed him and that I didn't have the balls or the integrity to do what was right. Can you fucking believe that? It was just business for chrissakes, not some holy mission." Jack paused for a moment and said, "It was real weird. He even told me one time that he regretted he gave me the name Jack. What the hell does that mean? And hell, he didn't even go to college!" Jack paused after his last statement. Uncomfortably, the visage of the vile, sneering Biggs, belittling Jack for not having an Ivy League degree or a fancy job on Wall St., entered his mind; his spine twitched. He squeezed his eyes shut and purged the thoughts, taking a long swig of the fiery wine.

Ian asked, "Did you love your father?"

After a mellow sigh, Jack said, "Yeah, of course I loved him. Hell, I worshiped him when I was a boy. We just drifted apart and after a while it got harder to feel deeply about him. He was a good provider and was never abusive or anything like that. He just seemed kind of cold and detached. But he was my dad, so I guess I always loved him."

"Do you think he loved you?" Ian quietly asked.

For several moments it appeared Jack hadn't heard the question as he was still and silent. Finally, he replied. "Yeah, he did. You can never know for sure I guess, but after having my own kids I don't know how any fairly normal parent couldn't love their child. You don't have a choice, you just love them, you know?"

Ian, sensing that Jack had more to say, stayed silent. After a minute, Jack continued, "Yeah, he loved me, there were times I could tell, particularly when I was young. He took me to a ball game once and he didn't even like baseball." Jack paused a moment, then said, "It was magical . . . I swear. But then . . . shit . . . I don't know."

Ian waited, then said softly, "Go on Jack." Jack took a deep drag off his cigarette.

He blew the smoke out of his lungs with a loud, powerful exhale and said, "I'm not sure if he loved me after I sold the company. Shit, I think he may even have hated me after that." Jack said the words with little emotion. He stubbed out his cigarette then added, "I never knew for sure though. He died just a week after the deal closed."

176

"Listen, mate," Ian said, "from what you've just described it sounds like the absolute wrong thing for you to do is not connect with your father. Who knows what you might learn about him and how that affected your life, and his?" Jack didn't reply, but considered Ian's words. They made sense, and Jack did feel strongly drawn to learning more about his father. Deep inside, almost buried in his subconscious, was a deep fear of what he may learn; of what it may possibly tell him about himself, about his father. Once again he tried to change the subject.

"You know how I told you my father never told me anything about his time on this island . . . even when I asked? He knew my passion for World War II history, but he still didn't talk about it. It was weird. He never supported that interest of mine, even kind of ridiculed it at times. I guess that's another reason I lost some respect for him and his service during the war."

"He really told you nothing?"

"Next to nothing . . . I only knew he was in the Navy. Like I've said, I always figured he was some sort of clerk type, or on some rust-bucket trolling the backwaters of the war, not a combat corpsman. He never told me a thing. He only lugged around that stupid rock I told you about."

Ian thought for a moment then, said, "I'm completely knackered mate and I must admit, a bit pissed on this bloody sake. There's still plenty of the stuff left though. I'll leave the bottle behind the Cave so some bugger doesn't pinch it. You do what you think is right; but I think you should invite your father for a drink. I could be wrong, mate. But like I said, from what you've told me about you and your father's lives, you may have been blessed with an opportunity . . . bloody hell, a sodding, fucking miracle even, a miracle provided by the spirits." Jack merely grunted and watched as Ian rose to a crouch and shuffled toward the doorway. He carefully clutched the *sake* bottle with both hands so as not to spill any during his unsteady exit.

"Hey, Doc," Jack said loudly, "you wanna hear another funny thing about my dad?"

"Sure," Ian mumbled.

"The company . . . the family company my dad started and I sold? Guess what it made?"

"Bloody great cakes and chocolates," the drunk doctor replied. "How the bloody hell would I know?"

Jack chuckled and said, "Wrong. Medical supplies . . . goddamn medical supplies! What a hoot, huh? He made 'em and now I'm stealing 'em. What a fucking hoot." Ian didn't reply. Jack watched him crawl out of the shelter and stagger toward the Cave, half drunk and half exhausted. He lit another cigarette and leaned his head back against the cool, moist soil of the dugout's walls. "Aww shit," he groaned. "Goddamn son of bitching shit." He talked out loud to himself, struggling with the dilemma his father's presence created.

"If it doesn't send you off the deep end, something good could come from meeting him. Damn . . . goddamn, buddy! What if you say the wrong thing and freak him out or something. Or he says something that freaks you out; something about him you don't want to know or something?"

He laughed out loud when he drunkenly pondered the fantastic absurdity his life had become. Here he was at 46, drunk in a bomb shelter on Guadalcanal, having a conversation with himself; a conversation that weighed the pros and cons of meeting his teenage father. His laughter grew louder and high pitched. Stress, exhaustion, and wine worked together to produce a marijuana-like hysteria. He toppled over and lay in the cool, moist soil of the dugout floor. His stomach muscles ached as his laughing reached the stage where he only emitted rasping grunts and squeaks. Suddenly the mania reversed itself, and his hysterics ceased in an instant. He lay quietly on the ground for a moment, feeling completely numb. He pulled himself up and exited the bomb shelter. He collected the *sake* bottle, paused for a moment, than entered the Cave.

13

Jack saw Ian on his poncho, already snoring loudly. His father and the Marines were clustered together in the back of the tent in lively discussion. A lone candle shone a dim, ghostly light on their gathering. All the men were lying on bedrolls, except his father. He sat cross-legged on a poncho he'd spread on the floor, his shirt balled into a pillow at one end. His young torso striped with sinewy musculature. Jack walked softly toward the group and sat on the ground nearby. He listened as the boys talked excitedly about returning to their unit, and what the future may have in store for them. It seemed they had completely forgotten the earlier tragedy in the hospital. They were so young, he thought. Still young enough to do this, to see their comrades maimed and killed, yet holding the belief that they themselves were invincible none the less. It seemed each boy had a different opinion of what was going to happen over the next days and weeks. The youthful, profanity-laced proclamations ranged from wildly optimistic to dourly pessimistic, from thoughtful logic to naïve fantasy. Tom was sitting quietly on the floor, listening to the boys talk. Jack could see his grinning father was enjoying the banter. Occasionally he'd guffaw at an outrageous comment that inevitably came forth in discussions such as these. However, his dad stayed out of the conversation and did not offer an opinion on their fate or how the campaign would play out. Jack smiled, recognizing well this trait. His father could only give so much of himself away. He knew the life stories of many of his employees, but they of course, knew little of him. Hell, he thought to himself wryly, I could never figure out if he was a Republican, Democrat, or something else.

Jack's emotions were numb; as if everything that had hammered his senses the last few hours had pulled some sort of psychic switch. It was, he thought, a blessed gift, and it gave him the strength to confront his father. "Hey," he stammered, "um . . . one of you guys named Macmillan?"

The boys ended their discussion and turned toward Jack. His father turned slowly and looked Jack straight in the eyes, unnerving him. "That'd be me," he replied. "What can I do for you?" Jack noticed his father raise and jut his chin out as he spoke. Jack had seen the old man do this countless times when a vendor or his accountants were in danger of pressing the wrong buttons. He concluded that for some reason, his father perceived him to be a possible threat. He quickly moved to reassure him. His dulled senses had him thinking clearly; as if his mind was able to completely focus on the issue at hand.

"Oh, nothing really . . . Lt Smith told me a guy in the tent has my last name and I was curious is all. My name's Macmillan . . . Jack Macmillan. I just thought, who knows, maybe we're related or something."

His father's head dropped and he smiled. "Oh, hey . . . no shit? How do you spell it?"

Jack spelled the name and his dad told him he spelled his exactly the same. He rose, stepped over to his son, and thrust out his hand. Jack slowly reached out, whereupon his father gripped his hand tightly, wearing a friendly grin. Jack dully stared at his father; his mouth hanging open. "I'm Tom," his father said. "It's nice to meet you. So where you from?"

Jack hesitated, his numbed emotions staving off panic. He coolly came up with a logical set of answers. "Chicago," he lied. "At least . . . that's where I've lived the last twenty years. I was born and raised across the lake in Grand Rapids, Michigan." Jack instinctively knew if he were to get close to his father, having the common connection of Grand Rapids would make it much easier. Tom's grip tightened and his eyes grew wide.

"No shit? You grew up in G.R.?" his father asked. Jack nodded and his father exclaimed, "Holy shit, maybe we are related! I'm from Sparta, just outside the city. You remember Sparta?"

"Hmm," Jack mumbled, stroking his chin for effect. "Let me think . . . it was a long time ago, probably before you were born. Is it northwest of town . . . a small farming community?"

"Exactly!"

"Yeah, I remember it. I think I remember my father taking us up there to pick berries at some farm. It was beautiful . . . I suppose that's why I remember it."

Tom nodded and eagerly told Jack that in fact his family owned a fruit farm and that he'd gone to Sparta High. When Tom asked him what high school he attended, Jack hesitated, then lied again, feeling the discussion might possibly drift too close to the lives they would share in the future. "Uh . . . Central . . . Grand Rapids Central, but like I said, a hell of a long time ago, so I don't think we'd know anyone in common."

When Tom began to try and determine if they could be related, Jack interrupted and invited him to the bomb shelter for a drink so they could talk in private. Tom eagerly accepted, then turned and urged his friends to get some sleep. "Nighty-night, you shit machines," he said. "It's back to work in the morning guys, so get some sleep." He assured them that he would be sleeping on the floor next to them if they needed him during the night. As he walked toward the exit, he told them to shake him extra hard due to the fact that he'd probably be drunk. A chorus of jeers and protests swept Tom and Jack out of the tent. Moments later they ducked into the bunker and sat on the floor. Jack lit the candle and set it between them. Like Ian, Tom howled when he took his first gulp of the wine. Jack assured him that it would taste better with each swig, and offered him a cigarette to mask the flavor of the wine.

"No thanks," Tom replied. "Those little bastards will kill you, I swear, but thanks for asking anyway." Jack grinned slightly and thought, that's him alright, so certain of his independently arrived at conclusions, and bloody minded enough to stick to them. Hell, Jack thought, in 1942 some still thought cigarettes were good for you.

Slowly getting drunk, Tom for the first time that night, Jack for the second, they quickly determined there was no way they could be related. Jack had conjured up fictitious relatives, including where they lived and worked. As he spoke, Jack noticed the expression on his father's face relax, a clear look of relief. Who, after all, would want to have the baggage of a newfound relative to deal with at a time and a place like this? Extended family, Jack thought, could be damned awkward in the most benign circumstances. No, what a man needed at a time and in a place like this were loyal friends, not relatives that could fuck with a mind that is already being fucked with enough. He decided to get his father talking about West Michigan, as he knew it was probably the thing that would most likely get him talking about himself and his family. "So," Jack asked, "how often did you get into Grand Rapids?"

"Not as much as you might think," Tom replied. "We went in a lot in the summer, but that was for work. We were just too damn busy on the farm and all, and sometimes it was hard to come up with the money for gas."

The gas issue surprised Jack. Hell he thought; it's only 15 miles. He shrugged off the comment and continued, "Well, as beautiful as I remember the fields around Sparta to be, you didn't miss much."

Tom's expression suddenly changed. His brow furrowed and his gaze fell to the floor. He said quietly, "Maybe . . . if I'd had the time I would have gone into town more often to shop and stuff, but it just wasn't possible. It was tough on the farm . . . real hard. I hated it."

Hated? Jack was, of course, anxious to find out what that was all about, but he was unnerved by his father's change in mood as he didn't want to lose the fragile connection he'd established. He decided to lighten things up. "Well, when the war's over, you can spend more time in town. Hell, maybe you'll even live there. Tell me though, the times you did go into town, what did you do?"

182

Tom sat up and a reflective grin creased his face. "At Christmastime, my mom would take us to the parade that went down uh . . . Fulton Street, I think it was. Afterwards, we'd go to Herpolsheimer's for breakfast and Christmas shopping. After things got real bad, you know the Depression and stuff, we skipped breakfast. Us kids would draw names and buy just one gift; and mom and dad wouldn't let us get them anything."

"Sounds like fun." Jack realized he was talking to his father as an elder would to a young man. It felt strange, but he reminded himself that his manner of speaking to his father was correct. He recalled his own trips downtown to the parade, and the hot chocolate with breakfast at Herpolsheimer's. The main difference between their experiences it seemed was that for Jack there was always plenty of money for food and gifts. Still, it was a comforting thought that he and his father had shared such a common, warm tradition. Back in the world he'd never known; his father never mentioned it and he'd never asked.

"It was a great time . . . hell, kinda like magic almost," Tom said. "It seemed like it was always snowing the morning of the Christmas parade . . . always." Jack, through the yellow glow of the candle, could see his dad was smiling, staring into the distance. He recalled how upset his father had been when Herpolsheimer's, a victim of the cloying, soulless malls, closed in the early 1980s. When he'd read the news of its closing in the paper, he poured himself a whiskey and stomped about the kitchen, telling Jack's mother how this was another sign of a declining civilization. Jack recalled his befuddled amusement at the time. His father hated to shop; in fact he couldn't recall him ever setting foot in the place; other than when he took him to the parade. He hadn't understood why his father cared. Jack had written it off as another of the old man's idiosyncrasies. He sighed; for the first time knowing the real reason.

Quietly he asked, "Where else did you go?"

"In the summer, when we were a little older, my sister Eliza*beth*, we called her Liz or Lizzy, and I would go to the farmer's market three times a week with a truck load of fruit to sell. That was fun too; hell anything to get some time off the farm was fun." Jack nodded and rubbed his eyes. Aunt Liz used to take him to the same market when he was young. They'd sample berries and peaches; she'd stop before each fruit display to tell him how it was grown and when it was harvested, answering each of his questions in detail. He smiled, imagining her and Tom, in their early teens, riding in an old truck, windows down, happily headed to town through the idyllic pastures and orchards.

Tom continued, "We'd get up before sunrise, load up the truck with crates of raspberries, blueberries, peaches, and strawberries. The sun would come up as we drove to town. Everything smelled so fresh and clean. It's kind of neat the way the dew sparkles all silver and stuff at daybreak, you know?" Jack nodded, but didn't reply as his experience with early morning dew was gained exclusively during early tee-off times at the club. Oft times he'd waited impatiently for the big rolling machine to clear it from the fairways so he and his partners could have their first bash at the little white ball. His father's sentimental reminiscing was welcome, but causing Jack some discomfort. He'd never talked to Jack like this back in the world and the incongruity of it had him self-consciously wondering why. Swigging off the bottle of wine he said, "That sounds really . . ."

"Oh yeah," Tom interrupted, "we'd also bring jars of this incredible strawberry jam my mom made. People would line up for miles to buy the stuff. It was good, I mean it was great!"

"I'm sure it was," Jack said quietly, his bottom lip trembling slightly. He remembered Grandma Mac's, as he called her, gooey, sweet tasting jam. He used to help her can the preserves at the small home his father had purchased for her on Giddings Street after they'd sold the farm. She'd give him a case of preserves to take home in his bike basket. Each season, as soon as the preserves were finished, he'd ride his bicycle to the bakery in Gaslight Village and buy a bag of fresh plain donuts. He'd race back home and slather gobs of the jam on the donuts. He knew very well why it had been so popular at the market. "Tell me more," Jack said in the tone of a beggar.

"Well, my brother used to take me fishing in the Grand River near a street I think was called Bridge. I never caught much on account Hank only let me fish from the bank. He was always afraid I'd fall in and get swept away or something."

"Well, after the war I'll bet Hank will let a combat medic fish in the river," Jack said cheerily. Suddenly, Tom closed his eyes and his mouth pursed shut. He grabbed the bottle from Jack and took a deep gulp. He wiped his mouth and looked at Jack for a long moment as if trying to decide to trust him with a secret.

Finally, he looked at the ground and muttered, "Hank is dead . . . no more fishing."

"Oh!" Jack blurted. Then, he remembered his mother, when he was a very young child, once talking about Dad's brother who had died on the farm long ago. She'd said, "Daddy never talks about it, so nor should we." The subject of his uncle, he'd never even known his name, never came up again, apparently, a largely forgotten event from the distant past. He silently cursed himself for not remembering it earlier in their discussion.

"I'm . . . uh . . . I'm real sorry Da-uh . . . Tom," he said.

"It's okay," Tom replied. He smiled thinly and added, "I'm over it . . . it happened 9 years ago after all." The pain that registered on Tom's face though, seemed to tell a different story. There was something else written on his father's face and Jack struggled to read it. Finally he realized what it was. It was shock. His brother's death, even after 9 years, still hadn't completely been accepted by him. Jack felt desperately sorry for him, and repressed an urge to reach out to him. It was a feeling for his father he couldn't recall ever having. They remained quiet for several minutes. Jack lit another cigarette and they traded hits off the bottle. Goaded by the wine and his curiosity, Jack asked another question.

"May I ask how your brother died?"

Tom frowned deeply and he drunkenly replied, "No . . . hell no," while defensively waving a hand. He said nothing more.

Jack, appalled, put his head between his knees and whispered, "You dumb ass, you drunken fucked up asshole." To his horror, he realized that Tom had heard him when he leaned over and placed a hand on Jack's shoulder.

"It's okay, bud," he said, "I jus' don't wanna talk about it, okay?"

"Okay . . . okay, I'm sorry," Jack said.

"Fuck it," Tom said with another wave of the hand. As Jack was taking a long pull off the bottle, Tom let out an ear splitting belch and blurted, "What do ya think uh the goddamn Dutch bastards in west Michigan? . . . the fuckheads."

Jack struggled to hold the gulp of wine in his mouth, but couldn't. It sprayed out of his mouth in a loud sputter. Laughing, he exclaimed, "Jesus Christ! I guess I don't have to ask you how you feel about 'em. Oh, and by the way, I'm half Dutch myself."

Jack wasn't lying this time. His father had, ironically, married a girl of Dutch descent. He had always known his father held the conservative Dutch immigrants and their heirs, who had built the city and still largely dominated it, in low esteem. He knew this from vague, but telling, comments muttered at the dinner table. On several occasions he'd referred to the local Dutch business community as the 'Dutch Mafia'. Jack had delighted in this and was intrigued by his mother's passive reaction to such comments. However, he'd never heard his father be quite so pointed, and was highly amused. Jack was also immensely enjoying his father's prodigious profanity. He could recall a few damns and hells, but very few. At no time did he remember his father dropping any fucks, shits, or goddamns.

"Oh shit, I'm sorry . . . uh, no offense. You see, I don't mean *all* the bastards, you know?" Tom slurred. "I mean the real preachy ones. The sanctimonious, self righteous bastards who think they shit carnations . . . those ones, ya know? The hypocrites . . . those types. The goddamn conniving ones who cheat at life during the week then go to church on Sunday and have some ordained collaborator forgive them and make them feel all special again, just because they bothered to show up and throw some dough in the bucket . . . or whatever you call it." Tom dragged a sleeve across his

186

mouth and added, "My dad, who did business with a lot of 'em always said, 'They're the first to look for an angle, and the last to pay their bills'.

Jack, laughing as he said it, let his father off the hook by telling him he understood. "My father used to say just about the same thing." He explained that he was raised Presbyterian, a truth, and that he found the clannish hypocrisy of the outwardly conservative Dutch descendants in the community off-putting. Still, he could see that Tom badly wanted to change the subject. He thought for a moment how he could oblige him, and remembered that he had been instantly struck by his young father's impressive vocabulary.

"You're pretty articulate for a guy your age, and no offense, but for someone who grew up on a farm. How'd that happen?"

"Left school at sixteen, and no offense taken. It's simple, I fuckin' read a ton," Tom said. "I love it more than just about any-thing else, 'cept maybe the rare times I'd go to the movies in Sparta. I was reading *The Jungle* by Sinclair Lewis while the other kids in my class were still trying to figure out *Dick and Jane*." Then, barely above a whisper, he added, "Don't read as much though since Hank died." Jack was stunned. He had seen his father read, but only the newspaper and technical journals that were related to the busi-ness. He had never known his father to read a book strictly for pleasure, or for that matter, go to the movies. His one interest in the arts was the theatre. He and Jack's mother often traveled to Chicago, Toronto, and New York to see stage productions. Jack had always attributed his lack of interest in most things outside the business and theatre as the product of a largely unimaginative, one-dimensional mind. Again, he was left wondering what had changed so drastically in his father between his youth and when Jack began to know him. Jack felt a deep urge, or more accurately a desperate need to know more about this young man, his father, swaying drunkenly before him.

Jack asked, "What do you want to do when you get out of the Navy?"

"Why the hell you think I joined the medical corps?" Tom replied. "I'm gonna be a doctor. A goddamn pediatric surgeon. It's my dream and I'm gonna do it."

"That's great," Jack said, hiding his surprise. His father, after all, hadn't realized this dream.

Tom continued, "I have to get things straightened out on the farm, then I'm going to college. You watch, bud. First one in my whole damn family."

"I'm sure you will," Jack said. Another abandoned goal, Jack thought. He certainly had the smarts and demeanor to achieve both. Was it money, the farm? He knew there could be no answer yet, not directly at least. He asked another question. "Why do you want to be a doc . . . a pediatric surgeon no less?"

"Firs', it's goddamn fascinating . . . the science and all. Second, I wanna help young people; cure 'em and stuff," Tom said. Quieter, almost under his breath, he added, "People like Hank . . . people like him."

Jack looked at his father, groping for words. He felt he should offer comfort in some way, but didn't know how. As well, he was still struggling to reconcile his teenage father with the one he'd known back in the world. What happened . . . what in hell happened? Jack decided he'd pushed him hard enough for now, and changed the subject.

"So you read *The Jungle*, huh?" he asked.

"Yeah, how 'bout you?"

"Yeah, I read it. I really liked it. What did you think of the Jurgis character?" For the next hour they debated the meaning of the book, the father, taking a more liberal view of the labor class' travails. Then they moved on to other books they had in common, particularly the works of a young writer named Hemingway. They scoffed and laughed good-naturedly at each other's opinions, and excitedly debated the merits of each book. Just as the father was giving the son a passionate discourse on why he felt Hemingway's books were too influenced by the writer's own ego, the loud clanging of a bell split the night. Moments later, the shelter was full of

Marines and Navy hospital staff. Tom saw his Marine buddies enter the bunker, turned to Jack, thrust out his hand and said, "It was great talking to you; it really was. We need to do it again." Jack noticed that the appearance of his mates seemed to have dulled his father's intoxication.

"Yeah, I enjoyed it," his disappointment obvious. "Thanks for the company."

"Hey," Tom said, "why don't you come out to my company area for a visit? We can talk some more and I can show you how a combat unit lives. I'm stuck with the Marines all day and I wouldn't mind some company from a corpsman; particularly an old Grand Rapids guy."

Jack eagerly accepted, "That'd be great, I'd love to. I have to go to the supply dump tomorrow. Maybe I can stop by on my way back. Where are you located?" Jack asked, though he already knew.

"On the bank of the Tenaru, a hundred yards or so from its mouth. C Company, 2nd Platoon. Lieutenant Grimes is our platoon leader. Hey, and if you can't make it tomorrow for some reason, be sure and come some other time, okay?" Jack was impressed and delighted at the obvious sincerity in Tom's invitation. He considered his attempt to connect with his father a resounding success.

"It's a deal," Jack replied. Tom crawled to the other side of the dugout to be with his comrades. Jack, knowing there was no danger, decided to leave the shelter and begin reading the medical book Ian had given him in the Cave.

Just as he was exiting, a voice boomed, "Hey, where you going, Jacko?" It was Turk. Jack ignored the question and clambered out the opening. "Jack!" Turk cackled. "You're too old to go out there darlin'. You'll get all fuckin' blowed up by them nasty Japs! Whose gonna tuck me in at night if your in a zillion pieces?" In spite of the emotions swirling within, he felt compelled to respond to Turk's heckling. He turned back and stuck his head through the entrance.

"I'll be fine, Turk," Jack shouted into the darkness. "All I'm gonna do is draw a big goddamn arrow out of candles so the bas-

tards know right where you're hiding . . . then I'm going to bed."
The boys laughed and hooted. Turk, Jack observed, laughed loudest of all.

As he walked toward the Cave, he heard the cough and rattle of the airborne intruder. Knowing the plane posed no danger, he entered the lean-to and laid down on his bedroll. Ian was still snoring, too drunk to have heard or minded the bell. Jack, extremely restless, carefully removed Ian's penlight from the breast pocket of his shirt. He snorted loudly, but did not wake up. Jack, the penlight clenched in his teeth, sat and read the first chapter of the medical book. It dealt with initial recognition of wound types and severity. He finished the section in ten minutes, but was still wide awake. He stared at the blank note page opposite the final page of the chapter, and was suddenly struck with an idea. Pulling a pencil from his rucksack he thought of Richard Tregaskis' diary. Smiling, he wrote in bold letters:

MY GUADALCANAL DIARY—JACK MACMILLAN

August 11, 1942
1st Battalion Naval Hospital
Company E
Guadalcanal—D+3

He looked for a long moment at what he'd written, pleased by the dramatic words. Then he began to record his thoughts on the coarse, light brown paper.

Yes, I am indeed here, it is 1942 and by all accounts I am not insane. Still can't believe what's happened to me. Don't think I will ever completely believe or accept it; how can one after all? I am trying not to overanalyze causes, reasons, metaphysical explanations, etc. I fear it would make me lose my mind; maybe literally. I almost feel if I thought too hard about it my brain would simply implode, shrivel up or something. Thank God for Doc—Lt. Ian Smith, M.D.,

Royal Aussie Navy. I would've likely gone mad by now if not for him . . .

. . . I miss Laura and kids terribly. Can't even think of possibility of not seeing them again and am telling myself often that I will. Strange though, I'm more at peace here than I have been back in the world. Even heat, food, creatures, Japs, not bothering me as much as it seems they should. Feel like I am focusing on something meaningful as horrible as this whole mess is. Have made friends already with Frank Cudlipp from San Francisco (unusual as a big chunk of the boys here are East-coasters due to the recruiting cycle) and Turk, don't know his real name; he's from south Philly . . .

. . . Getting all this on paper has settled me. Very tired now. Must go to prick Biggs' supply depot in morning, then a shift in the hospital.

He tucked the book and pencil into his sack and slipped the penlight back in Ian's pocket. Moments later, he was vaguely aware of the men returning from the shelter as he fell into a deep sleep.

14

When he woke the next morning, it was just coming dawn and torrents of rain lashed at the Cave. His head ached mightily; the residue of his two encounters with Ian's *sake*. He could still taste the heavy flavor of the wine in his mouth. Groaning, he leaned over the edge of his bedroll and spat into the dirt. Hearing a chuckle, he looked up and saw Ian, standing over him, grinning.

"Oh yeah, real funny, Doc," Jack muttered. "Christ, do I feel like shit. *Sake* is kind of like port . . . you go over the consumption line and you're hurting bad. You got anything for a wicked hangover, Doc?"

"I sure do; the best thing in the world for a hangover," Ian chirped.

"Let me have it then."

"It's bloody work, mate," Ian chuckled. He reached down for Jack's hand and said, "Rise and shine laddy; time to pay a visit to Mr. Biggs' heavenly depot."

With Ian's help, Jack slowly rose and rubbed his eyes. "Where's the goddamned coffee?" he asked.

"Very funny, Jack," Ian responded. "What I'd give for a bloody cup of tea myself. Guess our favorite hot beverages were not high on the Navy's list of priority items."

Jack and Ian walked together to the chow line. Jack took one look at the weeviled gray oats and prunes being offered and turned away with a groan. "I think I'll pass on breakfast, Doc. I'm gonna head straight out for the depot."

"Take Frank with you, he can be a pain in the arse when he wants to. The bloody Biggs bastard won't just have you to focus on." Jack protested, but Ian insisted that the young Californian accompany him. Jack was disappointed; he preferred to make the trip alone. He liked the feeling of freedom and responsibility and worried that a helper would detract from that. Grudgingly, he found Frank and they set off.

The truck clawed its way down the muddy track to the beach. Each dip and crater in the road set Jack's head pounding; his stomach churned. He was in no mood to converse, but regrettably, Frank was. He talked the whole way to the dump. The boy's incessant babbling made Jack feel worse and he tried to block it out. It reminded him of being stuck next to a chatty seatmate on a passenger jet as it rocked and shuddered in turbulent air. Turbulence, though intellectually he knew it irrational, frightened him badly and he would silently beg the person next to him to stop talking. There were times he felt an urge to scream . . . scream at them to stop their incessant prattle. He never had though; he'd only close his eyes and rest his head against the top of his seat, hoping the chatty neighbor would get the message. Jack felt like screaming for Frank to stop as well, but like his trips on jets, he didn't. Mercifully, Frank stopped talking when they pulled up outside the supply unit's tent. They jumped from the truck and Jack waved Frank over toward the dump. He wanted to scour the depot for the supplies on the list before they dealt with Biggs. To his satisfaction, he found it contained most of the supplies they needed. They walked back to the supply tent and entered. Wimpy, the doughy clerk, did a neck straining double-take when he saw Jack walk through the door. His eyes grew wide and he stammered, "What . . . what the hell do you want?"

"We're here for some supplies," Jack said. "Here's the list . . . do you still need to get approval from your CO?"

"Hell yes he does, old man!" a voice barked. Jack looked up and saw the arrogant captain standing just ten feet away. Biggs stood ramrod straight and again, had his hands on his hips. The look of anger from the previous day was gone, replaced by an evil smirk. Jack exhaled slowly, knowing that Biggs intended to make things difficult for him.

"Good morning, sir," Jack said politely. "Sir, I'm real sorry for the mix-up with the cots and typewriter yesterday. I truly am sorry you lost them, sir." Wimpy suddenly stood up, and without raising his eyes, mumbled that he had to retrieve something from the supply dump. As Wimpy beat a hasty retreat, Jack saw Biggs' face turn crimson; his hands dropped to his sides, balled into fists.

He took a step toward Jack and said, "Lost them like hell, you piece of shit! You stole them and both you and I know it, smartass! I slept in the goddamn dirt again last night because of you and I won't forget it!"

Jack was surprised when Frank interjected, "With all due respect, sir, I'm afraid you are mistaken. I've known Jack here since New River, he's a real straight shooter, sir, and he's always followed Navy regs to the letter." Frank smiled slightly and added, "I don't think he's capable of thievery, sir."

"Shut up, you little twat!" Biggs bellowed. "You speak when I tell you to, understand?"

Frank didn't so much as flinch and immediately said, "Yes, sir . . . sorry, sir. Perhaps it's best we just collect our supplies and leave, sir."

Biggs smirked and said, "Collect your supplies and leave you say? Well . . . let's have a look at your requisition, shall we?"

Jack handed him the list and after a cursory glance, Biggs said with a sneer, "Can't help you, gentlemen. We don't have any of the supplies on this list."

Frank bristled and started to speak. Jack stopped him by placing a hand on his arm. "Sir," Jack said, "with all due respect we checked out the dump before we came in so we wouldn't waste your valuable time. You've probably been so busy you weren't aware that you've received the items on our list. Most of them are there, sir, especially the real important ones like blood plasma."

194

Biggs eyes narrowed, and he lunged forward, placing his face inches in front of Jack's. "Listen, shoe shine boy," he said in a quavering voice. "Don't you dare tell me what I have or don't have! Even if I did have the stuff, I don't trade with thieves."

"Trade?" Frank blurted. "This isn't a dang market, sir. It's your job to make sure sick bays get the supplies they need! What kind of outfit are you running here . . . sir?"

At first Jack thought, "Oh great, Frank's really done it now." However, he noticed that the unexpected outburst from the pale, diminutive boy had a surprising, though brief impact on his nemesis. Biggs' face fell and he took a slight step back. For several moments, he seemed confused. Jack chuckled to himself and thought, "Gotcha! You're a sorrier piece of garbage than I thought."

Biggs quickly recovered and shouted, "How dare you talk to an officer that way, you little faggot! You give me one good reason why I shouldn't have you brought up on charges!"

Following Frank's cue, Jack said calmly but firmly, "Sir, two badly wounded Marines died in our hospital last night. We might have saved them if we'd had enough plasma. We need plasma, sir, and we intend to get it."

Biggs' face again contorted and for a moment he seemed stunned. After a seconds pause he sputtered, "Well, you can't have any supplies . . . we're uh . . . we're closed. Now get the hell out of here." Biggs turned and started to walk away. Jack laughed out loud at the captain's non-sensical pronouncement. Biggs stopped abruptly, then slowly turned around. "Are you laughing at me, sailor?" he asked. "You are both way over the line. Now get the hell out of here before I have you arrested!"

Jack guffawed and said, "Arrested for what, sir? Trying to procure supplies for a field hospital from an uncooperative supply officer? I don't think that would sit very well with your boss, do you, sir? Just sign the requisition, sir, and we'll be out of your hair."

Biggs stomped a foot on the ground and yelled, his voice highly pitched, "I'm Ivy League and an officer damn it! Not some old, uneducated retread like you! You treat me with respect, sailor! I will not sign that requisition . . . never, you hear? You're a goddamn thief and a traitor!" Jack suddenly recalled Wimpy's reaction the day before when he had successfully motivated him to keep his mouth shut. He knew instinctively that a similar approach with a man like Biggs would be at least as effective. Jack's face hardened as he took several steps forward and pierced Biggs' eyes with a furious glare.

"Sir," Jack said icily, "those two boys, the ones who died last night? They were good boys, sir. Young Marines who got torn to shreds by a Jap shell. Don't you dare call me a traitor, you pathetic son of a bitch!"

Biggs stiffened as his staff scurried for the door. Jack glanced at Frank and was pleased to see him vainly attempting to suppress a smirk. Biggs looked at Jack wild eyed and stammered, "That's it . . . that's it . . . you, you crazy bastard. I'm calling in the Shore Patrol. I'll give you're little shit sidekick here a break, but your ass is in the brig, mister!"

Jack took another step forward and said, "Not so fast there, sir. Like I said, those two boys were combat Marines. When our hospital guys tell their buddies we didn't have enough plasma to save them, and that you then prevented us from getting some more so we might save their own lives someday, I suspect they won't be too happy. Go ahead and have me arrested you fucking idiot. Enjoy the thought of it when you're laid up in our hospital with a broken face, sucking rotten Jap oats through a straw." He nodded causally toward Frank and said, "Frank here will do a real good job of taking care of you, won't you Frankie?"

Frank, rocking on his heels and smiling said, "Of course Jack; only the best for the good captain."

"That's a threat . . . you're threatening a superior," Biggs stammered. "I . . . I'll . . ."

Jack thrust the requisition toward Biggs and hissed, "Sign it, sir. Sign it and we'll be on our way." For several moments Biggs stared at the piece of paper, rage and frustration contorting his facial features. A knowing smile crossed Jack's face when Biggs slowly reached out and took the form. He leaned over a crate and furiously scribbled his signature on the document, muttering profanely all the while about white trash, the Shore Patrol, and the Navy.

When he was finished signing, he left the paper on the crate and growled, "Get the hell out of here, you fucking gangsters." He looked at Jack bitterly and said, "I'll take care of you later, shoe shine man. You can count on it."

Jack smiled politely, "Whatever, sir. My friend and I are just trying to do our jobs is all. Thanks for your cooperation, sir." Jack and Frank turned and walked toward the door. Jack, flushed with victory, stopped and turned back toward Biggs. He was standing with hands on hips again, fuming; trying hard to regain his dignity and sense of superiority. "You know, sir?" Jack said, "I never really cared for investment bankers. Most of 'em are too arrogant and egomaniacal to realize when they're being self-obsessed assholes and painting themselves into a corner. You know what else I found? I found that the smart ones, the really sharp bankers, were actually bloody stupid when it came to most things in life. Have a good day, sir." As he turned back toward the door, he heard the sound of a crate being kicked violently across the tent. He wondered for a fleeting moment whether the insult he'd just delivered could have once been said about *him* back in the world. Thankfully, as he stepped outside, Frank interrupted his thoughts.

"That was great!" he whispered. "Man oh man, that was the tops! I even liked how you slipped in Ian's 'bloody' word. "

"Thanks," Jack said. "I've had a lot of practice over the years. You can read guys like Biggs from a mile away. There's only one thing they really care about and that's their own hide. You threaten that and they make a lot of noises, but not much else. Besides, it's so early in this campaign and things are so disorganized. If he actually had the balls to try and have me arrested, he'd probably find it pretty hard to find anybody who gave a shit, and I'm sure he figured that out himself."

"Yeah, you're probably right."

"But hey, you put on a pretty good show yourself. He slapped the boy on the back and said, "Hell, Frankie, you were the one who tipped me off to the true nature of that wretched little man."

"I can't wait to get back to the hospital and tell the guys how we shut down that jerk!" Frank chirped.

The successful encounter with Biggs left Jack feeling exhilarated, as if he'd earned his first badge of honor. He'd been trying to play it cool, but Frank's statement put him over the top. He whooped, then spiked an imaginary football and shouted, "Oh yeah, man! Don't fuck with the E Company boys! You won't *ever* know how bad you'll hurt if you mess with those boys!" Frank, laughing loudly at Jack's boyish celebration, clapped him on the shoulder.

They quickly loaded up most of the supplies, but when they came to the blood plasma their work-pace slowed considerably. Glass bottles of dried plasma had been packed in simple 6 × 16 inch cardboard boxes marked—Blood Plasma. Accompanying crates held distilled water to be mixed with the powder. Ian had requested more plasma than the hospital would need for the foreseeable future. He explained that Marine Corps medical procedure required first line aid stations to apply to hospitals for their plasma; so much of the stores he'd acquired were to be inventoried and distributed to front line units as needed. The fragile, life saving bottles were in short supply on the island, so Frank and Jack handled the boxes as though they were precious artworks. They slowly lifted the boxes one at a time, and gently set them down in the bed of the truck. When they were finished loading, Frank braced the boxes of plasma with other crates and climbed into the back of the truck. Jack, still giddy, climbed into the cab, whistling, and started the engine.

Jack drove so slowly that the two mile trip took nearly fifteen minutes. He, mindlessly at first, began singing Creedence Clearwater's popular, *Fortunate Son*. It was only when he sang a particular stanza that he realized the irony of the lyrics, considering what had just occurred.

Some folks are born, silver spoon in hand,
Lord how they help themselves.

198

But when the taxman comes to the door,
Lord the house looks like a rummage sale.
It ain't me, It ain't me, I'm no millionaire's son.
It ain't me, It ain't me, I'm not the fortunate one.

His singing became quieter and less enthusiastic when he wondered at the meaning of the song. It was strange; he'd listened to the tune hundreds of times, but had never pondered its lyrics. When he finished singing, he squinted out the windscreen at Henderson Field, still thinking about the song's words. The morning sun was shining on the dusty runway, giving it a warm, golden cast. A single bulldozer beetled back and forth, working furiously to prepare the strip for the glorious aircraft that would bring thousands of young Americans back from the brink of destruction or a long and hellish incarceration. Many young men would die in those air machines, so that others could live. Larger machines would urgently deliver food and medicine and remove the badly wounded. He wasn't completely conscious of it yet, but the island was slowly changing him, slowly changing what he believed, what he didn't believe, and what he valued. Its inherent miseries—the heat, the disease, the minimal and abominable food supplies, the putrid jungles, and the specter of deadly combat—seemed to be awakening his soul from a long and deep slumber. For the first time, at the age of 46, he found himself wondering, with an assist from *CCR*, just who and what he'd been back in the world.

When they arrived back at the hospital, they started the slow process of transferring the plasma to one of the bomb shelters, then unloaded the rest of the gear. He and Frank worked feverishly, stocking the equipment. Some of it, things such as sterile dressings, drip tubes, syringes, narcotics, alcohol, and powdered medicines, they stored in the hospital itself. Items requiring less secure storage were placed to one side of the hospital and covered with a tarpaulin. At one point, Ian approached and asked how things had gone at the depot. Jack assured him everything went fine and that they had procured most of the supplies—and best of all, they'd acquired plenty of plasma. When Ian asked if he'd had any problems with Biggs, Jack, despite his previous promise of honesty, told Ian that the captain had been just fine. Upon hearing Jack's fib, Frank nervously turned away and busied himself unloading more supplies. Ian congratulated them and left. Frank, looking worried lectured him, "Jack, you just lied to Lt. Smith. I heard you promise him last time that you'd be honest with him. I don't know if this is right, Jack. I know what you said back at the depot, but what if he finds out what happened and realizes you lied to him again? Besides, he could cover for you if this thing blows up, you know? Maybe you should go talk to him."

"Listen, Frank, Doc has enough on his plate. It's just a little white lie for his own good. The point is we got the supplies and there's no need to bring anyone else into how we did it. Besides, what the hell is that asshole Biggs going to do? He can't report me because he signed the chit. If I were insubordinate, he wouldn't have done that, right?"

"Jack, c'mon," Frank said in exasperation. "He signed it because you threatened him."

"Oh, Frank, my boy, you have so much to learn and so little time," Jack sighed. "An egomaniac like Biggs isn't going to admit he signed a requisition because a lowly, forty-something hospitalman like me threatened him. Think about it."

"Yeah," Frank said, frowning, "maybe you're right. Cripes, I hope you are."

"No worries, Frank," Jack said.

As soon as they finished offloading, Jack said, "Let's get some lunch and head back out, Frankie boy." The events of the morning had dissipated his hangover and now he was ravenous.

"Okay," Frank said, "but where are we going?"

"The docs require a generator, so we're going to go get one."

"Oh yeah . . . okay." Frank hesitated a moment, then said, "Where are we going to find one though? Everyone on the island wants one of those things."

"We'll just drive around 'til we see one," Jack said matter-of-factly. "It's quite simple really."

Frank looked at Jack with a quizzical expression and asked, "What do we do if we just see one Jack? What are you thinking?"

"We'll jump off that bridge when we come to it," Jack said, not noticing he'd mangled the common phrase. Frank, of course, did.

Frank muttered quietly, "That's what I'm afraid of."

Jack looked askance at the boy for a moment, but he was still riding the high his confrontation with Biggs had produced. "You just stick with me Frank and you'll learn . . . I promise you."

Lunch was a rare treat: Spam. Jack detested Spam, but he was so famished, and anxious to commence the treasure hunt, he wolfed down a half tin full of the greasy loaf in less than a minute. Frustrated by Frank, jabbing and slowly picking at the meat product, Jack chided, "Jesus, Frank, you eat like an old lady at a church potluck. Let's get going. You can take your lunch with you."

Frank scrambled to his feet and apologized, "Sorry, Jack. I don't mind the taste, but the texture of this stuff just gets to me for some reason. I can't get over the feeling I'm eating some sort of organ or something. I actually prefer the Jap grub."

Jack immediately felt guilty for barking at his friend. "Okay, sorry . . . I'm just anxious to get back out there."

Frank set his mess tin on the ground, smiled and proclaimed, "Well then, let's go get us a generator." They jumped in the truck and roared off down the road.

After a few moments of silence, Jack, thinking out loud, said, "Frankie boy, you know, we're living history here . . . you realize that don't you?"

Frank reflected for a moment then said, "I guess you're right, I've never really thought of it that way. I've been seeing this as just a part of my life, an unexpected one for sure, but just something that my generation is experiencing and dealing with. It's hard I guess to see it from a larger perspective when you're living it yourself, but you're right, this probably will be considered historical, maybe even like Gettysburg or the Meuse-Argonne and the like. Hmm . . . interesting."

"We're a part of it . . . it makes us kind of special, don't you think?" Jack asked.

"Yeah, I can see that in a way I guess. Special as long as you don't get killed. If you get killed, you're not special, you're just dead. I mean, what's the point of being special if you can't know you're special, you know what I mean?"

"Yeah," Jack said quietly, a slight frown forming on his brow. "You're right, Frank . . . none of it means shit if you're dead. I never thought much . . . I mean the dead ones never seemed real to me, only the ones who survived."

"Uh . . . what?" Frank said. "You just lost me."

"Oh, nothing . . . just kinda' thinking out loud." Frank gratefully changed the subject to home and family while Jack drove close to Henderson where the support units, the units most likely to have generators, were located. The more they talked the more Jack was impressed by Frank's obvious intelligence and intensity, though he wished the teenager would lighten up a bit. Curious, he asked him what he wanted to do after the war was over.

Frank sat straight up in his seat and said, "That's easy. I'm going to Stanford's pre-med program. That's why I volunteered to be a corpsman. I'm going into cardiac care and I even know where I'm going to set up my practice."

"Wow, that's great," Jack said. "Where are you planning to go?"

"Marin County, on the other side of the Golden Gate Bridge. It'll keep me close enough to the hospitals in San Francisco as well as giving me an easy ride to my folk's place in the Napa Valley. The best of both worlds you might say."

"Hmm . . . Frank Cuddlipp, M.D.," Jack said. "That fits and I'm sure you'll make one hell of a cardiac doctor."

"Thanks, I think you're right, Jack," Frank replied flatly.

Jack, reflecting on Frank's reaction to his comments, thought "just like a surgeon." Saying Frank's name out loud with the added title jogged something deep in his memory. Frank Cudlipp he thought to himself. Dr. Frank Cudlipp . . . I've heard that somewhere. Suddenly, it hit him: The Franklin J. Cudlipp Cardiac Care and Research Center in Sausalito. He remembered reading an article about it in the *Grand Rapids Press*. It had been named, he recalled, after a man from the San Francisco Bay area. He also remembered that Dr. Cuddlipp had made his name in the development of heart artery bypass and other related procedures on the West Coast. Jack looked at Frank and thought, boy am I, or was I, right about him. He stared down the road, comparing Frank's coming life with his father's.

As Frank nattered on about the possibilities of what recent and future research could do to revolutionize cardiac care, Jack wondered why his father's dream of becoming an M.D. hadn't materialized. He knew with certainty that Frank would achieve his goals. How could he not after all? He had what it took, the smarts, the passion, and the pedigree. The only thing his father didn't have was the latter. He liked and admired Frank, but found himself feeling slightly resentful. Frank would achieve his dream as a world renowned cardiac care specialist; Tom would never come close to his. "God! What happened?" he whispered.

Suddenly Frank yelped, "There . . . there behind that shack; a generator!"

Jack slammed on the brakes and looked toward where Frank was pointing. Frank was right. A gray, gas powered generator was chugging away beside a nimble looking planked shack left behind by the Japanese. A crude, hand-painted sign was stuck in the ground near the entrance to the shack. The words on the sign read,

D Company Engineer Machine Shop
We Build/Fix anything, any time, on time

Jack sighed, "It's no good; this is a machine shop. We need to find a generator that's kind of being wasted. This shop is too important."

"Oh yeah, right," Frank replied dejectedly.

They drove on, and in quick succession found two more generators. In both cases though, Jack deemed them untouchable. One was at the refrigeration unit the Japs had built. The unit preserved various medical supplies and the few perishable foodstuffs. The other was another hospital. Finally, they drove by a small structure, jerry rigged with purloined timber and swatches of tarp and canvas. Sitting beside it was a gray generator. The sign in front of the structure, styled much like the one by the side of Tom's company area, read:

Press Tent—
All Broads Welcome

Frank squinched up his eyes and said, "You think that's where the newspaper guys live?"

"The correspondents?" Jack said. "That'd be my guess. How in hell do those guys rate a generator?" After a pause, Jack proposed, "Let's make sure it really is what it says on the sign. If it is, you let me handle everything, okay?"

"Okay," Frank replied, "but what if we get caught?"

"For chrissakes, would you please relax, Frank? This is a good deed we're doing; it's not an axe murder. Second, what are a bunch of news guys going to do to us? Write a story for *Life* magazine about two jerks who tried to steal their generator?" They left the truck, and walked directly into the tent. Two shirtless men were laying on bedrolls on their sides, writing. Other bedrolls, empty, were scattered about the tent. Writing tablets and balled up pieces of paper were sprinkled about carelessly. Jack spied several crude light stands, typewriters, and two balky electricity driven field phones. Knowing that most of the correspondents on the island spent much of their time with the combatants, he surmised that the tent was a makeshift media center where the reporters filed their stories, day and night. One of the men lazily looked toward them and asked, "What do ya' need fellas?"

"Uh, excuse me, are you guys correspondents?" Jack asked.

"Sure are, mac," the man answered.

"Oh good," Jack said with false relief, "we found you."

"What's up?"

"Some colonel told me to drive over here and try and find some of you guys. A *Catalina* is inbound and should land on the airfield in a while. He thought you guys would probably want to be there."

Both men sat bolt upright and together they asked, "No shit?"

"No shit," Jack responded. "You guys better high tail it over there."

The airfield was considered a key to the survival of the U.S. forces on the island. Without strong and consistent air cover, the Japanese would be able to land reinforcements in broad daylight with impunity. Their warships could stand offshore unimpeded, lobbing shells onto the Marine positions with the aid of direct sighting on targets. With limited heavy equipment, most of it left behind by the Japanese, the work went slowly and Henderson was still days away from being fully operational. Nevertheless, Jack had recalled that a PBY *Catalina* amphibious patrol plane risked a landing at the airfield on August 12th, the first aircraft to land there. So, he hadn't completely fibbed. There *was* an aircraft on its way to the island and it *was* a PBY. However, there was no colonel, and he hadn't the foggiest idea as to when the plane would actually land.

In an instant the two reporters had their shirts on and were out the door. Jack and Frank stood silent until they heard a jeep roar off in the direction of Henderson. "Like taking candy from a baby," Jack said coolly. He stumbled over a battered leather valise that was lying amongst the clutter. Black stenciled letters on the side of the case caught Jack's eye and he stopped, mesmerized.

TREGASKIS, R
INTERNATIONAL NEWS SERVICE

"Holy shit!" he gasped. He stood, staring in awe at the name on the case.

"What Jack? What is it?"

205

Frank's question snapped him back to real time and he stammered, "Oh uh, nothing . . . nothing really. I just uh, saw the name on that case and I thought I knew the guy, but I don't think I do."

"Oh. Hey, we better get the generator and blow out of here," Frank said.

"Yeah . . . yeah, let's get going," Jack muttered.

"You're out there right now, aren't you?" Jack thought to himself. "Out there on patrol, out there writing the book." The book he'd carried with him to his campsite on the Tenaru. He had checked it out from his neighborhood library when he was eight years old, then not wanting to give it up, his mother had purchased it. *Guadalcanal Diary* had affected him deeply and was a powerful catalyst in sparking his passion for studying WWII. A movie was made under the same title during the war but had been a disappointment to Jack. It had taken significant liberties with the book, being virtually unrecognizable as the same story. He hated how the movie studios altered the history of war to make what were already remarkable and tragic stories more appealing to the masses, often politically. Years later, some critics decried the book as overly propagandist and cleansed. Certainly, there was some truth in the claims, but as a boy the book had completely captured his imagination. To an eight year old it represented the epitome of manhood and male bonding; thousands of young Americans working together in desperate conditions to rid the world of a treacherous enemy. Besides, he conjectured, at the time the American public needed emotional incentives to steel them for the long, difficult conflict. Of course, just like the public in 1942, young Jack couldn't smell the rotting jungle and corpses, nor hear the screams of young men, their bodies torn and broken. Now though, he could. In the coming weeks this visceral awakening would grow, until it seemed it was nothing more than a world gone mad. The burgeoning, irresistible enlightenment the island was producing didn't discourage him from participating directly and selflessly in the deadly struggle. Instead, it was steadily instilling in him a need to help; to alleviate the human suffering of those caught in the manmade conflagration. It wasn't noble, glorious or profitable; it was simply the right thing to do.

Jack looked at Tregaskis' case one last time. The man had impacted Jack's life considerably and now he was filching his generator. He felt guilty, but only slightly. Tregaskis would have to write the book by candlelight or lantern he thought; the generator was needed to save the lives of his heroes. As they left the tent, Jack turned and whispered, "Thanks for the book, Dick, even if you didn't give the whole story. I understand; it was the best you could do . . . sorry about the generator though, pal."

Grunting and huffing, Jack and Frank lifted the generator into the truck and scrambled into the cab. Just as Jack engaged the gears, Frank shouted, "Stop!" Jack shifted into neutral, and before he could ask what the problem was, Frank was out of the truck, jogging back to the tent. He emerged moments later holding a field telephone.

"Field phone," he said, a cocky smirk on his face. "Now we can call the evac guys directly."

"Good thinking . . . for a California man," Jack chuckled. He put the truck in gear and sped off.

When they ground to a halt outside the hospital, Jack leaned out the window and yelled, "What's that you say? The hospital needs a generator and a phone? Not a problem boys! Frankie and I just happen to have top of the line models right here at your disposal!"

Ian, Dr. Goldman, and several others exited the tent. When Frank and Jack climbed out of the cab, both of the doctors shook their hands. "Good work, boys!" Dr. Goldman exclaimed. "I don't want to know how or where you got this stuff, but well done."

Jack and Frank grunted and breathed in short bursts as they hauled the generator out of the truck. They had to take a break when Jack, straining against the weight of the machine, expelled a loud fart that sent Frank into spasms of boyish laughter. Once the generator was finally placed astride the hospital, they unpacked electric lights, sterilizing equipment, and a small refrigeration unit they had picked up at the depot that morning. They wired those items, along with the field phone Frank had snatched, to the generator and started it up. Immediately after it sputtered to life, the two of them gleefully ran inside the hospital. They watched proudly as the bulbs in the light stands glowed brightly. The small refrigeration unit hummed. They rested their hands on the bottoms of the sterilizing machine and felt it grow warm.

"Everything seems to be working just fine," Jack said officiously. "Seeing as it's our baby, you and I will take responsibility for making sure the generator doesn't run out of gas, okay?"

"Of course," Frank replied.

Jack looked around the hospital. With the exception of a couple diarrhea cases, it was quiet. "Thanks for coming along, Frank. You were a big help."

"Hey, anytime Jack . . . it was really neat shopping with you." Jack smiled at the normally stoic boy, noting that he was one of the few who never referred to him as 'pops' or 'gramps'. He left the tent and, after a brief search, found Ian inspecting the supplies stacked beside the hospital. He'd pulled the canvas covers away from the stacks and stood before them, frowning.

"Hey, Doc," Jack said. "What're you staring at?"

"Oh, hey-o, mate," Ian said. "I'm just trying to think of a way we can prevent this stuff getting wet and rotting. When it really gets to raining on this bloody island, these scraps of canvas won't be worth a bloody damn." They studied the crated supplies in silence, trying to find a solution. Suddenly, an old photograph popped into Jack's head. It was grainy, black and white. He recalled exploring World War II sites late one night on the internet, and landing on a page relating to supply depots and distribution in the South Pacific. The picture was of a warehouse on Guadalcanal. The structure was rectangular with a peaked roof. The caption beneath the picture said it had been built weeks after the Marines had landed, and that it was constructed under the tutelage of local natives. The medical personnel had required the assistance of the locals, for the warehouse was unique, at least to the Americans. The materials used to build the structure were made entirely of grass and heavy sticks; crude for sure, but apparently highly effective.

Jack snapped his fingers and said, "I can solve you're problem, Doc." Jack had been looking forward to visiting his father, but the lure of taking care of the warehousing challenge was too great for him. He'd visit his father later in the day.

"What do you have in mind?"

"You'll see when I'm finished, Doc. I need some wheels."

Ian screwed up his face and said, "What?"

Jack said impatiently, "The truck?"

"What? What the bloody hell are you talking about?"

Jack sighed, then said, "I was going to ask you if I could take you're jeep and go visit Tom. But now I want to take the truck so I can work on this project. I can visit Tom tonight if it's okay with you. So, can I take the truck?"

Ian hesitated for a few seconds, then waved his hand at Jack saying, "Yes, yes, take the bloody truck already."

Jack turned and jogged toward the truck, Logjam thankfully nowhere in sight. He shouted, "Just leave everything up to me, Doc!" He excitedly hopped into the truck cab and sped off. After going a short distance, Jack spotted Frank and Turk sitting on either side of a palm stump. Lying on the stump was a deck of cards. He jammed on the brakes.

"Turk, Frank!" he shouted, "another mission boys! Hop up and I'll clue you in." The boys eagerly entered the truck cab and Jack roared off. He drove off toward Lunga village at a very high rate of speed. The three of them jostled and bounced as Jack explained the situation. When he was finished, both Frank and Turk were clearly pleased to have been included on Jack's little adventure. Before long, they arrived at the village. It was tiny and consisted of a couple dozen tin roofed shacks lined up near the waterfront. Some of the shack walls were made of crude wooden planks, others of woven grass. Several rickety wooden piers stretched out from the beach. The village had suffered badly during the Navy's pre-invasion bombardment and many of the huts were damaged and holed. Most of the inhabitants seemed to be carrying on as normal though.

Shirtless villagers were fishing off the piers, tending to gardens or simply sitting in small circles preparing meals or mending bits of damaged items. Naked toddlers frolicked in the surf and along the beach. Jack spied a very dark-skinned man with frizzed, gray speckled hair cleaning a catch of fish outside a nearby hut. He walked up to the man and knelt in front of him. The man looked at him briefly, then continued to serenely scrape the insides of a large, silvery fish. Jack knew the natives spoke a form of Pidgin English. He tried hard to recall some of the Pidgin words he'd learned as a boy while reading accounts of the campaign. Jack clumsily attempted to communicate with the old man.

"Um . . . helloum, mi tak . . . uh, to you-um. Mi wantem some helpum." Jack heard Frank and Turk behind him trying in vain to stifle laughter. He turned and glared at them which only served to heighten their amusement. He looked back at the old man and was pleased to see he had stopped cleaning the fish. Jack smiled and nodded, waiting for an answer. The old man only stared at him with watery, questioning eyes. Jack pushed on, determined to communicate.

"Uh . . . um, mi nidim helpum long soldia sick house. Yu helpum?" This time his attempt sent Frank and Turk into unconcealed hysterics.

To their surprise and Jack's delight however, the man smiled widely and tapped his head. "Mi save . . . mi save."

Jack looked up at Frank and Turk with a grin and mouthed, "Fuck you, boys." Then, the old man stood up, and gestured wildly with his hands.

"Yupela wetim hia long Peter," he said. "Mi go kisim long Peter pela long yu." At that the old man quickly shuffled off toward the beach. Jack watched as he walked onto one of the rickety piers and engaged a young man in discussion. He felt a hand slap him on the back.

"Holy shit, pops, I'm impressed," Turk said. "You're just full of surprises aren't you?" Jack ignored him, watching as the old man and his younger companion headed in their direction. "So what did he say?" Turk asked.

Without taking his eyes off the two natives, Jack replied, "I don't have the slightest fucking idea."

Moments later the old man returned. Jack noted that the older man's companion appeared to be in his teens. He was barefoot and wore only a yellowed cloth wrap around his waist. He was fairer skinned than his elder and his hair was brown, tinged slightly with orange. As they walked up to Jack the old man clutched the boy by his elbow, swept his other hand out toward Jack and said, "Yu tak long pela, Peter."

The boy nodded, turned toward Jack and said, "Isaac tells me that you would like help of some sort. What may we help you with, sir?" The boy's English was impeccable, his voice slightly affected with an English accent. Jack smiled and stuck out his hand. The boy gripped it lightly, smiling.

"So your name is Peter?" The boy nodded. "Where did you learn to speak such great English?"

The boy smiled proudly and said, "All the Marines ask me that, sir. I was raised by Christian missionaries from England. Then, until the Japs came, I worked for a British officer in the Protectorate Defense Force, a great man from Scotland. After the Japs landed, he headed south into the hills. I wanted to come with him but he said I was too young. So I came here to stay with Mr. Clemens'cook, Rachel."

Just as the name on the valise had stunned him momentarily, so too did the name the boy mentioned. He stared at Peter glassy eyed, quickly rolling the incredible story of the boy's former boss through his mind. Peter's quizzical look shook Jack out of his reverie. "I, uh assume you mean Martin Clemens?" Jack asked.

The boy excitedly replied, "Yes . . . yes, Captain Martin Clemens. Do you know him, sir? Is he alive? Has he come down from the hills?"

Jack, realizing his mistake, tried to think of a cover. Martin Clemens had been something of a legendary figure during the campaign, and Jack had been enchanted by tales of his brave and exotic adventures on the island. Clemens was a rough and ready young man, blessed with a remarkable degree of stamina, resilience and courage. He had gone to cover in the hills south of Henderson with a small group of intensely loyal natives. They barely avoided detection by Japanese patrols on several occasions and had witnessed the Marine landing from their elevated hideout several miles from the beach. Later, after Clemens walked out of the jungle, he and his men volunteered as scouts and guides for the Marines. The problem now though, was that Jack couldn't recall exactly what date Clemens had reached the Marine lines. He knew it was fairly early on, but didn't know if it had yet occurred. If the boy thought Clemens was in the Marine perimeter, he would surely seek to reunite with him.

"No . . . uh no," Jack stammered. "As far as I know he hasn't come down from the hills. I uh . . . I heard about him from some other locals. He sounds like quite a guy."

The boy frowned for a moment then said, "Oh, he is, sir. Captain Clemens is a great man . . . very great. I must say, sir, that I am a bit angry with him for leaving me behind, but I am still waiting for him to come down and collect me."

"Well, from what I've heard about him, I'm sure he's fine and will show up soon, real soon," Jack said.

"I hope you're right, sir."

Jack explained to Peter why he had come to the village. He pointed to a small grass hut and explained he wanted to build one like that, only bigger. He told him that the structure would be used to store and protect medical supplies from the elements; supplies, he explained, that would be used to treat Marines as well as native islanders. "There isn't an American on this island that knows how to build one of those," Jack said. "So we were wondering if some of the villagers would be willing to help us build the warehouse." As an afterthought Jack added, "We'll pay them, of course."

Peter smiled and said, "My people hate the Japs. They have been very hard on us and we are very happy you are here, sir. Of course we will help you."

The boy quickly translated Jack's request into pidgin for the old man. When he was done the man smiled, nodded his head, then grabbed Jack's hand and pumped it eagerly. The old man, Isaac, then turned to Peter and said, "Wanem bai American pela peim mi."

"I'm sorry, sir, but Isaac inquires as to what . . ."

"I think I know what he asked," Jack interrupted, grinning. The old man, apparently more business minded than his young cohort, had inquired as to what exactly the Americans would pay them for the job. Jack paused for a moment, pondering Isaac's question. Money was useless to them as there wasn't a local currency system. He considered food and clothing, but remembered the hardships the Marines would endure due to the shortage of these items. He tried to think of something the natives would appreciate and the Marines could do without. Suddenly, and without consulting Frank or Turk he blurted, "*Sake*, I think I know where I can get my hands on enough *sake* to throw one hell of a party for the workers."

"*Sake*?" Peter asked. "I'm sorry, sir, I don't know this word."

As Jack was describing the Japanese wine to the boy, a firm tug on his sleeve spun him around. "What Frank?" he asked impatiently.

Frank affixed Jack with a stern glare and whispered, "What the heck are you thinking, Jack? We can't give these people alcohol; it'd be wrong. Remember firewater and stuff with our Indians. Not only that, I have to believe the last thing the Marines want are a bunch of drunken natives wandering around the perimeter."

Jack stared at Frank numbly. He thought for a moment, cursed himself, then said, "You're absolutely right, damn you. I don't know what the hell I was thinking."

"I'll say," Turk muttered. "You try and give away any of our hooch again I'll pop you one in the fuckin' gums." Frank and Jack ignored Turk's comment as they tried to come up with an alternative. Jack described his concerns over giving them food and clothing that were badly needed by the American forces.

"I understand," Frank replied, "but we can spare a couple lousy bags of rice, can't we?" Jack considered the 10,000 Americans on the island and the hardships they were just beginning to suffer. He knew that all of them would lose large percentages of their body weight and that many would contract various diseases. However, he also knew that none of them would actually starve to death. He nodded at Frank, then turned back toward Isaac and Peter.

"Sorry," he said, "I was mistaken about the *sake*." Jack was further chagrined when he noticed a distinct look of relief cross the boy's face. "Upon completion of the job we'll give the workers two large bags of rice and several tins of fish." Peter translated Jack's offer for Isaac. When he finished, Isaac smiled, apparently satisfied with the deal, and once again shook Jack's hand. Then he was off, shouting urgent commands to certain inhabitants of the village. It wasn't long before twelve villagers stood in front them. The group represented a fair cross-section of Guadalcanal society. They were male and female, young and old, short and tall. Some were dressed in loincloths while others wore tattered and stained western style button-down short sleeve shirts. The men all carried machetes; the women some form of natural twine. The group stood quietly smiling, waiting for Jack to speak.

Jack said to Peter, "My pidgin's a little rusty. Would you mind translating for me?"

"Of course, sir," Peter replied.

Jack turned toward the group, cleared his throat and said, "Thank you very much for agreeing to work with us at the hospital. The warehouse, once it's completed, will help us keep our medicines and other supplies safe. That will be good for our patients and will save lives." Jack paused to allow Peter to translate. He watched with satisfaction as the villagers smiled and nodded eagerly. Jack lowered his gaze to the ground when he realized it had been over three years since he'd given a pep talk to a group of workers under his charge. He closed his eyes for a moment while he reflected on

214

the last one he had given to his workforce announcing the company was being sold. The speech had been delivered in a climate controlled 'clean room' where needles and plastic receptacles were mated, then packaged as finished syringes. The people who stood before him then were primarily dressed in pristine white lab coats. Others donned pressed khakis, brightly colored sweaters and polished loafers. He opened his eyes, raised his head, and looked at the villagers. Peter had stopped talking and they were patiently waiting for him to continue, still smiling. The sight froze Jack for a moment as he realized it wasn't just the manner of dress and location that set this talk apart from his last. It was clear the villagers were happy with Jack's message and were eager to be a part of his project. The group three years ago had displayed a far different countenance. The memory of silent, steely stares and heads shaking in disgust again produced the uncomfortable, yet hard to identify, gnawing at the base of his spine. As always, he quickly and completely purged the nagging memory from his mind. "Forget it, buddy," he whispered to himself. His focus returned to the villagers.

"We'll be traveling to the hospital in our truck," Jack said. "It's not a very long ride, but the road is very bumpy, so it'll be best if you sit on the floor the whole way. Again, thanks for your help, the guys and I really appreciate it." As Peter translated, Jack felt a need to say more, to add in his own way an historical perspective to the event. For to him, of course, it was history. He thought for a moment, and when Peter finished translating, he offered an earnest conclusion.

"I should add that it's not just me and the guys who appreciate your help," he said earnestly. "The United States Navy and Marine Corps also extend their thanks and gratitude. As well, the people of the United States greatly appreciate your efforts. By working together, we will rid the world of the imperialist tyranny that the Japanese Empire represents. I am honored to have the opportunity to work with you in this great endeavor. Let's go forward now and do our work. May God bless the United States and may God bless this village."

215

Jack heard a loud guffaw from behind. "Holy shit!" Turk giggled. "En-fucking-deavor? When did fucking Churchill get here? That has got to be the biggest load of crap I've. . . . ."

"Shut up, Turk," Frank interrupted.

Jack semi-consciously noted the exchange as he was watching very closely the reactions of the villagers to his words. The smiles slowly melted from their faces, as Peter translated, and were replaced by serious, prideful expressions. When Peter was finished, the villagers, smiling again, turned to Jack and raised their hands in the air shouting over and over, "USA good . . . Japs devil!" Jack beamed at the villagers and shook each of their hands before leading them to the truck. He noticed Frank looking at him quizzically. Turk wore a sneer of sorts and was shaking his head. Once the villagers were loaded in the back of the truck, Jack climbed into the cab and drove slowly back toward the hospital.

He waited for the ridicule that Turk would inevitably heap on him, but it was Frank who spoke first. "Uh . . . that was a swell speech, Jack," he said. "They seemed to enjoy it alright and all but . . . um . . . well, I guess I've never heard a corpsman talk like that. It kind of interested me . . . you know . . . why you said those things . . . um, what your goal was. They'd already agreed to help after all."

"Interested you?" Turk asked incredulously. "What's to be goddamned interested about? Jack's a nice guy and all, I'll admit. But he ain't normal like me and you, Frankie. Hell, he's a fuckin' nut job!"

"C'mon, Turk," Frank said, "I'll admit he's a little different. Remember he's a lot older than us . . . but I don't think he's unbalanced in any sort of clinical way."

"Well, I say he's loonier than a fuckin' loon."

"Listen," Frank reasoned. "Some would say his talk to the villagers may have been a bit dramatic . . . grandiose . . . slightly egocentric even, but that doesn't make him crazy."

"Grandi-what?" Turk squealed. "Speak English goddamn it!"

"Oh, cripes, never mind," Frank sighed.

Neither boy seemed to mind holding the debate over the state of Jack's sanity while he sat just inches away. Their seeming oblivion to his presence reminded Jack how young the boys were, and filled him with amused affection. The two young men could not have been more different in looks, background, or temperament. Yet still, somehow, on this wretched island so far from home, they had developed a friendship. A friendship, Jack knew, that very possibly would be the strongest bond either would forge in their lives. Jack knew this fact just as he knew when the enemy would attack or that many of the Marines wouldn't take their atabrine pills. He'd read about it for decades.

As Jack played the boy's banter back in his mind, he couldn't help but laugh out loud. The debate was so innocent, naïve in some ways, that Jack found it hilarious. Added to his amusement was the exhilaration he was feeling from his encounter with the villagers. Turk nodded toward Jack and said sarcastically, "Oh yeah, Frankie, you're right . . . he ain't crazy . . . no sir, not one little bit. No sir . . . laughin' out loud for not one fuckin' reason is very normal. Hell, we all do it all the time."

Turk's latest comment caused Jack to laugh even harder. He couldn't tell them, but both were wrong. He was pretty certain he was sane and though perhaps grandiose at times, his speech to the villagers was not egocentric. He couldn't tell them what had in truth driven the speech. First, it would be hard to explain. Second, if he could explain it, it would reveal too much about who he really was; where he was from . . . or more correctly *when* he was from. He couldn't tell them that speaking for the United States, engaged in a noble and desperate struggle against a country that had brutally attacked it, was the proudest moment of his life, in spite of the increasing revulsion he felt toward the human cost and misery of the struggle. It mattered not one wit to him that his audience had been a small ragtag group of native villagers as opposed to coiffed corporate heads or self-occupied politicians. He couldn't tell them that his call to arms, as given to the villagers, left Jack feeling exhilarated; much more so than any business conquest or new possession ever had. He also couldn't tell them the reasons for his intense feelings of satisfaction amidst all the misery. He couldn't tell them that for the first time in his life he was participating in something that really mattered, something purely human and relevant. He couldn't tell the boys any of this, so he merely smiled at them and said, "Who knows. Maybe I am a little crazy . . . aren't we all?"

"You might have a point there," Frank muttered.

"No . . . no fuckin' way," Turk enjoined. "I know fuckin' crazy when I see it, believe me." Jack and Frank knew that when Turk was exercised over something he used various forms of the word fuck, liberally. Actually, he always used these words a lot, but when he was exercised he used them . . . *a lot.* "You ain't never met my fuckin' Aunt Maria . . . lucky bastards," Turk continued. "Now Aunt Maria, boy; now that's fuckin' crazy for you. She'd sit on the sofa in our parlor all fuckin' day . . . she's lived with us ever since her husband hauled balls on her. She'd fuckin' sit there mewing and licking her paws . . . I mean hands . . . like a goddamn cat."

"Aw c'mon, Turk," Frank laughed. "No way I'm going to believe that one!" Turk, sitting next to the passenger window, quickly quarter-turned his body to face his friend. The move packed Frank tightly against Jack's side. The jungle slowly swept by over Turk's shoulders.

"I ain't shittin' you, Frank! She don't say one fuckin' word no more . . . she just purrs and meows . . . thinks she's a fuckin' cat, you know? No shit, I know crazy better'n anybody and, Jacko, you're wrong about us all being a little crazy. See, it's this way; there're normal, regular kind of fuckers, and there're crazy fuckers. Most of us, thank the Lord, are the first kind of fucker. Then you have the class of crazy fucker's like my Aunt . . . and Jack here. No sir, we're not all a little crazy . . . no fuckin' way." Both Jack and Frank smiled at Turk's crude discourse.

"That's absolutely brilliant, Turk," Frank said. After a pause, partially to recover from the barrage of profanity, Frank added, "Perhaps you should get Jack and your aunt together after the war."

"Hey! Great idea, Frankie," Turk replied enthusiastically. "Jack can stand in front of the sofa and make fancy speeches to Aunt Maria all day."

"Yeah," Frank said, beginning to laugh, "and when he says something she likes, she'll purr real smooth."

This sent Turk into loud fits of laughter. He pounded a fist on the dash board. "Oh shit yeah, Frank!" he howled. "And . . . and when he says something ole' Aunt Maria don't like, she'll hiss at him and claw at him and shit." Turk formed his hand into a claw and scraped the air, while at the same time emitting high pitched, feline-like sounds, "Raaare . . . raaare!"

Frank, normally stoic, was laughing so hard it seemed he would pass out for lack of oxygen. Tears spilled out the eyes of both boys. Jack was laughing too; not as hard as his friends, but hard. He was pleased that Frank had participated in making fun of him. It made him seem more human and less a vocation obsessed automaton; more willing to engage Jack as a pal. Until now, Jack thought, Frank had played the role of brilliant, but socially stilted, physician all too well. He reached over and first cuffed Frank, then Turk, on the backs of their heads.

After the laughter finally petered out, Jack said, "You're both assholes and I have just one question for you, Turk. If the whole world isn't a little crazy, then what in hell are we all doing on this stinking shit-hole island thousands of miles from home, trying to kill each other?"

"Touché Jack," Frank said, wiping the last tears from his eyes. Before Turk could formulate an answer, Jack heard singing coming from the back of the truck. He turned and looked through the small oval window at the villagers huddled on the truck bed. They were swaying back and forth as they sang.

Shall we gather at the river,
Where bright angels he has brought,
With its crystal tides forever
Flowing by the throne of God

At first, Jack was startled by the native's rendition of the old gospel hymn. The missionaries that had been present on the island for decades had taught them well. A smile creased Jack's face as he listened. "Incredible," he said under his breath. He contentedly hummed along with the refrain.

Yes, we'll gather at the river.
The beautiful, the beautiful, river.
Gather with the saints at the river,
That flows by the throne of God

Though sweat-soaked and hungry, surrounded by death, misery and the sour stench of the jungle, he said something else to himself, "You have to be the luckiest dude in the world, buddy," he whispered. In spite of missing his family, perhaps mourning him at that very moment back in the world, he truly felt incredibly lucky to be where he was and with who he was with. He realized, in spite of the human catastrophe occurring on the island, that he was happy, happier than he had ever been in his life. This acknowledgement unnerved him and he wondered what it meant, what it said about him as a man—as a husband and father. His thoughts were suddenly interrupted by a scream.

"Yee . . . hawwww!" Turk's muscular body jutted out the window like a ramrod, his arms waving wildly. They were entering the hospital area and Turk was anxious for his comrades to see what their secret mission had produced. "Hey! All you sad bags of horse shit who been itchin' your butts why'll me and my boys have been out workin' fuckin' miracles, listen up! We have, thanks mainly to my huge fuckin' brain, gotten us the finest group of locally trained construction engineers a bag of wormy rice can buy! You'll look on in wonder at their talents and skills!"

"Jesus Christ, Turk!" Jack huffed. "At least my speech was good." He reached over and grabbed Turk by the boots and shoved him the rest of the way out the window. He landed on the ground with a thud, followed by a violent curse. Peals of laughter rang out from a dozen or so men approaching the truck. Jack looked back at the natives and was delighted to see that they too were laughing at Turk's exit from the vehicle. Jack turned back just in time to see Turk's head pop up at the window, his face twisted with rage. For a moment, Jack regretted the prank as he feared the big man intended to do him harm.

"Goddamn it!" Turk screamed. "I should kick your fuckin' ass all the way back to the beach, you asshole!" Jack nervously looked at Frank and saw him covering his mouth with both hands and hunching down in his seat. His eyes were closed and his body was twitching with jerks of laughter. Jack looked back at Turk and saw him scowling at Frank. Turk, his face still red and contorted in anger, slowly turned and looked first at the Americans, then at the natives now standing in the truck bed. Both groups were still looking at Turk and laughing. Slowly, Turk's face lightened and before long he was laughing along with the rest.

Jack sighed with relief and said to Turk, "Man, am I glad you can take a joke. I thought for a minute you were going to kill me."

Turk smiled at Jack and replied, "Oh, I am gonna beat your ass off, Macmillan. Just not here in front of all these people." He winked at Jack haughtily and strode off. Jack hesitated in the truck for a moment, wondering if the boy meant it.

By now, the attention of the men surrounding the truck had turned to the group of villagers. Jack ignored the shouted questions of his comrades and slid out of the cab. He walked to the back of the truck and unlatched the gate. The dark, sparsely clothed islanders spilled out eagerly. The sight of their machetes and balls of crude twine elicited more questions from the group of American boys gawking at the strange scene. Jack wanted his project to remain secret as long as possible. He was taking great satisfaction from surprising and ultimately pleasing the men. The purpose for his gathering of the natives became known, though, just moments later. Ian strolled up, looked first at the natives, then at Jack, and at the natives again, finally fixing his gaze on Jack.

"What in bloody hell have you got cooking now, Jack?" Ian asked tersely.

Smiling, Jack replied, "It's a surprise, Doc."

Ian bristled, putting his hands on his hips, "Mate, there's a war going on around us, we don't have enough supplies and now there are a dozen natives with machetes standing outside my hospital. I'm not in the mood for surprises at the moment."

Jack's face reddened, once again set off balance by Ian's not giving him a pass in consideration of who he was and where he came from. He stammered, "Um . . . geez, sorry, Doc. You don't have to jump down my throat. I was just trying to add a little mystery or uh, um . . ."

"Just tell me what you're up to, mate," Ian interrupted. When Jack finished describing the project he'd planned, Ian's mood altered considerably. He smiled, slapped Jack on the back, and cheerfully ordered him to get to work. Turning his attention back to the project, Jack motioned the natives to follow him, then trudged to a muddy clearing twenty meters south of the tent. There he staked out the warehouse with small sticks to show the laborers where the walls were to be constructed. He borrowed Isaac's machete, hacked a small tree down, and trimmed it to a height of roughly ten feet. He stuck it in the ground at one corner of what was to be the warehouse. The islanders would use the pole as an indicator for how high to construct the walls. As Jack explained these things through Peter, the men and women before him only nodded, their ever-present smiles shining back at him. There was none of the chatter or endless questions that had been part of the process when addressing his well-educated office staff on a project. No ego games, politics, or petty bullshit. When he finished, the islanders simply waved and melted into the jungle. Jack stood in the mud, somewhat stunned. Shortly, he heard the sound of machetes striking wood and voices singing. Jack smiled when he recognized the song *What a Friend We Have In Jesus.* He sat on a fallen palm tree near the edge of the jungle and lit a cigarette. At that moment, it began to rain. The heavy downpour snuffed his cigarette out and drowned out the islander's melody. He considered taking refuge in the Cave but feared he might lose the respect of the

222

natives, so he stayed put. In what seemed just a few minutes the group walked out of the jungle carrying bundles of long sticks under their arms. After depositing them near the worksite they turned, waved again to Jack, and headed off down the road past the hospital. They appeared to be completely oblivious to the deluge. After a few moments confusion, Jack sprang up and jogged toward the group.

"Hey guys . . . hey, wait for me!" he shouted over the hissing rain. He caught up with Peter and asked him where they were going.

"Just a little ways down the road," Peter replied. "We saw a very fine field of grass from the truck. It is perfect for your medicines." He looked up at the sky, the rain bouncing off his face, then added, "Even very powerful rain such as this will be unable to touch your medicines, sir."

In a few minutes they arrived at the field the natives had spied from the truck. Acres of bright green, head-high grass stood dense and huddled, battered by the rain. The group began hacking at the base of the stalks and piled them on the road. Soon, a six-foot-high, thirty-foot-long mound of grass had been harvested. The natives gathered up bunches of grass and walked briskly back to the construction site. Jack gathered up his own bundle and struggled up the road. Unlike the bare feet of the islanders, the mud pulled at Jack's boots, making each step difficult. After several trips, Isaac indicated they had enough material. Slowly raising his hands from his sides and above his head like a preacher, he gave the order to commence construction of the warehouse. "Kirapim long wokim haus."

Moments later the rain stopped, leaving a steamy heaviness in the air. Jack worked alongside Peter, observing his techniques and doing his best to mimic them. The work was tedious and the heat was stifling. The breaths of air Jack gulped seemed to be imbued with solids. Salty drops stung his eyes and streams of sweat trickled uncomfortably down his back. Jack though, tolerated the heat much better now than he had several days prior at the 60th anniversary ceremonies on the ridge. While weaving a blade of grass between sticks, he looked in the direction of the ridge, for now, just outside the Marine's western perimeter. The area was devoid of manmade landmarks and the series of hills were covered with vegetation, so it was difficult to tell which hill was soon to become known as 73. It was there though, peaceful and quiet, largely unnoticed by the Marines or the Japanese. This, of course, would all change. He couldn't recall exactly when, but he thought it would be sometime in mid-October.

"Let's see," he whispered to himself, "its the 12th today . . . should be quiet when I go to the creek this evening." Jack cursed at a stubborn blade of grass then suddenly jerked his head up and looked north, toward the sea. "The 12th! Oh Jesus . . . goddamn it's August the 12th."

"Is there a problem, sir?" Peter asked.

Jack looked blankly at him for a moment, then replied, "Yeah . . . yeah there's something wrong. I've gotta go and try to fix it."

"Okay, sir, no problem," Peter said. "We'll be just fine here on our own. We should be done just before nightfall."

"Okay . . . okay, Peter . . . thanks," Jack replied in a daze. "If I'm not back, find Frank and he'll get the fish and rice for you." Jack jogged off in search of Ian. It was late afternoon, August 12, 1942, on Guadalcanal. A relatively quiet day punctuated at its end by a horror on the beach between Point Cruz and the Matanikau River. Jack had started when he suddenly realized that it was *Goettge patrol day*. He actually thought of it that way; this day was given to one thing in all the world, that being the slaughter of Colonel Goettge's foolish, slapdash patrol, several miles north and west of where he was standing.

Lt. Colonel Frank Goettge was the 1st Marine Division's intelligence officer. Having received a report from two captured Japanese naval ratings that a group of haggard Japanese soldiers were ready to surrender near Pt. Cruz, Goettege hastily assembled a 25 man patrol. They were lightly armed and would travel by sea in a ramp boat from Kukum village to the point, in hopes of bagging the prisoners for interrogation. Once landed, the group was mobile only in the sense of how fast they could walk or run. Goettge's planning and decision making regarding the patrol had always perplexed both Jack and esteemed military historians. First, why would he be so accepting of the enemy's story that he would only assemble a small force with very little firepower? Second, why did he come ashore at precisely the spot where earlier intelligence had indicated that a large, hostile force had assembled? Finally, he had no support if the patrol ran into trouble and no means of extraction. The ramp boat that had delivered them would be sent back to Kukum for the night. As Jack searched the hospital area for Ian, he recalled these things not with his normal historical curiosity, but with ever-rising anger and alarm. He had to do something to try to head off the slaughter of a platoon of his heroes. He found Ian in the Cave, lying on his bedroll doing paperwork.

Jack said breathlessly, "Doc, I've got to go somewhere in a hurry. Can I take the jeep?"

Ian looked up at Jack and after a slight hesitation said, "Crikey, mate, you look like you've seen a ghost. What's up?"

"I've got to go to Kukum right now! This is real important . . . there are lives at stake."

"Whoa there, mate. You'd better tell me what's going on."

Jack impatiently explained, "There's a 25 man Marine patrol leaving Kukum that's going to get ambushed near Pt. Cruz shortly after they land. The Japs are going to hack the wounded to death with sabers. It's a complete fuck-up and only three of the boys survive. I have to try to stop them from going. I can't remember for certain, but I think they're leaving at dusk."

Ian sprang up and quickly put his shirt and helmet on. "I'm not sure you trying to stop them is such a good idea, Jack, but we'll talk about it on the way." They ran to the jeep and sped off toward Kukum, Ian behind the wheel.

"Why in hell would you think this may be a bad idea?" Jack yelled over the roar of the jeep's engine.

"Well, first of all they may throw you in the nut house if you try to stop the patrol by telling them they'll all be killed. Then, what will you tell them when you turn out to be right? That it was a lucky guess? Or that you're a bloody time traveler and you know exactly what will happen on the island and when?"

"Well, maybe I should tell them, Doc." Jack shouted. "The thought scares the hell out of me . . . but it's not just this island, Doc, it's the whole war. I know what's going to happen during this war across the whole world." He laughed bitterly, "Jesus Christ, me, a middle-aged drunk from East Grand Rapids, could save millions of lives."

"You really need to think about that, mate. It sounds like a good idea, but I don't really think so," Ian said. "You know a lot more than just what's going to happen during the war. You know what's going to happen for the next 60 years. Are you sure that by apprising us of that information you'd make things better? Isn't it possible you could make things worse?" Jack paused and briefly considered Ian's comments. Then his mind was pulled back to the vision of Goettge's young Marines preparing at that very moment for their ill fated patrol.

Jack shrugged, "I don't know. I can't think about that just now. All I know is that I have to do something to try to stop this patrol . . . it's all I can do. I have to try, you understand?"

Ian squeezed Jack's shoulder, "I understand. We can discuss the bigger issues later, okay?"

"Sure, Doc . . . thanks."

They sped the rest of the way to Kukum in silence. When they pulled into the seaside village, Jack's stomach tightened and a deep frown creased his forehead as he immediately spotted a small group of Marines assembled on the beach, waiting to board a ramp boat. Standing on one of the wharves was a large, solid looking man with graying hair. He was speaking with a young Marine. "Goettge!" Jack gasped.

Ian followed his gaze and asked, "Is that the man you want to talk to?"

226

"Yeah," Jack rasped. The enormity of the situation made it difficult for Jack to find his voice. The sight of the patrol preparing to set out was both fascinating and horrifying at the same time. He wondered at the sight of the historic event, but was mortified over what was about to happen to all but 3 of the young Americans. He climbed out of the jeep and slowly walked toward the wharf. Beads of sweat began to form on his brow and roll down his cheeks. A wave of nausea churned in his stomach. The path to the wharf took him straight through the group of Marines clustered on the beach. Jack could not bear to look at their faces, but he heard their young, strong voices, joking and bantering about the usual things: girls, food . . . home. It was typical young American male banter, and it nearly broke his heart. Though he knew the odds of him dissuading Goettge were slim, the voices steeled him. He walked onto the wharf and approached the colonel. Goettge was in animated discussion with the Marine; waving his arms about. Jack stopped 5 feet short of them, took a breath and said, "Sir . . . Colonel, sir, may I have a word with you, sir?"

Goettge turned toward Jack; eyed him disdainfully for a moment, then barked, "Who are you?"

"Hospitalman Macmillan, sir; E Company, 1st Battalion Hospital at Henderson. I really need to have a word with you, sir."

Clearly annoyed Goettge snapped, "I'm just a little busy here, sailor, be quick about it." He turned to the Marine and ordered, "Sergeant, tell the men to prepare to board."

As the young sergeant brushed past him, Jack thought "Custer . . . Sergeant Custer . . . Goettge's aide." He, along with Goettge, would be the first to die if Jack failed to accomplish his mission.

"I assure you, sir, it's very important," Jack said.

"Go on then," Goettge said, impatiently giving Jack a backhanded wave.

Jack hesitated briefly, then decided it was best to just let the colonel have it, using his best military-speak. "Sir," he began, "with all due respect I urge you to stand down your force and delay your mission until further intelligence can be gathered regarding enemy deployment and field strength between the Matanikau and Pt. Cruz."

The colonel's brows rose in shock, but he quickly recovered and took several steps toward Jack. "And just why the hell would I or should I do that?" he hissed.

"Sir, if you take this patrol out, nearly all of your men will be slaughtered . . . including you, sir," Jack quietly explained. Goettge's face twisted in a look of mingled rage and amazement. The Marines on the beach had stopped their chatter, trying to hear the exchange. Goettge glanced back at them, then angrily grabbed Jack by the arm and pulled him farther down the wharf, away from the Marines.

"And just how in hell would you know that?" Goettge growled, barely containing his temper. Jack hesitated and felt Goettge's grip tighten painfully around his arm as he struggled to come up with an acceptable answer to the question. He glanced back at Ian standing near the jeep. Ian saw the look and immediately began to move toward the wharf. Jack stopped him with a vigorous shake of his head.

"Well, are you going to tell me, mister?" the colonel rumbled.

"I uh . . . I can't really, uh. Just please trust me. You have to trust me, sir. Please trust me."

"Listen, you rear area asshole!" Goettge yelled. "Get the hell out of here right now and stay the hell away from my brave boys, you crazy fucking bastard!" He dragged Jack roughly off the wharf, and shoved him up the beach so hard that he lost his balance and crashed to the sand. Loudly, so his men could hear, he yelled, "I'll deal with you when I get back, you goddamn lunatic!" He turned and stalked off toward the boat.

Jack slowly sat up in the sand and looked at the furious colonel. He replied quietly, "I'm not crazy, Colonel." Tears welled in his eyes as he added softly, "And, sir, you're not coming back, so you'll never ever 'deal' with me."

Jack watched helplessly as the patrol walked up the boat's ramp. One heavily freckled redhead stopped at the base of the ramp and turned toward him. Their eyes met and locked for several moments. The boy was not staring at Jack in amusement or sympathy, but with a strange intensity as if he was trying to see into Jack's soul. An order barked and the young man broke his gaze and clambered aboard. Having made the brief connection with the boy, Jack hoped he was one of the lucky three. The boat's engine growled to life and the boat slowly reversed off the beach. Ian knelt down next to Jack and put his arm around Jack's shoulders. "Sorry, mate," he said. "You did your best." As the boat turned west toward Pt. Cruz, Jack saw Goettge shoot him a last, hateful glare. The glare released all Jack's emotions and he sprang up, tears of rage and sadness rolling down his cheeks.

Quietly, at first, he hissed, "You fucking idiot . . . you stupid fucking idiot!" Then he raised his fist and shook it at the boat screaming, "You're a moron, Goettge! You just killed them, you son of a bitch. I'm glad you're going to die, you fucking asshole!" He rose and stomped toward the departing craft, continuing to rail at Goettge. He knew the colonel could not hear him over the roar of the boat's engine. Nevertheless, in his rage and grief he couldn't stop himself and continued screaming. A small crowd of villagers had gathered, curiously watching Jack's eruption. Finally, a nearby Marine officer shouted to Ian, "Get that man out of here and get him some help . . . now!"

Ian walked over and put his arm around Jack, gently guiding him toward the jeep. "Calm down now, mate," he said quietly, "you did everything you could." Ian's touch and words, as always, were soothing. They quickly extinguished Jack's outburst. The tears though, just like the other night in the bunker after the two boys died, flowed freely, unstoppable. He felt sick to his stomach. The slow drive back to the hospital was quiet. Ian seemed deep in thought. Jack's tears gradually dissipated and he stared blankly into the jungle. Again he was surprised that he could feel so much anger toward a Guadalcanal Marine. He had questioned Goettge's wisdom back in the world, but never his integrity. To Jack, he had still been a great man, having made the ultimate sacrifice fighting in the South Pacific. Now though, he seemed just another glory seeking, ego bloated, authority figure who was needlessly wasting young lives, lives that were very real to Jack now. His definition of hero had permanently been altered, and he was no longer curious regarding what war felt like. For now it seemed, it felt like murder.

When they arrived back at the hospital, Jack waited outside the Cave while Ian fetched a bottle of *sake*. Together, they walked toward the warehouse that the locals were constructing. When it came into view they marveled at the progress the villagers had made. The color of the building was deep green and the grass gave its walls and roof a texture so alluring that Jack felt an urge to rub his hands up and down its sides. The villagers appeared to be putting the finishing touches on the structure. The sight of the grass building improved Jack's mood, and for a moment he was able to put the patrol out of his mind. To Jack, the simple building was the most beautiful edifice he'd ever observed: more beautiful than Notre Dame in Paris or Westminster in London, grander than the Victor Emmanuel Memorial in Rome and nobler than Edinburgh Castle. The natives spotted him and asked in unison what he thought of their work.

"Beautiful!" Jack replied. "It's fantastic, people . . . excellent work!"

"Thank you, so much."

Ian chimed in with his appreciation while Peter happily translated. Jack walked toward one of the green walls. It was dense with woven grass and nowhere could Jack detect even the tiniest opening between the blades. He balled his hand into a fist and futilely tried to penetrate the grass wall. Peter was right he thought, the rain will only bounce and run off the peaked grass roof and the walls. He turned back toward Ian. As he did so, he noticed that Turk and Frank were standing near the warehouse entrance, trying to communicate with one of the natives. At their feet were 3 bags of rice and a dozen or so tins of fish. As Jack approached, both Turk and Frank turned to him smiling.

"These people did such a great job, Frankie and me decided to give them a fuckin' bonus," Turk said happily.

"Yeah," Frank added, "and boy do they deserve it." He grinned and shook his head. "Hardest working folks I've ever seen. They sing pretty good too . . . taught Turk and me some hymns."

"Hey, Jack," Frank said, "You should hear Turk sing *Amazing Grace*. Go on Turk, belt out a verse."

Jack smiled, "Not right now, guys." Though the building had lifted his gloom partially, he was still drained. Unlike a few hours ago, he wasn't in the mood for any lighthearted banter or horse-play. Turk, nevertheless, was apparently anxious to perform. Ignoring Jack's protests, he began to sing.

"Amazing Grace, how sweet the sound, that saved a wretch like me. I once was lost but now I'm found, was blind but now I see."

In an instant the crowd around the warehouse went silent. Jack listened in stunned awe. Turk's voice was rich and smooth, not the crude, gravelly baritone Jack would have expected. His sweet tenor wafted through the thick, hot air and lent a surreal quality to the gloaming. The hymn sounded unnaturally beautiful. And for the first time he not only heard, but *felt* the lyrics. The combination of both caused a lump to rise in his throat. He choked back tears, believing the small miracle to be a tribute in some way, to the young men dying at that moment near Pt. Cruz. After the first verse, Jack composed himself and looked at Frank wide-eyed. Frank, grinning proudly, winked at him and nodded his head slowly. When Turk finished, Frank slapped him on the back then led the group in a raucous round of applause.

"My gosh, Turk," Jack said, "Where in god's name did you learn to sing like that?"

Turk casually lit a cigarette and replied, "Fuck if I know."

Exasperated, Jack continued, "Well, have you been coached or taken voice lessons?"

"Yeah, that's right, I got me a fuckin' singing coach, in south Philly right around the corner on Mifflin street," Turk chortled. "I also got me my own massage girl to stroke my throat bones 'til they're all smooth and loose and shit. Makes the words come out real pretty."

"So you just naturally have this talent? I can't believe it."

"Hey I admit it, I like to sing, okay? Now quit givin' me the fuckin' business will ya? You're making me jumpy." Turk turned his back on Jack, puffing madly on his cigarette.

For a second, Jack was tempted to tell Turk then and there the depth of talent he possessed, and suggest he pursue it after the war. He decided though, that the rough and ready boy was probably embarrassed by his love for singing; tough Marines clumsily belted out bawdy ballads in dark, dingy barrooms. They did not sing opera sweetly or gospels with deep emotion. He decided to wait until they were alone together.

Jack took several moments to finish marveling at what he had just heard, then said, "Thanks for helping out guys, I appreciate it."

"Hey, no problem," Frank replied. "Turk and I had a ball and now we know how to build one of these things."

"So you guys helped them build it?"

"Sure," Turk grunted. "We ain't lazy ol' turds like yourself." Jack smiled and noted that Turk must be getting a bit bored as he had completed the statement without dropping one 'f-word.'

"Good one, you guys," Jack said. "I really appreciate it. Hey, can you two do me one more favor?"

"Depends on what it is," Turk replied warily.

"I was wondering if you guys wouldn't mind taking these people back to Ilu? Ian and I are going to meet to discuss supplies and such."

Turk snorted, "Oh, right . . . I guess that's why the lieutenant has that big fuckin' green bottle tucked up under his arm. I suppose you two are gonna extract the alcohol from it so we can use it in the hospital."

"Damn you're a sharp son of a bitch, Turk," Jack teased. "That is exactly what we're going to do."

Laughing, Frank interjected, "Of course we'll take them back. "They're our pals. Right, Turkey bird?"

Turk's head shot toward Frank so quickly that his cigarette inadvertently flew out of his mouth, causing Frank to duck. "I told you not to call me that, Cuntlip!"

It seemed that Jack, as he had in the truck departing Ilu, had suddenly gone invisible. Without a nod, the boys simply walked off to fetch the truck, all the while bickering back and forth about the insulting nicknames they'd bestowed on each other. Finally, Jack heard Frank rapidly screech, "Gobble, gobble!" Turk lunged toward his friend, but the diminutive boy was too quick. He took off down the road, Turk in lumbering, profane pursuit. From behind, Jack heard Ian yell, "Don't you dare hurt him, Turk!"

The boys returned with the truck several minutes later, chatting amiably; their dispute already forgotten. Ian motioned the villagers to the entrance of the warehouse. Once they were gathered, he thanked them warmly once again and announced, "I declare this bloody lovely structure shall be called the Emerald Palace!" At first, the natives were silent, but then Jack explained to Peter what an emerald and a palace were. Peter passed the meanings of the words on to the group and they all began to nod vigorously and smile at Ian and Jack, clearly pleased with the name. They then began to repeat the name over and over to each other, getting used to the sound of their new words. Finally, Jack led them to the truck where they started to load for the trip back to their village. Jack and Ian made it a point to shake the hand of each native and thank them again as they boarded the truck. The last to climb aboard was Peter. Jack shook his hand and rustled his coarse hair.

"Thanks, Peter, it was very good to get to know you," Jack said.

"You're welcome and thank you, sir," the boy replied. "Please, sir, a small favor?"

"No problem, what can I do for you, Peter?"

"If you see Mr. Clemens, please remind him that I am anxiously waiting for him. Please tell him he must come collect me as soon as possible. Okay, sir?"

"If I see him I will definitely give him the message."

"Thank you very much, sir," Peter replied. "You are very kind and great sir." Jack chuckled uncomfortably due to the boy's highly deferential manner when talking to him.

"Call me Jack . . . or Mr. Macmillan if you wish; whatever, but I'm no sir, okay?"

"Okay, Mr. Macmillan," Peter replied. As the truck pulled away in the rapidly fading light, Jack and Ian stood in the road waving. The natives eagerly waved back until the truck rounded the bend. Ian suggested they go inside the warehouse and christen it with the bottle of *sake.*

"I don't suppose it does any good to try to break this bottle on woven grass, mate; we'd be here for bloody eons," Ian rationalized. "I think our only recourse is to drink the stuff."

Jack nodded in agreement, "Sounds logical."

They opened the bottle and each took an extra long slug. Jack lit two cigarettes and a candle. They sat silently on the dirt floor surveying the interior of the warehouse; its grass walls and roof now turned a hue of brownish-orange by the candle. The color made the large blades of grass look as if they were dried cornstalks. They reminded him of the purple, brown, and golden displays of dried corn hung on many front doors back home in October, his and Laura's favorite month of the year. He lovingly recalled the chaotic, joyous Halloween nights that closed out the month. He enjoyed watching Grace and Joey, costumed and giddy as they prepared to trick-or-treat up and down the quiet streets of their neighborhood. He wondered if he would still be on the island on October 31st, helping patch up broken and torn marines, while his kids sallied forth on their treasure hunt. He tried to imagine how Laura would costume them this year, and who would help the kids carve their pumpkins; that had always been his job. He wondered if Joey would go as a soldier or a fireman, his usual preferences. The thought of his son in his miniature combat uniform unexpectedly conjured up a picture of the young redhead he had locked mournful eyes with on the beach at Kukum. All of a sudden, in his wasted mind, the picture changed. The young man heading up the boat ramp was now his son, plastic rifle, grenades and all. Joey was waving goodbye to him, his face alight with his goofy boy smile; as all the while Col. Goettge barked at him to hurry up. Jack moaned softly, buried his head in his hands, and wept. Not the convulsing sobs of the bomb shelter, or the enraged cries on the beach at Kukum, but a soft, gentle weeping. Ian, his arms wrapped around pulled up knees, quietly puffed on his cigarette in between gulps of wine. Save for Jack's muffled weeping, the new warehouse was quiet for several minutes. Finally, it was Jack who broke the silence.

"Jesus, I'm sorry again, Doc," he croaked. "I guess I'm turning into a real nancy boy. Christ, how many times is it now that I've bawled?"

"Don't be bloody silly, mate; we've had this discussion," Ian replied firmly. Ian paused then quietly asked, "Was it the patrol that got you going?"

"Partly," Jack said. He told Ian about the haunting eye-lock he'd had with the redhead, and how in his mind, he'd suddenly morphed into Joey. "Goddamn I miss my kids. I guess they're one of the reasons it was so hard to see those youngsters board that landing craft, you know?" He sighed and added, "I wish I were as strong as you, Doc."

"As strong as me you say? Bloody Christ, when are you going to quit underestimating yourself? To be honest it's getting bloody annoying. A weak man wouldn't be dealing with your situation in the manner you are. A weak man wouldn't have confronted Biggs. And you know what else? I bloody wish I could cry; I do. I haven't cried since they took me from my parents. I'm not sure why exactly. I guess something that horrible hasn't happened to me since, so a standard of sorts has been set for my tear makers, or some bloody such thing." Ian took a long pull off his cigarette and added, "Besides, for a man to cry when he feels very sad or angry isn't necessarily a sign of frailty; but a man who cannot cry during these times has a weakness in his character; that's me I reckon."

"Oh, c'mon, Doc," Jack said. "That's bullshit and you know it!" Jack eagerly seized the opportunity for once to be the one doing the bucking up. Ian just shook his head though, and waved Jack off.

"Just do me one favor, mate," Ian said, changing the subject. "If you feel the old tears getting ready to make another appearance and there are Marines around, pretend you don't know me, okay?"

Jack chuckled. "Okay, Doc, no problem." He lit another cigarette and decided he wasn't going to let his friend off the hook that easily. "You want to talk about it, Doc, about when they took you from your family?"

"Oh . . . there's not much to talk about, mate. Mostly, I try not to think about it. I think it would bloody well eat me up if I did. They just came one day . . . the government people. They said they were taking me for my own protection, that my mother and father didn't have the proper means of support to raise me in an acceptable fashion. It was bloody rubbish of course. I had light skin was all . . . the bastards. That was it, I never saw them again. I was luckier than others though, I suppose. At least I ended up in a home with decent people. They raised me as their own son and made sure I received a good education and the like. I suppose I love them, but I've never thought of them as my parents, just good people who raised me in a caring and proper manner."

"How is it you came to be a doctor?"

"The government wanted Abo docs to treat assimilated Abo's living western style in the cities. I qualified academically and I'd always been interested in medicine, so I was accepted. For some reason though, it never has been explained to me, they shipped me off to 'Blighty' for med school."

"Jesus Christ," Jack said. "What the hell do you do with your anger? Do you ever feel like you want to get revenge or something?"

"What's the point in letting anger eat you up. I've seen what that's done to some of my people, and it's never a nice picture. As for revenge? In a way I guess, I am going to seek some of that. When this bloody war's over I'm going back to my people, my real people, and live with them in the hills north of Adelaide. I'll use my medical skills to improve their lot, and my abiding belief in the Dreamtime to do all I can to preserve and restore my people's ways, not eradicate them like you whites, sorry, the Europeans, have tried to do. It's the best revenge I can think of."

Jack paused, then said, "I couldn't agree more, Doc. You have a hell of a lot to give to your people, Christ, any people for that matter. You've really been given a gift you know, and I can't think of a better way to use it."

"Thanks, mate. I must admit to you though that there are times I feel quite guilty about being here, participating in a war that has little or nothing to do with my people. Fighting alongside white men against a culture I have little knowledge of."

"Well, if it makes you feel any better you can bet the Japs would just love to get their hands on the riches your lands hold, and I doubt they'd be too polite in the process of seizing them. Things will come to light after the war about the lovely things the bastards did in China, the Philippines, the prison camps. It's not a pretty story."

"Yeah," Ian replied. "That's what I figured. I guess it's the lesser of two evils in a way. Seems like that's the choice a bloke has to make too bloody often in this world."

"Yeah . . . choices," Jack muttered. "You want to hear something really weird about choices?"

"Sure."

"Well, when I was driving along in the truck this morning, it suddenly dawned on me that I'm satisfied here, hell more satisfied than I've ever been in my life, in spite of the fact that I keep bawling like a baby." Jack continued, "I have experienced some hellish stuff, stuff I could never before have imagined. But even with all that, I don't know; I guess I feel that I'm not wasting myself. It's hard to explain but, and I feel like a shit for saying it, I'm fairly certain now that I'd choose to be here rather than back home with my family. How is that for a fucked up choice?"

Ian lay back on the ground and looked up at the grass ceiling, puffing slowly on his cigarette. After a few moments he said, "I can't know if it's an odd choice; bloody Christ, I'm not in your head, Jack. But I think I can safely say you shouldn't think you're a shit for feeling the way you do. Who knows, in your subconscious this might be some sort of penance."

"Penance," Jack muttered. He fingered his cigarette and took a drink of wine. His mind wandered to Tom hunkered down in a foxhole a couple miles to the southeast. He thought about his father's confusing life choices. He was silent for several minutes then suddenly blurted, "My father wanted, or wants to be, a doctor, a goddamn pediatric surgeon. Can you believe that?"

"Why is that so remarkable?" Ian asked.

"You should see him talk about it," Jack said. "You wanna' see purpose and passion? Talk to Tom about his future. The crazy thing is though, he isn't gonna be a doctor. He isn't even gonna go to college. He's gonna be successful alright, at least by most people's measures, but he'll never be a doctor. He's never gonna be what he's dreaming of being right now."

"Wasn't he passionate about his business?" Ian asked. "You said he was very attached to it and was very angry with you when you sold it, right?"

Jack thought for a moment, "In a way I guess; he cared deeply about his employees. Looking back, if he had a passion they were it, or at least they were what kept him going, kept him from complete despair. The way he treated them really didn't make good business sense, but somehow the company always put out great products on time and everything. When the more sophisticated multi-nationals started low-balling us, I think he mainly focused on keeping the business healthy enough to survive; profit generation or growth was definitely not a priority. He wouldn't compete head on, not wanting or needing to win, you know?

"Tell me, mate, in your opinion would the business have survived if you hadn't sold it?"

238

Jack squeezed his eyes shut tightly. "Yeah, if I'd run it like the old man it could have gone on forever. Hell, we had the best quality in all aspects of the business and there were hundreds of customers who'd never dream of leaving us. That's why the thing was so goddamn valuable. Problem is, I had no interest in running it like my dad did; not to mention the fact that I didn't have the same skill set he had."

"So that's why you sold the company?" Ian asked gently.

Jack opened his eyes and stared at the glowing candle for a moment, then said somberly, "You know, and this is going to sound strange, but I can't completely recall what drove me to so quickly sell the company. Hell, I knew Dad was horrified at the prospect, but I just kind of ignored that." Jack paused and sighed deeply, "God help me, it was a hell of a lot of money . . . 43 years old and not a care in the world."

"Well, who knows, mate" Ian said soothingly. "It's very possible you did precisely the right thing." Jack nodded slowly. Ian changed the focus of the discussion back to Jack's father. "So Tom was making and selling the materials that doctors would use while they were living *his* dream, right?" Ian asked. "He actually sold stuff directly to the sort of people he'd wanted to be?"

"Uh, what? Uh, yeah I guess . . . yeah that's right, except he didn't sell directly to them. He sold mainly to buyer types working for the big distributors."

"Wow," Ian said, "that would be pretty tough. Every day would be a reminder of your lost dream."

Jack and Ian went silent for several minutes, caught up in their own thoughts about Tom's future. Finally Ian said, "Do you have any idea why he didn't become a doctor?"

"None . . . I didn't even know he wanted to be one until yesterday," Jack replied flatly. He was in something of a daze. It was partially brought on by the wine, but mostly by a clear realization dawning after 40 years. After the war his father had lived his whole life with his shattered dream laid before him every day.

"You know, Jack," Ian continued, his voice slightly slurred. "You and your father really are a lot alike. I mean, it's not like you plan it that way or even ever talk about it . . . it just happens. I suppose it's probably genetic or some kind of . . ."

"What in the hell are you talking about, Doc?" Jack snapped. He snorted, shook his head and continued, "I'm about as different from my father as anyone could be. Jesus, Doc, maybe I need to cut off the *sake*."

For a time Ian said nothing, though secretly, Jack was eagerly waiting. Ian lit a cigarette and smoked it to a stub; then turned to Jack and said, "Jack, there's only one difference between you and your father that I can tell."

"Oh yeah, Doc?" Jack said, shifting uneasily, "And what would that be?"

"You got lucky and he didn't."

"Oh Christ! He could've sold the company any time and he didn't. It's not luck what I did with the company, it was good business."

"No, no, no, mate," Ian chided. "Not the bloody money and such stuff. Remember the Dreamtime and its values? That is all a society needs to live meaningful, happy lives."

"Well, that stuff as you call it, is a big part of life back in my world, so it obviously has some value for a lot of people when it comes to happiness," Jack grumbled. His tone belied irritation, but he avoided Ian's eyes.

"For some people, eh?" Ian asked. "How about for you?"

Jack took a hit from the bottle. He was annoyed by Ian's pestering. However, the good doctor had started a ball rolling that Jack couldn't ignore. "I don't know what you're trying to say, Doc . . . I'm confused."

"You told me a few minutes ago that you're happier here than any other time in your life," Ian reasoned. "You told me that you would rather be here on this stinking, miserable island instead of back in the world with all your bloody fancy stuff, right?

"Yeah, so?"

"Put two and two together, mate."

"Yeah . . . I guess . . . I . . . aw give it up, Doc. I'm not like my father. I mean, I retired at 43, I have a beautiful wife and kids, and I live in a great part of the country. Who the hell really knows why I seem to be happier here. Maybe it's just the chance to witness history, an adventure of sorts; you know, I'm getting a big kick out of it." As soon as the words came out of his mouth, he was confounded by the fact that he couldn't make any sense of what he'd just said. So, when Ian guffawed somewhat rudely, he wasn't too surprised.

"Oh yeah right-o, mate, and that's why you keep bawling when bad things happen . . . bad things that happen to people other than yourself or your family. You were dead back in the world, Jack. I've seen men like you in Sydney and London. I could see it in their faces and how they valued others, valued themselves. It's the opposite of a physical death. Their bodies are alive, but their souls are dead. Here, before your actual physical death, you've been given a second chance for your soul to live and flourish . . . to give all of yourself to something, not just mindlessly take. You are very fortunate. Don't close your mind and somehow try to make your prior existence something it was not. Let it go, mate."

Jack sat up, folded his arms across his knees and rested his forehead upon them. He slowly rocked to and fro, due partly to the *sake* and partly to the conflicting thoughts crisscrossing his tired mind. "Doc, you're a clever son of a bitch, but that doesn't mean you're always right."

"Perhaps not, but the Dreaming teaches us well," Ian replied, patting Jack on the shoulder.

"Fuck, fuck, fuck, fuck, fuck," Jack groaned slowly. "I'm like my father, huh? Shit, I don't know," Jack muttered wearily. He stared blankly at the floor, completely spent. He was too sad . . . too sad for the dead Marines near Pt. Cruz, too sad for his father. "I'm tired, Doc. I've had enough."

Ian patted him on the shoulder, "Sorry if I pushed you too far, mate."

"Nah," Jack replied, "you didn't go too far. Maybe you went a little too fast though."

As Jack stood up to leave, Ian stopped him, "Just one more thing before we bunk down. Remember our discussion on the way to Kukum? Have you thought about it at all . . . whether you should tell people what or who you are . . . you know, tell them what the future holds."

"Yeah, I thought about it after my little chat with shithead Goettge." Jack was still shocked and saddened by the experience at Kukum, and he still felt a strong resentment toward the colonel. Jack knew it was very likely that Goettge on the whole had been a good, intelligent man who'd simply made a mistake. For now though, he could only consider Col. Goettge with utter contempt.

"Well?" Ian asked, interrupting Jack's tired thoughts. "Am I supposed to ask you twenty bloody questions or something? What have you decided?"

"It's actually quite simple," Jack said wearily. "I know you don't want to know about the future, but I'm going to tell you a little story as an example. The Soviet Union is going to peacefully collapse, politically that is, in 1989. It'll be replaced by a democracy, or at least something akin to that. The collapse of the regime is basically the death knell for communist ideology around the world. Now say I tell the world this. What is that crazy fucker Stalin going to do when he gets this information . . . particularly after he learns he's going to croak in 1953? They'll have nukes long before 1953, so it could get real nasty. My coming out could literally blow up the world which, me thinks, makes the idea of coming out not such a good one."

"Makes sense," Ian said with obvious satisfaction, "but what the bloody hell is a nuke? Sounds like a type of flipping fish or something; the commies planning to attack with bloody fish then? Does evil know no bounds?"

Chuckling, Jack replied, "Nukes are definitely not fish, Doc. You don't want to know what they are, trust me, and you'll find out soon enough. The second reason I need to keep quiet is the very

242

simple fact that in spite of my rather supernatural appearance here, I ain't God, in fact I've never wanted to be God . . . though Frank did say he thinks I'm a bit grandiose at times . . . hmm." He rubbed his chin for affect.

Ian laughed, "It's definitely time for us to get some sleep, mate. I think we're getting a might punchy." He blew out the candle and, with arms draped over each other's shoulders, they trudged off to the Cave. In spite of his exhaustion, Jack decided to make a journal entry. He wanted to record the events of the day while they were still fresh. Once in the Cave, Jack fumbled around in his bedroll for the book, found it, then walked back to the Palace. He lay prone on his stomach and re-lit the candle. As he would in the days that followed, Jack launched his journal entry with a brief description of his day, followed by a detailed account of the day's events. In closing, he would record his private thoughts and include a brief agenda for the following day. Squinting hard to ward off his sleepiness, he opened the book and immediately began to write.

August 12, 1942—Guadalcanal

My fourth day on the island . . .

   . . . Missing Laura and the kids terribly—can't help but wonder how they're coping if I have actually gone missing back in the world. Hell, maybe I haven't; maybe there's two of me now; who knows? Jack '42 and Jack '02. It's too damned incredible this thing. Mustn't think about it for long or I get confused, frustrated—too agitated. How I came to be here is secondary to the fact that I am indeed . . . here. Whatever, too damn tired to think deeply about much of anything right now. . . .

   . . . Tomorrow—quick trip to asshole Biggs' supply depot in the a.m. to pick up more surgical gloves, (some jerk stole ours today, the nerve). Then, hospital shift and trip to the creek to see Dad. Also dreading the search, but

for some reason I feel a strong need to know if a redhead Marine I locked eyes with at Kukum was one of the three survivors from patrol. If not, I think those eyes will haunt me the rest of my days.

He folded the book shut and blew out the candle. His body and mind were heavy with an exhaustion of the like he'd never before felt and the Cave seemed miles away. He crossed his arms in the dirt beneath his face, then laid his head upon them. In 20 seconds he was sound asleep on the floor of the Palace. He slept so deeply that not even 'Louie the Louse' on his nightly sojourn stirred him.

15

Jack awoke an hour after dawn stiff, his middle age muscles aching from his work on the warehouse. As he finished a breakfast of boiled oats and glutinous prunes, he looked up at the sound of an approaching jeep. It pulled up next to the hospital 30 yards away and for a moment Jack's stomach tensed as he recognized the driver. At the same time he felt a burst of joy. He watched as his father hopped out of the jeep and half walked, half jogged into the hospital. Jack quickly rinsed his mess tin in already polluted water and followed him into the tent. Upon entering, he saw Tom talking to Ian. They were discussing the fact that Tom suspected a Marine in his unit had cracked several ribs. Tom was explaining how the injury occurred.

"Dumbass is from Ohio, right?" Jack heard Tom say. "Shit, I guess that explains most of it right there. In fact, I'm not calling him 'Dumbass' because he did this one foolish thing and hurt himself. Dumbass is actually his name, or at least his Marine name. If somebody tries using his real name nobody's gonna know who the fuck they're talking about. He's just Pvt. Dumbass, from Columbus fucking Ohio."

Jack, standing behind Tom, laughed out loud. He was still highly amused by his father's uncharacteristic and liberal use of profanity. It was the story of Pvt. Dumbass' origins though, that really got Jack laughing. Now that's the old man, Jack thought. The man—who had once boycotted California wine because of some affront by that state, real or imagined—had a way of categorizing whole groups of people, the vast majority of whom he would never meet. These categories were generally based on where a person was from or what they ate. For instance, he had often stated with deep conviction that vegetarians were not to be trusted. He was never able to explain why exactly, or for that matter, what those who eschewed meat might have in store for the world. He also had a thing about France, not wholly unusual, particularly amongst World War II vets. Tom's distaste for them though, was stronger than most; in part at least having to do with some business transactions he'd engaged in with them over the years. Jack chuckled to himself, recalling a time when he was a teen. His mother had harshly scolded his father at the dinner table after he'd referred to the French as 'the prostitutes of the world', and the country itself as 'a vast brothel'. His father hadn't a racist bone in his body, though in ways such as these he could certainly be described a bigot. Jack had always assumed it was an idiosyncratic need the old man had of keeping things neat and tidy when it came to understanding people with customs and experiences different from his own. What better way, his old man apparently believed, than classifying people by where they were from and what they ate. There was no real hostile intent in his father's oddities, and they no longer sparked shame or derision in Jack, but endearment and affection, a strange sort of pride. When Tom turned to find the source of the laugh, Jack's face shone with a grin that on a middle aged man could only be described as goofy.

"Hey, Macmillan!" Tom barked. "How the fuck you doing?" He thrust his hand out and they engaged in a warm handshake.

"I'm doing just fine, Macmillan," Jack replied.

"Hey, I missed you last night," Tom said. "You out gettin' laid or something?"

Jack was briefly taken aback by his father's crude question; he couldn't have imagined him saying such a thing back in the world. After a pause he replied, "Don't I wish. Naw, I had some unexpected business to take care of. How does this evening work for you?"

"Perfect! I'll make reservations at a nice little spot I know. Half past 6 okay for you?"

Jack eagerly said, "Outstanding, I'll bring my . . .

A loud, rolling cough interrupted him. "Gentlemen . . . I'm very sorry to disrupt the scheduling of your social calendars, but I'm bloody busy here," Ian said wryly. "Tom, finish telling me how Dumbshit, or whoever the bloody hell, got hurt, and I'll tell you how you should treat him or whether he needs to come here. After that, Jack can help you collect the supplies you've come here to get. Is that too much for you chaps?"

"Sorry, sir," Tom replied. "It's just that Jack here's my boy." Ian blinked rapidly several times at Tom's pronouncement and avoided eye contact with Jack. Tom added, "After all, he's not only a Michigan man, but he also has a superior last name."

"Okay, whatever . . . now finish telling me how your bloke got hurt."

"Okay, sir," Tom said. "Like I said, Dumbass is a *dumb ass*, right? We're sitting around last evening after chow, bored as hell, when ol' Dumbass suddenly comes up with a brilliant idea as to how to make a little money by way of wager." Tom paused for effect as well as to make sure his audience was paying attention. "The goddamn genius asks Murphy to grab a baseball . . . a few of the guys had been playing catch before chow . . . and they walk to a clearing near the tree line behind our position. Murph, you see, played minor league ball somewhere in Pennsylvania . . . Scranton, I think. They say he was a pretty damn good pitcher and if it weren't for the war he might be in the 'bigs' by now. Goddamn war fucks everything up, you know? In fact, Lieutenant Grimes and I were talking just this morning about the . . ."

"Please, Tom, please," Ian interrupted. "Just tell me what happened."

"Oh yeah, sorry, sir. Anyhow," Tom continued, "Dumbass apparently has, or maybe I should say had, this theory that pitchers can't hit a moving target on account they spend their whole lives trying to throw a ball over a stationary plate. So, he bets

Murph he can't hit him with that goddamn ball from 60 feet away. Murph takes the bet without hesitation. The catch in Dumbass' favor you see, or so he thinks, is that he'll be trotting along the edge of the tree line making it impossible for Murph to plunk him."

Jack's and Ian's smiles widened and they started chuckling, knowing full well how the story was to end. Tom, buoyed by the laughter, became more animated and gestured wildly with his hands. "Well, of course, all the boys are getting in on the action and money's changing hands all over the place and it's starting to look like Louis and Schmeling, you know?" Tom said. "So Dumbass walks about 30 paces to the side and Murph backs up sixty feet. Then Dumbass yells to Murph, 'Hey Murph, you big loser! Tell me when you're ready!'"

Tom then went into a pitcher's pre-windup stance. "After a few seconds, Murph shouts real cool, real calm like, 'I'm ready . . . shit-for-brains.' At that, Dumbass starts loping along the edge of the grove looking straight fucking ahead. He never looks at Murph, not once. It's like he's thinking if he doesn't look at Murph, then maybe Murph won't see him or something." Tom rocked back and lifted an imaginary ball, covered by an imaginary glove, over his head, then raised his front leg and said, "Anyhow, Dumbass is still running along the tree line and Murph goes into this gorgeous fucking wind up." Tom burst forward on his back leg and hurled the imaginary ball. "Well, Murph lets loose a fucking cannon shot and the second that ball left his hand, we all knew, we just knew right away, that poor Dumbass was in trouble. I even think I heard some of the boys who'd bet against Murph groan at that point; no shit, it was weird." Tom, clearly enjoying his performance continued, "Anyhow, that goddamn ball had eyes for poor old Dumbass. It was like the perfect BB shot and we all watched as the fucker slammed into his rib cage. When it did, the poor bastard let out this scream that was kinda half-pain and half-shock, you know?"

Shaking his head and smiling, Tom added, "He hit the ground like a sack of potatoes, boy." Then, Tom's face suddenly fell. "Poor sucker . . . I guess I should have stopped it me being a corpsman and all. Hell, all he was trying to do was lighten things up."

"Boys will be boys, mate," Ian chimed, wiping a tear from his eye. "Not one bloody thing in the world is ever going to change that fact. You check for any protrusions or indentations in the ribcage?"

"Yes, sir," Tom replied. "I didn't find anything."

"Does his breathing sound okay?"

"Clear as a bell, and he hasn't complained about any breathing difficulties, just that, in his words, 'it hurts like a goddamn motherfucking motherfucker son of a fucking bitch.'"

"My gosh, Doc," Jack blurted, "Turk's got a brother and he's here on the island!"

Ian laughed, "Bloody hell, anyone who can curse that exquisitely is a genius on some level."

Tom nodded in agreement, "Hmm . . . good point, sir."

"Okay," Ian said. "There's not much you can do for cracked ribs. They'll heal themselves fairly quickly and his pain will pretty much be gone in a few days. Give him some aspirin and tell him to use his bloody head in the future."

"Shit, Lieutenant," Tom joked as he and Jack headed toward the door, "if I tell him *that*, he'll bet Murph that he can't hit him in the head at 20 paces." Tom and Jack walked to the back of the tent to get the supplies Tom needed. While they unstacked and opened crates of atabrine, salt pills, and bandages, Jack proudly pointed the Emerald Palace out to him and told him the story of its construction. "Next time you come for supplies, we'll get them out of there."

"Great," Tom said politely. "Good job."

"Thanks." They finished loading an empty crate with the pills and dressings. Jack walked Tom to his jeep.

"See you tonight, okay?" Jack asked.

"You bet," Tom replied. "You sure you know where we are?"

"Yeah, I'm pretty sure. I know the Tenaru pretty well." He didn't tell his father that he'd already spied on him at the location.

"Okay, see you tonight."

"See you then," Jack replied. He watched Tom's jeep speed away until it disappeared around the bend. After the happy encounter in the tent between he, Ian, and Tom, Jack was even more excited about the day ahead.

He went back inside to let Ian know he was leaving for the supply depot and to see if the doctor needed any additional supplies. Ian didn't require anything else but cautioned him, "Now don't go tweaking the nose of that asshole at the depot, okay?"

In mock indignation, Jack put his hand on his chest and said dramatically, "Moi? Surely you jest Monsieur Cap-e-tain."

Ian smirked and shook his head, "You are an odd old bloke." He motioned toward the jeep, "On your way then."

Jack mounted the parked jeep and roared off at breakneck speed toward the depot still operating on the beach. He wondered when it would move inland to the airport. He couldn't recall, or never knew, when all the supply depots were moved off the beach and functioning in the vicinity of Henderson, but he figured it couldn't be too much longer. Five minutes or so after he left the hospital, he skidded to a halt outside Biggs' tent. As he leapt from the jeep, he saw Wimpy scurrying toward the tent door, all the while nervously glancing back at him. Jack followed him into the tent and saw Biggs and Wimpy in whispered conversation. When Biggs saw Jack, he whispered one more thing to the chubby boy and pushed him toward the door. As he brushed past, Jack noticed that the young man's face was taut.

Biggs took several steps toward Jack, a sneer on his face. "What the hell are you doing here, asshole?" he hissed.

As cheerily as possible, Jack replied, "Just here for some surgical gloves, sir."

"Yeah?" Biggs asked. "You plan on stealing anything this time?"

"I'm just here for the gloves, sir."

As Jack heard the door of the tent open behind him, Biggs' sneer turned to a hateful glare and he said, "We're clean out of gloves today mister. But I do have something special just for you."

250

Two men, Jack recognized them from his previous visits, suddenly appeared on either side of him, while several others in the tent beat hasty retreats out the door. Both men appeared very young, teenagers Jack thought. One was handsome, with sandy hair and deep blue eyes. The other was almost impossibly ugly with stained, crooked teeth, narrow eyes, a pug nose and matted black hair. Both were several inches shorter than Jack but the constant lifting of crates had studded their arms and chests with thick muscles. One of the men, the handsome one, wore a sneer on his face much like Biggs, his fists tightly clenched. The other though was fidgety, and seemed unable to look directly at Jack. Jack looked back at Biggs quizzically, concerned, but not frightened.

"Last time you were here I told you I'd take care of you later, right?" Biggs growled. "Well, it's later, asshole."

Jack looked at the two boys, then back at Biggs. Smiling nervously, he said, "What're you gonna do, Einstein, have these boys beat me up or something?" The words had just left his mouth when he heard a thunderous crack, followed instantly by a searing pain in his left ear. The blonde-haired boy had viciously slapped the side of his head with an open palm. The intense, fiery pain drove Jack to his knees. He felt no anger or fear, only a vague sense of confusion. He looked up at the boy who had dealt the blow and saw the boy's fist come crashing down toward his face. It seemed to be moving in slow motion, like a bullet filmed flying through the air in a modern Hollywood production. Jack could see it clearly, inching ever closer; but for some reason it seemed he couldn't move. He could move just fine of course, it's just that his mind was warping time. In fact, the fist smashed into his jaw a fraction of a second after it had been loosed, leaving Jack no time to react. The wicked punch knocked him to the floor and rattled his senses. His vision blurred, and it felt as if his body movements were impeded by heavy weights. Moments later, his head began to clear, but he was still in agony from the ear slap, and now the lower half of his face throbbed. He looked up to see the fuzzy figures of the two boys and Biggs hovering over him. The puncher was cackling away at Jack, but due to the roaring in his ears he couldn't decipher what the boy was saying; he was merely aware of the mocking tone. Biggs was smiling down at Jack, hands on hips, while the ugly soldier stood several steps back, a blank expression on his face. Jack still felt no fear and his confusion was slowly clearing.

Struggling to his knees, Jack rasped at Biggs, "You fucking coward!" At that, the blonde grabbed his shirt collar with one hand and pulled him to his feet. In almost the same motion he swung his other hand in a violent under-handed arc toward Jack's midsection. Unlike the ear slap and jaw-punch, this blow landed just below his ribcage quietly, as if the attacker had slammed a bag of sand. Once again, the blow sent Jack tumbling to the floor. The pain radiated out from the point of impact to all parts of his body, and he gasped loudly for air. Then, as Biggs watched, the two boys began to pummel him with their boondockers. His head, back, legs, and sides absorbed the kicks equally. The violence and chaos of the latest assault disoriented him to the point that he was no longer able to determine exactly what was happening. He was, however, able to discern that the ugly boy's blows were half-hearted and painless, unlike his comrades. Finally, after a half-minute or so, but what seemed like hours to Jack, Biggs called off the attack and knelt down beside him.

"Oh my," he said with mock concern, "you're a mess. You'd better go see a doctor, my friend. Know any good ones?" Tucked up in the fetal position, Jack's entire body ached and he could feel warm trickles of blood rolling slowly down the side of his face. Blood pooled in the little cup that the downward facing cheek formed inside his mouth. He heard painful, almost surreal groans emanating from somewhere in the tent, and for a moment he thought he was back at the hospital. Then, he realized the groans were coming from him.

"I hope you've learned your lesson, because I'd hate to have to fuck you up again," Biggs threatened.

Jack slowly turned his head toward him and painfully gasped, "You didn't fuck me up . . . your lackeys did."

"If we ever meet again I suspect you'll show me a little more respect and keep that shitty little mouth of yours in check, won't you old man?" In spite of his agony and rising anger, Jack nearly smiled at the irony in Biggs' ignorant comment for, in fact, Jack had just insulted him again, seconds before.

"Get this turd off my floor, men," Biggs ordered. As the two boys half-carried, half-dragged Jack toward the door Biggs shouted, "Oh, and tell your nigger doctor, or whatever the hell he is, to send someone else next time; you and I just don't seem to be getting along." After the two boys propped Jack behind the wheel of his jeep, the blonde, smirking, turned and headed back to the tent. The other boy lingered for a moment, wringing his hands. Just as he began to speak, Jack leaned over the edge of the jeep and vomited in the sand.

"Oh, shit," the boy said in a heavy Carolina drawl. "Jesus . . . I hope you're gonna be okay." He took a hanky from his back pocket and first wiped the vomit from around Jack's mouth then dabbed at the blood on his face and lips. "I'm real sorry about this, bud. I . . . uh . . . I didn't want to be a part of this but Captain Biggs said he'd have me on every shit detail for the rest of the war if I didn't go along. He'd do it too, believe me . . . son of a bitch has to be one of the meanest, most selfish, most goddamn foulest bastards that's ever walked this earth." After a pause he added, "I'm really sorry. Jesus, I guess in some ways you paid the price for me being too scared to stand up to that asshole. I'm sorry."

Jack nodded weakly, "Gotta go."

"Okay," the boy replied. "Take it easy driving bud; you're in pretty bad shape."

Without looking at the boy, Jack mumbled, "No shit." He started the jeep and drove off slowly down the beach. He was still a bit dizzy and nauseous from the beating, and his head and body ached. He never went much over 15 mph on his way back to the hospital as the bumps were too painful. As he passed soldiers along the beach and then cut up through the jungle, they'd glance at Jack, stop what they were doing, then stare until his bloody and bruised face was no longer visible. Jack was slightly embarrassed, but mostly he was feeling hatred toward Biggs; a hatred the intensity of which he'd never felt before. He was angry too, angry at the beating he'd just suffered and angry that he hadn't procured the surgical gloves. As well, he worried that Ian would decide that his supply days were over. When the jeep finally approached the Cave at the end of Jack's journey, standing on the side of the road watching him drive up was Ian himself. Smiling and waving at Jack as he approached, Ian stepped forward to greet him. As he did his smile disappeared and was slowly replaced by a deep frown.

"Bloody Christ!" he shouted. "What the hell happened?"

Jack slowly braked the jeep to a halt and muttered, "Fell down the goddamn stairs, Doc." Ian helped Jack painfully clamber out of the jeep. He led him into the hospital and laid him on one of the makeshift operating tables. He dabbed at Jack's wounds with a wet cloth, then checked for loose teeth and broken bones. While Ian was doing this, Jack told him the whole story, including the fact that he had lied to Ian about how things had gone on his previous visit to Biggs. He explained how he had received the blood plasma by threatening him, and how Biggs had told him that he would 'get him later.'

"Damn it, Jack!" Ian barked. "I told you not to lie to me! And just what in the bloody hell were you thinking threatening an officer like that?"

"I got the supplies, didn't I?"

"Not this time you didn't, mate . . . not this time."

At that moment Frank and Turk burst into the tent, apparently having heard of Jack's bloody arrival back at the hospital. Frank took one look at Jack and groaned, "Aww geez, Jack. It was that pig's butt Biggs, wasn't it? Man, you okay? You really look awful."

"Gee, thanks Frank," Jack replied. "Your bedside manner is exemplary. And it wasn't Biggs himself but two of his goons. Son of a bitch had a great time watching the show."

"Two!" Turk thundered. "That fucker had two fuckers do this to you . . . son of a fucking bitch! Takes two fuckers to beat up an

254

old man? I'll kill the fuckin' yellow bastard!" Turk performed something akin to a violent dance around the edge of the litter. He was furious, cursing and flailing his arms. Jack noticed Frank back away several paces. Though in pain, Turk's rage comforted Jack and increased his feelings of affection for the boy.

"Settle down, Turk," Ian said. "I'll take care of this with the Shore Patrol." Ian's voice, as usual, had a calming effect, but Turk was still fuming.

"With all due respect, sir, but you going to the fuckin' Shore Patrol ain't gonna accomplish fuckin' nothing," Turk said. "Frank told me about Jack threatening that asshole. What do you think the fuckin' cops are gonna do? Biggs is an officer and Jack is just a puny ass fuckin' hospitalman." Jack knew that Turk was right. The military police were not going to prosecute a case in which a low ranking thief and liar was beaten up by his peers, not an officer. The acting police on the island, Jack thought, had better things to worry about than a few boys knocking the stuffing out of each other. Jack looked at Ian as he worked on his face, and the frown he wore told him the doctor was thinking the same thing.

Turk continued, "No, yours truly is gonna take care of this one. My rule is, you fuck with my friend, you may as well be fuckin' with me. Me and some of the boys will just pay a little visit to this fuckin' depot and get things straightened out. I'm taking the truck." Turk turned to leave, but Ian stopped him.

"You're not going anywhere, Turk!" he snapped.

Turk whirled around and fixed Ian with an angry stare. "C'mon, Lieutenant, why the fuck not?" he demanded. "Jack got us a lot of important stuff by taking some risks and now he's paying the price. We can't let these fuckers get away with this . . . it'd be un-American!"

"Think, Turk," Ian replied, "the depot, for the time being, is our only source of supply. Our number one priority is caring for sick and wounded men, saving their lives. I'm just as angry about this as you, but there's nothing we can do about it right now without risking bigger problems."

"Doc's right, Turk," Jack said. "Believe me, I'd love to pay that asshole back in spades, but we're going to have to wait until that supply dump isn't so important to us." Turk looked at Jack, then Ian, then back at Jack with a look of rage and frustration. He violently kicked a pail across the tent and cursing loudly, stomped out the door.

"Sorry about this, Jack," Frank said. "We'll get Biggs' and the goons' numbers and take care of them later, okay?"

Jack smiled at Frank, "You bet, buddy."

"Well, I better go make sure Turk doesn't do something stupid," Frank sighed.

Ian nodded, "That is an excellent idea." Frank patted Jack gently on the shoulder, then turned and walked out the door.

"Poor Turk," Ian lamented. "He really wanted to kick somebody's arse."

Jack smiled painfully, "Yeah, I think he's more upset about this than I am."

"Turk's wired a bit too tight I suppose, but he really likes you," Ian said while swabbing blood from Jack's nostrils.

"You think so?" Jack asked. "Let's see, yesterday alone he accused me of being crazy, then he told me he was going to kill me, then he called me a lazy old turd. Yeah . . . maybe you're right, Doc."

Ian chuckled, "Both of those boys like you Jack . . . Turk and Frank. I think they admire you and look up to you. This is a scary place if you hadn't noticed. Add to that the fact that they're away from home for the first time and you have a situation where young people need someone to look up to or hang on to. Besides, just look what you've accomplished; the supplies you've acquired with your thievery and the construction of the Palace . . . and now you've taken a bloody great thrashing for the unit. You're becoming a bit of a legend already, whether you like it or not. As well, even though you're one of them, you're different and not just because of your age."

"Different in what way?" Jack asked warily.

"It's hard to explain but some people, just by the way they talk and carry themselves help make those around them believe that in the end, everything will be alright, everything. Don't ask me to explain it beyond that because I can't. It's too bloody bad you pretty much wasted it back in the world, mate." Jack stared at the ceiling while Ian tended to his injuries. He took no offense at Ian's last comment. He would have the day before, but not now. It seemed the island was guiding him, teaching him. Ian was right, it was a waste; so much had been wasted. "Hell, you must've known a few people who had those sorts of intangibles back in the states," Ian added.

"Kind of," Jack said. After a deep sigh he continued, "People always used to say the same sort of things about my dad . . . business associates, friends and even Laura. I never got it though, never saw it."

"Like I said to you last night, mate, your father and you are a lot alike."

16

They were silent for a minute or two until Ian said somberly, "You're recollection of the Goettge patrol was spot on: three sur-vivors. They have them over at the D Company aid station. I heard that Goettge was the first to get it . . . maybe there is a merciful god in heaven after all. He didn't have to witness the slaughter."

"He did get it first," Jack said flatly. "Half his face was blown off." Jack decided that as soon as Ian was done working on his injuries, he would walk the short distance to the battalion hospital and see if he could find the redhead amongst the survivors.

"Okay, I've patched you up as best I can," Ian said. "I want you to spend the rest of the day here taking it easy."

"I've got a shift, Doc, and then I'm going out to see Tom," Jack protested. "I've got bruised ribs and whether I'm lying here or mov-ing around it's still going to hurt, right?"

"We can't be certain you don't have some internal bleeding just yet, so I want to keep an eye on you."

"Oh, c'mon, Doc, I'm not bleeding internally. Those bastards didn't kick me that hard; besides, my blood pressure would be indi-cating it already."

"A few days in a field hospital and now you're a bloody surgeon, eh mate?" Ian asked half mockingly. "No, you stay right here."

Jack knew it was useless trying to shift Ian, so he decided that once the doctor was away or distracted, he'd slip out of the tent. "Okay, Doc," Jack said. "You're the boss." To Jack's dismay, Ian sat down at a nearby crate and started doing paperwork. As he watched Ian work, the exhaustion the beating had produced overwhelmed him. He fought it at first, but in a few minutes he fell into a deep sleep.

When he awoke his head was still pounding. He looked at his watch and groaned; he'd been asleep for four hours. "Shit . . . goddamn it," he groaned. He raised his hands to his face and gently probed his injuries. After lying still for a minute with his eyes closed, he opened them and searched the tent for Ian. To his relief the doctor was nowhere in sight, so Jack slowly raised himself and slid off the cot. He hobbled out the door and headed up the road toward Company D's hospital. As he walked and shook off the effects of his nap, he began to feel better. The throbbing in his head subsided and the movement seemed to alleviate the aches in his ribcage. "See, you don't know everything, Doc," he muttered to himself.

He reached the Company D aid station in 10 minutes. It looked much like Company E's hospital. The two crude structures, along with their meager medical equipment, represented the only things remotely resembling organized surgical facilities on the island. Jack couldn't recall exactly, but it would be weeks, if not months, before the Navy would deliver medical equipment of the quantity and quality needed for optimal care. He paused for a moment outside the entrance, lit a cigarette and puzzled over how he'd catch a glimpse of the three survivors without them seeing him. He couldn't take the risk that they might recognize him and remember his warning on the beach the previous day. As he puffed on his cigarette, men were coming and going through the door of the hospital. A young man wearing a surgical mask around his neck stepped outside and stood next to Jack. He pulled out a cigarette, then patted his pockets. "Shit, I lost my damn lighter again." Turning toward Jack he said, "Hey, mac, you got a light?"

"Sure," Jack said. As he was lighting the boy's cigarette, Jack noticed that he was staring at him.

"Hey, shouldn't you be inside?" he asked Jack. "Patients are allowed to smoke inside you know."

"I'm not a patient," Jack replied.

"Oh," the young man said sheepishly. "Hope the other guy looks as bad as you do, bud."

"Guys," Jack corrected. "I got mugged by some supply ass-holes." Male pride, as with many other ambitious men, had at times aided him in his endeavors back in the world and at other times had unwittingly sabotaged him. This pride was very much intact in spite of his journey, if not heightened. He needed the young man to understand that he'd been ganged up on, though he knew very well that just one would have been enough to do the job.

"That stinks . . . the bastards," the boy replied sympathetically.

"Yeah," Jack said. "Hey, I heard you have the 3 guys who survived the ambush on that patrol last night."

"Yeah, they're right inside. One of the guys told us he escaped by swimming out to sea while the Japs plinked away at him. He said he looked back once at the patrol and saw the fuckers hacking our guys up with swords . . . dirty little bastards."

"Yeah, I know," Jack said. "Hell, I figure it's going to backfire on the sons of bitches. It'll just mean our guys are going to fight harder and that we never move without very heavy firepower." Jack paused then continued, "A friend of mine was a good pal of one of the guys on that patrol. The guy was real young looking: freckle-faced and red hair. Any of those guys look like that?"

The young man frowned and Jack immediately knew the answer to his question. "No, I'm sorry for your friend, bud, but none of those guys look anything like that."

"Okay . . . thanks," Jack said quietly. He flicked his cigarette away, and without another word trudged off in the direction he came. When he arrived back at the hospital the first person he saw was Frank, transferring supplies from the back of the hospital to the Palace.

"Lt. Smith wants you to report to him immediately," Frank advised. "He didn't seem too happy about you wandering off."

"He'll get over it," Jack shrugged. "Where is he?"

"He's with some patients. We just got three cases of dysentery and he's checking them out."

As soon as Jack entered the hospital, Ian barked, "Damn it, Jack, I told you to stay down. What in bloody hell do you think you're doing?"

"Sorry, Doc, but I had a good sleep and when I woke up I was feeling a lot better. The walk up to D Company actually helped a lot."

Ian's look immediately softened. The men stared at each other for a moment, then Jack slowly shook his head.

"Sorry, mate."

"It's okay. I think freaking out at the beach was a catharsis of sorts. For some reason it helped me accept that I can't change much and that it doesn't do me or anyone else any good to get too upset about it."

Ian nodded, "You've changed things in little ways, mate. That's all one good man can really do and you're right, as god-awful as it is, all we can do is our best and try and not let it break us. Now give me a hand with these new patients. They're in pretty bad shape so we need to keep a close eye on them, and from what you've told me this is just the start."

"That's right, Doc. There's going to be a lot of this coming in from now on and we're going to start getting our first malaria cases any day now."

"Bloody marvelous," Ian muttered.

Jack spent what was left of the afternoon working alongside Ian in the hospital. When Jack asked to borrow the jeep to go visit Tom, Ian suggested they first pay a visit to one of the supply dumps at Henderson and pick up a couple cases of Japanese beer for him to take along. Jack was delighted at the offer. On the way to the dump, Ian explained that a supply sergeant who worked there owed him a favor having to do with some sort of, as Ian put it, 'penis virus', he had treated while onboard ship. The man had supplied Ian with the *sake* they had enjoyed earlier, and now he eagerly greeted Ian and happily complied with the doctor's request. After dropping Ian off at the hospital, Jack made the short drive to the Tenaru. Once there, he slowly chugged his way downstream, peering at each cluster of Marines dug in on the creek bank. Just as he arrived at the spot where he had spied on Tom, he heard a shout.

"Hey, Macmillan!" his father's voice boomed. "Over here, buddy!" Directly ahead, Jack saw Tom standing and waving his arms wildly. Jack waved back and steered the jeep toward him. When he pulled up alongside him, the smile on Tom's face suddenly vanished.

"Jesus Christ! What in hell happened to you?" Tom asked.

Jack smiled wearily, "Knife fight with a dozen Japs. One of the little fuckers got away . . . damn it."

"No seriously, you're messed up pretty bad; tell me what happened."

Jack pointed proudly to the cases of beer, "A little gift for you and your friends. After we crack a couple of these and sit down somewhere, I'll tell you the whole glorious story."

Scrambling into the jeep, Tom replied in a hushed voice, "Not a good idea. If the boys catch a whiff of that beer they'll be all over us. In fact, I'm surprised they haven't sniffed it out already. Let's drive a ways into the grove." Jack was touched by Tom's obvious concern as well as his desire to hear Jack's story uninterrupted. As he pulled into the grove, Tom's face was taut and he was frowning. After a hundred yards or so, Jack brought the jeep to a halt and reached into one of the beer cases pulling out two brown bottles.

"Shit," Jack muttered, "I don't have anything to open these with."

"No problem," Tom said still frowning. Tom lowered each bottle to his waist and deftly popped the caps off with his Navy issue belt buckle.

"Looks like you've done that a few times before."

A fleeting smile appeared on Tom's face as he replied, "Just a few. Now tell me what happened." In between sips of the warm, yet surprisingly tasty, beer Jack told the whole story of his run-ins with

Biggs and how they had culminated in the beating that morning. When he relayed the parts about how he had first duped, then threatened, Biggs into releasing supplies, Tom laughed and nodded approvingly. When Jack finished, his father clapped him on the back.

"First, that is one great story, pal, at least up 'til the part where you get the shit kicked out of you. You're a brave son of a bitch to fuck with an officer like that." Strangely, to Jack, his father seemed excited, almost giddy. Tom continued, "Second, I think that asshole needs to learn some manners and to not fuck around with guys from Michigan. Let's head back to my squad area. I'll introduce you to some of the boys and Lieutenant Grimes. We'll all have a few beers and we'll see how they feel about the situation with Mr. Diggs."

"Biggs." Jack corrected as he started the jeep.

"Biggs, shmiggs," Tom replied. "It doesn't matter much on account the fucker may be dead tomorrow if I know my guys—and especially Lt. Grimes'—way of thinking. Add to that the fact that after you lay those beers on 'em they're going to be extra motivated."

Jack didn't quite know what to make of his father's comments. Surely, they wouldn't consider taking some sort of revenge on Biggs, a Marine officer, for a stranger, beer or not. Just the thought though, filled Jack with anticipation. After clearing the coconut grove, Tom pointed Jack to a cluster of five foxholes on the riverbank. The holes were just big enough to hold two men each. "Those are my guys right over there; we're part of Lt. Grimes 2nd platoon. Pull up right next to them so no one else sees us unloading the beer. We'll pass it all out to my guys right away, that way it's every man for himself when it comes to protecting it from scavengers." When the jeep came to a stop Tom summoned quietly, but urgently, "Beer call, boys!"

A young Marine looked up wide-eyed, "No shit?"

"No shit, boy. Finest beer ever made in Japan. They tell me fucking Tojo himself brewed it and it all comes courtesy of my special buddy here," Tom said nodding toward Jack. "Some of you shit-squirters may remember him from when you were being sissies in the sick bay the other day. He's a corpsman there."

As the boys, eight of them, crowded excitedly around the jeep, Jack recognized several of the gastro victims. "Hey, how you doin', doc?" one of the boys asked. "Geez, you get hit by a bus or something?"

"Shut-up, Lou . . . it isn't funny," Tom snipped. "He's gonna tell the story of what happened as soon as we get the beers passed out. You're not gonna believe this shit." Tom suddenly stood up in the jeep and started slowly turning his head in search of something. After a few moments he stopped turning and yelled, "Hey Lieutenant . . . Lt. Grimes! You got a minute, sir?"

"I'll be there in a few, Tommy," Jack heard a voice shout. Tom sat back down and introduced Jack to his squad mates. He told them about their shared last names and West Michigan connections. Then he pointed, proudly Jack thought, to each one and gave their names.

"Sergeant Jackson, meet Jack Macmillan." He continued with the introductions and each time he named one of his mates, the boy would smile and eagerly offer his hand. He delivered their names with an obvious tone of affection.

"Murph . . . Ski . . . Big Mikey . . . Dumbass . . . Lou . . . Danny, and last but certainly least, Scozzolari, or Scooz as we call him." When he introduced Scozzolari, Jack froze for a moment, staring at the young man. Anthony Scozzolari looked very different than he had nearly a week ago at the ceremony on Skyline Ridge. He had a full head of thick black hair, was slender; his skin unblemished and olive tinted. He was handsome, but in an unconventional sense. His nose was slightly too large, dark eyes slightly too small. Jack now had the answer to the mystery of the unnerving gaze Mr. Scozzolari had laid upon him several times during his speech and the stammers that had accompanied them. Though the encounter with the young Scozzolari was haunting, Jack recovered quickly as he was enjoying the moment immensely. It wasn't just that he was meet-

264

ing his father's buddies, it was more. Other than the first horrific morning, it was his first direct encounter with combat Marines in the field. These were his real heroes, the men whose bravery and toughness he had wondered at for so long. Men who had somehow tolerated near starvation and the hell of the jungle, yet still fought to the death a brave and tenacious enemy. Unlike the Marines on his first day, this group was welcoming him as a friend and comrade. Jack knew his liquid gift likely added some encouragement to their warm greetings, but still, on the whole, it seemed genuine. It felt right and good that as things on the island worsened, he would be sharing many of the same hardships and risks as would his heroes, with his father. When the introductions were over, Jack sat in the jeep, smiling as broadly as his swollen, cracked lips would allow.

"Nice to meet you guys," he said. He grabbed a case of beer from the back and set it on his lap. The boys murmured excitedly, pleasing Jack immensely. "Let's see," he continued, "there are 10 of us, so we each get 2 beers with 4 leftover, and Tom and I have already had one of ours."

"No," Tom corrected, "we have to count in Lt. Grimes' so there'll just be 2 left over. What do you want to do with the extras? They're your beers after all."

As Jack was passing out the bottles he said, "Hell, I don't know. Why don't you come up with something?" Just as he finished saying this, he found himself passing bottles to the apparently woeful boy known as Dumbass. The boy grinned broadly but was bent at an angle at the waist, favoring his cracked ribs.

Dumbass took the bottles chattering, "Oh, sweet Mother of Mary, sir! I ain't had a fucking brew since goddamn Wallington."

"It's Wellington, shithead, not Wallington," Ski corrected.

"Oh yeah," Dumbass muttered, smiling cheerfully. For a moment Jack felt sorry for the boy and his face clouded. But then he noticed Ski's grin as he reached over and gave Dumbass a playful, affectionate shove. Dumbass looked at Ski and began to chuckle.

Scozzolari, having already opened and taken a big chug of his beer, looked at Jack, belched loudly, and announced, "Ol' Dumbass may have a mostly hollow cranium, but he's one hell of a Marine . . . a good man, right guys?" The other boys nodded. Jack figured 'Scooz' must have seen the concern on his face and felt it necessary that Jack understand the true feelings the squad held toward the young Ohioan, despite the seemingly cruel nickname they had bestowed upon him.

"How are the ribs young man?" Jack asked. Although Scooz had allayed his concern regarding it, Jack still couldn't bring himself to call the boy by his Marine name.

"Feeling a little better, sir," Dumbass replied. "Still hurts pretty damn bad though, sir."

"I'm not a 'sir'. I'm just a plain old corpsman."

"Oh wow . . . you're really old," Dumbass said flatly.

"Thanks so much for that," Jack quipped with exaggerated sarcasm. "But because you're still in pain, you get one of the extra beers." Dumbass' happy yelp was drowned out by cries of protest from the other men. Jack raised his hands and said, "We'll pass the last bottle around and everyone can have a swig." This calmed the men, but Jack could still hear some mutters of good-natured discontent. Then a new voice rang out.

"What's up, Tommy?" the voice inquired. Jack turned and saw another young Marine approaching the group. He was a slight man with several days of dark stubble shading his face. His uniform seemed to droop around his body and the steel pot he wore appeared to engulf much of his head. Yet still, Jack noticed, the man carried himself confidently and he could sense an air of fortitude and competence about him.

Tom introduced Grimes to Jack, explaining how they had gotten to know one another. Then he pointed to Jack's face, "As you can see, sir, he took a real thumping this morning. I think you and the boys might wanna hear about it."

The lieutenant gazed at Jack's battered face for a moment, then said, "Sure . . . let's go sit on the riverbank." After they were seated,

266

Jack started to tell the same story he had told to Tom minutes earlier. This time though he took his time, adding more detail and drama to the telling. The men sat rapt throughout the story. When he finished he was very pleased with the effect it had on the men. Curses and vendettas rent the air. After a moment or two, Lt. Grimes spoke, "Quiet men." He took a long, slow drag off his cigarette, turned to Jack and asked, "You say this depot is on the beach a thousand yards or so east of here?"

"Yes, sir, that's right," Jack replied.

"Well," the lieutenant continued, flicking his cigarette into the creek, "I think we need to take a stroll down the beach in the morning and pay the good Mr. Biggs and his chums a little visit."

"Gosh . . . really?" Jack asked incredulously. He was awed by the fact that a World War II Marine combat unit would deign to come to his aid. "That . . . that would be great, Lieutenant. I'd owe you guys a big one."

"You just keep bringing the beer, bud, and you're paid up, okay? Besides, this isn't just about you. I've only been in the Corps for a year, but I've seen a lot and assholes like Biggs—I don't give a shit what their rank—need to learn that it doesn't pay to withhold Corps supplies or play goddamn politics with them. By late tomorrow morning, I suspect he'll have learned that lesson."

"Great, Lieutenant; thanks a million," Jack gushed. He was excited at the possibility for revenge, but just as important he knew that with the involvement of a Marine combat unit, there was nothing Biggs could do in retaliation, and he would be forced to work with Jack in a fair manner.

"Can you be here at 0800 in the morning?" Grimes asked.

Jack thought for a moment, then replied, "Sure, that shouldn't be a problem."

"Good. Okay men," Lt. Grimes said addressing the group. "Be ready to move out at 0800 for the supply depot . . . combat loaded. Sarge," Grimes said looking at the man named Jackson, "make sure your people are in their holes at dusk, locked and loaded. I'll be back to check on you guys in an hour or so."

"Yes, sir," Jackson replied.

Grimes shook Jack's hand, "Thanks for the beer, sailor. See you at 0800." At that, the lieutenant stuffed his remaining beer bottle in the side pocket of his dungarees and walked off toward a squad of Marines downstream.

After Lt. Grimes departed, the little group of men buzzed with excitement over the next morning's mission. It was a much needed diversion from the monotony of sentry duty, relieved occasionally by tense but largely uneventful patrolling beyond the perimeter. At least this time, they said, they might actually accomplish something. Plus, they couldn't wait to see an officer humiliated.

"I wouldn't be surprised if Lt. Grimes makes the fucker cry," Danny chirped.

"Knowing that asshole and his type, it wouldn't surprise me a bit," Jack said. "I'll be one happy fella when that shithead is put in his proper place."

"Well I hope he stays there," Lou said. "These officers cover each other's asses real good. Take Morehead for chrissakes!" Lou turned to Jack and grumbled, "Captain Morehead is our chicken-shit company commander. A Naval Academy jerk-off who thinks he's fuckin' Napoleon and that we're just a bunch of simple shits who don't deserve to breathe the same air as him. It's like you said, Ski, thank god we got Lt. Grimes. He protects us from Captain More-fucking-dick-head and the other high society bastards. We'd be screwed without him; and the rest of these platoon leaders is nothing more than snot-nosed ninety day wonders, totally useless. We should count our blessings, boys." Murmurs of agreement rose from the group.

Tom ended the conversation by announcing, "Hey, it's time for chow." The men pulled C-rations, rapidly becoming rare on the island, out of a box and opened them. Jack drew meat stew and biscuits. The meat in it was nearly indistinguishable as such. The beer helped wash down the gray, rubbery chunks and additives. While they ate they continued to discuss the planned visit to Biggs' depot the next morning. Then the subject inevitably shifted to home.

They talked about the usual stuff: girls, sports, food, and motion pictures. It was lighthearted, often greatly embellished banter. Jack leaned back against the river bank, slowly finishing the last of his beer and reveling in the stories the boys told of their lives in 1930s and '40s America.

"Aw c'mon," Louie groaned, "there's no fuckin' way that that homo Crosby can sing better than Frankie Sinatra. You gotta be outta your skull, Mikey."

"You just think that 'cause you're from Hoboken, like Sinatra is," Danny retorted. "If you were from the Bronx like me, you wouldn't be so fucking stupid."

"Aw fuck it," Louie groused. "You guys just don't know shit about music . . . that's the problem." Taking a deep breath, he added, "God, I wish I knew how the Yankees are doing."

"Who fucking cares?" Big Mikey huffed. "The Red Sox are going to win it all anyway."

"Oh now that's a good one, Mikey!" Danny chortled. "Williams is a great ballplayer, I'll admit, but they ain't done shit since the last war. In fact, I bet you they don't win another Series never."

"The Cubs," Ski interjected.

"What?!" Big Mikey and Louie yelled in unison.

"Yeah, the Cubs. You fancy pants East Coasters are going to get steamrollered by the Cubbies."

"You're an idiot, Ski," Big Mikey said. "Now I know for sure where not to place my bet, because you've never been right about nothing."

"Listen, you morons, ain't nobody gonna beat the Yankees this year and you know it!" Louie pronounced emphatically. This effectively ended the discussion, primarily Jack decided, due to the fact that the majority of the boys were Yankee fans. All the while, Jack noticed that Tom would laugh and smile at the boy's cracks and jibes, but never joined in. Then, he heard Murph and Dumbass having their own discussion.

"So what's it like, Murph?" Dumbass asked.

"What's what like?"

"You know, getting laid. I heard you telling Scooz about some girl you, you know . . . poked on the ball field in Scranton."

"Poked?" Murph chuckled, rolled his eyes and then asked, "So you never been laid?"

"Not even close, boy. I ain't never even touched a damn tit." Jack was amused and touched by the boy's honesty. He heard Murph chuckle again, then realized the other boys were also eavesdropping on the conversation.

"It's goddamn magic," Murph said. "Especially the first few times. I mean the first time you're holding a tit in your hand you just can't believe it. I mean, it's like it's not real or something and the nipple is kinda glowing at you, I swear, it goddamn glows." Murph paused to take a deep swig of beer then continued. "Then there's third base . . . oh my god. First time there was the happiest moment of my life; I guaran-fuckin'-tee you. I can't even describe it to you; you're just gonna have to experience it yourself boy."

"Wow," Dumbass said dreamily.

Inevitably the others chimed in with their own experiences and with advice for Dumbass as to how he might go about getting laid. Jack smiled to himself, suspecting that most of the boys hadn't much more experience in the matter than Dumbass, excepting perhaps one or two of them drunkenly groping with aged hookers in New River before shipping out. He hoped they would all survive to enjoy the beautiful, lonely young ladies of Melbourne, where they were to be sent when they were relieved in December. He knew their extended stay at the Melbourne cricket ground would represent some of the happiest days of their lives. As the banter continued, Jack stared across to the other side of the creek, then downstream. The fading light was blending the foliage together in a grayish murk. Suddenly, he recalled that in 6 nights the blackness of the jungle would, in a frightening instant, give way to the eerie green light of flares. The bank across from him, and in particular the sandbar, would explode with teems of wildly screaming enemy soldiers intent on killing the Marines and retaking the airfield. His father and the other boys would be within yards of where the heavy

270

blows of the enemy attack would fall. The battle, though largely one-sided and a clear victory for the Marines, would be a horror that few, if any, on the island could imagine. He involuntarily shuddered, then had his thoughts interrupted by Sgt. Jackson.

"Okay, girls, time to tuck in for the night. You know the drill, helmets and boots on at all times. Your weapons are locked and loaded and no, and I mean no, smoking. If I catch one of you knuckleheads sleeping while you're on OP, I'll wring your goddamn neck."

The boys gulped down the last of their beer, then grudgingly went about the task of hunkering down for the night, securing their small section of the eastern perimeter. Jack happily accepted an invitation to Tom's foxhole. It measured 4–5 ft. in diameter and 4 ft. deep, and contained adequate space for two men. Tom explained that as the squad corpsman, he insisted on having his own foxhole in case he were to have to work on a wounded comrade under fire. The lack of a foxhole buddy was certainly less secure, Jack knew, and it must have made the long, black nights even more lonely and frightening. It was another sign of his father's commitment to the well being of his squad mates. Jack climbed in first, then Tom crawled in beside him. They sat shoulder to shoulder and quietly talked. It wouldn't have mattered if they could have positioned themselves to look at each other's faces, for suddenly it seemed, it had gone pitch black.

"You're squad seems like a great bunch of guys," Jack said.

"The whole platoon is great. Best bunch in the world as far as I'm concerned," Tom replied. "There isn't a one of 'em I wouldn't do just about anything for."

"That's great," Jack said. "You're a very lucky guy." Jack meant it. Thinking back on the conversations near the river, he envied the obvious closeness of the squad. There didn't seem to be one boy who didn't fit and wasn't liked by the others. It was remarkable how much they knew about each other and, in spite of the constant razzing, how much they cared about what was going on in each other's lives.

271

"Yeah, I suppose you're right. I got lucky, I guess."

"It's not just that," Jack said. "You guys have been thrown together in a pretty tough situation, from boot camp all the way to this shitty piece of real estate. Add to that the fact that you're all trying to achieve the same goal and you have the ingredients that really bond men together."

"Uh-huh," Tom said flatly. Tom's seemingly uncomfortable reply left Jack feeling foolish. He reminded himself that his father was only nineteen, and that his little discourse on male bonding might cause him unease. Back in the world, his father had never been comfortable with touchy-feely issues. So, the question Tom asked next surprised him.

"How about you, Jack?" Tom inquired.

"What do you mean?"

"You know, have you ever had a real close group of friends? Guys that you'd risk your life for if you had to, because you know they'd risk theirs for you?"

After a pause, Jack replied, "No . . . I mean, not yet . . . I mean . . . ah . . . here on the island could be my first time."

"Could be?"

"Yeah, I didn't ship here with my unit so I'm still getting to know them, but I've already made some real good friends." Jack didn't, or perhaps couldn't, admit to his father that after 5 short days he already considered them the closest friends he'd ever had.

"Tell me about 'em," Tom said. Jack eagerly described Ian, Turk, and Frank. Tom laughed heartily over some of Turk's antics and philosophies, and was curious as to what kind of doctor Ian was. His interest deepened when Jack told him Ian had received his medical training in London. After answering a number of questions regarding Ian's medical skills and practices, Jack told Tom about Frank's deeply convicted goal of becoming a heart surgeon after the war.

"I think he's gonna' make it, too," Jack said. "He has everything working in his favor. He's bright, focused, determined, and has the personality that makes for a great surgeon. His parents are professors at Stanford, which I'm sure isn't going to hurt him any."

"No, I don't suppose it will," Tom agreed. After a pause, he chuckled, then added, "It's a lot like my situation. Medical schools are just dying to admit the sons of drunken fruit farmers." Jack took a moment to recover from his surprise. His Grandpa Macmillan had died eight years before he was born. Tom had occasionally spoken of his father, William Ferguson Macmillan, but mostly anecdotally and endearingly. He never had anything negative to say, and had certainly never spoken of his father being an alcoholic.

Haltingly, Jack asked, "Your father, he uh, he drinks too much?"

"If you think a fifth of scotch whiskey a day is too much, then yes, he drinks too much," Tom replied without bitterness. "He was always a heavy drinker, but when Hank died he just went straight to the bottom of the barrel and I guess that's where he intends to stay."

"That's tough," Jack said softly, heartbroken for his father. A few moments later he asked, "How well does your family cope with it, his drinking I mean?"

"Okay, I guess," Tom replied. "Thankfully, Dad's a gentle, kinda dopy drunk, so it never gets nasty or anything. It means a whole lot more work for Liz and me on the farm for sure. Dad works, but doesn't get much of anything done. It's toughest on my mom." Jack's Grandma Macmillan, Granny Mac he called her, had always seemed so happy, almost carefree. He couldn't imagine her living with a drunk, particularly after the death of her eldest son. In her eyes, the pain must have shone; it must have been there. Jack had never seen it though; he'd never had a reason to really look.

"How is it toughest on your mom?" Jack whispered.

"She's basically all alone," Tom explained. "I mean, my dad's there, but he really isn't, you know? I mean, it's not him anymore, it's just his body. His personality and soul are altered, or even erased each day by the goddamn whiskey. It stinks, but I try not to blame him, with Hank and all." Jack fought off an urge to hug his father. He unconsciously took a cigarette out and lit his lighter.

"No, no . . . shit!" Tom gasped.

"Put that light out you fuckin' idiot!" Sgt. Jackson yelled. Jack quickly extinguished the flame.

"Oh Christ . . . I'm uh . . . I'm sorry," Jack whispered. Jack was horrified that once again his own absent-mindedness could have endangered a group of marines, this time a group including his own father. He didn't have long to think about it though, for suddenly he felt a hand roughly grab his shirt and jostle him tightly up against Tom.

"Which one of you fuckin' nurses just lit that?" Jackson hissed. Jack could feel the Sergeant's hot breath on the back of his neck.

"I did," both Tom and Jack said at once.

"Who did? Macmillan?"

"Yes," they both replied again.

"Goddamn it! Two fuckin' Macmillans in one fuckin' hole! This is fucked up!" Sgt. Jackson rasped violently. "Now Macmillan . . . my Macmillan I mean . . . who lit the fucking light?"

"I did, Sarge, I'm real sorry," Tom confessed. "I just lost my head for a minute." Jack began to protest, but Tom elbowed him in his already aching ribs, taking his breath away.

"Yeah, well, you keep pullin' dumbshit stunts like that and you'll lose your head for real."

"Sorry, Sarge, it won't happen again." Jack felt Jackson's grip loosen, then fall away.

"Use your fuckin' noodle from now on, Mac," Jackson said, the anger leaving his voice. "You're just lucky you're a corpsman and I like you, or I'd have your ass over a barrel in the morning."

"Thanks, Sarge . . . sorry again," Tom said sincerely.

"You ladies have 20 more minutes then Jack here needs to head back to his unit. Oh and thanks again for the beer, pal," he added.

"Sure," Jack said uncertainly. They heard the sergeant crawl back toward his foxhole.

"What'd you do that for?" Jack whispered tersely. "I don't need you to take the fall for me."

"Don't sweat it, bud. It's like he said, he likes me and I'm the squad medic. He wasn't gonna do anything more than scream at me. Lt. Grimes will chew me out in the morning, but after that it'll be forgotten. If we had told him it was you, he would have tossed you out of here and never let you back." Jack, though, still felt terrible about his latest failure and his father taking the heat for him made him feel all the more inadequate. He slunk down in the hole, silently cursing himself.

As if reading Jack's thoughts, Tom said, "Hey, forget about it. Shit like this happens all the time. Usually it's one of the boys getting caught trying to sneak a smoke though. People do dumb things all the time, they get yelled at, then get on with doing what they're doing. You're a good guy and I like talking to you. I didn't mind taking the rap for you. Don't worry about it, okay?"

Tom's words helped Jack put his mistake in its proper perspective. He'd read of blunders even experienced soldiers had made that were considerably more serious than his, Colonel Goettge for one, he thought bitterly. "Okay," Jack said, "thanks for taking the heat for me. I owe you one." He was pleased by Tom's description of him as a 'good guy'. This, though, was tempered by a certain sadness the rest of his comment caused. His father had said he liked talking to him; back in the world it had been something they rarely did outside of work, unless they were drinking, and even then it was mostly about the company.

They sat in silence for several minutes, listening to the sounds of the black jungle. Birds shrieked in the trees; lizards, crabs, and rats rattled the brush. Occasionally, a crocodile could be heard splashing into the creek. Each time one did, Jack started. Murmurs, whispers, and periodic bursts of muffled laughter emanated from unseen foxholes, providing a surreal backdrop to the haunting symphony of the jungle. Jack was reminded again what would occur at this place in six days time. Out of the screeching, dark jungle the enemy would descend upon his father and the Marines like a hissing, writhing serpent. He removed the thought from his mind by re-starting their conversation.

"So you were saying your father's drinking is tough on your mom?" Jack asked.

"Yeah. It's tough on my little sister, too. I think it's hard for her to understand, and she takes it more personally than I do." Jack recalled the conversations about life on the farm he'd had with his Aunt Liz, the last one occurring just a few weeks before he'd departed for Guadalcanal. Unlike his father, she loved to talk about the farm. But like her brother, she never talked about her father's drinking or anything negative regarding their lives for that matter. It was as if she and her brother had had an idyllic, perfect childhood. And she never, not once, talked of Hank's death. Jack hesitated for a moment, unsure as to whether he should ask Tom a question he knew would be unwelcome. Finally, he decided it was a question, he in a way, had a duty to ask again.

"Your brother . . . Hank," Jack said quietly.

Tom was silent for several seconds, then said warily, "Yeah?"

"I know you don't like to talk about it, but do you want to, or uh, can I ask again how he died?"

For what seemed ages, Tom remained silent. Then Jack heard a quiet sigh and Tom said, "I guess I'd need a whole lot more than two beers to talk about that."

"It was pretty rough, huh?"

"Yeah, it was rough." Tom volunteered nothing more and Jack assumed that once again, the matter was closed to further discussion. But then, his father surprised him.

"Hank was my hero . . . Lizzy's's too. He was only 13 when he died, but he was already one of those kids that other kids just naturally follow. You know the type?"

"Sure do," Jack replied. "But they're few and far between."

"You're damn right there. Hank was a one-of-a-kind man. Man," he chuckled ruefully, "he was 13 and I think of him as a man. He'd do anything for Ma and us. I was only 10 years old but he treated me like a son—played ball with me when he didn't feel like it, taught me to fish. He'd read to Liz and me every night for an hour or more, even after Liz and I had learned to read ourselves . . . that's how I fell in love with reading. He wasn't just a second father to us; he was something more than that . . . it's hard to explain."

276

"I think I understand," Jack lied.

"We buried him on the farm. Ma couldn't stand the thought of him being away from her in some cemetery."

"I'm real sorry," Jack said softly.

Tom didn't say anything else for a minute or two. Jack could sense, almost hear, his father's mind struggling to say something more. Finally, he did. In a tortured whisper he blurted, "I killed him . . . I killed Hank." He'd made the statement rapidly, his words crisp and clipped. It was as if the faster he said it, the less painful it would be. Involuntarily, Jack gasped. He silently chastised himself, then desperately grasped for something to say.

"Oh . . . c'mon," he stammered, "I'm sure that's not the case."

"What the hell do you mean that's not the case?" Tom said bitterly. "You weren't there goddamn it!"

"I'm sorry . . . sorry." They sat in silence for several moments as Jack tried to recover from the shock of his father's horrifying pronouncement, vainly searching for something to say.

Tom though, spoke first, "Sorry for biting your head off, Jack."

"No problem . . . I deserved it," Jack replied softly.

After a pause, Tom continued, "I've never talked to anybody about this, nobody. I'm not sure why I'm telling you now; it just seems that I should. It's easy to talk to you about this sort of stuff for some reason." Jack sensed Tom shifting uncomfortably. Tom confirmed it by saying, "It's kind of strange I guess."

"It's not strange at all. I take it as a compliment." Jack's heart was pounding and conflicting emotions whirled in his mind. He felt sorry for his father, but also felt anger that he'd never talked to him about such matters back in the world. "Why?" he screamed in his mind. "Why did we throw away all those years? And over what?"

His thoughts were abruptly wiped from his mind when Tom suddenly blurted, "He bled to death." Then, in the same staccato rhythm as before, he told the terrible story of his brother's passing. "We were in the apple orchard, a couple hundred yards in. Hank and I were cutting dead limbs off the trees with a pole saw." Tom paused for a moment then said, his eyes squeezed shut, "Hank had climbed to the top of a tree to take down a tangled branch. I'd gone back to the barrow to get something, and without thinking I'd propped the pole saw up in the tree pointing straight up at him. As I was walking back from the barrow I saw him start to move to a large branch. He slipped . . . he . . . he." Tom took a deep breath and paused.

"Go on, buddy, you can tell me," Jack softly urged his father.

Tom immediately continued, "On his way down the tip of the saw caught one of his thighs and went in all the way to the bone. The branches broke his fall and he landed pretty soft; but I saw blood turning his overalls red."

"Jesus," Jack said, "he was 13 and you were what, 10?"

"Yeah," Tom said quietly. "We were both young, but that doesn't give you the right to fuck up, does it?" Jack, remembering Tom's reaction when he last challenged his opinion on the incident, decided he wouldn't respond, at least not until he heard the full story. "Hank started turning pale and at first seemed kind of stunned or something. I unhooked his overalls and pulled them down to get a better look at the wound. It wasn't real big but blood was just, Jesus Christ, it was just gushing out. I went a little crazy then . . . crying and screaming at Hank to tell me what to do. That seemed to wake him up and he grabbed me by the arm, real calm like, and told me to make a tourniquet. He was talking to me real gentle, you know, encouraging me. I took off my shirt, notched it with that goddamn pole saw, then tore a long strip out of it. Hank told me where to tie it and I did; I pulled that fucker as tight as I could. I stopped crying when the bleeding seemed to slow way down. Hank told me to go get Pa. I ran as fast as I could, screaming for my dad the whole way. It seemed like fucking hours, but I cleared the orchard just as Pa came bursting out of the house. I told him what happened and we went running back to Hank. He yelled back at Mom to follow us in the truck. When we got to where we could see Hank, I knew something was wrong. He wasn't moving and he looked . . . he, uh Jesus, he looked bad. We ran up to him and Dad started screaming his name and shaking him. Ma came up in the truck and when she saw him she started screaming too. Then I started screaming and crying and

278

shit." Jack heard Tom softly groan. Tom stopped talking so Jack assumed the story was done.

"It doesn't sound to me like you did anything wrong," Jack said, feeling a desperate need to comfort his father. "You made the tourniquet and got it on him as fast as you could."

"I left the fucking saw in the tree!"

"You were ten for godsakes, and what were the odds that Hank was going to fall? It was a freak accident, nobody's fault."

"It doesn't matter, I fucked up. It was my fault he was so badly injured and then I was too stupid to save him."

"Listen I'm not trying to patronize you, but I think you're wrong, Tom," Jack said firmly. "You were just a kid. Hell, I think under the circumstances, it was quite an accomplishment just to get the tourniquet on him. What else could you have done?"

Tom didn't say anything and Jack could hear him crying softly. The only other time he'd seen his dad cry was after Jack sold the company. He didn't know it, but he'd hear his father's gentle weeping one more time while on the island.

"No, thanks for trying to make me feel better, but I fucked up alright." Tom replied. "You see . . . I ah . . . when I looked down at his leg, when my Ma and Pa were screaming and crying and shit, that's when I saw it. The goddamn tourniquet was laying loose around his leg; hell, it was barely even tied. I fucked up the knot."

Jack paused for a moment, taking in the new information and briefly reflecting on how damaging such an appalling trauma would have been on a young boy's psyche. "Tom, you were a boy chrissake. You did your best."

"Hah!" Tom spat. "You can't just fuck up and say, 'oops, I just killed my brother, but it's okay because I'm just a kid'." Tom, no longer crying, added angrily, "I'll tell you this; I'll never again be in a situation where I'm not fully prepared to help somebody who's hurt badly . . . never . . . I fucking swear."

"Is that why you're a medic?" Jack asked. "Is that why you want to be a pediatric surgeon; so you can save kids like your brother?"

Tom sighed and said, "Yeah, I suppose it is."

"You can't save 'em all you know, buddy. Sometimes it's just not meant to be."

"I know that; I'm not some crazy fucker trying to bring my brother back to life or something. I know I can't save 'em all, but I can save a lot, and at the same time I won't kill anybody for lack of preparation or proper effort, like I did with Hank."

Jack was about to protest when Sgt. Jackson stuck his head in their hole, "Okay, time to break it up. Pops needs to get back to his unit."

Tom turned to his son and patted him on the shoulder, "Thanks for coming out, Jack. Sorry to lay this thing about my brother on you though."

Jack felt an urge to hug him. Amazingly though, just like back in the world, he couldn't. He only replied, "Don't mention it; it's good to talk about things." It was advice he'd never followed himself—particularly with his father.

"Okay, thanks," Tom said. "Oh, and thanks too for the beer, pal."

"Glad to do it. Thank *you* for your help with Biggs. I'm really looking forward to tomorrow."

"Me too . . . should be a hoot."

Jack groped in the dark for his father's hand. He found it and they gripped each others hands tightly. It was exactly the same type of handshake he and his father exchanged back in the world after long separations . . . never a hug or embrace, just a warm, manly handshake. "See you in the morning, Tom," Jack said quietly.

"In the morning, buddy."

Jack pulled himself out of the hole and walked toward the jeep. The blackness forced him to walk slowly with his arms outstretched, feeling for the vehicle. Finally, his hands touched the hood of the jeep. At that moment, two thunderous bangs in rapid succession boomed just yards away. Jack screamed and threw himself to the ground. Several other shots followed further down the line, then the firing ceased. Jack's heart was thumping wildly and his ears were ringing. His panicked breaths came in rapid, shallow gulps.

"Ladies, ladies, ladies!" A voice boomed. It was Sgt. Jackson. "You're gettin' your goddamn panties all tied up in knots! There ain't nothin' out there! Discipline ladies . . . discipline." Several moments passed, then more quietly he said, "That was you wasn't it, Scooz?"

"Uh, yeah, sorry, Sarge," a voice sheepishly replied. "I thought I saw something."

"Well thanks a lot, you wop bastard," Jackson huffed. "I was sound asleep dreamin' my head was caught between Mae West's tits and you just ruined it, you idiot!"

Up and down the line, laughter wafted from foxholes. Jack, chuckling along, rose to his feet on shaky legs. He climbed in the jeep and called out, "See you in the morning, guys." Out of the darkness a chorus of cheery "thanks for the beers" and "see you in the morning" rang forth. Though still shocked and saddened at what he'd learned about his father, he managed a satisfied smile; he was delighted with his new friends. He slowly pulled away, the blackout covers on his headlamps allowing just enough light by which to navigate. As he squinted through the dark, he felt a sudden sense of sadness for the boys he had just left. Somehow, it felt wrong that he was leaving his father and his mates alone in the dark jungle. Just then, a terrific downpour commenced. The huge drops hissed through the air and in seconds everything was sodden.

"Poor bastards," he mumbled, thinking of his father and his friends sitting in holes now filling with rainwater and mud. Jack slowed the jeep to navigate the gruel-like track, and his thoughts returned to the stupefying, tragic story his father had told him of his brother's death. He couldn't know for certain what impact it had on his father's later life, but he knew it must have been significant. He thought of nothing else on the trip back to the hospital. When he finally arrived, he entered the Cave and saw Frank and Turk lying on their stomachs, playing cards by the light of a stubby candle. He noticed Dr. Goldman asleep on his bedroll at the other end of the Cave. Ian, then, would be on duty in the hospital. Just as he lowered the grass door, he heard the rain stop.

"Goddamn figures," he muttered out loud.

Turk looked up at Jack, stared for a moment, then said, "Wow . . . you are really having a bad day aren't you?"

"Tell me about it."

Turk looked at Jack quizzically then said, "Why the fuck should I tell you about it? It was your day . . . not mine." Turk rolled his eyes and shook his head slowly. "Whoa . . . you still say he ain't fuckin' crazy, Frankie?"

"Never mind, Turk," Jack said wearily. "It's just a figure of speech."

"Whatever you say, Jacko. Hey, I still say you and Lt. Smith are wrong about that fuckin' supply asshole. I still say we go kick some ass. It's the . . . the . . . the . . ."

"Principle?" Frank asked.

"Yeah, that's it, Frankie. It's the fuckin' principle, you know?"

"I agree with you Turk, but we can't put the hospital at risk," Jack countered. Then smirking, he added, "That's why I've found a way of getting back at the son of a bitch without him ever even thinking of trying to interfere with our supplies." The two boys sat up and listened to Jack's story regarding his visit to Tom's unit, and how they were planning to go to Biggs' depot for a little chat. When he finished, Frank grinned broadly and Turk whooped with delight.

"Oh, that is going to be a kick," Frank said. "Biggs is going to poop his pants! Boy, I wish I could see that."

"Well, I'm gonna see it!" Turk proclaimed. "I got nothin' goin' in the morning. I'm coming with you, Jack . . . no fuckin' way ol' Turk is gonna miss this fuckin' hoe down." By his verbiage, Turk was clearly excited.

Jack smiled, "That's fine if you want, Turk. I've got to go talk to Lt. Smith and see if I can borrow a vehicle. We'll leave at 0730 if I can get one. If not we'll walk over at 0700."

As he exited the Cave, he heard Turk say to Frank, "Did I really just hear you say 'poop his pants'? What the hell is that? A fuckin' man just don't talk that way, Frank. Ain't you ever gonna fuckin' cuss? Just once maybe? It ain't American; I'm fuckin' telling you, Frankie." When Jack was halfway to the hospital, he could still hear the boys bickering.

Jack found Ian in the hospital checking on the dysentery cases.

"Hey, Doc," Jack said.

"Hello there, mate. How was your visit with Tom?"

"Just fine."

Jack told Ian the story of Tom's drunken father. However, he didn't tell him the painful, shocking discussion he'd had with Tom regarding his brother. He felt it was a private issue between father and son, one which formed a unique bond. He concluded by telling him the plans Lt. Grimes had for Biggs in the morning.

Ian was clearly pleased, "That is bloody marvelous! I wish I could come along. Hell, I bet this guy not only stops messing with us but actually bends over backwards every time someone from E Company comes calling."

"I bet you're right. I hate to ask, Doc, but is it possible for me to have the jeep again?"

"Of course, mate, I consider this official business."

"Thanks, Doc."

Jack and Ian chatted while they both worked on the dysentery patients. Jack emptied bedpans and wiped the men down with a wet cloth while Ian did blood pressure and temperature checks. After Jack's tumultuous day, the quiet of the tent and the warm, golden glow of the single light bulb suspended above brought a much welcome sense of peace. Caring for the ill Marines while talking to his friend delivered a warm, almost cozy feeling. It was the happiest moment of his day and he didn't want it to end. As soon as Ian was done with his rounds, though, he announced that he had a meeting to attend at the regimental aid station. He finished his paper work and bid Jack a good night. Jack walked back to the

283

Cave, chatted with Frank and Turk for a while, then retrieved his journal. He laid on his stomach and began to write.

August 13, 1942

Very weird day. Biggs had me beat up for stealing med supplies and dissing him. Tomorrow, the asshole pays . . .

. . . Redhead Marine from Goettge patrol didn't make it—damn sad and awful. Feel like I knew him for some reason. Have to get used to this. I can't freak every time someone dies—I'll go crazy. I know men will die and there's nothing I can do about it. This war is not what I thought it was. Cause is just, sure, but now the actual method used, war, essentially seems so stupid, so wasteful. The Marines are just normal boys, who more than anything else, just want to go home. Was it worth it at all, the war? Don't know, of course, but sitting here right now it is hard to imagine it is—was. Very confusing for me and has me asking questions I've never once considered.

Right now, God help me, I'm planning to be with Tom and his squad the night of Tenaru River battle. Will try hard not to chicken out. Gunshots tonight at Tom's unit—nearly shit my pants. Hope I can hack it. Question: if I get killed here do I really die or do I go back to the world? Think there is chance I would go back so will try and get courage from that theory.

Tomorrow—take care of asshole, then hospital shift. Perhaps visit Tom's unit again in the evening, if possible.

17

The next morning Jack and Turk excitedly wolfed down boiled oats, a prune each, then roared off to meet Tom's squad. On the way, Jack taught Turk how to sing Creedence's, *Green River*. Turk whooped after Jack sang the song through the first time; he loved it. Jack was amazed at how quickly he picked up the lyrics. He sang the song with gusto and his voice was smoother and richer than John Fogerty's, though the song lost little of its soulfulness. Somehow, the boy instinctively applied the twangy, southern inflection that was Forgerty's style. Jack slowly passed by the side of a long column of Marines as Turk loudly sang,

Well, take me back down where cool water flows, yeah.
Let me remember things I love,
Stoppin' at the log where catfish bite,
Walkin' along the river road at night,
Barefoot girls, dancin' in the moonlight.

The Marines hooted and cheered. Jack beat his thumbs on the steering wheel in time with the music. He mimicked the twangy guitar riffs that separated stanzas and lines, using "nong-a-nong-a" and "niow-niow" as the basis for the guitar's sound.

I can hear the bullfrog callin' me.
Nyaww.
Wonder if my rope's still hangin' to the tree.

Love to kick my feet 'way down the shallow water.
Shoefly, Dragonfly get back t' your mother.
Pick up a flat rock, skip it across green river.

Welllllll!

The cheers from the Marine column rose in pitch, but hadn't a chance of drowning out Turk's voice.

Up at Cody's camp I spent my day, oh,
With flat car riders and cross-tie walkers.
Old Cody, junior took me over,
Said, "You're gonna find the world is smould'rin'.
And if you get lost come home to Green River."

Welllll!
Come on home.

The Marines in the column whistled and applauded when Turk finished the song. Turk, his face beaming, raised his hands above his head, held them together and shook them like a victorious fighter. Jack assured him that there were many similar songs he could teach him and Turk seemed eager.

When they arrived at Tom's squad area, Jack was surprised to see that Grimes' entire 2nd Platoon, 27 men, was preparing to march. The lieutenant, he thought, must want to make a big impression on Biggs. Jack saw Tom talking with Grimes, Jackson, and Big Mikey. He and Turk walked up and greeted the group, "Morning, guys. Morning, Lieutenant."

"Morning, Jack," Tom said. "You ready to ride?"

"You bet." Pointing to Turk he said, "This is a friend of mine from the hospital; name's Turk. He wasn't gonna miss the show at any cost. Turk, this is my . . . this is Tom, Big Mikey, Sgt. Jackson, and last but not least, the man who made this little expedition possible, Lt. Grimes." Turk exchanged greetings and handshakes with the others, then Lt. Grimes explained what the procedure would be.

"Jack, you and Turk probably aren't up to marching all the way there and back in this goddamn heat, so you take your jeep . . . I'll ride with you." Jack glanced over and as he expected, Turk was grimacing. "The rest of the men will march in double column. When we get there. . . ."

"Excuse me, sir," Turk blurted.

"What is it, sailor?"

"Sir, if it's okay with you, sir, I'd rather not ride in the jeep. I'd rather walk with the other guys. I ain't an old fucker like Jack and I'll hold my own just fine on the march . . . I fuckin' promise, sir."

The lieutenant stared at Turk for a moment, a knowing grin slowly forming on his face. "Okay mister, that's no problem at all, and from now until this mission is over, you are officially a member of the 2nd platoon." Jack knew this would delight Turk, which in turn delighted him. He marveled at the sensitivity and savvy of the otherwise tough, young lieutenant. He was a natural born leader, a very rare breed of man.

Turk was apparently speechless, for he only cast darting glances at the others in the group, beaming widely. Jack chucked Turk on the shoulder and said, "Turk, you can do your little macho-man bit, but I'm no damn fool . . . I'm riding." Turning to the lieutenant he asked, "Can Tom here ride with us?"

"Sure."

"Hey thanks, Jack," Tom said. "I'm no fool either."

"Me too?" Big Mikey asked.

"Why not," Grimes replied wearily. "But don't come whining to me when the other guys are giving you a bunch of shit."

"Fuckin' sissies . . . uh, not you, sir," Sgt. Jackson muttered.

Jack slumped, and in an exaggerated whiny voice he said, "But it's just so, so hot and humid and sticky and stuff. I just hate to get all sweaty and icky and for sure my bunions would violently inflate. Then, one of you big strong Marines would have to carry me."

Lt. Grimes and Tom laughed, but Jackson only stared at him, apparently perplexed. Turk leaned over toward the sergeant, tapped his head and said in a low tone, "Fuckin' pops ain't all there, Sarge. Think the first war fucked up his brain some."

"Holy Christ, I guess so. Turk, you march with me."

Again Turk beamed, then leaned toward Jack, his face hardening. He whispered aggressively, "What's a fuckin' macho-man? You called me that . . . what's it mean?"

"It's a compliment, Turk . . . don't worry about it," Jack said impatiently.

"It'd better be."

"Anyhow," Lt. Grimes interrupted. "When we get there, I'll have Biggs assemble his men. No one says a word but me, got it? This guy out ranks us, which I don't think will be a problem, but we have to handle it carefully." Lt. Grimes then ordered Jackson to form the platoon into two parallel columns. Jackson walked away and immediately began barking out profane orders, Turk trailing close behind. The riders mounted the jeep, with Grimes taking the wheel. To Jack's surprise, and before the column began to move, he roared off toward the sand bar at the end of the creek, turned and sped east along the beach.

"Aren't we going to ride alongside the men?" Jack asked.

"Naw, it's too damn hard working the clutch and the gas pedal in the sand at walking speed. We'll stop short of the depot and wait for them." A few minutes later the depot lay just a hundred yards ahead, and the lieutenant braked the jeep to a halt. Jack offered Grimes a cigarette and asked him what he planned to do when the war was over.

"Build bridges," Grimes replied confidently. "I'm going to finish up my engineering degree at Pitt, get my masters at MIT, I hope, and then build bridges. Don't care too much about money or any of that. I just want to build bridges, always have."

"Interesting," Jack said. "You sure seem zeroed in; why bridges?"

"I've always loved them. To me they're like beautiful works of art. Every cable, strut, and rivet fascinates me. I can look at one all day, you know, study its lines and analyze what's holding the thing up. I grew up in Pittsburgh and I loved exploring the road and rail

288

bridges over the Susquehanna and the Monongahela. In fact, I nearly got squashed by a C&O freight train one day when I completely lost myself in an unusual welding pattern attaching a strut to the bridge. Good thing it was summer, I would've died in that river in the winter." Jack chuckled as Grimes took a long drag off his cigarette and continued, "Our country's going to need them, too. I believe this war is going to create a boom. I want to be a part of building the infrastructure that'll support it, not just be a link in the money chain."

Jack was very impressed by the young officer. Back in the world he would have been threatened by such a man, unwilling to cede any sense of commercial acuity. Strangely, Grimes left him with no such feelings. In fact, all he really felt was a deep sense of pride in his fellow American.

Grimes continued, "Tom told me you both grew up in Michigan."

"That's right."

"Well, one of my dreams is to build you guys a bridge that would join your lower peninsula with the upper peninsula. I can't remember the name of the area, but I'd love to be a part of building that bridge."

"Mackinac," Jack said, "the straits of Mackinac."

"Yeah, that's it. I've already worked on some designs in school for a five-mile-long dual suspension bridge there. Think of it, a five-mile-long suspension bridge. Would that be something or what? Of course, you never know if the government would actually fund such a thing."

"Oh, I think they will, sir," Jack said confidently. Lt. Grimes then gave a fascinating lecture on how the Golden Gate Bridge in San Francisco had been constructed. He'd gone all the way to California and back by bus during a school break at Pitt just to see it and the dual level Bay Bridge. His eyes lit up when he described their curves and lines. The lecture ended when the rest of the platoon marched up.

"It's about time you boys got here," Tom razzed. "You collectin' seashells on the way?"

"Fuck you, Tommy," Jackson huffed.

Lt. Grimes turned to the platoon, "Okay men, let's go meet Mr. Biggs . . . and remember, I do the talking."

Moments later, the column halted in front of the supply tent. A group of men were standing outside smoking cigarettes. Jack's eyes narrowed when he recognized the handsome blonde boy who had beaten him. He pulled his helmet lower over his face as he feared the boy would run if he recognized him.

"One of you imbeciles fetch Captain Biggs for me," Lt. Grimes ordered gruffly. "I need to talk to him." Jack saw Wimpy, wide-eyed, break away from the group and go inside the tent. The other men continued to smoke their cigarettes but were clearly unsettled. The demeanor of the lieutenant and the silent, glaring, heavily armed platoon cast a menacing pall. A moment later, Biggs walked out of the tent, stopped suddenly, and slowly surveyed the scene. Twenty-seven armed, grimy, hard looking Marines stood just yards away, all of them staring sternly straight at *him*. The four riders still sat in the jeep.

"You Biggs?" Grimes asked.

"I'm *Captain*, Earnest Biggs, CO. Who are you?"

"Assemble your men, Biggs . . . all of them."

"What? Who the hell are you . . . what do you want?"

"Fuck that!" Grimes barked. "I said assemble your men."

"This . . . this is outrageous. I demand to know what your business is. I'm a Marine Corps officer and by the looks of you I detect a hint of insubordination here."

Grimes' eyes flashed with anger and he shouted, "I'm fucking General MacArthur! Assemble your men now or I'm going to get out of this jeep and shove my bayonet up your fucking ass. Assemble your men . . . now!"

Some of the supply men began to mutter and curse. One of them said loudly, "This is bullshit. Who the hell do you assholes think you are?" With alarming quickness, Dumbass sprang forward and doubled the speaker over with a rifle butt to his midsection. He slowly sank to the ground, groaning loudly.

Dumbass looked down at the fallen supply man and sneered, "We're Marines, fuckface!" The chatter amongst the supply men came to an abrupt halt. A look of fear and anger spread across Biggs' face and he quickly ordered Wimpy to assemble the members of the depot's unit. Jack was enjoying watching Biggs squirm. He kept glancing over at the blonde, keeping an eye on him. Tom leaned over his shoulder and whispered, "You see the guys that beat you up? Don't point . . . just describe the fuckers."

"I see one of 'em." Jack told Tom where the blonde was standing and what he looked like. After a few moments Tom said, "Okay, I got 'im." Then Turk walked up and asked the same question. It was Tom who replied. "He sees one of 'em and he's mine, Turk, sorry."

Jack looked at Tom with chagrin. His father apparently intended to exact revenge for him and it made him uncomfortable. "It's my fight, Tom, I'll take care of him," Jack argued. Turk guffawed loudly.

"C'mon, pops," he said. "You got fuckin' boobs for chrissakes. These guys are half your age. They'll kill you."

Tom visibly winced, but agreed with Turk. "The good news is that Lt. Grimes told us Biggs is yours. We'll handle these other guys. Hell man, when was the last time you were in a fight anyhow?" A hell of a long time ago, Jack thought. Besides, he had only been in a few fistfights growing up. It wasn't due to any fear of physical injury, but more a fear of being humiliated. He'd also felt it embarrassing to be in the situation in the first place; beneath him in a way. His father had always told him that intelligent, right-minded people didn't fight or resort to violence unless absolutely necessary. Yet here he was, eager to exact revenge for his son. Biggs interrupted Jack's thoughts.

His chin still jutted, but his nerves were betrayed by a slight quaver in his voice, "I demand you tell me who you are and why you're here."

"Shut the fuck up!" Grimes barked. Men were beginning to gather around the tent, staring nervously at the Marines. When it appeared they had all assembled, Lt. Grimes leaned over and put his arm around Jack. "This is a good buddy of mine." For the first time, Biggs' eyes rested on Jack's bruised face. A look of surprise, then uncertainty, crossed his face and he reddened. Jack glanced over at the blonde just in time to see him turn and begin to walk into the jungle. Tom had also noticed the attempted escape.

"Scooz!" he shouted, pointing at the blonde.

Scozzolari immediately raised his rifle and shouted, "You take one more step, dickhead, and I'll put a slug in your bony ass!" The blonde stopped and slowly turned around. Tom walked over and stood in front of him.

Turk leaned over and asked, "You see the other one yet?" Jack surveyed the supply men and quickly found the ugly boy. He pointed him out to Turk.

"Remember, I said one of the attackers never hit me and apologized afterwards. He's the one so go easy on him, okay?"

"But the fucker was kicking you, right?"

"They were half-hearted kicks, not nearly as vicious as the other guy's."

"Okay. I'll talk to him and just shove him around a little."

"Okay, good."

Biggs was trying hard to recover the situation. He pointed at Jack accusingly, "The thief, the man who stole supplies. Why is he . . . ?"

Grimes shot out of the jeep and stormed up to Biggs shouting, "Don't give me that crap you chicken shit, son of a bitch!" Biggs slumped slightly. "You're the fucking thief, you bastard! When you withhold medical supplies you're withholding them from me and the men standing behind me, you understand that, shit for brains? We hardly have any supplies as it is and assholes like you are withholding stuff? I ought to shoot you dead right here!"

Jack had conjured up the most menacing scowl he could, but in reality, was working hard not to laugh out loud at Biggs' obvious discomfort. He was visibly terrified, but he was doing his best to maintain his composure, "I'm sorry, but you're mistaken, I . . .."

292

"*You're* sorry, you motherfucker!" Grimes thundered. Pointing to Jack he continued, "You withheld vital supplies from wounded Marines and when this good man tried to work around that fact, you had your goons beat the stuffing out of him! You didn't even have the balls to do it yourself." At that, Jack saw a commotion out of the corner of his eye. He turned just in time to see his father take an angry step toward the blonde. The boy looked terrified, but clenched his fists and spread his legs, preparing to defend himself. The last move was a mistake. Tom quickly swung his booted right leg up as if punting a football. The boot crashed into the boy's groin. He grabbed at his crotch and emitted a brief, animal-like howl. As Tom's foot came down, his right arm shot out and he smashed his fist into the boy's nose. The blow made a loud crack and blood immediately exploded from the injury. The blonde sank to the ground, screaming in agony.

"Hmm, don't that fucker scream just like a girl?" Turk said as he casually trudged off toward the other attacker. He stopped in front of him and did what he said he would do; he engaged the ugly man in what appeared to be a relatively passive discussion. Then, after several moments, Turk crossed one arm across his chest and rested the elbow of the other on it, cupping his cheek in his hand. Turk nodded his head thoughtfully several times as the ugly boy explained himself, then dropped his hands to his sides. An instant later, so quick it didn't register until well after the blow was struck, Turk's fist shot up toward the ugly boy's face and connected solidly with his mouth. The sound of Turk's blow did not have the gunshot effect of Tom's; it was duller, almost squishy Jack thought. The boy's eyes screwed shut in pain and he crouched with his arms straight out, staggering backwards like a drunk trying to maintain his balance. As he pedaled awkwardly backward, Jack saw him spit several rusty colored teeth out in sprays of blood. Finally, he tumbled onto his back, moaning.

Grimes and Biggs had stopped their dialogue to observe the action. When Jack looked back at them, he saw that Biggs had gone pale. He looked at Turk and saw him kneeling over his victim. Turk pulled his medical kit out and began to gently clean and bandage the boy's mouth. When he was done, he lifted the boy to his feet, put his arm around him and guided him to the jeep. As Turk walked past, Jack said with a wry smile, "That was quite a shove, Turk."

"I talked to the son of a bitch like I said," Turk said defensively. "You were right; he didn't do nothin' too wrong. I just felt bad for him with those mossy fuckin' teeth of his. Thought I'd help him get rid of some of the smelly little bastards. Too bad about the busted jaw though; but hey, I ain't never said I was a fuckin' dentist." The boy was in agony, but Jack felt only slight remorse. As Turk said, he had kicked him and did nothing to stop the beating. At that, Tom walked up with the blonde, lightly pressing a cloth against his nose.

"Broken nose," Tom said. "You'll have to take him to your aid station too." The two injured supply men hunched in the back of the jeep, moaning in unison. Jack turned back toward Biggs and saw that Grimes had turned a crate on its side and was directing him to sit on it. He slowly and reluctantly sat down. Grimes turned to Jack and motioned him over.

"Come here, Jack. Biggs has just been telling me he's a big man on Wall Street, just like his old man. Says he grew up in a penthouse on Park Avenue and that he knows a lot of important people, even people in Hollywood he says. So I'm thinking someone as high society as Mr. Biggs here could always use special grooming." Jack eagerly approached, but his smile vanished when he saw Lt. Grimes pull a straight razor out of his pants pocket and slowly unfold it. Grinning, he rubbed his index finger softly up and down the blade. Biggs cursed and tried to get off the crate. A Marine standing behind him roughly forced him back down with the length of his rifle.

"What the hell are you people doing?" Biggs asked wide-eyed. "Are you going to cut off one my ears like they say you animals do? You . . . you can't do this. I'm an officer in the United States Marine Corps! You'll be arrested, you . . ."

"Would you please shut the fuck up," Grimes said wearily. "I'm tired of you're creepy little voice. Now take your goddamn medicine like a man."

In a way, Jack would've loved to cut Biggs' ear off; he detested him that much. But he knew he could never actually do it. He wondered what Grimes had in mind and locked eyes with him. The lieutenant, his back to Biggs, winked at Jack, leaned over, and whispered something in Jack's ear. He handed Jack a small tin and the razor. Smirking, Jack walked over to Biggs and leaned over him. Waving the straight razor in front of his face he said, "Alright darling, let's get you all pretty and perky." Biggs was sweating profusely and his left eye was twitching. Jack looked up at the Marine standing behind Biggs, "Hold his head still will you, I'd hate to cut off the wrong goddamn thing."

Turk yelled, "Cut his fuckin' cock off!" The Marines laughed. Jack dipped his fingers into the tin Grimes had given him. When he pulled them out, the ends were covered with a beige cream. In two quick swipes he spread the cream over Biggs' eyebrows, then happily whistling, proceeded to shave Biggs' lower forehead bare. When he was finished, he wiped Biggs' brow clean with his sleeve, then stepped back and admired his work. Turning to the platoon and smiling proudly, he pointed at Biggs with both hands palms up, and announced, "Gentlemen, the sauciest officer on Guadalcanal, Captain Earnest N. Biggs, United States Marine Corps, formerly of Park Avenue, New York."

The men laughed and hooted raucously. Jack noticed that even some of the supply men were sniggering, some stifling outright laughs. Jack felt more empowered, and somehow more free, than he ever had. He held the razor and tin over his head in triumph, then bowed deeply to the appreciative audience. He looked at Biggs and chuckled. Without eyebrows, the dark haired captain looked both comical and frightening, like some Hollywood space alien, Jack decided. He also thought the shave gave Biggs a permanent look of being startled. The effect was exaggerated by Biggs' tanned face. Where two dark furrows of hair were moments ago, there were now strips of white that seemed to be glowing in contrast to the surrounding skin.

After the laughter and catcalls died, Lt. Grimes walked up to

Biggs, crouched down and hissed, "Now you listen to me, sir, and you listen closely. If I hear of you fucking with this man or anyone else from his hospital, or for that matter anybody on this island, we'll be back. And next time we won't be such good sports."

"You're . . . you're in big trouble, mister," Biggs answered, his voice shaking.

"Oh really?" Grimes dripped. "What are you going to do, dumb shit? Tell your superior officer? Hell, he probably hates your sniveling little ass as it is. You going to tell the Shore Patrol? What an enlightening investigation that would be, if they'd actually be interested enough to bother holding one. When they found us, *if* they actually could, and we told them why we paid you this little visit, I wonder what kind of things they'd find in your files, or when they talk to some of your men, hmm? I know your type; you're as dirty as pig shit. No, you fucked yourself, Biggs. You fucked yourself real good." Biggs clenched his jaw and looked down at the ground, tears welling in his eyes.

Grimes stood up and shouted, "All right Marines, form up and prepare to move out."

Jack walked up to Biggs and stared at him for a moment. Then he placed his index and middle finger just above Biggs' bare brows and firmly pushed his head back until he tumbled backwards and sprawled in the sand. As he walked away, Jack crowed, "I told you investment bankers are ignorant bastards." Biggs lay in the sand glaring hatefully up at him. Jack was unable to conjure up the slightest amount of sympathy for the man. But then something strange, and never before experienced, happened. The wide smile on his face suddenly evaporated as a picture of him telling the employees of his family company that it was being sold popped into his brain. He turned away from Biggs quickly, wondering if any of them would have happily given him similar treatment if given the opportunity. He strode off toward Lt. Grimes whispering urgently to himself, "No comparison, buddy . . . none. This guy is a sicko, you were just a good, aggressive businessman, bud . . . don't sweat it." By the time he'd reached Lt. Grimes, he'd completely purged the self-doubt from his mind.

18

"Thanks a lot, Lieutenant. I really can't tell you what this means to me." Jack said to Grimes.

"No sweat, Macmillan. I doubt if he's going to give you guys much trouble from now on, but if he does, let me know."

"You're sure there won't be any trouble over this, sir?"

"There are 10,000 Marines on this island. We'd be tough to find even if they wanted to. Besides, we just did a little grooming. We didn't hurt him. I'm pretty certain we won't hear a thing," Grimes assured him.

"You're probably right," Jack agreed. "You want a lift back to your position?"

"No thanks; you need to get those fellas to the hospital."

"Yeah, Tom and Turk really nailed 'em." Jack offered his hand to the lieutenant, and after saying goodbye, he turned toward the platoon, now lined up in two rows for the march back to their positions. "Thanks guys. I, and everyone at the E Company hospital, appreciate it! I'll see you soon."

"No, thank *you,* bud!" Dumbass yelled. "This was funner than huntin' squirrels with you're dick hanging out!"

"What?" several boys wondered in unison.

Jack smiled, "I think I know what you mean D.A. Uh . . . maybe not."

Tom and Jack shook hands. "Thanks a lot, pal," Jack said.

"Hey, no sweat. You come visit whenever you can, Macmillan, beer or no beer. But obviously, if I had a choice . . ."

Jack laughed, "I'll see what I can do, but in any case, I will definitely be visiting again . . . soon."

He mounted the jeep, waved goodbye, then drove off down the beach at low speed. The two supply men in the back emitted occasional moans. Nodding his head toward the back of the jeep, Turk said, "At least my guy's gonna get a shiny new set a' fuckin' choppers."

"Yeah," Jack guffawed. "Dr. Turk's revolutionary new dental procedure for periodontal disease, guaranteed to work every time! You carefully walk up to the patient, then, as hard as you can, hit them in the mouth with a goddamn baseball bat!"

"Hell yeah!" Turk squealed. Jack's alliteration inspired Turk to break out in a rousing rendition of *Take Me out to the Ballgame*. When he finished the song, Jack asked him to keep singing. Turk stunned him with a perfectly delivered example of *God Save the Queen*. Jack listened to the music and wondered about Turk. For someone outwardly as simple as he, Turk was remarkably complex and interesting, completely unlike the one-dimensional characters Jack had been accustomed to back in the world . . . incredibly profane, yet exceedingly gentle with his patients. Savagely striking a man, then moments later happily and beautifully singing two songs that couldn't be farther apart in their origins. After a week, Jack still didn't know his real name or much about his past.

"Where in the hell did you learn that?" Jack asked.

Turk smiled, "My neighbors back home in Philly was fuckin' limeys. I was pals with one of the boys and he taught me the tune. It's one of my favorites for some reason, you know, seeing that it's an alien song or whatever you call it. It's . . . it's . . . kinda grand and proud and all, you know? Makes you think them fuckin' limeys won't never be beat . . . not like them French fucks."

"Yeah . . . yeah, you're right, Turk. I've never thought about it that way." Jack shook his head wondering whether Turk's last statement confirmed a lack of intelligence or a sort of diction-challenged genius. He couldn't help but, for some reason, lean toward the latter.

"So what did you do back in Philly, before the war I mean?" Jack asked.

"Odd jobs when I could get 'em. Mostly ran numbers for the bookies and played dice in the street the rest of the time."

"Interesting. You looking forward to getting back there?"

"Yeah. I'll tell you one fuckin' thing, Jack. South Philly is the center of the whole goddamn world and I live in the best neighborhood in South Philly . . . no shit."

"How about family?"

Jack noticed Turk's face cloud over. "My old man was an asshole, used to beat the shit out of me and my ma . . . that is until he up and hauled fuckin' ass in '37. Ain't seen him since."

"Sorry to hear that," Jack said softly.

"It's okay, hell, it was actually good the bastard left, you know? I got three older sisters and they're real good. They was always after me for gettin' into fights and runnin' numbers and shit, but it was just because they cared. They looked after me and ma real good."

"It's good your mother has them while you're out here."

Turk's face fell and he stared out to sea. After several moments without altering his gaze, he said in a strangely casual way, "Nah, just before we shipped out of New River I got word from Maria, she's my oldest sis, that Ma was dead. It was real quick I guess, some sort of infection. We were quarantined before shipping out, so the fuckin' Navy wouldn't let me go to the funeral."

"My gosh, Turk," Jack gasped. "I am really sorry. Jesus man, that's as tough as it gets."

Turk brushed a hand through the air and said, "Ah, it's fuckin' life, you know? I ain't gonna whine about it." Turk's demeanor clearly demonstrated he no longer wished to talk about his painful memories.

"I don't even know your real name; what is it?" Jack asked.

Turk rolled his eyes, "Jesus you're a nosy little shit, and I'll kill your ass if you laugh. If you just got to know, it's Victor De la Rose.

Some fuckin' comedian in my family changed the 'a' to an 'e' after they got off the fuckin' boat from Portugal. We been defendin' our honor ever since." In spite of the sad stories Turk had just told him, Jack couldn't prevent a snicker from escaping.

"Fuck you," Turk muttered.

"Sorry, bud. How did you get the name Turk?"

"Would you quit givin' me the fuckin' business? Who are you, J. fuckin' Edgar Hoover?"

"I'm just trying to find out a little more about you," Jack replied. "That's what friends do you know."

Turk frowned and, looking concerned, said, "Sorry for biting your head off, Jack. I just don't like to talk much about myself, okay? It don't mean we ain't friends, does it?"

"Of course not. That's not what I meant."

"Okay, good. I don't wanna have busted that fucker's jaw for nothin'." Jack and Turk looked at each other for a moment, then burst out laughing. Jack grabbed the back of Turk's neck and shook him affectionately. Together, they broke out in a happy rendition of *Green River*. When they had finished, Jack taught Turk two more Creedence songs: *Run through the Jungle* and *Who'll Stop the Rain*. Again, Jack was amazed at how quickly Turk acquired the tunes and their lyrics. He begged Jack to teach him more.

When they arrived back at the hospital, most of the staff, including Ian, crowded excitedly around the jeep. Some of the men chuckled, while others were silent, when they saw the condition of the two men Tom and Turk had 'educated'. Jack was expecting Turk to dramatically recall the event for his unit mates with much embellishment and braggadocio. Strangely though, "Problem solved boys," was Turk's only comment.

As the hospitalmen clapped, Turk and Jack gingerly helped the injured boys out of the jeep and into the hospital. They laid the men down on the saw-horsed stretchers and Ian let out a low whistle. "Wow, it looks as though these blokes really learned a lesson. What did the Marines do? Bash 'em with their bloody rifle butts?"

"Nope," Jack answered. "Two punches: one broken nose and one broken jaw."

Turk pointed to the blonde and added, "Oh and I don't think that feller's fuckin' balls are feelin' too peachy neither."

Jack chuckled, "Oh that's right; make it two punches and one boot."

"Very efficient," Ian remarked. "Someone knew what they were doing."

Jack looked at Turk and smiled, "Hell, Doc, one of em . . ."

"Them Marines are tough sir, I fuckin' assure you," Turk interrupted. Turk looked at Jack and shook his head rapidly. Jack nodded and said nothing more.

Ian manipulated the blonde's nose, straightening it as best he could. Then he carefully stuffed cotton gauze inside his nostrils. Throughout the procedure the boy winced and groaned. Two black rings had already formed around his eyes and, in spite of Ian's efforts, the boy's nose still bent slightly to the right. It was swollen to twice its normal size from the blow Jack's father had delivered, and the boy was now a hideous cartoon of his former handsome self. Jack felt no real pity for him; but he also felt the young man was suffering enough for his crime, so he neither apologized nor tormented him further. When Ian finished, he gave him some aspirin, then moved on to the ugly boy, who, much to his misfortune, had grown considerably uglier after his encounter with Turk. While Ian worked on his jaw, Jack gingerly cleaned dried blood from his face and hands.

After examining the boy's jaw, Ian radioed the battalion hospital and asked for an oral surgeon who was stationed there. Within minutes, the doctor, surprisingly old Jack thought, was working on the boy's jaw, wiring it to his upper plate. When the young man's moans deepened, Turk gave him a dose of morphine and within a minute he was silent and groggy. After the oral surgeon was finished, the boy fell completely asleep. Turk, trying hard not to disturb him, wiped gently at the boy's lips and around his mouth. He then applied a small dressing over a portion of the boy's lower lip that had been split by his own blow. As Jack watched Turk work, he overheard Ian and the oral surgeon talking about how the young man had been injured.

"I'm not exactly sure what happened," Ian lied. "Some sort of fight between the Navy and Marines. Happens all the time, it's just too bad it had to happen while we're in the middle of a bloody war."

"Yeah, like we aren't going to have enough to deal with," the oral surgeon agreed. "But boys will be boys I guess. Christ, they're so young . . . poor buggers. They should be fighting over girls outside the ice cream shop, not over some silliness on this cesspool of an island. Hell, I'm only 45, not exactly ancient, but I'm old enough to be their father." The doctor smiled and added, "Hell, I'm probably old enough to be you're father!"

Jack was shocked to hear that the oral surgeon was a year younger than he. He'd felt for certain the man was at least in his mid-50's. He looked at him more closely, then realized what had misled him. For the last week, and with the exception of Col. Goettge, the men Jack had been constantly exposed to and interacted with were very young. They had become his close friends and companions and he increasingly identified with them; he was, in a way, becoming one of them. He hadn't looked in a mirror since he had left the world, so his appearance, in his imagination, matched more closely his Marine and Navy friends than the doctor's. Looking at the surgeon though, he easily recalled his aging skin, growing jowls and thinning hair. "Jesus," he whispered to himself, "no wonder everyone was so pissed that Biggs had me beat up." Still, he considered his deluded transformation a blessing. He needed to feel young . . . to be one of them as much as possible.

The two doctors decided that the jaw case should be moved out to ship. Ian would construct some sort of protective device to fit over the blonde's nose, and he would be sent back to the supply depot immediately.

At approximately 1400, the hospital received its first two malaria cases and one case of dengue fever—'breakbone' fever the

302

Marines would call it later, due to the throbbing aches it produced throughout the body. When the malaria cases arrived, the mosquito borne virus was in burn mode for both men. Frank took their temperatures and announced that both hovered at 105 degrees. The pasty boys were sweating profusely. Jack tried as best as he could to keep the men hydrated, and wiped down their bodies with wet cloths. An hour after they arrived, the virus changed its method of misery in one of the boys. He began to shiver with severe chills, even though it was hot and humid in the tent. After a half hour of this, the young man became delirious, babbling nonsense and groaning. At first Jack felt frustrated by his inability to do much of anything for him. After a while though, he became used to the sights and sounds of delirium and largely, just like everyone else, became accustomed to the symptoms of the disease. He knew that until things heated up on the battlefield they would continue to receive malaria, gastroenteritis, dengue, and dysentery cases almost exclusively.

In the early evening, more malaria and dysentery cases arrived. The great and awful diseases, that would cause more casualties amongst the American soldiers than the enemy, had invaded the Marine ranks and were spreading from foxhole to foxhole. Jack spent the rest of his day in the hospital, too busy and worn out to pay a visit to Tom and his squad. Aching and completely exhausted, he fell fast asleep while making his journal entry in the Cave.

August 14, 1942

Good day; great day! Took care of Biggs and his two goons . . .

. . . . Saw a doctor my age today, thought he looked ancient at first, but finally realized he looked no older than me. These men are so young! I knew they were, but never really thought about it and what it meant. Question: what would happen if all nations were required to field armies

of people only 40 and over? Would fix problem of war quickly would be my guess.

The Marines, the vast majority at least, are hard and tough, though imbued with honor, bravery and loyalty. Part training and part growing up in the '30s I suppose. We grew up soft and easy, I'm not sure if we would have been as honorable and dedicated as these boys. Seems opposite should be true with all we were given, strange. We are so much more focused on material goods and instant gratification than these boys on the island. Though their young lives have been physically difficult, there is much more stress back in the world. Stress that we don't even recognize as such. All the must do's. Must have this and that; must vacation here and there; must have kids in training for this sport or that. There is more pressure as the world moves faster and gets more impersonal and cold. It makes me sad to see their misery and suffering and know that their grandchildren will be better off financially because of their sacrifice, but not emotionally or spiritually. Jesus, I'm starting to sound like Ian. Must be really tired.

Too busy to visit Tom tonight. Need to figure way to pinch beer for squad. Am too tired to think about tomorrow.

19

For the next four days Jack followed a fairly set routine. In the mornings he'd make a run to Biggs' supply depot. It had moved from Red Beach to just down the road near the battalion hospital. Jack had badgered Ian into putting him back in charge of supplies. Biggs refused to talk to Jack when he was at the depot, choosing only to fix him with an evil looking glare. Jack figured this was his way of trying to restore some shred of dignity and machismo. In spite of the glare, Biggs still looked like a car had backfired when he was walking by, though a five o'clock shadow was beginning to sprout on his brow. Tellingly, Jack no longer needed Biggs' signature on his requisitions. For himself, Jack took great care to treat the staff at the depot with respect and avoid any sort of provocation. It wasn't difficult, for they were exceedingly cooperative.

After depositing and inventorying supplies in the Emerald Palace, Jack would take up his shift in the hospital. Contact with the enemy was still rare, so the casualties were mainly victims of disease or accidents. He spent much of his time working with and talking to Ian. The hours they spent together brought them ever closer. Jack would finish his shift around dinner time, then head for the Tenaru and spend some time with Tom and his squad mates. Turk insisted on coming each time. At first Jack resisted, but then happily relented when Turk bribed him with his access to a mysterious and seemingly endless supply of beer and *sake*. When they couldn't borrow the hospital's jeep, they'd walk the distance, roughly a mile each way, lugging the cases of contraband on their shoulders. The oppressive heat required rest stops at least every hundred yards, making the journey up to an hour long. They'd make the trip on a direct line by diagonally cutting across Henderson's 160 ft. wide runway, then pass through the coconut grove. At night it was cooler, and they'd jog or walk quickly back through the dark, screeching groves and jungle, often singing CCR's *Run through the Jungle*, to keep their nerves steady. Turk always sang the lines—

Whoa thought it was a nightmare,
Lo, it's all so true,
They told me, "don't go walkin' slow
'cause devil's on the loose."

Better run through the jungle,
Better run through the jungle,
Better run through the jungle,
Whoa, don't look back to see.

—a little louder and with more emotion than the others. After returning to the hospital, Jack would sit with Ian in the Cave or a bomb shelter, talking about the war, care for the men, but mostly about life and its various challenges and meaning. The Japanese Navy was now cruising, unmolested, up the 'Slot' on a nightly basis and shelling the perimeter. They did relatively little damage, but it was terrifying. Unlike 'Louie the Louse', Jack had no idea where the shells may land, so he'd take cover with the others when the Jap destroyers and cruisers opened up.

On his visits to the Tenaru, Jack watched with amusement as Dumbass and Turk predictably and quickly struck up a close, remarkably profane relationship. They would move around the platoon area almost as one, jawing, belching, and generally creating some form of turmoil, mostly joyous, wherever they stopped. During a visit on the 17th, Tom noticed the two friends hunkered down in Dumbass' foxhole, sipping beer and talking seriously in hushed tones. Occasionally, one or the other would snicker and duck his

306

head. Jack wondered what the strange behavior meant. It wasn't long before he found out. It turned out Dumbass had a plan. Jack and the others watched it unfold.

Sporting serious looks, the boys clambered out of their hole and strode toward Jack. "Hey, Jacko," Turk hailed. "It ain't a problem if me and Dumbass borrow the jeep for a little while, is it?" Jack eyed the boys warily, both looking at him with wide-eyed innocence.

"Depends; what are you planning to do with it?"

"Um, we gotta go get some supplies," Dumbass replied. "Sgt. Jackson asked us to. It'll be real quick."

Jack looked at them a little longer. He didn't believe them for one second, but he could see no real harm in letting them take the jeep. "Oh, alright . . . but don't do anything stupid, okay?"

"No fuckin' way, Jacko," Turk said, slapping Jack on the shoulder. The two boys quickly walked back to Dumbass' hole, grabbed their shirts, and Dumbass, strangely, a long stick of some sort. They jogged to the jeep, hopped in, and sped off in the direction of the beach. After a half hour they had not returned and Jack was getting slightly antsy. Then he heard hollers and whoops. He looked down the road toward the beach and saw the two boys in the jeep, shouting wildly, smoking big cigars.

"Yeeehawww!" Turk yelled.

Dumbass held up the stick and waved it back and forth. Jack noticed a string was attached to one end of it. Then, as the jeep swerved and jitterbugged its way closer, he saw that the vehicle was different, misshapen with lumpy protuberances. He looked closer. The boys had somehow attached at least 15 grayish-blue, kapok life jackets to it. One, stuck to a tire, was taking a terrific beating. Others were tied to all four sides of the jeep. Another was tied to the steering wheel. Just before they reached where Jack was standing, they turned 90 degrees . . . toward the stagnant Tenaru.

"Oh hell yeah, boys!" Dumbass screamed. "We gonna have us a fuckin' fish fry!" As they zoomed past Jack, Dumbass looked at him and yelled, "You got a swell boat, Jack!" Jack saw that Dumbass had fashioned a crude hook to the end of the string that now dangled from the stick. What looked to be one of the gray, rubbery chunks of meat from a C-ration was impaled on the hook. Turk was driving the jeep, chomping his big cigar . . . laughing and yelling. The other boys in the platoon area, realizing what was going on, were on their feet, waving their arms and cheering wildly. Just before he launched the modified jeep upon the waters of the creek, Turk bellowed, "Anchors aweigh, motherfuckers! The USS *Turkass* is underway!"

In horror Jack yelled, "Hey. . . . no! No you goddamn idiots . . . that's the doctor's jeep!" It was too late. The jeep plunged into the murky waters of the creek, creating a small tidal wave that roiled the normally calm waters of the river. In a matter of seconds, it sank to the bottom. Once it had settled, the only things still visible were the two boys' heads, reminding Jack of a pair of ducks floating on a pond. Sodden cigars still jutted from their clenched teeth. Incredibly, Dumbass still held the fishing pole above his head, the impaled meat chunk invisible below the surface. "I don't believe it," Jack groaned. "He's fishing goddamn it . . . he's actually fishing." Jack buried his face in his hands and mumbled, "I'm fucked." The other Marines, including Sgt. Jackson, had gone completely wild, slapping backs and cheering the two boys in the water. Then a sharp, angry voice rose above the happy din.

"Goddamn it, you morons! What the hell do you think you're doing?" It was Lt. Grimes. He stormed up to the creek's edge, his face red and twisted with rage. Jack could not recall seeing any other man quite this angry in all his life. "That's Corps property you shitheads! Shit . . . fuck! Shitfuck! We're on an enemy island, short on equipment, and you dumb shits pull a stunt like this? I ought to shoot your stupid asses right now!" Turk and Dumbass said nothing at first; they just sheepishly stared back at the furious lieutenant. The only sound was the gurgle of air bubbles rising from the sunken jeep, as several awkward seconds passed, the fishing line still dangling in the water.

Finally, Dumbass spoke, "But Turk and I already figgered you'd get the first trout, sir. We was even gonna fry the bastard up for you."

Grimes' mouth fell open slightly, and after a shocked pause he grunted, "Trout? What the . . . there isn't a trout within . . ." After a pause, he groaned and threw his arms up in the air. "Ah fuck it," he muttered. Dumbass' announcement had completely disarmed him. Jack watched, thinking he could actually see the anger exiting Grimes' body. Finally, unable to help himself, the lieutenant burst out laughing. Soon, the platoon area rocked once again with laughter and cheers. Even Jack couldn't help himself and, though worried about the jeep, joined in the merriment. After a minute, Turk stood up on the seat of the jeep and raised his hands. Slowly, the platoon quieted down. Then he stretched his arms out, preacher-like.

"Men," he shouted, "in honor of this very special day, a day in which we've seen the launch of the most beautiful ship in the United States fuckin' Navy, the USS *Turkass*, I'd like to sing a song. A song about the greatest Navy in the world, no matter what them dirty fuckin' Japs have to say about it."

In his beautiful, rich voice Turk began singing the Navy hymn, *Anchors Aweigh*. At first some of the other boys joined in, but they quickly stopped when they heard Turk's voice. As he finished, loud cheers once again erupted. Turk and Dumbass swam ashore and were mobbed by the platoon members. A grinning Lt. Grimes shook their hands. Then he ordered the two to get the jeep out of the water. Their platoon mates, without being asked, jumped in to help. They shouted and splashed in the water, reminding Jack again that they were just boys, not historical supermen. A rope was attached to the back of the jeep, and all the men, including Jack, pulled. The jeep quickly popped out of the water and the men excitedly crowded around it. Turk climbed in, closed his eyes, folded his hands, pointed his head toward the sky and pretended to say a brief prayer. He crossed himself, then tried to start the jeep. After a few coughs and grinds the rugged little vehicle fired to life. Jack sighed with relief and a new round of cheers broke out. On the way back to the hospital that night, Turk begged Jack to swear he'd never tell Ian the story of he and Dumbass' fishing expedition. Reluctantly, Jack agreed.

20

Aug. 18th marked the first bit of real aerial excitement for the men in the area of Henderson Field. Other than the occasional noontime nuisance raids, when the Japanese raiders for the most part sprinkled a few bombs ineffectively around the airfield, the Marines had escaped any major aerial onslaught. Now that would all change. The Japanese conducted their first major daytime air raid targeting Henderson. Jack knew the attack was coming, but only that it would come during daylight hours, not the exact hour itself. The raid on the 18th, like the previous smaller raids, would be uncontested. Jack was working in the hospital shortly after noon when he heard the alarm bell ringing at the Pagoda. Ian ordered the men to carry the patients on litters to the bomb shelters, then, as he had during every other raid, walked over to Jack.

"Any reason to worry on this one, mate?" Ian asked.

"Naw, not really, Doc. This is going to be the biggest yet, and they'll actually hit the airfield this time, but no one in this area is going to get hurt. Should be quite a show; you want to watch it with me?"

"Sure, as soon as I'm sure all the men are in the shelters, I'll join you outside the Cave. That's actually a good idea. The boys are getting a mite jumpy over these bloody raids. It makes them feel a little vulnerable and helpless when they see the nasty little buggers swanning about overhead like they're at the bloody Sydney Air

Show. When the boys see that we're not too concerned about the raids, they might feel a little better about their prospects."

Jack helped carry litters to the bomb shelter, and was coming out as Frank was going in. "Hey . . . where're you going, Jack? Everyone's in the shelter."

"Doc Smith and I are going to watch the show outside the Cave."

"Jeepers creepers; Turk's right . . . you are crazy. But what about Doc . . . what's his excuse?"

"We're not too worried, Frank. The Jap fliers couldn't . . . uh, can't hit a cow in the ass with a snow shovel."

"Well isn't that the problem?"

"What do you mean, Frank?"

"Well, I don't really think the Japs are up there right now saying to each other, 'Okay, now remember, our target is Macmillan and Lt. Smith. We'll find 'em and blow 'em up.' No, their target is the airfield; you get my drift Jack?"

"No, I can't say as I do."

Frank, exasperated, rolled his eyes and continued, "If their target is the airfield and they can't hit what they're aiming at, then it's possible they'll hit you and Doc just sitting there smoking your dumb cigarettes." Jack, of course, couldn't tell him that the bombs wouldn't harm them. He simply carried on with the false bravado.

Jack smiled cockily, "The Japs wouldn't dare mess with me and the doc, Frankie." Just then they heard the faint sound of aircraft engines out to sea. It started out as a low rumble, then grew to a higher pitched, but throaty growl. Jack looked up and saw eight white, wispy contrails snaking out of the north, pointing directly at him. Frank saw them, too.

"Okay, I've seen enough," he said. "You guys are nuts. You really should take shelter."

Jack looked down at Frank and saw the look of concern on his face. For a moment he felt badly that he couldn't reassure the boy that the bombs about to be dropped would fall loudly, yet harmlessly. He only said, "We'll be fine, Frank; you go get in the shelter."

311

Frank rolled his eyes again, and stalked off as Jack once again lifted his gaze to the heavens.

"Betties," he said quietly to himself, "un-fucking-believable. Goddamn Betty bombers . . . God help me but this is fantastic, incredible."

"Talking to yourself, old cobber?" Jack heard Ian ask.

Jack looked down at the doctor and said, "Hell, yes I am." Pointing to the approaching planes, he said, "Those are Betties; two engine Jap heavy bombers. They had great range, but were lightly armored; you could darn near bring them down with a pea shooter. Their crews called 'em the 'Flying Cigar' because they would invariably burst into flame when hit. I've been reading about them and looking at pictures of them for almost 40 years . . . my god."

They sat down under the shade of a palm tree and watched the bombers draw nearer. "Look, you can really see the planes now!" Jack exclaimed. The bombers were being very cautious; they were making their attack from 25,000, feet but their cream-colored bellies were easy to spot against the blue sky. The formation of planes, along with their gauzy contrails, was a beautiful sight. Sunlight glinting off the Perspex noses of the bombers added a twinkling affect. The tight formations of four aircraft each, and their slow movement through the sky, added grace to beauty. When the bombers seemed to be directly overhead, the rumbling growl of sixteen powerful radial engines reverberated and was a reminder that the bombers were a menacing, destructive force. Moments later this was confirmed by the whistle and rattle of falling bombs.

A cluster of sixteen bombs fell just two-hundred yards away—much, much closer than Jack was expecting. They saw huge explosions over by the airstrip, and the concussions battered their chest and ears. The bombs made horrible, otherworldly crashing sounds when they landed, and the ground quaked. It was as if the island, or at least Henderson, was coming apart in a spasm of violence. In spite of the fact that he was quite certain he'd be safe, Jack was stunned by the maelstrom. Now, as he'd read, he understood clearly why the Marines had been so terrified of the aerial assaults. They created a feeling of utter helplessness and exposure. He knew the second cluster would be falling shortly. He and Ian locked widened eyes for a second, then, without saying a word, they rose together and sprinted for the bomb shelter. Just as they dove inside, the next stick of bombs fell. They huddled on the ground of the shelter with the others until they were certain the explosions were over.

When they sat up, they heard laughter and a voice cackle, "Yeehaw! Well if it ain't that big old hero, Jacky Macmillan!" It was Turk. "What's a matter, Jacko, get a little too fuckin' hot for you out there? Frankie told me what you and the lieutenant were gonna do." Turk turned toward Ian and said, "No offense, sir, but may I kindly suggest that you don't listen to Jack no more? I told you the fucker's crazy, sir."

Suddenly, Ian started laughing. It started as a chuckle then built to a full blown belly laugh. "You might be right, Turk," he choked. "Bloody hell, Jack, the look on your face after that first stick of bombs fell was bloody brilliant."

Jack began to laugh too, and added, "You weren't exactly the picture of calm, sir."

"Shit, and no offense again, sir," Turk interjected, "but you should have seen the fuckin' look on *both* your faces when you come divin' in here. It was like you was being chased by Eleanor Roosevelt, she bein' all naked and shit." By now, everyone in the bunker was laughing raucously. When the all clear sounded, the men spilled out of the shelter. For all the noise and violence, the bombs, other than pocking the airstrip with a couple craters, had all fallen harmlessly in open fields. Still laughing, and relieved to be safe, they returned their patients back to the hospital.

When they were done, hunger, more intense than Jack had ever felt, assaulted him. He'd noted that the flab around his waist had shrunk considerably. The younger men were losing weight, too. General Vandegrift had decreed just days after the landings that one meal a day was to be cut from the men's diet. The battalion hospital mess delivered meals mid-morning consisting of C-rations, spam, or captured Japanese rations, then again just before dusk.

Stacking supplies in the Palace, and his journeys carrying cases of beer to the Tenaru, had whipped Jack into the best shape of his life. But the exercise, heat, and lack of food was causing him to lose weight at a rapid pace. By the 18th, Jack's tenth day since departing the 'world', he estimated he'd lost fifteen pounds.

August 18, 1942

Good day in the hospital and at the Tenaru. All the men are losing weight from lack of supplies, the goddamn heat and the digging/ marching and such. My God this island is a miserable, hellish place. I'd read about it but you have to be here to really understand its foulness. The rats, lizards, land crab, crocs etc. and the foul stench of this place, not to mention shit-like mud, was previously unimaginable . . .

. . . Tom hasn't said anything about Hank since he told me what happened on the farm. I don't want to push him . . . don't want him to shut me out. It's amazing in a way, but we have become good friends. We talk for hours about the war, medicine, and books. He loves hearing about my kids . . . Jesus, his grandkids. I tell him real stories about Joey and Grace, but change their names. He thinks, like the others, (other than Ian) that I'm a school teacher in Chicago who signed up to do my part after serving in the first war. Don't know why I told them I was a schoolteacher; suppose I should have just told them I was a businessman. Anyhow, am sincerely treasuring my time with Dad. Everything is different now.

Tomorrow—supply run in morning, then hospital shift and a visit to Tom. Looking forward to the 20th as the first U.S. fighters and bombers land at Henderson. Can't wait and will definitely be there—should be quite a show from what I've read. Seeing the pilots and the Wildcats and

314

Dauntlesses will probably blow my mind. Amidst all this horror and misery I still feel lucky, grateful. It is quite a paradox really, but Ian has helped me keep it in perspective and I don't feel as guilty as I did a week ago. Goodnight, Laura, Joe, and Grace. I love you with all my heart; and I miss you.

21

August 19th was a routine day excepting a light air raid at noon followed by the nightly, yet largely ineffectual, visit by the Jap navy. The next day was much different though, with the drama of the first squadrons of Marine combat aircraft landing at Henderson adding to the specter of the looming battle at the Tenaru. Jack's excitement over the long anticipated arrival of the desperately needed airplanes was tempered by the anxiety and dread he felt regarding his first taste of combat. He would not be re-enacting the battle fueled by a quart of bourbon this time. It would be real. On the morning of the 20th, he became increasingly jumpy and nervous. After making the supply run and stacking the goods in the Palace, Jack invited Ian to lunch. They sat down in a bomb shelter and shared a mess tin of mushy Japanese rice. For the last week, Jack had reminded Ian daily of the battle that was to come.

"You remember what's going to happen tonight, right?" Jack asked.

"How the bloody hell could I forget?"

"Can I have the jeep for the night?"

Ian turned slowly toward Jack and stared at him for several moments before answering, "You're not going anywhere near that battle, mate. You're not trained for combat and we need you here."

"I have to go," Jack said firmly. "Put yourself in my shoes, Ian. It's my father out there for godsakes. Think about it. Besides, I can help with the wounded and bring a couple criticals back in the jeep when the fight's over."

Ian lit a cigarette and stared at the floor for several seconds. Then he looked up at Jack and said, "You're right mate. If you feel this is what you need to do, then do it; just don't do anything bloody stupid."

"Me do something stupid, Doc? No fucking way." Jack clapped Ian on the back and they walked back to the hospital to begin their shift.

Jack tried to take his mind off what was to occur in the blackness of the next morning. It was becoming ever more difficult. He instinctively knew that once he was with his father and squad at the creek, his nerves would settle some, so he repeatedly checked his watch, wishing the time away. He welcomed the arrival of the first American combat aircraft, not only for its historical significance, but for the fact that it would offer him a distraction, albeit brief, from the impending battle. When his shift was done, he gathered Ian, Frank, and Turk and explained that he had heard some planes were scheduled to land. They piled excitedly into the jeep and made the quick trip to Henderson.

The rumor that Marine warplanes were inbound had swept the area around Henderson and hundreds of men had gathered looking skyward, straining to hear the sound of engines. Ever since Admiral Fletcher had withdrawn his three carriers on the 8th, the skies had belonged to the Japanese, and thus the seas as well. The lack of air cover and an offensive air capability, caused the Marines to feel they had been virtually abandoned—that they were expendable. It seemed to them that the Japanese, when they were ready, could quite simply park their Navy offshore, darken the skies with Betties and Zeroes, and land fresh troops at will. To many Marines of all ranks, their defeat, and quite possibly their death, seemed inevitable as long as they were subject to Japanese air domination. So it was an enthusiastic and buzzing crowd that Jack and the others joined at Henderson.

"How many you think there will be?" Jack heard a fuzzy-faced boy ask a friend.

"I don't know," his buddy replied, "but right now I'd give anything to see just one of the beautiful bastards parked on this strip!"

Moments later a faint buzzing noise could be heard to the northeast. As the noise grew louder men began to yell and cheer. Then a voice cautioned, "What if they're Japs?" This quieted the men down for a time and the crowd only listened as the buzzing grew louder. The sound of these engines had a higher pitch than that of the Betties the day before.

"Holy shit, it sounds like every goddamn wasp and hornet in the world is headed our way," Turk excitedly exclaimed.

Finally, the planes appeared out over Ironbottom Sound. In an instant, the crowd of young Marines erupted in wild cheers and shouts. Helmets and campaign hats flew in the air. "Wildcats! Jesus, aren't they goddamn beautiful?" a Marine shouted.

"Dauntlesses too!" screamed another. "You Japs are fucked; you hear me? Fucked!"

Jack was holding his hands triumphantly in the air, yelling and cheering along with the others. Ian was a bit more subdued, but he too was cheering the new arrivals. Frank and Turk were arm in arm, jumping up and down, waving at the planes. Frank was happily waving, shouting "Welcome . . . welcome!" Turk was inexplicably yelling over and over, "Fuckin' bitches! Fuckin' bitches!"

A Marine was counting, "15 . . . 16 . . . 17 . . . 18 . . . 19. Nineteen Wildcats . . . nineteen of the beauts!" And to Jack they were beautiful. On his numerous trips through Chicago's O'Hare airport he would often make his way to the terminal that displayed a restored Wildcat. Lt. Butch O'Hare, a Chicago native, had won the Medal of Honor flying a Wildcat during the war. He was later killed in action, and the city named its airport after him. The restored Wildcat was placed in a terminal there in his honor. Most people would walk by the stubby fighter barely, if at all, giving it a glance. Jack though, each time he laid over at the airport, would slowly circle it—looking at every detail, from the tires to the gun ports. When he walked beneath the engine, he tried to smell the grease and aviation gasoline . . . sometimes, he swore he could. Now, nineteen spanking new Wildcats were circling him, their paint scheme just like that of the Wildcat at O'Hare. Light blue on the bottom, dark blue on top. "God they're gorgeous," Jack muttered.

Another Marine broke Jack's trance by yelling, "10 . . . 11 . . . 12. Twelve Dauntlesses, boy!"

Jack turned toward the twelve dive bombers flying over their heads, perpendicular to the runway. Their paint scheme mimicked that of the Wildcats. He could clearly see the pilots in open canopies, their leather helmets and goggles sheltering them from the slipstream. Behind the pilots sat a machine gunner facing to the rear. Suddenly, one of the Dauntlesses peeled off, swung sharply around and flew very low down the length of the runway. The men went wild, and many, like Jack, had tears in their eyes. As he watched the Dauntless complete its sprint down the runway, he said quietly to himself, "Welcome to Guadalcanal Major Mangrum. So glad you're here."

Major Richard Mangrum, one of the heroes of the Battle of Midway several months before, swung his plane back around, and on this pass, settled his Dauntless down on the dusty runway. As the men continued to cheer, Jack saw an older looking man rush to greet Mangrum as he stepped down from his cockpit. Jack recognized him as General Archer Vandegrift, the head of the ground forces on the island. After that, a plane landed every half minute or so, each time eliciting renewed bursts of cheers. Jack noticed that the pilots seemed a bit surprised by the highly emotional reception they were getting. They didn't appreciate yet that the young men cheering for them saw them not just as fellow Marines, but as saviors—an airborne cavalry arriving not a moment too soon. After the Dauntlesses landed, Major John L. Smith led the stubby, Wildcat fighters over the field in a massed formation pass that thumped in Jack's chest and ears. He was screaming at the top of his lungs, jumping up and down like the others as each Wildcat settled to earth. When all the planes had landed and shut down their engines, the silence seemed disorienting in a way; almost as if the atmosphere had somehow been altered by the arrival of the fearsome war machines. In some ways, Jack thought, it had. Vandegrift rushed over to Major Smith and gave him the same warm welcome he'd given Mangrum.

The Marines closed around the fighter pilots, shouting welcomes and telling them what to do to the Jap flyers when they made an appearance. Along with the joy he felt, Jack felt an intense burst of pride that once again brought tears to his eyes. He'd never felt anything closely resembling it. His mood darkened, though, when gazing at the gallant young fliers, he couldn't help but think that many of them would be dead in a matter of days and weeks. They looked so young and invincible that it was hard to imagine the violent, often lonely deaths they would suffer. They would save Guadalcanal; they would save thousands of young Americans. But, of course, the dead ones would never know it. It was indeed the ultimate sacrifice, but one that Jack now struggled to find any pure reason for. They were still his heroes, but no longer simply brave and valiant warriors. Now, they were noble victors and tragic victims all at once. After a few words from Vandegrift, Mangrum, and Smith, the happy crowd dispersed and returned to their duties.

As they made their way back to the hospital, Jack's feelings of excitement over the landings waned, and were slowly replaced with the same sense of fear and dread he'd felt earlier. Time seemed to be racing toward the impending battle at the Tenaru. He'd often wondered what it would be like to experience pitched battle . . . what his feelings would be as he anticipated the fight. He'd always believed it would be frightening, yet not truly understanding what that meant, what it really meant to know other humans were trying to kill you in unspeakably violent ways. As the battle loomed, everything was different than he'd imagined . . . much different. Young men, the great portion of their lives still to be lived, were going to die or be horribly maimed. He wondered what the dead men were doing at that moment. Perhaps they were reading, carousing with friends, or trying to catch a nap, completely unaware of the awful fate that awaited them just hours from now. They weren't just statistics in a book any more. God forbid, Jack thought, some of them may even be boys I know. Nothing about it was remotely as he'd fantasized. There was an amateur historian's sense of curiosity as to what the battle would look and sound like, but mostly just a deep sense of dread and sadness. Knowing he wouldn't be making a journal entry that night, he entered one as soon as he arrived back at the hospital.

August 20, 1942

The Wildcats and Dauntlesses landing at Henderson were fantastic! Just now returned. Weird, I was so proud even though I knew it was going to happen. What a day! The boys were going nuts—very special. Recognized Marion Carl there too. He looked so young and handsome climbing out of his Wildcat. One of top aces on island—will be shot down and rescued by natives (in a few weeks I think). Made me sad to think of him being murdered a few years ago by some punk in Oregon. Carl was in his 80s and a scumbag kid broke into his house and killed him with a shotgun when Carl moved to protect his wife. A goddamn hero even as an old man. Pisses me off when I think about it. Makes me wonder what is wrong with us . . .

. . . Still real jumpy about tonight. Told Doc I needed to be there; he understood after a bit of a protest. God I hope I do well. I'll just keep telling myself that if I get shot, worse thing that happens will be a trip back to the world. Not ready to leave really, but would if I have to. Think Dad will do well.

22

After Jack finished his entry, he volunteered to take a second shift in the hospital to help keep him occupied. As time passed, he became increasingly nervous. His mouth dried, his knees weakened, and he frequently stepped outside the tent to calm his spinning head. When 6 o'clock came, the end of his shift, he sprinted out of the tent and headed for the Emerald Palace. There he grabbed a field medical kit from the inventory and checked it's contents . . . two battle dressings, gauze, a tourniquet, four morphine syrettes, cotton swabs, surgical tape, one container sulfa powder, salt pills, tincture of iodine, and as an almost black irony, Jack thought . . . aspirin. Then he went to the Cave and retrieved his helmet and a bottle of *sake* he'd asked Ian to procure for him. As he was walking toward the jeep a voice shouted, "Hey, Jack! Where you going . . . out to the squad? You ain't trying to leave without me now, are you?

"Shit!" Jack exclaimed under his breath. It was Turk.

Jack turned around, "Uh . . . yeah, Turk . . . I'm going, but you can't come, not tonight."

Turk's face screwed up and he demanded, "Why the fuck not? I got two fuckin' cases of beer for the guys."

"Um . . . Doc says he uh, needs you here," Jack muttered.

"Oh, bullshit!"

"No, I'm serious, Turk . . . go ask him."

Turk thought for a moment, then said, "I'll do just that. You wait here."

As soon as Turk stepped inside the tent Jack leapt into the jeep, revved the engine, then sped off in a spray of orange dirt. He knew that Ian would figure out what was going on and back up his story, but he didn't want to deal with Turk's whining and insults. As he pulled away, Turk, hearing the engine, flew out of the tent. Over the roar of the motor Jack could hear him screaming as he chased after the jeep. "You fuckin' asshole, Jack! I'll never fuckin' trust you again, you fuckin' cheater! You ain't my friend no more, you stupid old bastard!"

In spite of his nerves, Jack was chuckling to himself as the jeep rounded the bend. He was pretty sure he'd be able to patch things up with Turk upon his return. The boy wasn't as tough as he acted. Without fully realizing it, he drove to the squad area much faster than normal. He was completely oblivious to squads of Marines cursing him as he sped by kicking up choking dust. As he closed on the creek, he nervously checked the contents of his kit again. His stomach was churning with nausea, and his breathing came in short shallow gulps. When he arrived, he was surprised to see Dumbass, still clearly suffering symptoms of malaria, walking wearily toward him. "Hey Jack, how you doin'?"

"Doing just fine, D.A. What're you doing up? You look terrible."

The boy ignored Jack's question and asked excitedly, "Did you hear about Captain Brush's patrol?"

"No . . . I uh . . . no," Jack stammered. He'd forgotten about the Brush patrol. Feigning ignorance he asked, "What happened?"

"Well, he's on patrol with about 60 guys and the native scouts tell him there's a Jap patrol approaching. Well, ol' Brushie goes right on the attack; they flank the fuckers and wipe 'em out."

"Good show," Jack said.

"But guess what else?" Dumbass said, grinning.

"What?"

"They were new troops, army pukes, not the navy fuckers or termites we've mostly seen. They had on fresh uniforms and boots

323

and stuff so they musta just landed." Dumbass' eyes sparkled and he added, "Captain Brush said the fuckers may be headed this way and that there're plenty more of 'em."

"And that's good?"

"Fuck, yes it's good. We're gonna finally have a fight . . . a real fight. Not shootin' at some starvin' Jap sailor or termite, or the tree that goddamn Scooz keeps thinkin' is moving. We're finally gonna do what we came here to do."

Jack smiled at the boy. He wondered how eager he'd be for a fight in the morning after his first taste of the carnage. "I'm not sure you're exactly in tip top fighting shape D.A. If they do attack you may have to sit this one out."

"Hah!" Dumbass spat. "A lousy fuckin' cold ain't gonna keep me away from my boys, especially when a fight's brewin'."

"You've got malaria, D.A.," Jack said in exaggerated exasperation. "Goddamn malaria . . . not a head cold. My god look at you . . . you've turned yellow."

A new voice interrupted them, "What are you doing here?" It was Tom.

Tom and Jack shook hands, then Jack said, "I'm off duty; what, I need a pass now to visit you guys?"

"Of course not; it's just that the Japs may be headed this way, so you probably shouldn't be here."

"They may not attack," Jack said. "Besides, I brought a field aid kit, so I can help out if they do."

"Hey, you brought a field kit?" Dumbass interjected, "I thought you said you hadn't heard about the Japs."

Jack quickly recovered saying, "I hadn't heard about the patrol, but I had heard that the Japs were on the move east of the Tenaru."

"Well, it's all moot anyway," said Tom. "Sarge will kick you out before dark. The Japs only attack at night."

"I wouldn't be so sure of that," Jack said slyly. He held up the *sake* bottle and showed it to Tom and Dumbass.

Tom chuckled, "You're a clever old pecker."

"Got beer?" Dumbass asked.

"Sorry D.A., not tonight," Jack replied. "My source is temporarily sidelined."

"Hey, ladies!" a voice boomed. Jack turned and saw Sgt. Jackson approaching. His muscled, shirtless body was stained with dirt. His spiny crew cut glistened with sweat; his trousers were soaked. "Having a little coffee klatch, are we?"

"Just talking to Jack, Sarge," Dumbass replied.

"Listen, Dumbass," Jackson barked, "if you don't lie down and stay there like I keep fucking telling you, I'm gonna send you back to sick bay!"

"It ain't no fun lying on your fuckin' ass all day you know, Sarge."

"Well then," the sergeant said with mock sweetness, "I'll order up a young native girl and some vodka gimlets so his highness don't get too bored."

Dumbass cheerily replied, "Now that sounds like just what I . . ."

"Get in your fucking hole . . . now!" Jackson shouted.

Dumbass sullenly trudged off to his hole, and Jackson turned to face Jack and Tom, smirking. "Well if it ain't the lovely and talented Macmillan sisters; once again doing what they do best . . . having a little chat!" Jack and Tom laughed.

"It ain't funny, boys. Do I look like I just waltzed off the 18th green? Huh? No, I been diggin' deep holes with the other boys so's when the Japs pay us a visit we don't get our goddamn melons shot full a' holes."

"What do you want us to do, Sarge?" Tom asked.

"Well, I suspect you boys are a bit too fragile for digging. We finally got wire. One spool, and they say that's all there's left on the whole goddamn island. I want to make it count. You can string that right along the riverbank." Pointing to a large wooden spool lying on the ground he said, "The wires there; the stakes are with it. We don't have any hammers, so you'll have to drive the stakes with a rock. I want you to string directly across from that abandoned amphib tractor right clear to that dead croc over there."

"Oh," Jack said, "you mean from reptile to reptile then."

Jackson looked at him quizzically for a moment then said, "You really ain't very funny, bub."

Tom whimpered and asked, "Ooh, what if I get poked by that nasty looking wire, Sarge? It would hurt so, so bad." Like two mischievous boys, father and son snickered at each other's comments.

Jackson rolled his eyes, "You ain't funny neither, dickhead. Now get to work."

Jack and Tom rolled the spool of barbed wire and stakes down to waters edge. They found a couple of heavy rocks for hammers, and began to drive the stakes into the sand at five foot intervals. The stakes were sturdy and the top ends had been formed into small curly-Qs that they wove the wire through. After several minutes, Jack asked, "So, uh, are you scared?"

"Scared about what?"

"Scared about the Japs maybe attacking."

"No, not really." Tom reflected for a moment then said, "Really, I'm just scared about one thing."

"What's that?"

Tom's face clouded over. "I'm scared about being scared; you know, too scared to do my job properly. I couldn't handle it if I fucked up . . . I'd rather be killed."

"You're going to do just fine. Trust an old man, you're not the sort who'd run from a fight or your responsibility, no matter how dicey it gets."

"I hope you're right."

"I'm always right, pal," Jack said. He sighed involuntarily, as he recalled his father referring to him using that same affectionate term when he was a young boy. For some reason, the memory sent a wave of sadness through him. He shook it off and attacked the wire stringing job with much gusto. It was exhilarating for him to be doing something to prepare for battle—to protect the marines, to protect his father. When they were done, Jack's hands were bloodied by multiple abrasions and punctures. Tom's were unscathed.

"Jesus Christ!" Tom yelped. "You're just supposed to string the wire, not feel it up! Sit down, I'll be right back." Tom retrieved the medical kit from his foxhole, and they sat on the creek bank admiring their job as he went to work on his son's hands. Tom gently cleaned Jack's wounds, then taped small bandages over them. As he worked, he whistled popular tunes of the day. The only one Jack recognized was *Chattanooga Choo-Choo.* Watching his father work intently on his hands, he was suddenly taken back to the early '60s at a cottage their family had rented up north on Big Star Lake. Jack and Tom had gone fishing for perch early one morning. The sunrise fishing trips were the happiest memories Jack had with his father. They would set out in a small aluminum boat, just as the sun rose over the oaks and pines lining the eastern side of the lake. A small, five horsepower motor was attached to the stern. They would chug their way to the other side of the lake where it was said the fishing was best. He could still smell the blue-gray exhaust emitted by the sputtering little engine. On this particular venture, Jack had cast a hook through the top of his middle finger. While he screamed in agony and fear, his father tried in vain to calm him. Tom steered the craft back to the cottage as fast as the little engine could propel them and carried Jack inside. Once there, his father had carefully cut off the looped end of the hook, pulled it out, gently washed the wound and bandaged it. All the while his father had whistled, just as he was doing now. Jack looked at the finger he had hooked so long ago. He could still see the little bump of skin, lighter than that surrounding it, where the barbed hook had pierced him. He looked again at his young father, still whistling. Suddenly, uncontrollably, his throat caught and tears welled in his eyes. He turned away so Tom wouldn't see and struggled to compose himself.

"Alrighty," Tom said without warning. "You're all patched up, pal."

Jack quickly dragged a sleeve across his face and turned toward his father, though he averted his eyes. "Uh, thanks, man . . . I appreciate it," he stammered.

"No problem."

Suddenly, twenty-five yards downstream, they noticed a commotion. A circle of Marines were crowded around something on the ground. They were hollering and screaming. Every so often the circle of men would rapidly bow out at a point, then collapse back in. Jack and Tom strolled over to investigate. Jack pushed his way into the group and to his surprise, saw Big Mikey trying, with some success, to ride a crocodile. At first, Jack laughed, but then he spotted Scooz on the other side of the circle. A sense of panic and horror suddenly struck him as he recalled Scozzolari's story on Hill 73. His horror turned to rage—rage against the indiscriminate killing machine that would snuff out the life of this jovial, good natured boy on the hell-island named Peleliu. He broke toward Big Mikey screaming, "Get off that croc, goddamn it . . . get off!" He slammed into the side of the boy, knocking him off the reptile. They both tumbled into the water, then Big Mikey quickly sprang up. He stood over Jack with clenched fists, blood oozing from one of them, just as Scooz had described.

"What the hell did you do that for?" Big Mikey bellowed. "Are you fucking crazy?" Jack only stared up at him, panting; there was nothing to say. The other men stood with mouths agape; including his father. "I oughta put your lights out, old man!" Jack slowly stood up, his rage replaced by sorrow.

"I'm sorry," he said quietly to the boy. He turned and slowly trudged back toward Tom's hole; the Marines watched him silently as his father quickly followed. Tom sat down on the rim of the hole, looking down at his son.

"What the hell was that all about?" he asked. "You a big animal lover or something?"

Jack, staring blankly at the creek, lit a cigarette and replied, "Yeah, something like that."

"You're lucky Big Mikey didn't clobber you."

"You'd better go patch up his hand. The croc's skin gashed it when I shoved him," Jack replied flatly.

Tom stared at Jack for several seconds, then said, "I will, but first tell me what . . ."

At that moment Sgt. Jackson, to Jack's relief, loudly interrupted their discussion. "Alright you pinheads, the lieutenant wants everybody in their fighting positions, locked and loaded!"

Jack heard Louie whine, "Aw geez, it ain't even dark yet."

"I don't give a fuck if the sun's shining out your asshole, Lou! The lieutenant says get in your hole, so get in your fucking hole." Then Jackson turned to Ski and Danny, "You two take Listening Post first. Dumbass and Murph, you guys relieve them at 0200." Jack looked at the LP smack on the edge of the creek, just behind the wire they had strung, 25 yards forward of the main line of resistance. Dumbass and Murph would be sitting alone, out front, when the battle started. He shifted his gaze to the other side of the water. The trees and shrubs on the other bank looked menacing and horrible. In his imagination the vegetation seemed to be hissing and snarling, causing him to shudder. Then Jackson said, "Lt. Grimes will be by in a little bit to check on you, so look alive, girl scouts!"

Jack watched sadly as Tom walked over to Big Mikey and applied a bandage to his wound. They were quickly involved in animated discussion; Tom nodding his head at once, then shaking it, then nodding again. "Trying to convince him I'm not a crazy old fucker, I suspect," Jack said out loud. He wasn't embarrassed by his action, though he regretted it. He'd simply felt a need to do something, no matter how illogical. To him the croc represented violent, needless, premature death. He did the only thing he could do. He acted instinctively and got the boy off the croc. But he knew it wouldn't change anything. Big Mikey would never see the shores of his home again, never marry and experience the matchless joy of having children . . . grandchildren.

Tom was heading back to his hole when Sgt. Jackson shouted, "Hey, Macmillan!"

Tom turned, "Yeah, Sarge?"

"No goddamn it!" Jackson growled. "Macmillan the old."

"Oh, uh, what do you need?" Jack replied dully.

"I need you to get the fuck out of here," Jackson barked.

"Why?" Jack asked. "It's early."

"Why does everyone keep telling me what time it is, goddamn it? Just do as I say, okay?"

Jack rose and approached the sergeant, "Can I talk to you over by the jeep?" Jack winked and added, "It'll be worth your time."

Jackson eyed him suspiciously, "Oh, what the hell . . . okay."

When they got to the jeep, Jack showed Jackson the bottle of *sake*, "I'll trade this for a night with the squad . . . deal?"

Jackson's eyes shone and he immediately agreed, "Fuck yeah. It's a deal! You can get your ass shot off as often as you'd like, as long as you keep the hooch flowin' in my direction. Besides," he said cheerily, "yah can't never have enough docs around."

"My thoughts exactly," Jack said. Jackson reached for the bottle, but Jack pulled it back. "There's just one catch, Sarge."

Jackson's brow furrowed, "And just what the hell is that?"

"You don't get drunk tonight."

Jackson's eyes grew large. "What the fuck good is the stuff then?"

"You can get drunk tomorrow when I'm gone, okay? I don't want to be here if you get in trouble with Grimes, you know?"

Jackson stroked his chin for several moments, then said reluctantly, "Well . . . I guess I see your point. Okay, I agree." Jack handed him the bottle and, somewhat dejected, Jackson trudged off. After a few moments, and without turning, he waved a hand and muttered a half-hearted thanks.

When Jack returned to Tom's hole he told him the story. Jack was pleased when it sent his father into a fit of laughter. They talked until it was completely dark. Tom thankfully, sensitively Jack thought, never brought up the incident with Big Mikey and the croc. After an hour, Tom decided he'd better try and grab some sleep. Jack, knowing he wouldn't be able to fall asleep, sat in the hole and waited . . . waited for the killing to begin. He felt nauseous and light-headed, although he wasn't as nervous as he'd been at the hospital. He felt safer and less anxious with his father by his side. At midnight, a sentry fired a shot at some unseen target. The bang

330

of the Springfield caused Jack to jolt hard. His movements woke up Tom and they listened together as sporadic gunfire carried on for several more minutes. Simultaneously, scuttlebutt quickly moved up and down the line that sentry outposts on the opposite bank of the river were being pulled back, due to an inordinate amount of unusual sounds. When it quieted down, Tom went back to sleep. Jack's inability to read his watch in the blackness caused him great anxiety. Several times he was tempted to spark his lighter, but the fear of a Japanese soldier spotting it overrode his gnawing desire to gauge when the battle would start. A soldier, Jack thought eerily, who may be at that very moment crouching, unseen on the other side of the creek . . . waiting, stalking. The night began to take on a surreal, other worldly quality. It just seemed incredible, almost a farce of sorts, that shortly the young men positioned on either side of the creek would begin to kill each other over a dusty strip of land on an island none of them had heard of until shortly before they'd arrived. He looked toward the creek mouth, squinting hard into the darkness. He was unable to make out Schimd's, Rivers', and Diamond's machine gun embrasure. Still, using his memory of the location of the worn monument to the men back in the world, he estimated where they were located.

A heavy sense of dread pressed on him with each passing minute. He felt fear, but not for his own safety. He feared what he was about to see and how he would react to it. However, a part of him, a part he worked hard to suppress, was excited at the prospect of witnessing the battle. Not just from an historical perspective, but from seeing combat, from smelling and hearing it. He knew it would be horrible, but it was irresistible. As the time for the battle drew near, his throat became dry and choked, and he struggled to breathe normally, his body soaked in sweat. He heard his father softly snoring. He envied Tom and the Marines. They were blissfully unawares, not sitting alone in agony, waiting for the slaughter. Finally, at 0200, it started.

The only decisive warning the Marines received were piercing screams and taunts from the other side of the creek, punctuated by cracks of rifle fire. A high-pitched, banshee-like voice pierced the heavy air. "Maline, you die tonight! Maline, eat shit!" Jack shuddered at the shrill howling. Several Marines hollered back. "Fuck you, you fish head eating monkeys!" one yelled. Other Marines sporadically and blindly fired into the dark jungle.

Then, oddly, the jungle went completely silent for several moments, as if death were taking a deep breath before it exploded on the young men. After several muffled explosions, the jungle and creek were suddenly bathed in eerie green light as flares were flung skyward. Holding his breath, Jack slowly peeked over the rim of his foxhole. He could see the other men doing the same. Jack looked toward the mouth of the creek and its sandbar two-hundred-fifty feet away. He, of course, knew what he'd see, but was still stunned by the scene unfolding. A bustling mass of Japanese soldiers, their bayonets glinting in the green light, were moving quickly across the sand bar toward the Marine positions. High pitched shrieks and war cries burst from the enemy, increasing the nightmare quality of this early morning on the Tenaru. Jack screamed, "Oh God . . . it's happening! It's happening!" Tom crouched beside him, quietly watching. Jack momentarily felt ashamed by his outburst, but forgot it quickly as the Marine lines exploded in a maelstrom of rifle and machine gun fire.

Japanese soldiers were slowly falling to the ground in clumps atop the sandbar. Then, two Marine 37mm cannons coughed, raking the attackers with body-shredding canister shot; the death clumps grew steadily. The boys in Tom's squad were adding to the din, firing their Springfields downstream at the enemy. Danny was pumping rounds from his BAR toward the sand spit in short bursts. Jack looked over at the LP and was somewhat surprised to see Murph and Dumbass still manning it. He would have thought they'd have high-tailed it back to the main lines when the attack started. Dumbass was on his knees, banging away with his rifle and screaming at the Japanese. He could see his jaw working furiously, but couldn't hear what he was yelling over the indescribable din of battle. For a moment he felt as though he would unravel; completely lose his ability to think rationally. Jack tried to summon courage from D.A., and by using the old technique. "You can do it, buddy," he whispered to himself. "Just hang in there, bud." He felt as though he was outside his body; watching the battle, but detached from it, like an angel or a ghost. As in a dream, he heard Tom shouting, telling him something. He looked and saw his father's lips moving up and down in slow motion. "What . . . what?" Jack yelled in confusion.

Tom put a hand on Jack's shoulder. His touch calmed Jack and he regained much of his focus. He clearly heard his father say, "When we start taking fire, be sure and keep your ears and eyes open. I'll take the first casualty. If I need help I'll wave you over; if not, you take the next, okay?"

"Yeah . . . okay," Jack shouted. Jack noted that his father had said 'when' we start taking fire, not if. He lowered his head into the foxhole and rubbed his eyes roughly, still trying to shake the surreal feeling of being physically detached from the swirling battle. He raised his head back up and looked at the Japanese attack. He only saw a few survivors breach the wire just yards in front of the Marine positions. A few last desperate shots were taken before several of them, bayonets affixed to their rifles, dropped into Marine fighting holes. Jack clearly saw one man jump into a hole, then moments later, come flopping back out again; limp, dead. Firing slowly died as the last of the enemy, very few now, were routed out of the Marine positions and off the sandbar. Jack knew the battle was far from over, but the temporary calm allowed him to take stock of himself and the others.

Cheers arose all around the perimeter, and he saw Dumbass and Murph, still at the LP laughing and slapping each other on the back. He couldn't understand why Sgt. Jackson wasn't pulling them back. Perhaps, he thought, they wanted observers as close as possible to the other side of the creek to give warning if the enemy tried to swim or boat across. With the light from the flares it seemed pointless and risky. And they hadn't been doing much observing or listening either; just shooting. The other boys were rearranging gear and reloading their weapons. Flares continuously hurtled into the sky. Jack jumped when Tom yelled, "Everyone okay?" Affirmatives, most including some form of profanity, flew back. The boys were giddy with the excitement of their first engagement. The enemy had been shredded, while they themselves were left unscathed. Loud cheering and taunts rolled up and down the Marine line, lending a collegiate type atmosphere to the night. Jack though, knew it couldn't last. He wasn't young and he wasn't a Marine. He didn't see things the way young men did.

He looked back at the sandbar. "It's different," he mumbled, in a daze. "It's different."

"Sure is," Tom replied grimly. "The scenery's a little different than it was a little while ago, huh?" Tom had misunderstood his meaning. Combat—the fighting, the dying. It was all very different than he'd imagined or understood. A half hour ago he was anxious to experience it. Now, even though he hadn't directly been involved, he felt he'd seen enough. Mostly it was the violence, the monstrously raw, sickening violence that one could never imagine if one hadn't seen, smelled and heard it. He had always believed that it was only what men *saw* during battle that caused fear and dread . . . what caused some of them to lose their minds. But there was much more. The chaotic sounds of the battle; the screams, explosions, and gunfire held a shattering violence all their own. The acrid smell of cordite and burned flesh mixed with duller smells of blood, and feces from shattered intestines, added to the horror. The plaintive wails and moans of wounded men wafting over the quiet battlefield punctuated the slaughter with sadness and misery. Jack crouched in the hole for nearly an hour, horrified, yet transfixed by the sounds and smells of the engagement. He shuddered and looked to the other side of the creek as new war cries sounded.

"Here they come again!" a voice screamed. Officers and noncoms barked orders while privates and corporals encouraged each other with their own battle cries. Jack whipped his head around toward the sandbar. They were coming again. More of them this

My Father's Keeper

time: screaming again, dying again. The Marines pumped rifle and machine gun rounds into the clustered pack of men, and the 37mm's scythed down whole chunks of humans with each shot. Still in something of a daze, Jack watched as the attack impaled itself on the Marine lines. Marine mortar and artillery pounded the Japanese. The Japanese answered with their 75mm artillery and knee mortars. On this attack more of the enemy cleared the wire in front of the Marine lines, and this time American screams of pain mixed with those of the Japanese. Knowing that he was just yards from where his countrymen were being killed only added to the desperate desolation Jack felt. "It's goddamn primitive," he whispered. "Goddamn . . . this is crazy . . . goddamned insane. The people at home don't know, don't have a fucking clue. If they did . . ." His thoughts were interrupted by an unusual sound. A Marine machine gun fired off several hundred consecutive rounds rather than the normal short bursts used to maximize accuracy. "Jesus Christ!" Jack said out loud, "They just killed Johnny Rivers. Now the bastards are going to get Schmid's eyes."

"What did you say?" Tom asked.

Jack, wild eyed, turned toward his father and said, "Oh nothing, never mind." Then he suddenly grunted, "I've got to do something." Tom vainly lunged at him as he scrambled out of the foxhole and began to run toward the mouth of the creek.

"Hey!" Tom shouted. "Get back here, Jack! Have you lost your fucking mind?"

As he ran past Sgt. Jackson's hole, he heard him shout, "What the fuck? Macmillan, get your stupid ass back here!" Jack ignored him. "You're on your own, you crazy fuck!"

As Jack had drunkenly mimicked on the morning of his journey, Privates Johnny Rivers, Al Schmid, and Cpl. Leroy Diamond were manning a .30-caliber machine gun set directly in the path of the attacking enemy. Rivers, a promising welterweight, had been at the trigger when a bullet struck him in the face, killing him instantly, and freezing his finger on the trigger. As Jack drew nearer, he identified the machine gun embrasure, the same spot he

335

had honored at the weathered, fauna-entangled obelisk just a few weeks before. He knew Diamond would be firing the gun now, but would fall wounded at any moment. Instantly, Schmid, a 19-year-old from Philadelphia, would take control of the gun. Moments later a grenade would explode at the front of their embrasure, blinding Schmid permanently. Schmid would continue to man the gun, though, firing in the direction his wounded buddy commanded.

Jack was sprinting toward the bunker as fast as a 46-year-old could, but as it had during the first attack, he and the battle seemed to be moving in slow motion. He could see the fiery explosions of grenades and mortars, and the twinkling of rifle and machine gun fire, yet strangely could no longer hear them. Like before, he consciously knew he was witnessing the battle, but felt the same detachment. All he heard were his own rasping grunts. He wasn't charging across the battlefield for any sort of personal glory or gain. He was simply desiring to find a way to help the young men he'd previously seen as invincible, completely immune to the horrors of indiscriminate slaughter. Now though, the island had taught him that they were merely flesh and blood, not supermen, young boys who, for the most part, just wanted to complete their government appointed duties and return back home. They did not deserve to have their limbs ripped off, their eyes blinded, or their lives snuffed out. Jack's self-appointed mission, therefore, was to save Schmid's eyes, if he could. He remembered his and Ian's discussions regarding attempts to change history. But, he reasoned with himself in the slow motion slurry of the battle, this wasn't history. It was just a boy's eyes. Strangely, now that he was actually participating in the action, all fear had left him. Then, a seemingly illogical sense of exhilaration swept over him. The battle was insane and brutal, but strangely, he felt a clear sense of freedom and vitality. The unexpected feelings produced an involuntary shriek of what could only be described as joy.

"Yes . . . Yes!" he screamed over the din. Peering at the bunker, he could see someone furiously working the machine gun. "Schmid!" Jack screamed. "Schmid, you've got to . . ." the crash of a mortar round exploding in front of the bunker cut him off. He instantly felt a heavy slap on his cheek, and the bomb's concussion knocked him to the ground, his ears roaring. He'd come within fifteen yards of the position, but was too late. Stunned, he lay still for a moment, then slowly rose to his knees. An enemy machine gunner opened up, and sprays of dirt crisscrossed in front of him. He splayed out on the ground, grinding his face into the soil. His senses, as well as his hearing, gradually returned and the slow motion, silent pace of the action reverted back to real time, frenetic and fierce.

The mortar and machine gun fire had shattered his exhilaration, yet he managed to force himself to lift his head slightly and look in the direction of the bunker. Just yards from Schmid's position he saw a Japanese soldier plunge into a foxhole and bayonet a young Marine clear through the throat. The dying boy's foxhole mate reacted quickly, loosing a full clip of sub-machine gun fire into the enemy's midsection. The sheer animal violence of the fight sent rolling waves of nausea through his stomach. His heart felt as though it would burst in his chest. He glanced once more at the bunker and saw that the machine gun was working again, a blind man at the trigger. Feelings of frustration mixed with intense pride produced tears that etched jagged white lines as they rolled down his grimy, trembling face. The thought of rising up was terrifying and seemingly irrational. But having read countless accounts of men pinned down in battle, he knew he had to move, and after inhaling a deep gulp of air, he tore himself off the ground. Crouching low, he sprinted back toward Tom and the others. He made the trek back at least as quickly as he'd made the one out . . . this time driven by fear. As he entered the squad area, he heard Jackson mock, "You seen a fucking ghost or somethin'? Best you let us do the fightin', pops."

In a blur, Jack saw his father leaning out of his hole, offering out a guiding hand. He dove into Tom's hole at full speed. Inertia carried his legs past his body and he ended up on his back in the hole—his legs stuck straight up along the back edge, his boots peaking above the rim. Jack looked up and saw Tom staring down at him in wonder.

337

"What in the hell was all that?" Tom asked angrily. "First Big Mikey and the croc, and now this? You okay?"

Jack thought for a moment, then shakily replied, "I thought I saw someone go down."

Tom reached over and gingerly fingered Jack's cheek. "Hey, you're hit." It was only then that Jack felt the stinging pain in his cheek. He reached up and felt a jagged piece of metal protruding from his skin.

"Mortar," Jack mumbled. He noticed that the firing had died. The second Japanese attempt to penetrate the Marines had resulted in bloody failure. Jack hoped that a corpsman had reached Schmid and Diamond by now, and at least given them some sort of comfort. He felt badly that he hadn't been able to save Schmid's eyes, and he realized his wild charge had probably been a stupid thing to do. But he was proud of himself for making an effort to help, as well as having the courage to make the attempt. Though still shaking with fear, a smile briefly flickered across his face.

"It's not bad, but maybe it's enough to get a lesson through your thick skull," his father gently admonished. "Christ, you're lucky to be alive. Our job is here with the squad, not out there, you dummy. Besides, I told you I'd take the first casualty, didn't I? You've got to follow procedure out here or you'll fuck up and get killed or get someone else killed."

"Sorry," Jack said. After several moments of thought he frowned and said, "Hey, help me convince Jackson and Grimes it won't happen again. I don't want to be banned from visiting you . . . uh, visiting you guys."

"I'm not sure if I should, but I guess it was pretty brave of you, and nothing bad came out of it other than this little nip on your cheek. I'd hate for you to be banned as well. But you have to promise not to scare the shit out of me again."

Jack, pleased by his father's affectionate words, said solemnly, "I promise. I've learned a lesson. God knows, nowadays it seems that's about all I'm doing."

"Good," Tom said. Then with a chuckle, he added, "But oh

man, I wish you could've seen the look on your face when you re-entered the squad area. It almost made your shenanigan all worth it."

As if on cue, Jack heard D.A. shout happily, "Hey Tommy, did you get all the shit cleaned outta Jack's trousers?" Laughter burst from the squad's foxholes.

"Hey, Jack!" Scozzolari called. "Them nasty fuckin' Japs didn't rape you did they? I heard they love to screw nurses the most!" More laughter followed. The good-natured ribbing, as well as Jack's pride, settled him and tempered the disappointment in his failed mission.

"Listen up, men," Jack yelled with exaggerated importance. "I've finished reconnoitering the area to our front. I had to clear out a few hotspots, but it's safe for you boys now." Profane guffaws rose from the surrounding holes.

"Hey guys," Tom shouted, "you're not going to believe this, but Jack picked himself up a beautiful little wound."

"No shit?" several of the boys asked at once.

"No shit," Tom replied. "His cheek stopped a mortar fragment. He'll be wearing a purple heart on his chest and a little jagged scar on his face. The broads won't be able to keep their hands off him."

Combat wounded, Jack thought. "If only the old man could see me now," he whispered to himself. It was ironic, for the last three years he'd convinced himself that he could care less what the old man had thought of him.

His ponderings were interrupted by the sound of Dumbass muttering loudly. "Shit," he said. "Life ain't no fuckin' fair. Fucker's an old man *and* a goddamn nurse. I gotta get me a wound like that or I ain't never gonna get laid, boy."

"You'll get there, bud," Murphy replied. "And you won't be an ancient specimen like Jack there." Murphy's comment and his father's simultaneous removal of the mortar fragment caused Jack to wince. Tom shook some sulfa on the wound and bandaged it, assuring Jack it would be fine until morning when he could have Ian stitch it up at the hospital.

Before Jack could say anything, a rapid, rhythmic cracking sound burst from the abandoned amphibian tractor mired in the Tenaru. Jack and Tom watched, transfixed for a second or two as the ground around the squad's holes was stitched by machine gun fire. Then they both flung themselves on the bottom of the hole. Jack heard Lt. Grimes yell, "The bastards have got up in the amphib with an MG! Stay down!" The Japanese machine gun crew directed most of their fire toward the Marine positions at the head of the river, but occasionally traversed their gun toward Jack and the others, keeping them pinned down.

As Jack screwed his head into the bottom of the hole, Tom shouted, "Well, I guess our war's started! Unbelievable. Bastards must've swum across the river carrying a machine gun! Those fucking monkeys have got some balls!"

"They're brainwashed," Jack said in a muffled voice. "Just like the goddamn al-Qaeda."

"They're what?" Tom asked. "Who?" The time warped exchange was interrupted by a series of desperate shouts.

"Goddamn it! Murph's hit . . . Murph's hit! Corpsman up . . . corpsman up!" The boy yelling was Dumbass. Remaining at the forward LP had left them exposed to textbook enfilade fire from the enemy machine gun. Murph must have raised himself above the precipice of his foxhole at the wrong time.

An instant after D.A.'s panicked shouts, Tom sprang out of the hole and was running toward the LP. As he left, he screamed, "Murph's hit! Covering fire . . . Covering fire!" The entire platoon opened up on the amphibious tractor, but the gunner kept firing. His aim, thankfully, was affected by the Marine bullets pinging on the armor of the vehicle. Jack desperately peered over the edge of his hole and watched Tom's dash. Geysers of dirt kicked up at his heels as the Japanese machine gunner tried to catch his bullets up to him. Watching his father sprint the 25 yards left Jack breathless. He sighed with relief when he saw Tom drop safely into Murph and D.A.'s hole. Jack descended, but each time the enemy machine gunner stopped firing to reload or redirect his fire toward the

340

beach, he'd lift his eyes just above the edge of the hole and gaze at the LP. During a lull he was first shocked, than horrified to see D.A. standing upright, shooting at the amphibian, all the while screaming maniacally.

"You goddamn fuckin' motherfuckers! You messed up Murph's pitching arm! I'm gonna kill you fuckers!"

The battle turned to slow motion again. Jack screamed, "Get down D.A . . . get down! Goddamn it, get down!" He was conscious of his words but couldn't hear them. Tom was desperately trying to pull D.A. down. Sgt. Jackson heard Jack scream and looked out to see what was happening. His shouts added to the frightening chaos.

"Goddamn it, Dumbass! You get your fucking ass back down in that hole right now!" Dumbass didn't respond. He simply stood, reloaded his rifle, then furiously worked the bolt as he fired off round after round.

Jack felt a sense of helplessness as never before. Yet he was mesmerized by the sight of the loyal boy, in a blind rage, taking on the machine gun. Sickeningly, he knew what the only outcome could be, but he couldn't take his eyes off the dreadful scene. The machine gunner, inevitably, found the boy from Ohio and squeezed off a burst. Jack watched as the bullets slammed into him. His body jerked violently and his helmet flew off, yet still he stood. It wasn't until Jack was halfway to the LP that he was even conscious he'd left his hole. He heard, though it seemed a distant echo, Sgt. Jackson scream, "Corpsman up . . . Covering fire!" Finally, Dumbass crumpled down into the foxhole. When Jack was within 10 feet of the hole, the machine gunner spotted him and loosed off a short burst. He heard the bullets crack and whine as they passed overhead. He jumped safely into the foxhole.

Tom was rolling a bandage around Murph's shoulder, while at the same time nudging Dumbass over with his knee, trying to assess the severity of his wounds. After Jack flopped into the congested, bloody hole, Tom looked at him with a deep intensity, but devoid of panic or fear. He yelled, "There's not enough room in this hole to work on both of them without that gun knocking the crap out of us. Murph's hit hard, but he's going to be okay if we can get him back in the next few hours. I'm not so sure about Dumbass." Jack nodded wildly, feeling manic, fully acceding to his father's calm leadership. Dumbass was moaning softly. "We gotta get him back to our hole," Tom continued. "I'm gonna give Murph a shot of morphine and he should be fine here for a while . . . the bleeding isn't too bad."

Murphy begged, "Go . . . go goddamn it! I'm fine; just take care of him!" Tears of rage and anguish rolled down Murph's face. "Goddamn those fuckers! Go, Tommy . . . go take care of him, I'm fine. As soon as I'm sure the gunner is distracted, I'll haul ass to the rear, but you guys go now!"

Tom nodded and said to Jack, "Grab on." They each hooked an arm under one of the D.A.'s armpits, then Tom bellowed, "Taking him out! Covering fire . . . covering fire!"

They heard Sgt. Jackson yell, "Covering fire on the amphib! Don't stop shooting 'til they're under cover!"

Once again the platoon massed fire on the amphib, and Tom and Jack scrambled out of the hole together. Hunching low, they dragged Dumbass toward their foxhole. The covering fire was effective, distracting the Japanese gunner. When they were halfway to the hole, a thundering clap knocked them to the ground. A mortar, or something, had destroyed the amphib along with its occupants. The battlefield was quiet again as Jack and Tom rose to their knees. "Gun's knocked out!" Tom said breathlessly. "We'll work on him right here." Jack heard Sgt. Jackson tell the other men to stay in their holes and keep down. He, however, scurried over to where Jack and Tom had stopped. He crouched down next to the three men, watching quietly.

Jack and Tom knelt on either side of Dumbass. He was staring up at them pleadingly, no longer moaning, but his breathing labored and raspy. Tom reached down and ripped Dumbass' shirt open. He looked at the boy's chest and groaned, "Oh Jesus . . . Jesus, Dumbass, they fucked you up bad, buddy." Jack looked down and saw three bullet holes, one in his stomach and two in the right side of his chest. The holes were small, Jack thought. Compared to the other injuries he had seen near this spot on his first day, as well as those in the hospital, the bullet holes seemed relatively benign, non-threatening.

Jack meant it when he said, "You're gonna be fine D.A. They're just tiny little holes, bud."

Tom glanced quickly at Jack, then said, "Uh . . . yeah, I was just kidding about them fucking you up bad, buddy. You'll be fine." Jack heard Tom curse himself under his breath. Tom took a plasma bottle attached to his webbing and handed it to Jack. Jack held the bottle above his head as Tom inserted the needle tipped tube into Dumbass' arm. Dumbass was losing blood quickly, and Jack felt a great sense of pride in his father for having the knowledge and foresight to have plasma available at the front, against normal procedure.

A new firefight erupted near the sandbar, and Jack glanced in that direction. He could see the Marines firing into the surf and recalled that Col. Ichiki had sent the last waves of his shock troops into the sea in an attempt to flank the Marine positions guarding the Tenaru. This attack failed as well, in another spasm of grotesque violence. Apparently unbeknownst to the inept Col. Ichiki, the Marine lines took a ninety degree turn to the west at the beach. The Japanese soldiers were again slaughtered in their dozens by withering fire from the Marine positions on the beach. Ichiki's force had largely spent itself as an offensive force as the first glimmers of dawn were appearing to the east. Jack looked back at Dumbass and saw tears forming in his eyes.

"I don't wanna die, Tommy," he groaned. Tom had the fore and middle fingers of his left hand on the boy's neck, checking his pulse.

"You're not going to die," Tom assured him. He looked at Jack and shook his head in frustration.

Dumbass started to shake, his breathing becoming more raspy and difficult. He reached up and grabbed Jack by the collar. "Oh goddamn, I don't wanna die, Tommy," he gasped. "I just wanna go home."

"It's Jack, D.A. Try and stay calm, buddy." Jack gently held the boy's shoulders as still as he could. Blood dribbled from Dumbass' mouth and he was trying hard to focus his eyes. He coughed several times, sending sprays of blood into Tom and Jack's faces. Dumbass lifted his head off the ground, his voice barely above a whisper, "Oh god, Tommy . . . god." His grip on Jack's collar tightened, making it difficult to hold the plasma bottle steady. Jack glanced at his father working furiously to stanch the blood. He looked back down at D.A. and saw that his eyes were getting glassy. For the first time, to his shock and horror, Jack realized that the boy might actually die. D.A's hand fell away from Jack's collar, and his body seemed to relax.

"How's Murph?" he asked.

"Murph's fine, just a nick," Tom replied. At that moment, Dumbass inhaled deeply, more a gasp than anything, and his eyes rolled to the back of his head.

"C'mon, Dumbass!" Tom implored. "Don't give up, buddy . . . the plasma's flowing . . . don't give up!" Jack noticed that Tom had stopped working on the wounded boy and realized that here, in 1942, on a remote island in the middle of the jungle, there was nothing else that could be done. Sgt. Jackson was hovering over them, still silent. Dumbass convulsed and more blood gurgled from his mouth. "Jesus Christ!" Tom said a moment later. "No pulse . . . I can't get a goddamn pulse!" Jack looked at Dumbass' face. His mouth was agape, his eyes half-open, unseeing. Jack instinctively leaned over and began to blow into Dumbass' mouth.

"What are you doing?" Tom asked. Jack knew that CPR had not yet been developed, but he carried on; he had no choice. Tom let him go, apparently figuring that Jack knew something he didn't. As Jack conducted mouth-to-mouth, he could taste the boy's salty blood on his tongue. He could feel it covering his cheeks and chin. Still he blew, muttering 'c'mons' and 'pleases' in between breaths. He blew until Tom gently grabbed his shoulders and pulled him to his knees.

"He's gone, Jack. He never had a chance." Jack looked down at D.A., unable to accept that the lively boy was dead. He knelt again and prepared once more to blow life into the boy, but Tom wrapped an arm around his shoulder tightly, holding him at bay. Then his father wiped the dead boy's blood off his face with a cloth, and said in an officious, unnerving tone, "We were prepared; we worked quickly, efficiently and used our training. We did everything we could to save him. He never had a chance . . . not with those wounds. And thanks for covering for me when I first saw how bad he was hurt. I shouldn't have reacted that way; it won't happen again, I assure you." Jack didn't tell him he'd truly believed what he'd told the boy, that he would survive. He just nodded and struggled to get control of his emotions. He knew he had to be strong. As if reading his mind, Tom said, "This isn't going to be the last time. We've got to be able to move on quickly if we're going to do our jobs properly." Tom's sudden, cold professionalism was impressive, yet at the same time, alarming.

Jack, motivated by his father's stoicism, quickly composed himself and noticed that Jackson was still standing over the dead boy, staring. He realized that though the sergeant was tough and grizzled, it was very likely this was the first man he'd ever lost in combat. Jack broke from his father's embrace, leaned toward Jackson and said, "I'm real sorry." At that moment, Lt. Grimes joined them, having made sure the amphibious tractor was secure.

"We have a KIA?" the grim faced lieutenant asked.

"I'm afraid so, sir," Tom said, nodding toward the body.

The lieutenant shook his head, spat in the dirt, and muttered, "Aw Christ . . . Christ . . . poor kid. Jesus Christ!"

"I didn't pull 'em back," Jackson muttered flatly, still staring at the dead boy. "I should've pulled 'em back."

"C'mon Jackson, they knew they could come back as soon as we took fire," Lt. Grimes said.

"We didn't take direct fire, sir, until that MG opened up from the tractor," Jackson replied. "I should've pulled 'em back as soon as the Japs attacked downstream."

"It's not your fault," Grimes said tersely. "You didn't know the bastards would swim the stream." Jackson looked increasingly

345

shattered and dispirited. It was a shocking transformation from just minutes ago.

"Yeah, Sarge," Tom said. "What the hell are you thinking? It was Dumbass who fucked up by exposing himself to the Jap gunner."

It wasn't a cruel thing to say, Jack thought, but it was hard . . . cold. Tom, obsessed with caring for his Marine comrades, now seemed strangely detached from the tragedy that had taken one of their lives.

"No, I fucked up," Jackson quietly said. "I killed him and messed up Murph to boot." Tom cursed loudly, shook his head in disgust and stalked off toward Murphy. Jack was perplexed at Tom's intolerance of Jackson's guilt and remorse, considering his own regarding Hank's death. He thought back to the time, as a boy, when he broke his cousin's leg while playing football in a foot of snow in the backyard. On the way to the hospital, his cousin's cries and moans had driven him to tears and he kept apologizing to his parents. For a time his father was silent, but then exploded.

"Listen, you little baby! You were playing, he got hurt! Quit feeling sorry for yourself, damn it! This sort of stuff happens, so quit acting like a sissy!" Jack had done his best to muffle his sobs while his mother, sitting between the boys, cradled him. He never understood why his dad was so angry at him for being upset. Now, it was beginning to make sense. Not sense really, because there was not really any sense in it. It was more that he was coming to understand the origins of his father's occasional, yet harsh and distant, attitude toward his own family. His dad, he was beginning to suspect, had been scarred by Hank's death so deeply that a part of him had become irrational, even paranoid in a way.

The rising sun was beginning to filter through the grove on the other side of the river as Tom broke the news of D.A.'s death to Murph. When Murph dropped his head, Tom cradled it on his shoulder and held it there. Jack shook his head in amazement. One minute his father was disgusted with Sgt. Jackson for taking responsibility for the death of one of his men, the next he was tenderly comforting a friend of the dead man.

Jack turned back toward Jackson and saw that Lt. Grimes had a twisted wad of the sergeant's shirt in his hand, and was speaking to him with a quiet intensity, their noses only an inch apart. The only words Jack could make out were, "Now get your shit together! You've got other men to look after!" Grimes' exhortations had an immediate effect on Jackson. Within minutes he was his normal self, getting the men reorganized, trying to take their minds off their buddy's death. Jack pondered whether any man, thinking himself somehow responsible for the death of a comrade and the maiming of another, could truly ever get over it. He could only bury it deeply, holding its gnawing specter at bay. There had actually been three casualties caused by the machine gun. He just couldn't see Sgt. Jackson's wounds. He wondered how many old men back in the world were trying, still trying, to manage the war-induced demons in their souls. He wondered too, how many were misunderstood, or perhaps largely unknown, by their own families.

His thoughts were interrupted when he saw Murph and Tom trudging slowly past. "I'm taking Murph to the forward aid station," Tom said. "I'll be back soon, but for now, if we get any other shit, you handle it, okay?"

Jack looked at his father, sadly at first, then took a deep breath and said, with as much confidence as he could muster, "Yeah, no problem."

Just as Tom and Murph began to head to the rear, Lt. Grimes approached, "Hey, Macmillans."

"Yes, sir?" they answered.

"I saw how you guys handled yourselves when we got hit. Outstanding work. That was tough stuff, both of you. It makes a big difference when the boys know someone will be there to help if they're hit, no matter what. Good job."

Jack held his breath as Grimes walked away. He was still deeply shocked and grieving, but Grimes' words nevertheless filled him with pride and relief. He managed a thin smile. He looked at his father; his expression hadn't changed a bit. Tom said sternly, "I gotta get going with Murph."

347

"Okay," Jack replied. "Hey, tell them to evac him to my hospital, okay?"

"Great idea, I'll do that." Then he nodded toward D.A., his pallor turning yellow, and said, "Could you do me a favor and move him behind the lines and cover him up? I'll get Graves Registration to come up as soon as they can. Get someone to help you."

"Okay," Jack said somberly.

Jack turned and looked at the body for a moment, "What's his name?"

It was Murphy who replied, in a quavering voice, "Douglas Ames. That's where we got his nickname . . . from his initials. Some people thought it was mean, but he kinda liked it for some reason." After a pause he choked, "But, I think we should just call him D.A. from now on like you did, you know?"

"Yeah, I think that's a good idea, Murph," Jack replied. "You take care, and hopefully I'll see you later today."

He watched Tom and Murphy slowly walk away until they disappeared into the coconut grove. He stood over the body of Douglas Ames for several moments. He couldn't bear to ask any of the other squad members to help him carry their dead friend behind the lines, so, alone he hooked his hands under the boy's armpits. As he did a tropical squall quickly turned the soil to a thick gruel. Grunting and straining, he dragged D.A. in tortured bursts a couple feet at a time. Leaning for maximum leverage, his face was only inches from the dead boy's. The visage of the lifeless face, one eye closed, the other half open, along with the undignified manner in which he was moving him, roiled Jack's emotions. He thought of D.A.'s comment just before he died, regarding the fear that he'd never get laid. As he dragged the body, he was suddenly wracked by deep sobs.

"What a waste . . . oh, Jesus help us, what a stupid waste!" he sobbed out loud. "I'm sorry D.A . . . I'm so sorry." Finally, exhausted, he left the body near his jeep, parked just off the road. He took a poncho from the back and gently draped it over the dead boy. Kneeling in the mud, he took a moment to collect himself then softly said, "Goodbye . . . good luck, D.A." He wearily pulled himself to his feet and slowly trudged back to Tom's hole. As he did, he gazed out toward the sand spit. He could see grotesque, twisted piles of dead Japanese on the sandbar. Occasional bursts of machine gun and rifle fire cracked from the Marine lines as Japanese survivors moved amongst palms across the river. But for the most part, the fighting for the Marines holding the line was largely over. Jack knew that come late morning, Lt. Colonel Cresswell's battalion would rollup the surviving Japanese troops, corner them opposite what the Marines would christen Hell's Point, and annihilate them. It was a great victory for the Americans. Nearly eight-hundred Japanese had been killed to the Marines' thirty-four. More important than the lopsided casualty figures, however, was the effect the victory had on the psyches of the Americans and Japanese alike. For the first time in the war, an American force had held fast against a strong, motivated Japanese force and routed it. The Marines had fought hard and bravely. After their early defeats, many American military men, as well as the public, had secretly questioned how they stacked up to what seemed to be a superior enemy. No more though. The Marines had proven that, in fact, it was likely the opposite was true. The Japanese, on the other hand, had learned that the Americans fought tenaciously and skillfully, given the proper weaponry and leadership. As well, the average Japanese foot soldier must have questioned the wisdom and skill of his leaders when men were pointlessly, stupidly even, cast forward in human waves against a line of well-entrenched, well-armed defenders. Though relatively small in the context of other World War II battles, the Tenaru, nonetheless, had broad implications regarding the prosecution of the war. Jack shook his head slowly, still horrified by what he had just experienced, but in awe as well. He was grieving for the dead, mainly D.A. As hellish the specter though, he still believed he was where he should be.

Jack slumped in his father's foxhole as Marine artillery shells crashed in the jungle across the creek. Ever so often, muffled screams echoed from the other side as the battle took on a more distant and surreal quality. He was startled when someone plopped heavily down beside him. It was his father, returned from the aid station. "Jesus! You scared the hell out of me," Jack said.

"Sorry about that."

"Did you get Murph to the aid station okay?"

"No problem," Tom said

"What about his wound . . . how bad is it?"

"Well, his baseball days are certainly over. He'll need some reconstructive surgery on his shoulder and it looked like the bullet, or bullets, tore a lot of the flesh off the upper part of his arm. A plastic surgeon should be able to take care of that. It's amazing what they can do these days."

Jack sighed as he gazed over at the empty listening post where the two boys had been hit. Murph, he knew, would have gladly given up his baseball career if it had meant his friend could live. "How's he doing with D.A.?"

"He's busted up a bit, but Murph's tough; he'll be alright."

"How're you doing?" Jack asked softly.

"I'm fine," Tom replied quickly.

"You sure? I mean, I thought with Hank and stuff . . ."

"This war, D.A., the Marines, all of this shit has nothing to do with Hank," Tom said impatiently. Jack, grieving for his father as well, pressed on.

"Christ, it was hard as hell on me, Tom; I can't imagine what you . . ."

"The Japs killed D.A. and I killed Hank; there's a big difference. D.A.'s dead; nothing's going to change that, and I have a very important job to do. If I let one death distract me, I might fuck up and I don't ever plan to fuck up again, understand?"

"I guess," Jack said reluctantly. He thought about Tom's comment. For a moment he wondered why anyone going into the medical profession would set such an unrealistic, even irrational, goal for himself.

Suddenly, Tom asked, "What in hell do you think Jackson's problem was? Jesus, and he's got us thinking he's some sort of tough guy. What a fucking baby." Jack blinked rapidly several times and thought carefully for a few moments about what he would say in reply. The sun was rising behind the palms, shedding a bright light on the torn ground and corpses. Sharp cracks from rifles and bursts of machine gun fire, their tracers arcing to and fro, once again cut through the jungle. The artillery barrage had lifted.

"I don't understand why you're so angry at Sgt. Jackson," Jack said cautiously. "You said it wasn't his fault."

Tom rolled his eyes. "Of course it was his goddamned fault! He should have pulled those guys in immediately. It was his job and he fucked it up."

Jack's eyes widened. "So why did you tell him it wasn't his fault?"

"Because that's what you tell someone when they fuck up and kill somebody. You go along with it and don't mope around, 'oh poor little me', like he's doing." You can feel sad, sure; that's normal. But it happened, you learn your lesson, and you move on . . . it's that simple."

"You really think it's that simple?" Jack asked.

"Of course it is. After all, I'm living proof, right?"

Jack blinked again. "But what if it isn't? What if it isn't that simple, I mean?"

"It *is* that simple goddamn it; that's all there is to it."

Jack sunk lower into the hole, frustrated at his father's unwillingness to explore his own emotions. After a while, Tom drifted off into a restless, writhing sleep. Jack only stared out toward the sand spit, exhausted; but his swirling emotions impeding sleep.

23

An hour later, Jack wearily climbed out of the foxhole and stretched. Though he would have liked to stay with the squad, he knew the hospital would be full of wounded Marines and he was anxious to return and help out. He was looking forward to being back with Ian and the others, but especially Ian. He felt as though, for his own emotional health, he needed to talk to him about the battle and D.A. . . . about his father. Without eating, he said good-bye to Tom and the others, then climbed into his jeep. He noticed sadly that D.A.'s body was still lying on the side of the road. He quickly looked away, started the jeep, and drove off, not for the hospital, but to the head of the creek.

He pulled up just behind the Marine positions at what had already been christened Hell's Point and got out of the jeep. Gunshots could still be heard, but only on the other side of the creek. In the distance he heard the metallic squeak of tank treads and the throaty roar of their diesel engines. Cresswell's 1st of the 1st were grinding the surviving Japanese down, sometimes literally with the treads of their Stuart tanks.

The battle site was torn with mortar and grenade craters. Jack could see several shattered Marine embrasures, including Schmid's, as well as one of the 37mm guns, twisted and charred. The smell of cordite, mixed with the smell of blood and feces, hung heavy in the air. The smell of rotting flesh already tainted the air with its indescribably foul stench. Most Marines were out of their holes, milling about . . . some talking somberly, others excitedly, about the battle. He looked over at the sandbar and saw hundreds of dead Japanese piled on top of one another. Thousands of monstrous insects feeding on the freshly dead corpses created a loud, constant buzz. Brown, spiny crabs scuttled amongst the heaps of torn remains. In the surf, dozens of sharks, lured by the scent of blood, swarmed violently about, devouring floating corpses. To his horror he saw a shark nearly beach itself and sink its teeth into the leg of a dead Japanese soldier. The predator violently writhed and flapped its tail in the surf, successfully dragging its meal out to sea. Jack choked back vomit, but stood transfixed, unable to tear his eyes from the scene . . . a scene that went beyond hellish. In fact, Jack thought numbly, there simply wasn't a word man had created that could aptly describe what lay before him. Macabre, ghoulish, gory . . . none of them were sufficient.

Two grunting, gasping Marines broke his trance as they struggled past him carrying a loaded poncho. Jack looked down and saw a dead boy, his eyes slightly open, his skin colored by death. The young man's face was unscathed. He saw something glimmer around the dead boy's neck. It was a shiny silver pendant in the shape of an English-style B. Jack gasped and recoiled a step, it was the enthusiastic, eager boy from South Boston; the boy who'd invited him to Fenway Park after the war. He had been Jack's first patient. His name, Jack thought, what was his name? Leonard . . . yeah, Lenny Chesnek. Jack sadly followed the makeshift litter with his eyes. "Jesus Christ," he whispered to himself, rubbing his tired eyes. "This is so fucked up." He watched as they laid the boy down at the end of a row of corpses. He stared for a moment, then turned away to go in search of an officer. He was learning to abhor foul and senseless death, but also learning to cope with it, cope like all men had for thousands of years after battles. He grieved for the boy from Boston, but his eyes remained dry. He trudged off and found a Marine captain talking on a radio.

"There's hundreds of Jap stiffs right in front of me," the captain was saying. "It was the goddamnest thing I've ever seen; they just kept coming and we kept mowing 'em down. They're laying out there in huge piles and some of 'em aren't dead, so we're being extra careful. You should have seen those bastards fight though, Ed." Jack assumed he was talking to Lt. Colonel Edwin Pollack, the highly respected CO of the 2nd Battalion, 1st Marines. "It was incredible," the captain said. "I mean they had to know they were all going to die, but they just kept coming." Jack waited patiently as the man listened to his superior say something over the phone. "That's right," the captain continued. "I've never heard of this kind of fighting, Ed. They're goddamn crazy; but as long as they're willing to cluster up and parade nicely right into the muzzles of our guns, I guess we shouldn't complain." After exchanging goodbyes, the captain hung up.

"Excuse me, sir," Jack said. "I'm with E Company, 1st Medical Battalion and I'm headed back to my hospital. I was wondering if there are any wounded I can take with me?"

The captain wearily rubbed his eyes, then replied, "No, they've all been evacuated, but thanks for asking."

"No problem," Jack replied. He turned to leave but the captain stopped him.

"Wait a minute. There is someone you can take." He turned to a Marine sitting on the rim of his foxhole cleaning his rifle." "Mahoney, bring Jarvis up, will ya?"

"Yes, sir," Mahoney replied.

The captain turned back toward Jack and said, "A case of the nerves. He was right in the thick of it and a few of his buddies got killed. He's always been a bit squirrelly, but Christ, it was one hell of a fight, so I guess you can't blame him. He's not a coward; he's just not as tough as the other boys. He hasn't said one word since the second attack."

Moments later Mahoney walked up with his arm around a very young Marine. Jack took one look at the boy and knew it had to be Jarvis. The young man was staring straight ahead with an utterly vacant expression on his face. His mouth was half open and he walked uncertainly, as if he were drunk. His uniform was blood stained and filthy. Streaks of clean skin ran down his cheeks where tears had washed away residues of dirt and gunpowder. Jack immediately felt badly for the boy. After having seen the fighting and watching D.A. die, he completely understood how any man could and inevitably would, given the time, break under the strain. Jack moved forward and said to Mahoney, "I've got him." He wrapped his arm tightly around the boy's shoulders and guided him toward the jeep. He put him in and slowly drove off, leaving the killing ground. On the way back to the hospital, he tried to soothe the young man.

"You're going to be just fine, Marine. You just need to clean up and get some rest." Every few moments he'd say, "It'll all be fine. You're going to be just fine, pal." The boy though, only stared straight ahead glassy-eyed, muted it seemed, by the horror he'd witnessed. It was therefore a relief, though somewhat uncomfortable, when Jack pulled up in front of the D Company aid station, where a neuro-psychiatric team was housed. He gently led the boy to triage, wished him luck, then anxiously roared off.

When the jeep came to a halt, the door of the E Company hospital flung open and Ian strode out. "You're alive," he said, grinning broadly. His face darkened though when he noticed Jack's appearance. The bandage on his cheek was smeared with mud and his body was covered in blood and grime. Jack quickly clambered out of the jeep and without thinking, hugged Ian tightly. Surprised, Ian quipped, "It's good to see you too, mate."

"Sorry, Doc," Jack said sheepishly. "After last night and this morning I'm just damn glad to be back here. It's awful, Doc, it really is hell just like they say. The platoon lost one guy, Douglas Ames; the other boys called him Dumbass." Ian's expression remained unchanged. "Remember? The kid who got plunked in the ribs by the baseball."

Ian's eyes widened, "Oh bloody Christ . . . that's Turk's buddy, isn't it?"

"Yeah; I'll tell him as soon as I can. I don't look forward to it."

"Well, don't rush," Ian replied, pointing behind him at the hospital. "They started coming in a little after 3 a.m. and they haven't stopped. We're full up and busy as hell. In fact, I've got to get back to work, so we'll have to talk about your night later."

"Okay, Doc. I'll get to work, too," Jack said. When he walked through the door, he stutter-stepped. The hospital's appearance had changed dramatically since he had left it the previous evening. Wounded Marines, more than 20, lay throughout the tent. Some, the most badly wounded, were on the sawhorse-supported litters; others with lesser injuries were laying or sitting on the floor. Most were smoking. Hospitalmen streamed amongst the wounded, assessing their conditions in a non-stop triage. On occasion, one of the lesser wounded would suddenly become a priority case and would quickly be moved to an elevated litter for attention from the doctors. Soft moans rose from some of the men on the litters. Dr. Goldman was working on one Marine who'd been shot in the abdomen. He was working quickly, almost roughly, Jack thought. But he knew they had to get the boy patched up as quickly and efficiently as possible so he could be transported offshore for more extensive care. With the fighting over, by evening, the hospital would have far fewer patients. Many would have been sent to a ship, while others would have already returned to their units. As Jack scanned the wretched, almost primitive scene, he realized that the entire hospital staff was at work in the crowded tent.

"Shit!" he suddenly hissed. His eyes had come to rest on a corpsman and a wounded Marine. Tears glistened on the cheeks of both. It was Turk and Murph. "You dumbshit," he said to himself. "You should have thought of this." He quickly strode over and put his arm around Turk.

"I'm sorry, pal," Jack said.

After a pause, Turk turned away and said bitterly, "I mighta saved him damn it!"

"Tom and I did everything we could for him, Turk. You know that."

"I'm sure, but still, maybe it would've been different if I'd been there."

356

"Turk, he . . ."

"Never again!" Turk interrupted firmly. "Never again, Jack! Don't you never fuckin' leave me behind again when you go up to the line; you understand?"

Jack, his arm still around the shoulders of his heartbroken friend, replied softly, "Yeah, I understand. I won't do it again; I promise." Jack patted Turk on the back and asked Murph how he was doing.

"I'm fine. Doc Smith changed my dressing and cleaned the wound out real good. He said I was going to be fine. Now I'm just waiting for a ride to the beach."

"Do they have you on morphine?" Jack asked.

"Yeah, that's some good stuff; keeps making me fall asleep though."

"That's good, Murph, the sleep's good for you." Then he forced a smile and added, "Well, at least your war's over. It won't be long and you'll be back in, where is it . . . Baltimore?"

Jack was taken off guard when Murph glared at him and argued, "The fuck you say my war's over. I'm not just going to fire off a few clips, get winged, watch my best friend get killed by those dirty little bastards and say, 'oh that's it, time to call it a war'. No fucking way . . . I'll be back to settle the score with the fucking bastards. I'm coming back, bud; you can count on it."

Having spent time with the closely knit young men, Jack wasn't surprised by the proclamation. He forced a smile and said, "Well, for the Japs' sake, I hope you're wrong." Jack knew that Murphy's shoulder and upper arm were shattered. It was obvious that he would be discharged by the Marine Corps after what would likely be a very long convalescence. His war was definitely, irrevocably over. For now though, Jack was happy to play along with Murph's delusion. "I'll be looking for you then when we march on Tokyo, okay? We'll have a beer or ten."

Murph smiled weakly, "It's a deal."

They shook left-handed and Jack added, "You take care of yourself, Murph. Sorry again about D.A."

357

"I'm sorry, too. Take it easy, Jack."

The next several hours flew by as Jack changed bedpans, cleaned, swabbed, and redressed wounds, and cleaned dirty, blood stained skin. By early evening, things had begun to slow down. Only half the peak number of patients remained. At 1900, Dr. Goldman gave half of the staff relief from the hospital, including Ian and Jack. Dr. Goldman and the others would carry on in the hospital until 0200, when the rested staff would spell them. Jack and Ian wearily shuffled through the dusk toward the Cave, and sat down on a coconut log near its entrance. Jack thought back on the last twenty-four hours and what he had seen and done. Despite his lingering grief over D.A.'s death, and revulsion at the life-grinding violence, he was satisfied that he had performed well. "You ain't blowing it, bud," he said out loud.

"Blowing what, mate?" Ian asked.

"Oh nothing really," Jack replied. "Just giving myself a little pat on the back."

"Yeah? That's good, mate," Ian said, holding a bottle of *sake* out to Jack. "Have a drink, but we need to go easy tonight as we're on duty at 0200."

"No thanks, Doc. Not tonight." He couldn't remember the last time he'd turned down a drink under any circumstance.

"Suit yourself," Ian replied. They each lit a cigarette and Ian asked, "What's the pat for then?"

"Well, it was painful to hear what you said last week about me and my dad being a lot alike and that the only real difference is that I got lucky. Remember that discussion?"

"Sure I remember it, but my intent was not to hurt."

"I know," Jack replied softly

For the first time, Jack told Ian the story about his Uncle Hank's death and about his drunken grandfather, and the difficult life on the farm. He hadn't told Ian the stories before as it seemed something that should be shared exclusively between father and son. The last night though, had changed everything; he needed to talk. He described his father's reaction to D.A.'s death.

"Bloody Christ. What do you make of all that?"

"I don't know for sure, but I've got to try and figure out why he didn't pursue a medical career. Christ, think about it, a career in pediatrics! That could have given Hank's death some sort of meaning."

"Whoa, whoa there, mate. It's not my business, but are you trying to find a way to alter your father's future?"

"Why the hell wouldn't I?"

"Well, first is you and your family. You'd be altering their futures, maybe even their existence; don't you think? You are his son, not his mentor, after all."

After a long pause, Jack said, "Christ I don't know . . . I almost feel like I'd be sacrificing him, or at least his happiness." Jack could never put the existence of his own children in jeopardy. He felt a vague sense of relief, but dropped his head.

Ian, staring at him intently, asked, "What is it, mate?"

"It all seems so stupid and meaningless now."

"What does?"

"What I did back in the world."

"Don't be too hard on yourself," Ian replied. "I'll never understand the western man's ways. But I see the way you take risks for the lads and work in the hospital 'til you nearly drop. It seems sometimes that you would die for them; die for them on this bloody island so far from your world."

"Yeah, this island," Jack muttered. "This goddamn crap hole of an island." Jack sat silent for a moment, then said, "Doc, do you believe that your people, the ones who still live in the old way, are superior to us?"

After a slight hesitation, Ian replied, "Superior no; wiser yes. We think and live more simply, but we see more deeply. There is a spiritual reason for everything we do. In your world, a world I've lived in, true spiritualism is almost completely absent in everyday life. That's why we're sitting here on this bloody crap hole, as you call it, trying to kill each other with only a vague sense of why. You're caught in cultural and political machines that are so vast and complex that one simple human can never really figure it all out."

"Yeah," Jack said quietly. After thinking for several moments, he said, "You know, I went my whole life thinking I was superior to my dad, tougher, more progressive. I resented his melancholy and detachment, but now, shit, now it seems he's a better man than me; I guess he always was. Hell, it's not even a contest."

Ian interrupted his thoughts with a slap on the shoulder and said, "It's not supposed to be a bloody contest! Besides, you can't judge the quality or value of your life or anyone else's until they're gone. You're still a young man . . . sort of."

Jack smiled wryly, "Right now I feel goddamn ancient. What's say we hit the hay?" They trudged to the Cave and laid down on their bedrolls. Jack clenched a penlight in his teeth and began recording his daily journal entry.

August 21, 1942

Tenaru battle over—very rough, even rougher than I, or anyone I'd guess, could imagine. It is very different than I'd always thought it would be: louder, smells are awful, violent beyond anything I thought humanly possible. Utter chaos, violence, and horror. Don't know why people have to experience war to figure out how dreadful it is. It is a cliché of sorts, but now I truly believe that if the men initiating war actually had to participate in it, there would be no more wars. . . .

. . . Very disturbed about Dad. Sgt. Jackson felt responsible for D.A.'s death and Dad reacted very strangely to that. Was very angry and derisive. It wasn't rational and I am certain much of it is connected to Hank. I never considered him a tragic figure, but I am looking at things much differently now. Christ! I wish I was wiser, or at least more aware, back in the world.

360

Too tired to think anymore.

Tomorrow—shift at 0200, sleep if I can, another hospital shift, out to the Tenaru. Turk and I are bringing the boys some brews. Still can't figure where the hell Turk is getting the stuff. Will be very hard, particularly on Turk, when D.A. doesn't come bounding up to us like always.

24

The next day, Jack's 2nd shift ended late in the afternoon. Ian had accompanied an injured Marine to Kukum for transport to a ship. The man had broken his back by falling from a coconut tree while in search of his breakfast. So far the Marine wasn't paralyzed, and Ian wanted to make sure he had as gentle a ride to the beach as possible. With Ian using the jeep to transport his patient, Jack and Turk were left to walk the three quarters of a mile to the Tenaru to visit with Tom and his squad mates. Flight operations were underway at Henderson, making the 250 foot diagonal shortcut across Henderson's runway a bit tricky. Jack and Turk were each carrying a case of beer and the hot sun was beating down on them. The air was so thick and wet that Jack felt as though he was swallowing it, not inhaling. He continually shifted the case of beer from the top of his shoulder to under his arm, then up to the top of his helmet, like Indian women carry urns of water from the village well. The shifting didn't do much good, and after the short distance to the edge of the runway, Jack was fatigued and dripping with sweat. They stood to the side of the runway, watching as a dozen Wildcats and Dauntlesses lined up for take off, grateful for the rest. As they waited, Jack took off his sweat-drenched shirt and tied it around his head to keep the sweat out of his eyes. Turk looked at Jack and said merrily, "Hey great news, Jacko!"

"What great news?" Jack asked wearily.

"Your tits is shrinking!" Jack rolled his eyes, slowly shaking his head, too hot and tired to bother formulating an appropriate response.

The planes began rolling, one at a time, down the runway. By the time each Wildcat reached the spot where Jack and Turk were standing, the plane would just be rotating off the Marsden-matted runway. The Dauntlesses would rotate another 150 feet down the runway. As each plane roared by, Jack gave the pilots a vigorous thumbs up. "Yeah!" he squealed boyishly when one of the pilots saw him and returned the salute. They waited until all the planes had flown out of sight, then slowly began to make their way across the runway. Suddenly, they heard a shout from behind.

"Clear the runway you goddamn idiots! Are you shitheads blind? There's a C-47 on final!" Jack whipped his head around to the south. In their excitement over the departure of the patrol, they had forgotten to check to see if any planes were arriving.

"Jesus Christ!" Jack yelled. The big cargo plane was just touching down and barreling straight at them. "Let's go, Turk!" he screamed. Like thieves, they ran as best they could carrying their loads across the landing strip. But when they were two-thirds of the way across, the toe of Jack's boot caught on a section of the holed, Marsden matting, and he crashed to the ground. His box of beer broke open, spilling some of its contents. Jack watched wide-eyed as the C-47 grew larger, its steel propellers chopping the air. He sprang up, grabbed the damaged box and took off for the edge of the runway. After several paces, he was shocked to see Turk running past him in the opposite direction.

"You left some fuckin' beers goddamn it!" Turk hollered above the growing, thrumming roar of the plane's two huge piston engines.

Jack stopped running and yelled, "Forget the beer, goddamn it! Let's go!" Turk ignored him, kneeled down, took off his helmet and dropped several bottles of beer in.

"Turk, forget the beer, goddamn it! We gotta go, man!" Turk kept anxiously glancing back at the plane. His helmet was full, so he was using the bottom of his shirt as a basket for the remaining bottles. Finally, he staggered to his feet, holding his helmet in one hand and the bottom of his shirt in the other. "Hurry . . . hurry, damn it!" Jack screamed. Turk was running, but in mincing, baby-like steps, so as not to endanger his cargo. The plane was only 100 feet away when Turk reached Jack. They scurried off toward the edge of the runway. When the plane roared past them, Jack could feel the rush of the vortex, created by the wing tip, brush his neck. When they reached the scrub at the side of the airstrip, they sat down to rest and looked back at the path they had taken. A man stood directly across from them, shaking his fist and yelling. Jack figured he was the one who had shouted the warning. They watched the furious man for a moment, then looked at each other and burst out laughing. Neither had laughed since D.A. had died. It felt good.

"What in god's name were you thinking?" Jack asked.

"What do ya mean?" Turk said, his eyes bulging. "What the fuck were *you* thinking? We never, ever, leave a fallen beer on the fuckin' field of battle. We're the U.S. fuckin' Navy; we always go back for the beer. You messed up . . . but don't worry bud, I won't tell nobody." Turk's statement, along with the sight of the man still standing on the other side of the runway, hands on hips caused Jack to laugh harder. He was gasping for breath and wiping at his eyes. Tears came to Turk's eyes too, and for several moments neither could speak; they both clutched their bellies and writhed on the ground.

Finally Turk choked, "Oh shit, Jack, it was like when you and Doc Smith got bombed by the Japs, except better. The sight of you all fuckin' splayed out, your eyes just about poppin' out of your head they was so big . . . oh shit . . . oh Jesus . . . I'll remember that for the rest of my fuckin' life!"

"Yeah, well the sight of you cramming beers into your helmet and shirt while a goddamn C-47's about to slice and dice you will give me some fine memories, too." After a pause he added, "Oh Jesus, I can't remember when I've laughed this hard. I just hope the beers are worth risking your life for, pal."

Turk stopped laughing and looked at Jack with a thin smile. "They're worth it. After yesterday and Dumbass, I mean D.A., and Murph and all, I think the guys will really appreciate it."

"Yeah . . . yeah, you're right." He then momentarily drifted away, thinking of his children back in the world, silently praying that they would never have to endure the same violent, wretched challenges that the youngsters which of he was now bound were coping with. He wrenched himself from the worrying, sad thoughts, and refocused on the grief-stricken boy sprawled in front him.

"Good job," Jack said weakly. His voice gained more confidence and bombast. "You saved the beer and you saved the day. Now let's get these babies to the squad."

Turk ingeniously took off his shirt and tied off the sleeves. He filled the sleeves up with the wayward bottles of beer. The rest of the way, Jack carried the damaged case in one hand and the shirt, by its tail, in the other. He was pleased to learn that the arrangement was actually easier on him than carrying one full case. They stopped several times along the way to rest, yet still by the time they arrived at Tom's squad area, he felt as though he might collapse. Jack set the beer down and dropped to one knee, propping his head up at the bridge of his nose with his thumb and index finger. A wave of nausea swept over him and his head spun. After several moments he leaned over and vomited on the ground. Turk stood next to him, hands on hips, breathing heavily, although not heavy enough to suppress a chuckle.

"Hey!" Jack heard Scooz shout. "Jack and Turk are here and they look like shit! Jack's kinda gray, you know, kinda like the Yankees away uniforms, kinda . . . hey . . . wait a minute . . . is that . . . could that be what it looks like?" Turk smiled wearily and nodded. Jack looked up at the boy. Scooz was grinning broadly, and in his excitement was compulsively running a hand through his jet black, wavy hair. Though only 18, he sported a heavy black stubble. To Jack, he seemed like an eager young puppy, full of life and energy. He thought back to Scooz's speech on Hill 73 two weeks ago. It had been delivered in a feeble, gravelly voice, and only a glimmer of his youthful enthusiasm remained. The contrast between the boy and the old man was stark and induced a momentary feeling of melancholy. But, Jack thought, the lively boy had survived; he'd made it and lived a long life. Troubled, even perhaps tormented at times by his memories of the war and his lost comrades for sure, but he'd made it. D.A. was dead; a full sixty years before his friend gave the speech on the ridge just a few miles from where he'd been cut down. The randomness of it all seemed unfair, cruel. But Jack, still grieving, smiled at Scooz, thankful that he knew at least one of them, besides his father, would survive the war.

"Beer call, boys!" Scooz shouted, bringing Jack back to the Marines present . . . his past. Scooz ambled up to Turk and Jack and shook their hands vigorously. "Just kiddin' about you guys looking like shit," he said smarmily.

"Fuck you, Scozzolari," Jack said. "You smelled out the beer and now you can't help but get your nose up our asses."

Scooz gasped, put a hand to his chest and said, "Oh, Jack . . . you've wounded me. I don't just love you for your beer . . . there's so much more."

Jack rolled his eyes, "There's no need to kiss my butt anyway. Turk here's the beer man; a beer man with a mysterious and seemingly endless source of supply. Kiss his ass; leave mine alone."

"Point taken," Scooz replied, stroking his chin thoughtfully. "Okay. Jack, only you look like shit. Turk here looks like Errol fucking Flynn."

By now all the boys, including Tom, were crowding around, welcoming Turk and Jack. Jack looked carefully at Turk. He was smiling, but Jack could clearly see the pain in his eyes. His best pal and Murphy were the only ones missing. They carried the beer to the creek bank and sat down, Jack next to Tom. After they had each opened a bottle of beer, Jack asked, "How's it going guys?

"Shitty," Sgt. Jackson responded. "We been sitting here all day on our keisters doing goddamn nothing." Pointing to the jungle on the other side of the creek, he continued, "1st Battalion is havin' all the fun and they weren't anywhere near the battle last night. We've

366

been listenin' to 'em all day herding the Japs into a corner down near the beach while we sit here pickin' our fuckin' noses. The firing stopped a little while ago. I think they got all the bastards."

Jack looked toward the sandbar and the heaps of rotting corpses. Fortunately, the wind was blowing straight along the beach, keeping the smell of the bodies clear of their position. Jack could clearly see Marines walking amongst the corpses, hunting for souvenirs and checking for wounded. Suddenly a shot rang out, and Jack saw a Marine go down. Another shot, another Marine fell. Jack grimly recalled what was happening. Wounded, suicidal Japanese soldiers were trying to take a Marine with them. Jack remembered that the Marine response to the surprising treachery was to line up a group of riflemen and fire into the clumps of bodies.

"The fuckin' baboons are shooting our guys!" Lou yelled.

"Motherfucking savages!" Big Mikey bellowed.

"I need to bag me some of them fuckers!" Jackson raged. The sergeant's eyes were wild with fury, his body taut, veins bulging. Shirtless, he grabbed his Tommy gun and sprinted toward the sandbar.

Others started to follow, but a voice shouted, "Stay where you are!" Jack turned and saw Lt. Grimes standing just a few yards away. When he turned back, Jackson had reached the area just west of the sandbar. He joined a group of Marines lying prone in the sand at the edge of the creek. An officer barked an order and the men began firing Springfields, Colt .45 pistols and BAR's into the putrid mass of dead and dying Japanese soldiers. Sgt. Jackson loaded clip after clip into his sub-Tommy, firing madly into the mound of enemy soldiers. Bodies jerked and convulsed as bullets slammed into them. Pieces of flesh and bone were torn off and flung through the air, most splashing in the sea behind, sending the sharks into a renewed spasm of frenzy. Jack knew that the action the Marines were taking was justified and necessary to ensure their safety, and he felt little sympathy for the Japanese. But the gruesomeness compelled him to look away. He shriveled into the bottom of his hole.

"Gotta do it, pal," Tom said quietly, squatting down beside him. "The bastards didn't leave us any choice."

"I know," Jack replied. "It's just so goddamn awful, like a horror movie coming to life or something. Not just this, the whole thing: the battle, the wounded, the screams. This just kind of punctuates the whole crazy fucking mess." Jack paused for a moment then added, "I wonder if this'll make Sgt. Jackson feel better about D.A.?"

"I wouldn't count on it," Tom replied. "In a way it'll just make him angrier. The only thing that really works is to just get rid of it. That's what he needs to do, but I'm not sure he's strong enough."

"Get rid of it?"

"Yeah, throw the fucker away. You can do that you know. You just banish the memory; remove it from your mind. Sure, there are times the fucker will try and sneak back in, but all you do is zap the son of a bitch."

"Zap it . . . with what?" Jack asked as the firing at the Point gradually petered out.

"I like to think of it as a brain ray that your mind fires, that . . . oh never mind, I uh . . . I'm . . . just forget it. I'm not making sense." Tom pursed his lips and looked away.

"No," Jack said. "You're making perfect sense. I guess I'm just not sure what you're describing is a healthy technique for someone's emotional . . ."

"Not that crap again!" Tom spat. "Jesus Christ, Jack, sometimes you can really get on a guy's nerves. I never should've told you about Hank." Jack dropped his gaze to the ground, hurt by his father's angry words. He recalled the discussion with Ian the previous evening, about letting his father's emotional difficulties be. Tom's stubborn, angry reaction to Jack's latest attempt to help made it easier. After an awkward pause lasting a full minute, Tom spoke.

"I'm sorry, Jack. I just don't like to be analyzed, you know?"

"I've kind of figured that out," Jack replied. He forced a smile, then said, "No problem, bud. I know I can be a pain in the ass at times."

The firing at the sandbar had ceased, and shortly thereafter Jack and the others saw Sgt. Jackson marching back toward the squad area. No one said anything to him when he sat down and rejoined the group. He bitterly muttered one word after a deep swig of beer, "Fuckers." Moments later, a heavy downpour engulfed them. The men wrapped themselves in ponchos and gathered together as Turk loudly, but smoothly, sang the mournful song, *Who'll Stop the Rain.*

Long as I remember, the rain been comin' down.
Clouds of myst'ry pourin', confusion on the ground.
Good men through the ages tryin' to find the sun;

Turk had taught them the song on a previous visit and they'd expertly learned to join in on the refrain, the infusion of their deep voices combined with the hissing rain creating a haunting, yet beautiful harmony.

And I wonder, still I wonder who'll stop the rain.

The rain splattered off their helmets and ponchos and they all huddled together in a tight knot, providing a sort of comfort from the deluge.

Heard the singers playin', how we cheered for more.
The crowd had rushed together, tryin' to keep warm.
Still the rain kept pourin', fallin' on my ears.

Once again the entire squad joined the refrain:

And I wonder, still I wonder who'll stop the rain.

When they finished singing, the men sat silently, dealing with the misery of the downpour and mud as well as memories of the previous night. The silence was broken when Lou asked somberly, "Hey, Jack, did Murph get sent to your hospital?"

"Yeah, he did," Jack said.

"How's he doing?" Big Mikey asked.

Jack nodded toward Turk and said, "Turk's been taking real good care of him, haven't you?"

"He's okay," Turk said. "His baseball career is over, but he don't care too much about that right now. He just wants to get the surgeries and stuff out of the way so he can come back out here and kill Japs. Murph's fuckin' pissed, boy." Everyone, except Jackson, murmured comments supporting Murphy's goal. Jack remained silent regarding his true condition.

As the tropical squall abated, the boys began to tell amusing, affectionate stories about Murphy. Ski said, "Remember that time at Parris Island when Murph put that scorpion in that strange fucker's bunk. What was his name? A big farm boy from Georgia . . . Darnell, that was his name. Wonder what happened to that goldbrickin' son of a bitch? Probably pealing potatoes on some rust bucket by now." The boys laughed at the memories of the prank.

Louie recalled another incident, "How about the time in that bar in Wellington when that dame, the redhead, dumped a pint of beer over Murph's head? He never did tell us what he'd said to her. God she was pissed, and ol' Murph just carried on drinking, all wet and shit like nothin' had happened. Hell, he didn't even bother to towel himself off."

Before long of course, the subject inevitably turned to D.A. Jack, smiling, leaned back against a sandbag, closed his eyes and listened to the warm, funny stories about the squad's dead buddy. They each talked about the first time they'd met D.A. and how enthusiastic and friendly he'd been. They reminisced too about D.A.'s bet with Murph, and the time Turk and he went fishing in the creek in a jeep. They told stories about a boy who was a faithful friend and a fierce protector of the members of his squad and platoon. A boy who, though not very bright in the conventional sense, had an innate, remarkable sense of the mood of his mates and what to do to positively affect it.

Finally, Big Mikey summed up by saying somberly, "He cared, boy. D.A cared for each one of us more than he cared for himself; hell, that's what really got him killed I guess."

"Yeah," Scooz added. "He was the best. He was the best of us, wasn't he?" Heads slowly bobbed up and down. Jack looked over at

370

Turk and saw that tears had welled in his eyes. Once again the young man was proving he wasn't nearly as tough as he would have others believe. Turk noticed Jack staring and quickly wiped his arm across his eyes. He cleared his throat and suddenly sprang to his feet.

"Well," Turk said loudly, "Jack and I can't just sit out here all night wastin' time with you sons a' bitches. There's a war goin' on, you know. C'mon Jack, it's time to head back." Turk's sudden pronouncement surprised Jack, and several of the boys protested.

"We don't have to head back just yet, Turk," Jack contended.

"Yeah we do. I got shit to do back at the hospital and I ain't lettin' an old fucker like you walk back all by his lonesome, so c'mon."

Jack looked at Turk for a moment and saw there was a certain desperation in his eyes. "Okay," he said quietly, "I'm coming." They said their goodbyes and slowly made their way through the coconut grove.

They walked in silence for several minutes, then Turk quickly blurted, "I ain't coming back out here with you no more. I'll still get you the beer and I still want you to bring me if you're goin' into a combat situation."

"Why not, why don't you want to visit the squad?" Jack asked.

"Just don't fuckin' want to."

"Tell me the reason, Turk," Jack softly said.

Turk thought for a moment, wondering it seemed, if he should tell Jack what was bothering him. Finally he said, "I'm no good at it."

"No good at what?"

"The dyin' and people gettin' hurt. I'm no good at it. I mean in the hospital it ain't a problem . . . I don't know those boys so it don't bother me so much. Dumbass though, I ain't gonna call him D.A., Jack. I only known him as Dumbass. Anyhow, we was close pals and now he's dead. It's fucked up."

"Your feelings are very normal, I should think," Jack said. He winced at the condescending nature of his pronouncement, as he remembered Tom's foxhole rebukes.

"Normal or not, I don't fuckin' like it. I realized all of a sudden when we were sittin' there talkin' that Dumbass was the first, but sure as hell he won't be the last. I like all those guys, but I don't wanna be friends with 'em like I was with Dumbass."

"I see," Jack said. "So you're afraid you'll get too close to them if you keep coming back?"

"Yeah, that's about right." Turk paused then added, "This is just between me and you, okay?"

"Of course."

"I mean, I don't really feel bad about it," Turk continued. "I'm sure a lot a guys feel the same way; like your friend, Tom, for example." Jack's head jerked up and he stared at Turk for a few moments.

"What did you say?"

"I said it don't fuckin' bother me much, but I still don't want everybody . . ."

"No, not that," Jack interrupted. "What did you say about Tom?"

"Oh. I noticed he don't get too close to the boys. I mean he's a great guy and real nice to everyone and all, but its pretty fuckin' obvious he keeps his distance. Makes even more sense when you consider he's the doc and all. Hell, you're his best pal and you ain't even a part of the platoon. I'm surprised you didn't notice it."

"I uh . . . I guess I just wasn't paying attention," Jack said quietly. In fact, he had noticed Tom's distance from the other boys, but had assumed it was simply his nature, for it fit well with the man he had known back in the world. He'd been so focused on his father and their relationship, that he'd never really given much thought to Tom's relationship with his squad mates.

Turk added, "It's kinda odd that Tom was that way before his first battle, before anybody died. It was like he knew what it would be like or somethin'. Hell, I sure didn't."

"He knew . . . God knows he knew," Jack muttered somberly to himself.

"How's that?"

"Uh . . . never mind." For years Jack had pitied himself over his father's seeming cold-hearted detachment. He shook his head and loudly sighed. When they arrived back at the hospital, Jack found Ian in the Cave, preparing to get some sleep. Jack told him about his visit with the squad, the stories about Murph and D.A., and what he'd realized about his father . . . with Turk's help. True to his word, Jack mentioned nothing of the difficulty Turk had had with the visit.

"You're learning a lot, eh mate?" Ian said when Jack finished. Jack somberly nodded his head then patted his friend on the knee, "Get some sleep, Doc." Within minutes Ian was snoring quietly. Jack laid on his stomach and wearily scrawled an entry in his journal.

August 22, 1942—still on the Canal.

Two shifts in hospital today. By end of 2nd shift most wounded from Tenaru battle evac'ed. More malaria and dysentery cases coming in plus one appendicitis. Moved him quickly offshore for emergency appendectomy. Weird, after awful battle and dead and wounded, it was actually pleasant to see a malady not caused by man or the stinking island . . .

. . . The boys told stories about Murph and D.A., very touching and sincere. They're good boys; can't help but keep wondering who will survive the war and if any of them are still alive back in the world. The only one I know of for sure is Scooz. Big Mikey; goddamn it. It's so hard to think of him stuck out here for two more years only to get his life snuffed out on Peleliu. I pray he lives a lot of life during the 9 months the boys are in Melbourne after this mess . . .

. . . Learned from Lt. Grimes when I was out at the creek today, that the company commander, Captain Morehead, I think he said was the guy's name, was nowhere to be

seen during the battle and well after it was over. When he did show, he pulled a bunch of chicken-shit shenanigans that he probably was hoping would cover his dereliction. It really pissed the boys off. Strange thing is, just like Biggs, I bet he really believes he's hot shit!!

Ironic that for all my life I would've considered men such as these to be giants as long as they'd worn a uniform during the war, yet could not, or would not, consider my father in the same way. There is so much I didn't know about Dad, or simply did not, or could not, see. I was thinking on the way back from the creek about how he ran the company. He treated his employees so well—so much patience. I think now that he saw them as a great responsibility of his, perhaps the most important of his life. Dad saw his job as not just to pay them, but to enrich their lives. All the things such as the company trips, lunch concerts, birthday parties, hospital visits, funerals, seemed overreaching and pointless to me, but they were a part of Dad's philosophies and what he saw as his purpose.

Tomorrow—morning and evening shifts in hospital. Supply run in between to replenish after today. Try to get out and see Dad.

25

An epic sea battle was fought on August 24–25. The clash, involving carrier aircraft from both sides, became known as the Battle of the Eastern Solomon's. Jack and the other men on the island heard about the battle, but were little effected by it, as the action took place several hundred miles north and west of their location. The battle was a clear American victory; the Japanese carrier pilot corps having been decimated. However, the victory did not stop the Japanese from landing reinforcements, it only delayed them. On August 30, under the command of General Kiyotake Kawaguchi, they began to swarm ashore at Taivu Point, 10 miles to the east of the Marine perimeter. It would take them nearly two weeks to form up in strength and march into position for the next attempt to take Henderson. The intervening period was relatively quiet, save for several heavy air raids on the airfield and the daily shelling by enemy cruisers and destroyers; none of which did much damage, other than to the men's psyches. As well, Marine patrols occasionally skirmished with the survivors of the Ichiki detachment and a foray by the First Battalion, Fifth Marines across the Matanikau led to two Marine deaths and several wounded.

Jack had a front row seat for a colossal air battle that was fought over Henderson on the 30th, between Japanese carrier planes and Marine Wildcats. A squadron of newly arrived Army Air Forces P-400 Bell Airacobras would also participate in the aerial fray. Jack knew the P-400s, lacking an effective supercharging system, were no match for the Japanese Zero fighters. He, along with hundreds of others, cheered the Wildcats as they hurtled down on the Japanese fighters, sending eight of them spinning into the sea. Likewise, he turned away when each of four overmatched Army Airacobras were downed by the Zeroes. He recalled, with much relief, that the Army aircraft would be limited to ground attack roles after the actions of that day.

His time during this period followed a fairly consistent routine. Each day he served two 6-hour shifts in the hospital. The work was mostly mundane, as virtually all the hospital's patients were victims of disease. He'd take the opportunity during breaks to go and visit Tom at the creek. They spent much time together, chatting about home, medical procedures, or playing Euchre. Tom never mentioned Hank again and seemed to enjoy telling Jack about his plans for medical school and a practice at Blodgett Hospital, just a short walk from where Jack lived back in the world. These discussions were maddening, but Jack played along, giving what he knew was futile encouragement. As Jack was leaving the Tenaru one evening, Tom said to him, "I never thought an old guy like you would be my best pal." A lump formed in Jack's throat and he could only nod. He forced a smile and simply strode off through the coconut grove. He and his father had become something he'd never imagined possible . . . best friends.

Turk, true to his word, never again accompanied Jack on his visits, though as promised, he kept the squad well supplied with beer. One evening, as Jack was preparing to haul a heavy case to the squad, Turk surprised him with a gift. Jack was walking past the hospital with the case of beer slung on his shoulder, when he heard a shout from the Emerald Palace.

"Hey, you old bastard; you're gonna kill yourself haulin' that fuckin' beer through the jungle!" Jack saw Turk wearing a wide grin, the ends of his mouth turned up so high that his smile had a goofy aspect to it. He was standing at the entrance of the warehouse.

"Screw you, pal!" Jack shouted. "I may be older, but I'm a man of action."

"I been busy, too," Turk said cheerily. "Come see what I been workin' on."

"Later, Turk."

"No," Turk implored, "you really got to see what I fuckin' done." Jack looked at him and couldn't resist the boy's pleading eyes. He set the beer down and trudged to the Palace entrance.

"Okay, what is it?"

"You wait here," Turk said excitedly as he ducked into the warehouse. A moment later he reappeared, a crude, makeshift wagon trailing behind him. He was pulling it along using a shaved tree branch attached to an empty blood plasma crate. A looped handle made of surgical tubing was threaded through a hole that had been punched in the top of the branch. All metal, spoked wheels were attached to the bottom of the crate. *Pops Brew Wagon—We Deliver* had been crudely painted on the side in what appeared to be tincture of iodine. A smile spread across Jack's face and he thrust his hand out and vigorously shook Turk's.

"Geez, thanks a lot, Turk," Jack gushed. "What a decent thing for you to do; thanks a lot."

"Test drive it," Turk said proudly. "Put the beer in there and see how she does." Jack set the case of beer in the empty crate and pulled it in a circle around Turk. The wagon's wheels squeaked as they turned but, other than that, it functioned perfectly. Turk never took his pride-filled eyes off the wagon during its short circular journey.

"It's fantastic . . . perfect!" Jack proclaimed. "Where in heck did you get the wheels for the thing?"

"It ain't a fuckin' 'thing', Jack," Turk huffed, slightly annoyed. "It's a piece of goddamn engineering genius."

"Yes, you're so right. I'm sorry."

"Anyhow," Turk said, "I liberated them wheels from some sort of heavy Jap cart. I don't know what the fuckin' Japs used it for, but some of the boys up around the Pagoda, supply and motor pool types, was usin' it as some sort of fuckin' portable bath. Can you believe that shit? I seen it and I thought to myself, 'them clever

377

fuckin' sons a bitches'. Then I think to myself, Turk old boy, I wonder if you could ever be as clever as them bastards. Well, there's the answer," Turk concluded, pointing at the wagon.

"You are clever indeed," Jack said. "Thanks a lot, pal. This is going to add years to my life." He trundled off toward Henderson, the wheels of the wagon squeaking pleasantly. Whistling, he ignored the odd stares of Marines as he passed and happily made his way toward the creek. The flat metal wheels rolled easily over the soil, and the slow rhythm of their squeaks seemed to give life to the little wagon, as if it were a companion on the journey, chattering away as Turk had on prior visits. When Jack ran across Henderson's runway, the low squeaks turned to high pitched squeals, urging him to the other side. Having arrived at the squad's position, in considerably better shape than his previous journeys, he proudly showed off his new possession. Tom and his mates were duly impressed. They asked Jack to pass on their sincere appreciation to Turk.

Jack's visit with his father that night was typical of all his visits over the quiet period. They'd sit on the creek bank with the squad, talking and joking, until just before dark. Then the two would retire to Tom's hole for an hour or so before Jack went back to the hospital. Jack had given up trying to ease his father's emotional problems and decided to simply enjoy their time together. As they sat in the foxhole talking, Jack asked Tom if he was anxious to get married and start a family.

"Hell no!" Tom declared. "I'm going to have to focus everything on college, then med school. I don't have a clue how I'm going to pay for it all, and I sure as heck can't be weighed down by a family just yet."

"Understood," Jack said. "How about later then?"

"Sure," Tom replied. "I've always loved kids; hell I'm going into pediatrics, aren't I?" After a brief pause Tom muttered, "I'd think it'd be kind of hard to have your own kids though." He quickly added, "I still want to have them though."

"Hard in what way? You get used to diapers and all that shit, no pun there, by the way."

Tom chuckled nervously and said, "I'm a worrier I guess. It just seems that I'd be worried about 'em every minute, you know?"

"Yeah, I know, and believe me, you do worry about them a lot. But not all the time, and the worrying and all the other stuff is worth what they give to you anyway."

"Oh, I'm sure it is, it's just that I . . . uh . . . oh never mind."

"No, go ahead with what you were about to say."

"I . . . uh . . . would just hate to see something bad happen to them. I'd worry about that. Like I said, I'm a worrier."

"You'll be fine," Jack assured. "You just have to relax." Jack said this in spite of vaguely understanding Tom would never really be able to. He also briefly considered the fact that he'd been an only child. He shifted uncomfortably in the foxhole and changed the subject. They passed the remainder of the evening, and the evenings that followed, talking easily and comfortably about most things. As his father had done with him back in the world, Jack told his dad little of his past, or at least very little that was true. He was too ashamed and worried how his father might react. It was, Jack thought wryly to himself, 'the future repeating itself in the past.'

26

The rain was falling in torrents early on the evening of September 5th as Tom and Jack huddled together in the foxhole. They'd been laughing at Scooz who'd stripped naked, made a Tarzan-like yell, then taken a running start and slid rapidly on his belly through the mud, straight into Louie and Big Mikey's foxhole. Scooz's naked body had draped over the two boys, writhing and cursing in their hole.

"Get off me, you goddamn wop!" Big Mikey bellowed.

"Ahh, goddamn you . . . that's disgusting Scooz!" Louie yelled. "Your dick touched the back of my neck . . . shit!" Finally, they'd flung him out of the hole to raucous cheers from the entire platoon. He stood up, his front half covered with mud, and bowed toward Jack and Tom; then turned the other way and bowed again.

"Goddamn," Tom muttered. "That son of a bitch has got one hairy ass."

Several days before, Scooz had been reprimanded by Lt. Grimes for entering the mess line wearing only his boondockers and helmet, innocently clutching his mess tin. Above the predictable din, Jack had heard Grimes wearily shout, "Scozzolari, put your goddamn trousers back on! Christ, it's like running a goddamn nursery school sometimes."

After the hilarity of Scooz' latest antics, father and son sat quietly, each lost in his own thoughts. The feeling of his father pressed

tightly against him provided warmth as well as a sense of content-
ment. He pondered each of their lives and how different they'd
been. He believed more than ever that his father was a better man
than he; at least back in the world. Jack contemplated ways in
which he could 'catch-up' if he ever made it back.

"Tom?" he asked quietly.

"Yeah?"

"Do you think a man who hasn't lived his life well . . . uh, who
hasn't really had things in the right order and stuff . . . do you think
that man can change things or make amends of sorts?"

Tom was silent for a moment as he pondered the question, then
he said, "I'm not sure where that question came from, but yes,
absolutely I believe a man can change his ways and make up for the
past. Not in a Charles Dickens sort of way or anything, but in a
quiet, unselfish way." He took a long pause, then added, "I mean,
you know, I'm no Bible guy, but if you cheated at your job or were
greedy or didn't treat your family well, there are definitely ways
you could atone. Why, you looking for absolution or something?"

Jack laughed lightly and said, "Nah, not absolution. Hell that's
just a nice and tidy way for people to clear their conscience. No, I
guess I'm looking for something more substantial."

"Jesus, Jack," Tom said. "You think too deeply about shit sometimes, you know? I wonder if I'll be like that when I'm old . . . oh
geez, sorry for that."

Jack laughed, "Maybe I do, but these days I just can't seem to
help myself."

"You want to tell me what about your life has got you asking this
sort of question?"

Jack was caught off guard. He quickly sputtered, "Uh, no. No, it
would bore the hell out of you."

"You sure?"

"Yeah, I'm sure." Jack squirmed uncomfortably. He was prepared to talk to anyone about his past, anyone but his father. He
blurted, "I gotta get back to the hospital. I'm on night shift." It had
stopped raining and Jack made the lonely trek back through the

grove and across the runway; the empty beer wagon sublimely wailing.

September 5, 1942

Same old, same old at hospital. Lots of malaria, dysentery, some dengue now too. Custom will change in a week when the ridge fight starts. Night shift tonight—4 a.m. now.

Tokyo Express (that's what they/we call the ships that shell us every night) knocked crap out of us last night. Scared the hell out of me, though I was pretty sure we would be okay. I have read so often of how it is to be under artillery bombardment. I have never heard one description that does justice to the terror and desperation you feel; there are simply no words.

Heard we strafed Japs good this morning trying to land in barges. Think I remember this. But, I know many are getting ashore. Battle of Edson's Ridge is a week away. Jap's will attack ridge that is south and east of Henderson about a mile. Two night battle, very brutal fight, many dead. Jap's will come within whisker of breaking through to airfield . . .

. . . Laura, you may never read this journal though I pray every day that somehow you will, but this passage is for you and the kids. I think you would be proud of me. I fear (though you would never admit it) that it would truly be the first time ever. God I miss you and the kids. I now know that you and they are really all that matters and should matter to anyone, that and living a true and honorable life (as corny as that may sound). Nothing else matters or for that matter is even real. Everything else is goddamn Vegas; everything, I think. Guess I'm turning into an old cynic but I think this island would have the same effect on lots of folks my age. I am so sorry for the man I was,

particularly since my dad died. My drinking and hobnobbing must have been awful for you. You want to hear something funny? Since I left paradise and arrived here in hell I have felt no compulsion to drink. I have only done so for social purposes on a few occasions. Why couldn't I see it? Why couldn't I see anything? This dark and foul island combined with what I've learned about Dad has opened my eyes to what I was to you as a husband and as a father to my kids. I hope it's not too late. Just please know that I love you and the kids beyond words. The greatest gift I could be given is if someday you read these words and understand that they are from deep in my heart.

Tomorrow—consecutive shifts in afternoon and evening. Won't be able to go see Dad. Up at 9. Palace needs repairs and heard some more hospital cots have arrived. Think we will need some more for the ridge battle. Will go see if Biggs can cough some up. Ran into him at D Company yesterday. His eyebrows are sprouting nicely, only looks mildly astonished now.

27

When Jack woke the next morning, he popped into the hospital to ask Dr. Goldman for the jeep. After getting permission, he turned to leave. He glanced at a new patient lying on a cot, then stopped in his tracks. It was Wimpy from Biggs' depot. He was shirtless and a bandage covered a baseball-sized area above his belly button. He was sound asleep. Jack turned to Dr. Goldman and asked, "What happened to this guy?"

"Gunshot wound."

Jack looked back at the chubby boy. "I know this guy," he said. "Did a Jap infiltrate his position or something?"

"I wish I could say that was the case," Dr. Goldman said dourly. "It was friendly fire. We're transporting him to the beach in a half-hour or so. He's in pretty bad shape but I'm quite certain the surgeons onboard can save him."

Minutes later, Jack pulled up to Biggs' supply depot, curious as to how the boy was wounded. As he strode toward the tent, the door opened, Biggs tramped out, two armed Marines escorting him. He was cursing bitterly, looking straight down at the ground. Jack stood in silence as the procession passed and mounted a nearby jeep. Other men milled around watching. One standing a few feet from Jack spat, shook his head, and cursed. "Fucking piece of shit," he muttered.

Jack turned to the man and asked, "What the hell is going on?"

The man looked at Jack, his eyes widening in recognition.

He paused for a moment, then said, "Well, you of all people will be pleased to know they're finally shipping the goddamn prick off the island."

"Jesus, did he have something to do with Wimpy getting shot?"

"That's right. Doesn't surprise you, does it?" the man said bitterly. "He woke up last night and heard a commotion near that pile of supplies over there and he figures someone, a Jap or a Marine, is helping themselves to his precious stash of shit. So he pulls his .45, sneaks up behind the guy and puts a bullet in his back. Turns out it was poor Wimps just out taking a piss. Can you believe that shit? Shot him in the back!"

Jack shook his head slowly. "What a goddamn lunatic," he said. As the jeep pulled past Jack on its way to the beach, Biggs locked eyes with him. Jack shook his head in disgust. A look of anger spread across Biggs' face. He jutted his chin out and mouthed, "Fuck you."

"Nice shot asshole!" Jack shouted. "Have a good life you piece of shit!" Biggs looked away. Jack turned toward Biggs' former charges and said bitterly, "Good riddance to bad rubbish!" They all murmured in agreement. He then assured them that Dr. Goldman believed Wimpy would make it. As he walked back toward the supply dump, he spotted the handsome boy whose nose had been broken by his father. The boy's eyes were wreathed in fading bruises; his nose still bent a tad to the right. Jack nodded slightly and the boy responded in kind. After helping himself to ten cots, Jack drove back to the hospital. He was sorry Wimpy had been hurt, but was pleased that Biggs was gone. He wasn't one of us and never will be, Jack thought. The thought brought an ironic, unconscious smile to his face.

28

Two mornings later, on September 7, Jack was busy, along with Turk and Frank, setting up the new cots in the hospital. A truck full of Marines had overturned on a ridgeline the day Jack had picked up the cots, flooding the hospital with patients. There were some broken bones, lacerations, and gashes, but fortunately no one was killed. Still, Jack and the others had to wait two days to set them up, as it was impossible to rearrange the existing cots without causing considerable discomfort to the injured Marines. While they worked, Turk sang a beautiful version of *Lodi*.

> *Just about a year ago, I set out on the road,*
> *Seekin' my fame and fortune, lookin' for a pot of gold*
> *Things got bad, and things got worse, I guess you'll know*
>   *the tune.*
> *Oh! Lord, stuck in Lodi again . . .*

Jack looked at Frank, who was slowly bobbing his head in rhythm with Turk's singing. When he saw Jack watching, a big smile creased his face and he said, "What could be better than having an honest job and old Turk singing while you're doing it?"

Jack smiled back and replied, "Not much, Frankie, not much at all." He watched the two boys work, his smile still in place. After D.A. was killed, Turk and Frank had grown even closer. They still had their squabbles, but had become nearly inseparable: the effete, future world-famous surgeon from Palo Alto, and the burly, coarse, boy from South Philly. Jack shook his head in wonderment. It was clear the boys, opposites in so many ways, had developed a real love for one another. Jack wondered if the two would remain close or stay in touch with each other after the war. Then, as an afterthought, 'That is, if they both survive.' The concept made him shudder, for he loved the boys himself. It wasn't the love he felt for Laura, or the deep, unconditional love he felt for his children. It was a love borne out of shared peril, privation, and complete dependency on one another. They were non-combatants in a sense, but on Guadalcanal in the early days, there really was no such thing. After a month on the island, living and suffering with his heroes, they no longer seemed larger than life to him. Among the many good people, there were thieves, liars, deviants, and cruel young men . . . a cross-section of 1940s America. He no longer studied them in awe, for now he was of them. He, like they, had weaknesses and failings, but on the island, they all needed each other regardless of pasts or personalities. He no longer worshipped them; he had simply learned to love them.

> *. . . Rode in on a Greyhound, I'll be walkin' out if I go.*
> *I was just passin' through, must be seven months or more.*
> *I ran out of time and money, looks like they took my friends.*
> *Oh! Lord, I'm stuck in Lodi again . . .*

Jack's thoughts were interrupted when he saw Frank suddenly drop to the floor and scrabble around in the corner. The boy then sat still and chuckled in a low, devious sort of way. Jack was perplexed until Frank looked at him, his eyes gleaming, and held up his hand. In it he clutched a wriggling, three-foot-long snake. Like so much on the island, it was olive-green, but with dark-red, evil looking eyes. Jack followed Frank's eyes over to Turk, who was bent over, meticulously unfolding and placing cots at perfect 90-degree angles to the tent wall.

> *The man from the magazine, said I was on my way.*
> *Somewhere I lost connections, I ran out of songs to play.*

387

*I came into town, a one night stand, looks like my plans
    fell through.*
Oh! Lord, stuck in Lodi again . . .

Jack watched as Frank crept over and placed the reptile in a
tightly folded cot that Turk would set up next to the others. When
Frank walked back past him, Jack pursed his lips and wagged his
finger at him. He felt a little sorry for Turk, he was so terrified of
snakes; but the show, sure to be spectacular, was irresistible. They
waited as Turk finished up a cot then, unawares, moved to the one
containing the snake.

. . . If I only had a dollar, for every song I've sung.
Every time I had to play, while people sat there drunk.
You know I'd catch the next train, back to where I live.
Oh! Lord, I'm stuck in Lodi again.
Oh! Lord, I'm stuck in Lodi again.

As the song ended, Turk picked up the cot and began to unfold
it while holding it in the air, just above his head. Suddenly, his body
jerked, and for a second, went completely rigid, as if it'd been
struck with a high voltage electrical shock. Next, he reflexively
threw the cot up and away, while emitting what was, to Jack, the
most frightful scream he'd ever heard from anyone. He quickly followed the first scream with another. Jack watched in amused consternation as the green snake flipped out of the cot, sailed up,
rotated once in the air, and started down. Down, it seemed, in slow
motion, then incredibly coming to rest, neatly draped on Turk's left
shoulder. After a brief hesitation, while his nerves and brain sent
urgent messages back and forth, Turk went into a spastic dance, his
vocal chords temporarily frozen by utter fear. Jack watched in
amazement at the jerky but speedy movements of the boy. Turk's
dance was an effort to dislodge the snake, without having to actually touch it. After several moments, and still voiceless, Turk successfully ejected the snake. His face was taut with terror, and as he
sprinted for the door, his vocal chords restarted. "God . . . oh

God!" he screamed. "Fuck! Oh, Christ . . . oh Fuck!" Jack could see that Turk was no longer aware of his surroundings, his only conscious thought being to get away from the snake. They watched him run down the road a ways, then stop and sit in the middle of it, carefully surveying the surrounding soil.

Jack turned toward Frank. He found him clutching his mid-section, slowly sinking to the ground. His face was bright red and tears streamed from his eyes. He was laughing so hard he was barely making a sound, just little squeaks, punctuated occasionally by gasps of air. He curled into the fetal position, continuing to rasp and squeak. For a moment, Jack wondered if it was possible for a man to laugh himself to death. Finally, when Frank began to regain some measure of control, Jack, wearing a slight smile, said, "That was real nasty, Frankie boy. You may have scarred him for life." Jack felt even sorrier for Turk than he had before the incident. The snake's unexpected landing spot had been an unfortunate break for him. It turned a scary-phobia moment into a horror show for the boy. Still, Jack thought, it had been pretty funny.

Frank wiped away tears and said, "Naw, he'll be fine, he just needs a little time." Frank paused to further compose himself, then said, "Oh jeepers; that was the funniest darn thing I've ever seen. Did you see him jumping around like some . . . some sort of elec-trified Merrie Melodies cartoon guy? Oh geez, I think I may have peed a little in my pants."

"Are you going to tell him you put the snake in the cot?" Jack asked.

"Of course," Frank replied. "I wouldn't do something like that to the big ape and then try and hide. Heck, even if he kills me, it'll still have been worth it."

Just then, they heard Turk outside the tent ask in a wary, highly pitched voice, "Hey, Frank, Jack . . . you guys still in there?"

"Yeah, we're in here," Jack replied.

"Where's the fuckin' snake?"

Frank looked around and found the snake curled up near a crate. "He's still in here."

"Jesus Christ!" They heard Turk scuffle away from the tent.

"Don't worry, buddy, I'll get him out," Frank yelled. Jack could tell by Frank's words and tone of voice that he too was starting to feel badly for his friend.

When Frank walked out the door holding the snake, Turk backpedaled even farther yelling, "Goddamn it, Frank, watch out!" Frank turned and headed toward the jungle behind the tent. After a few steps Turk yelled, "Kill the fucker, Frank."

"There's no reason for that. Don't worry; I'm going to let him go a long way from here."

"Fuckin' kill it, please, Frank. I need to know that fucker is dead or I won't never sleep again."

Frank stared at Turk, unsure as what to do. Finally, Jack stepped forward, took the snake from Frank's hands, held it down on the ground and cut off its head. "Good, thanks, Jack," Turk muttered. "Man do I fuckin' hate them fuckers."

Frank, looking slightly stressed, took several steps toward Turk and quietly said, "I'm sorry, Turk. I didn't mean to spook you that bad, buddy. It was just a joke."

At first a look of surprise dawned on Turk's face, then quickly turned to a deep frown. "You fuckin' did this, Frank? You put that fucker in the cot?"

"I'm real sorry, Turk." Still though, Frank couldn't stifle a chuckle.

Turk's frown immediately became a look of rage, and Frank stepped back several paces. "I can't fuckin' believe you did this!" Turk howled, stepping toward his friend. "You know I have to kill you now, Frank, don't you?"

Somewhat concerned, Jack shouted, "Run Frank!" Frank turned and sprinted up the road. Turk followed, bellowing profanely.

"Don't hurt him, Turk!" Jack yelled. "Remember, you guys are friends!"

Without looking back, Turk shouted, "That little turd ain't my fuckin' friend no more!" Jack chuckled as he watched the two boys

390

disappear around the bend. If he caught him, he knew Turk would punish Frank in some way, but it wouldn't be too serious, and before long they'd be fast pals again. He turned and headed back to the hospital. Just as he reached the door, he heard a jeep approaching. He looked up and was delighted to see his father at the wheel. He waved and Tom replied in kind, but weakly. The jeep halted in front of Jack, and he noticed Tom was frowning.

"How you doing?" Jack asked cheerfully.

"I'm here for sulfa," he muttered flatly. Then, in almost the same breath, he added, "Lt. Grimes is dead."

For several moments, Jack stood in stunned silence; his mind bending. Finally he managed to stammer, "What? That can't be . . . Lt. Grimes? Oh my god, I . . . I can't believe it. I always thought he was the one guy . . ."

"So did we all," Tom interrupted dolefully.

Like a prisoner of war, Jack raised his hands and rested them on top of his head. He gazed skyward. "How . . . How did it happen?"

"Jap sniper," Tom said. "1st and 2nd platoon were on patrol a mile or so west of Koli Point. We'd just entered a small clearing in the jungle when a shot rang out . . . one lousy fucking shot, nothing else. Lieutenant Grimes took the bullet in his forehead. He died instantly."

"Aw, Jesus, I . . . I can't believe it." Jack said. "He seemed invincible. How are the guys doing with it?"

"They're pretty busted up. Grimes was one of the few officers they really liked and respected. They're not only sad, but scared about fighting without him around. Just pray that his replacement isn't another stupidass coward like Morehead." Jack remembered the grieving, pimple-faced boy who'd lost his captain during the strafing attack on the first morning. A heavy sadness swept over him; not just for Grimes, but for his father and the rest of the boys.

"Did they get the sniper?"

"Hell, yes they did," Tom grunted, a hint of satisfaction in his voice. "Scooz, Big Mikey, and Danny went right after that fucker, didn't even know if he was alone or was one of hundreds. They chased him out onto the beach, and the bastard ran through the surf, trying to escape. Danny carries a Thompson and he's real good with it. That fucking rodent must've had 15 holes in him. The captain ordered some of the boys to bury him; that is, after he hauled his yellow ass up from the back of the line. They weren't too pleased about that; they wanted to leave the son of a bitch where he was."

"Goddamn," Jack groaned, "Why Grimes? He was a man . . . a good man." Jack thought back to the visit that Grimes had organized on Biggs' depot. He wondered what comforts Biggs was enjoying on some ship offshore, awaiting a new assignment stateside, while Lt. Grimes lay in some maggot-filled grave near the beach, no children or grandchildren in his future. No beautiful bridges soaring above the nations waterways. The grand bridge joining the northern and southern peninsulas of Michigan would be built, but Grimes, as he had dreamed, would not be there to help.

Suddenly, a series of snapshots quickly rolled through Jack's mind. It was spring, 1964, and he was sitting next to his mother on a ferry taking them from Mackinac City to historic Mackinac Island. They were sitting on a bench in the heated lounge. The course the ferry took ran roughly parallel to the magnificent five-mile suspension bridge built in the 1950s. When the ferry pulled out, Jack's father had walked out on deck and leaned on the rail, in spite of the brisk spring air and spray arising from the choppy waters of the straits. Jack had watched his father for several minutes, staring at the bridge . . . frowning, shivering. He'd left his mother's side and walked out on deck.

"What ya doing, Dad? Come inside, it's real warm in there." It seemed his father hadn't heard. "C'mon Dad, let's go inside," he urged, tugging at his father's windbreaker.

His father, his face drawn, looked down at Jack and said tersely, "Go back inside and sit with your mother."

"But I'll stay out here with . . ."

"Now!" his father barked. Jack retreated to the lounge, tears spilling from his eyes. His mother cradled him for the rest of the journey, while his father stood at the rail, never taking his eyes off

392

the bridge until the ferry docked. Jack had been deeply hurt and confused by his father's angry brush-off. Now he understood; he understood completely. A sudden rage overcame him and he slammed his fists down on the hood of Tom's jeep.

"Goddamn it!" he yelled, tears welling in his eyes. "This is so fucked up! We shouldn't be sending our good men out here; there aren't enough of them! It should be men like your captain and Biggs . . . and me, even! Not people like Grimes!"

Tom stepped out of the Jeep and put his arm around his son. "Take it easy, Jack . . . settle down, and don't you dare lump yourself together with men like that. You're in a completely different league."

Jack quickly composed himself and apologized, "Jesus, I'm sorry. I'm, uh, a bit of a gusher, I guess."

"Geez, there's nothing wrong with letting it out once in a while and hell, you're older and not trained like us, so you shouldn't expect yourself to be quite as resilient."

"Sweet Mother of Christ," Jack muttered. "How the hell do you train someone to handle this?" He paused for a moment, his reddened eyes gazing across Henderson toward Edson's Ridge. "I uh . . . just tell the guys I'm real sorry about Lt. Grimes, okay?"

"I will." Tom patted him on the back and said, "Now, how about a hand rustling up some sulfa? The jungle is a nightmare on even the smallest nicks and cuts. Some of the boys have picked up some nasty infections and leg ulcers." It struck Jack how they all, including himself, were quickly learning to allow brief moments for grieving, then quickly move back to their duties. Jack retrieved a box containing packets of sulfa and put it in the back of the jeep. Tom hopped in and asked, "Hey, you coming out tonight?"

"Yeah, sure . . . I'll bring some beer. I'm sure the guys could use it."

"That'd be great. See you tonight."

"See you then." Jack watched sadly as Tom pulled away. He felt an urge to shout out to his father, to beg him to stay for a while, but instead he turned toward the hospital and went to work.

After his noon shift at the hospital was over, Jack loaded up the beer wagon, adding two bottles of *sake* Ian had donated, and slowly made his way to the Tenaru. The sound of the wagon entering the company area lured Tom's squad out, as well as a man he hadn't met. The stranger strode up to him, smiling smugly; a Colt .45 on his hip. Rifles hung on the slumped shoulders of the boys, and there wasn't the gaiety that normally accompanied Jack's visits. He knew instinctively that the man must be Captain Morehead. He was making his first appearance at beer call, more than likely Jack thought, because Lt. Grimes was no longer around. Jack felt an intense and immediate dislike for the man, and his intuition had him bracing for a confrontation. He reached into the wagon and pulled out the bottles of *sake*. He handed them to Lou. "Something a little extra for you boys today," he said, smiling wanly.

Morehead frowned and announced, "I'm Captain Morehead, CO, and I'll have those bottles."

Jack looked squarely at the officer and said, "Hospitalman Jack Macmillan, sir. Nice to meet you, but the hooch is just for this squad . . . sorry, sir."

Morehead's eyebrows arched and his mouth fell open. "What the hell did you just say, mister?" The words exited his mouth at a high pitch, an odd sort of squeaking.

"I said I don't have anything for you, sir. I just have enough for the squad."

Morehead gaped incredulously. "If this is a joke it isn't very damn funny!"

The two locked eyes. Jack's expression was blank; unbending. "Sorry, sir, but no joke."

The captain's eyes blazed. He took an angry step toward Jack and shouted, "I forbid it! I forbid my men consuming alcoholic beverages other than the occasional beer, you understand? The *sake* is mine!" He lunged toward Lou and attempted to snatch the bottle from him. Lou stepped to the side and swung the bottles behind his back. "Goddamn it!" Morehead yelled. "You're all going on report! By god, every single one of you!"

394

"Sir," Jack said calmly. "Firstly, the *sake* isn't yours, it's mine. Secondly, these boys lost their leader and friend this morning, if you may recall, and I'm sharing what I have with them and that's it."

"You little prick!" Morehead screeched. "Give me those bottles!" He put his hand on his sidearm as if to un-holster it. Jack froze. Then from behind he heard several rhythmic, metallic crunches. They were the sounds of bolts on Springfield rifles being rammed home. Morehead's eyes widened. Other members of the platoon had gathered round. All glared silently at their captain. Sweat streamed down the sides of his face. He looked around at the men and slowly moved his hand away from the pistol. He took several steps backward and stammered weakly, "You men . . . you . . . ."

"You may report me to Colonel Pollack if you wish, sir," Jack interrupted." Pollack was a good and fair officer, Jack remembered. He knew instinctively that Morehead would be taking a huge risk by going to Pollack. It was very likely that Pollack would see *him* as the real culprit in the fracas, considering the events of the day. Jack could tell by the worried look on Morehead's face that he was mulling the same possibility. After several moments, and without another word, the captain slowly turned and stalked off into the coconut grove. There was no rejoicing amongst the men. Led by Jack, they strode slowly to the edge of the creek and sat down. Only one comment was made regarding the face-off. It came from his father.

"You have a way with those in authority, Jack old boy," Tom said. "I bet you were hell on your ma and pa." Jack blinked quickly and forced a smile. The incident between Jack and Captain Morehead was never spoken of again. The captain became ever more scarce and no longer bothered the men. Days later, he was relieved by Colonel Pollack and sent home for reasons not explained to the members of the unit.

Jack stayed late talking with the squad, mainly about Lt. Grimes. Some of the boys still seemed to be in a state of shock over the loss of their leader. Others were grief-stricken and apprehensive. Grimes' replacement had not yet arrived, and there was much anxiety over what sort of man they would get. They were young, but they knew they had been very lucky to have Grimes. Jack did his best to assure them they would be okay, and he reminded them that the most important thing was that they take care of each other. It didn't seem to do much good, but Jack kept trying; with Grimes dead, he felt a need to act as a reassuring father figure. When it was time to get in the foxholes, he went with Tom and they talked until shortly before midnight. Then they both fell asleep, leaning against one another. Jack woke several hours later when a heavy squall soaked them. He cursed, quickly bade Tom farewell, and hustled back to the hospital for his first shift. During a break, he made his journal entry for the previous day.

September 8, 1942

Lt. Grimes was KIA yesterday—Jap sniper. Still can't believe it. Am not quite as sad as when D.A. died, but much more shocked. Hard to explain. He was just one man but it feels like we took a huge beating from the Japs. He seemed too strong and too in control to be killed. It just doesn't seem real . . .

. . . Hope the guys can get over Lt. Grimes quickly, me too. Wishful thinking maybe. Tried to comfort and reassure them being their elder and all. Feel kind of stupid now as I feel I did little good and can't truly understand what they're feeling. Tom seemed okay, not like after D.A. though. I think losing Grimes has shaken him just as much as the others . . .

. . . Frank scared the living devil out of Turk this morning.

. . . Next time I saw them they were chattering away like schoolgirls, but Frank was gently kneading his ears, which were fiery red. When Turk finally caught him, he'd boxed his ears with two simultaneous blows. For some reason picture of Turk clapping his large paws together

396

and them being stopped from joining by the sides of diminutive Frank's head is amusing. I chuckle as I write this.

Lots of air action again today. It is almost becoming routine. Our boys are doing well against the Japs. Saw a Wildcat dive away from two pursuing Zeroes that had gotten behind him. The heavier Wildcat pulled quickly away from the Japs who must have been cursing in frustration as they finally peeled off and broke off the pursuit. Much laughing and cheering.

Rest of today—finish first shift then afternoon shift. In between, Ian has asked me to locate and pinch a chair with stout backrest. (Think I'll try the Pagoda.) Dr. Goldman screwed up his back lifting litter out of truck. Having trouble standing for long periods so will treat patients sitting down when he can. Refuses bed rest. Very withdrawn but a good doc. Out to river this evening. Beer continues to flow from mystery source via Turk.

In between shifts, Jack drove up to the Pagoda. He entered the crude structure and was immediately frozen by the sight of Brigadier General Roy S. Geiger, head of flight operations on the island. Jack immediately recognized the grizzled old flier from pictures he had seen. The no-nonsense, World War I bomber pilot stood ramrod straight, talking gruffly to one of his subordinates. His sharp features and close-cropped silver hair gave him a regal countenance. Jack paused for a moment in the doorway and listened to their conversation.

"Sir, they're living like rats in those soggy tents north of the runway," the subordinate said. "They sleep in the mud, or at least they try to, during the Jap bombardments at night. The starchy, protein overloaded chow they're getting is causing intestinal gas and cramps at high altitudes that are nearly debilitating. Add to all that the fact that they're in almost constant combat and you have a very difficult situation. The strain is wearing on them, sir. I'm not sure how much harder we can push them."

"Listen," Geiger said gruffly, "I know it's tough, Toby; tougher than it's ever been for any group of American pilots, but we have to keep pushing. We do have to somehow scrap this defensive rut we're in though, and let the boys play a little offense. That will help tremendously and I'm working on it. In the meantime I want each man to clearly understand his duty and to fulfill it . . . or die trying, understand?"

"Yes, General," the man named Toby replied.

"In the meantime, see what you can get them in the way of better chow and maybe some fresh fruit."

As Jack slid past the two officers, it was hard for him to take his eyes off the general. In a couple weeks, he knew the 57-year old officer would take a Dauntless up himself, and dive-bomb an enemy position as an example to his men. Geiger would also be the first Marine aviator to command an entire army in the field later in the war on Okinawa. Two years after the war, as cancer slowly drained the life from his body, he refused to stop serving his beloved Marine Corps and country. He worked right up until he died. Jack had always admired him, but he felt no remorse over his plan to steal one of the rare chairs on the island. After all, Jack's reverence was held mostly for the young men doing the fighting on the ground and in the air, not the generals directing the battle. He simply couldn't understand how the older, god-like by military standards, general officers could send their younger fellows to their deaths. He didn't consider them bad people, but how does one play golf or bridge, or enjoy a fine meal after they've directed thousands of young people to violent deaths? What kind of man stays sane? He had to give Geiger credit though; he didn't mind getting directly involved in the scrap from time to time. But the juxtaposition of most senior officers relative safety, their public relation machines and massive egos, set against the tens of thousands of anonymous deaths suffered by the young foot soldiers, seamen, and fliers, once seemed to him a simple and little pondered fact of our hierarchal based society. Now though, after weeks on the island, Jack thought it perverse. He shook the thoughts from his head and refocused on his mission.

After Jack passed the two men by, he saw a sturdily built chair sitting in front of an overturned crate. He walked over and hesitated near the chair, checking to make sure everyone in the room was distracted. Most were poring over maps and documents. Jack quickly lifted the chair off the ground and started out the door. Just as he passed by the two men again, Geiger turned rapidly and the two bumped lightly against one another. "Sir . . . I'm very sorry, sir," Jack stammered. "I uh . . . I . . . they asked me to repair this chair, sir."

"I don't give a goddamn about a chair, son," Geiger replied. "Just get the hell out of my way."

"Oh . . . yes, sir. Sorry sir." Jack stepped aside and the general impatiently strode away. As Jack walked back to the jeep, clutching the chair, he chuckled. He whispered to himself, "You just stole a general's chair and while you were doing it he called you son . . . Christ." After delivering the purloined chair to the hospital, Jack started his second shift.

29

At 6 o'clock he trudged to the Tenaru, pulling a load of beer. When he arrived, he saw Tom and the entire platoon gathered around a small group of natives by the side of the road. He walked up to the group and asked his father what was going on. Tom, smiling, gestured toward the natives and said, "They're a family. They're making the rounds trying to see who has Bibles and if we want to sell them. It's pretty neat; they're going to distribute them to their fellow villagers still hiding up in the hills. Apparently the Japs destroyed all their old ones along with just about everything else they had."

Jack looked at the native family. Besides the parents, there were two adolescent boys and a small girl. Jack guessed her to be about six or seven. They were all smiling and the little girl was tossing a small coconut up in the air. She looked at Jack; he smiled and gave a little wave. He ached for his own children. Jack turned back to Tom and asked, "What does a Bible go for here?"

"A piece of fresh fish and some sort of strange fruit, papaya, I think. The men say it's real tasty."

"Wow, good deal." Jack watched as several Marines eagerly traded their Bibles for the foodstuffs. He could tell by the looks on their faces, and the tones of their voices, that the reason they were selling their Bibles had little to do with what they received in exchange. Conversely, Jack observed a group of Marines standing off to the side, watching the proceedings with sneering looks of distaste. The men trading ignored a fellow Marine who muttered, "I don't trade with goddamn niggers." Just as Jack was about to tell the man off, he noticed a jeep roaring up the road. Suddenly, out of the corner of his eye he saw the little girl bobble her coconut. She lunged for it, propelling it forward, away from her. It thudded to the ground and rolled into the road. She immediately sprang after it.

"No!" Jack screamed. "Get back!"

He moved toward the little girl, now bent over in the road, but it seemed as though his feet were weighted with iron balls. He heard the jeep driver curse as he locked his brakes. He screamed a last warning, "Move!" It was too late. The driver had managed to slow the jeep considerably, but it hit the little girl just as she rose, clutching the coconut. Her scream was cut short when the jeep's grill banged her chest, folding her throat over the edge. The impact sent her flying back several feet. The jeep stopped with its chassis covering the lower half of her body. Everyone froze for a moment, then pandemonium. Marines cursed and the girl's parents screamed. Jack and Tom rushed to the girl and knelt beside her.

"Back up!" Tom yelled. The girl was wide-eyed and conscious, but strangely silent. Tom began to run his hands lightly over her chest to check for broken ribs, while his son dabbed at some deep lacerations the jeep's grill had sliced into her chest. "I don't feel anything. She may have gotten lucky," Tom said. The girl's parents had knelt down beside each leg and were gently stroking them, talking softly to their daughter, reassuring her. Tom moved up to her face and examined her eyes. She still wasn't making a sound, but her eyes were wild with fear. Suddenly, Tom jerked his head down and placed his ear on her mouth and put a hand on her chest. A second later he shot up, "She's not breathing!" Her parents began to whimper and plead. Tom stuck a finger down the girl's throat then gently placed a hand on her neck. "Shit!" he hissed. "Her upper larynx is crushed. Jack, get me out a scalpel and some sulfa. Louie! Where's Lou, goddamn it?"

"Right here, Mac." Lou replied from behind. "What do you need?"

"Go get your pipe, unscrew the stem and give it to Jack, now!" Lou scrambled off toward his hole. Tom looked across the girl's chest at Jack, his eyes showing great confidence and purpose.

"Jack, we're gonna do a tracheotomy. It's her only chance; you with me?"

"I'm with you," Jack said quietly.

"Okay, I'm going to make the incision right here," Tom said rapid-fire, while touching a spot on her lower throat. "It's gonna bleed so you keeping wiping it. When Louie gets back with the pipe stem, you sterilize it with your lighter. When I'm done cutting, dump a load of sulfa on the incision and rub it inside the cut a little, understand?"

"Understood."

"Okay, give my scalpel a burn." Jack ignited his lighter and held it under the knife. Jack looked at his father and felt a burst of pride. He was in complete control, calmly yet quickly working to save the girl's life. He watched as Tom leaned over and carefully made an incision in her throat. Blood flowed out of the cut and Jack, working around his father's hand, wiped it away with gauze. Louie returned with the pipe stem and Jack sterilized it. Less than a minute had passed since the jeep hit the little girl.

Jack quickly dumped some sulfa on the girl's cut and rubbed it in as deeply as he could. Then, Tom took the pipe stem from him and placed it in the incision he'd made. He wiggled and pushed it as the little girl's parents began to moan quietly, begging Tom and Jack to save their child. "Plis dokta pela. Plis helpim pikinini bilong mi. Fiksim bilong em plis!"

After a moment, Tom said, "There, it's in." He bent over the girl and blew several times into the pipe stem in an attempt to fill her lungs with air. To Jack's horror, he saw that each time he blew, Tom's own cheeks filled with air. The tube was blocked. Tom lifted his head and pulled the makeshift tube out. He blew through one end and his breath hissed out the other side. "Goddamn it!" He roughly put his finger in the incision he'd made, felt around for several seconds, then muttered in agony, "Shit! The incision

402

isn't deep enough." He lunged for the scalpel. "Oh Jesus . . . Jesus Christ!"

The girl's eyes were glassy and beginning to bulge. She writhed in panic. Jack held her as still as he could. He looked at his father and saw that Tom's calm confidence had abandoned him. He was wild eyed, his hands shaking uncontrollably.

"Its okay, buddy," Jack urged "You're doing fine." Tom re-entered the initial incision with the scalpel. He rapidly cut deeper into the girl's throat, then held the scalpel perpendicular to the incision and pushed down on it to make sure he was through. He tossed the scalpel aside and attempted to reinsert the pipe stem. Tom was struggling desperately with the tube. His unsteady hands and the fact that the second, rougher cut had loosened tissues on the sides of the incision, combined to make the insertion difficult. The girl's parents wailed ever louder.

"Get them the hell away!" Tom yelled. Big Mikey and Sgt. Jackson tried to escort the parents away, but they refused to move. Jack felt terrible for the little girl and her family, but for his father as well. He desperately wanted to do something to help, but he could only watch and give encouragement.

"Easy does it, Tom," Jack coaxed. "You're doing fine, buddy."

Finally, Tom forced the pipe stem through the opening, then quickly blew into it. This time the girl's lungs took air. Moments later though, it slowly seeped back out through the pipe stem. Jack touched the side of her neck to check for a pulse but felt nothing. The sound of the air escaping emitted a quiet, yet haunting whistle. The girl's chest fell, but did not rise again until Tom blew into the pipe stem a second time. Again the awful whistle; again the falling chest. This went on for nearly ten minutes . . . Tom blowing, the whistles, then nothing. The little girl was dead. Jack leaned over the child and placed a hand on his father's shoulder. "Tom, she's gone," he said quietly. "You did everything you could, buddy."

"Sulfa, Jack . . . sulfa . . . I'm ready for the, I'm ready . . ." Tom murmured in a daze. His eyes were wide, staring at the girl in desperation. Then slowly, his jaw slackened and his shoulders slumped as if some terrible weight had been pressed upon them.

"Tom," Jack said more firmly. "She's gone, buddy. You did good, it just wasn't meant to be." Tom looked up at him, his face pale, his eyes belying an unspeakable pain. He looked down at the dead girl for several moments. Then, without saying a word, he rose, turned, and staggered toward his foxhole. Jack was stunned for a moment. He wondered what the demons in his father's head were saying to him . . . taunting, torturing him perhaps, with dark memories and self-recriminations. Jack took off his shirt and covered the little girl. He wanted to go to his father, but knew he first had to take care of the girl's family. The mother and father, along with their sons, huddled next to her, sobbing, swaying back and forth. He approached them and said softly, "I'm sorry. We did everything we could. I'm very sorry."

The father straightened up, composed himself, and said in a strong voice, "Mi famili bringim pikinini bilong mi long Koli ples." Although the village, Koli, was abandoned, Jack figured that is where they wanted to bury her. The father picked up his dead daughter, and the grief stricken family began to slowly trudge down the road toward the beach. As Jack was watching them leave, a jeep approached, and a Marine chaplain climbed out, apparently having been contacted by radio. Jack explained what had happened. The chaplain told him he'd give the family a ride back to their village and do what he could for them in the way of comfort. Jack thanked him, then turned and walked toward Tom's hole. Tom was slumped down in the hole, staring straight at the dirt wall. Jack settled into the foxhole, put his hand on his father's shoulder, and softly asked, "How you doing?"

"Oh . . . Jack," Tom said in a daze.

"You okay?" Jack asked.

"I'm uh . . . I'm fine," he mumbled.

"You sure?"

"I'm fine." He'd lifted his eyes but was staring out to sea, his skin still pale. It seemed that every muscle in his face had slackened, and his entire face had fallen. He didn't look at Jack, not once. "It's probably time for you to head back to the hospital," he said dully.

"Naw, it's still light out. I'll stay with you a while."

"No . . . no. I want to be alone."

"But a little company might do you some good. I could even stay . . ."

"Just go, please . . . just go."

Jack hesitated. He wanted to stay with his father and console him, but he decided the best thing to do would be to accede to Tom's wishes. "Alright," he said. "You take care of yourself." Jack lingered for a moment, then leaned over and put his hand on his father's neck. "It's okay, pal. It's okay. You did your best."

"Yeah . . . my best," Tom whispered hauntingly.

"I'll try to come out tomorrow, okay?"

"Yeah."

30

Afted his slow, sad walk back to the hospital, he immediately sought out Ian. He told him the horrible story of the little girl and his father. When he finished, Ian sighed, "What a bloody tragedy."

"No shit," Jack replied.

Jack squeezed his eyes shut, tilted his head back and groaned, "God Ian, I was such a selfish prick. I only saw my dad's moroseness and distance from the standpoint of how it affected me. I never really thought about him or why he was that way. Christ," he spat bitterly, "no wonder he didn't want to talk about the war."

Ian stroked his chin for a moment, then said, "Listen, you've had a rough day. What say we retire to the shelter and have a nip of the grog?"

"Okay," Jack said wearily. Just like after the Tenaru battle, he felt no compulsion to drink. It was an effective bonding tool and nothing more. While they sipped *sake* and smoked, Ian entertained Jack with descriptions and stories about London during the Blitz. The tales were enthralling and thankfully took his mind off his father and the day's events. Countless times on business trips, Jack had wandered the streets of London, wondering what the city was like during the early years of the war: what the people ate, what their homes looked like, what the Luftwaffe bombers droning over the city must have sounded like. He tried to imagine the thunderous crashing of bombs and the thumping tattoo of anti-aircraft guns. Now, while the city was still at war and Ian's memories still fresh, he described what it had been like, right down to the smells and sounds during and after a raid. He described the devastation and squalor of the East End, and the relatively intact neighborhoods of Knightsbride, Chelsea, and Mayfair. It seemed much the same as Jack had read, yet darker, depressing, not the defiant, glorious adventure Hollywood and period media had depicted. The island, and Ian's first-hand descriptions, conspired to make the Blitz visceral and real for the first time in his life. He sat mesmerized by the horror Ian described until they had finished the entire bottle of *sake*. They were both tipsy and stumbled their way back to the tent. Jack decided he was too drunk and weary to write a second passage in his journal, so he crashed onto his bedroll and was asleep in seconds.

Over the next several days, things remained relatively quiet. However, Marine patrols and Martin Clemens' scouts were increasingly making brief, sharp contacts with Japanese troops on the move. Jack had been unable to track Clemens and he wondered if he and the native boy, Peter, had been reunited. Jack was the only American on the island who knew for certain when and where the next attempt at taking the airfield would occur. This changed however on September 11. Japanese bombers flew over and dropped bombs on a ridge southeast of Henderson, where Colonel Edson and his Marine Raiders and parachutists had dug in, supposedly to rest, after their desperate struggle on the adjacent island of Tulagi, as well as constant patrolling along the Matanikau River. It was a clear hint as to where the Japanese intended to land their next blow. Eleven Marines, thinking the target was Henderson as usual, were caught out in the open and lost their lives. The attack raised the anxiety level in the Marine perimeter considerably. Everyone knew the Japanese would attack with more troops than they had at the Tenaru, and there was real concern that this time the Marines would not be able to hold. They were all thinking and talking about the consequences of a Japanese breakthrough. Would it be a quick, violent death, or a slow, hellish one hiding out in the jungle? Would the Japanese take prisoners? And if so, would they be murdered? Would they starve to death, or die from disease? Would they go mad?

Jack, as much as he wanted to, couldn't comfort them. He couldn't tell them that although the issue would be in doubt for some time and that the Japanese would come close to breaking through, in the end, the Marines would hold in a valiant, bloody effort. He couldn't tell them that the inept Japanese Army intelligence section had vastly underestimated Marine strength on the island, and wouldn't send a force large enough to accomplish their objectives. He simply went about his work and remained silent as the boys around him, at the hospital and the Tenaru, chattered nervously about the impending battle. Though he knew the Marines would prevail and that he wouldn't be directly involved in the fighting, the same sense of dread he'd felt before the first battle rose ever higher. A haunting feeling of the enemy creeping in the dark, closing on the perimeter . . . on him and his friends . . . swarmed his senses. On the night of the 11th, walking back to the hospital after visiting Tom at the creek, a crackling rustle from a nearby tangle of vegetation startled him. Previously, he would have assumed it was a harmless creature and ignored it. Now though, and without the support of Turk, he panicked and ran the rest of the way, his wagon trailing behind, protesting with high-pitched squeals. The storm was gathering.

September 11, 1942

9/11—59 years earlier. Can't help but reflect today on how different world is then, than now, or vice versa, or whatever. Things in many ways are easier for those back in the world today yet in many ways more difficult. Talking to the young Marines here is very different than talking to young adults back in the world. As ghastly as this whole thing is, as well the Great Depression, the boys have more hope for the future for themselves as well that of their

country and the world. Their outlook and desires are sim-
pler and more grounded in the basic needs to live a satis-
fying life, i.e. family, comfortable home, food on the table.
There is no mad scramble to acquire as much as they can;
no self-pity-no feelings of entitlement. (God knows, I'm an
expert on this stuff.) They haven't been bombarded with
all the trash and marketing crap that our young people
have. Drugs for kids as easy to attain as a candy bar at the
drug store. I admire this generation, however, the idea
that it was on their watch where much of this crap began
to percolate as well in some cases, occur, nags at me. I try
to make sense of it but I can't. Perhaps it is just the natu-
ral human condition and cycle. Who knows? Hell, just six
weeks ago I would have hardly seen or cared about the
problems, much less wasted time thinking about them.

On to the day's news. Jap bombers hit Edson's Ridge.
Didn't remember that. 11 killed, 14 wounded. We treated
some of wounded. Very bad. Boys weren't expecting Japs
to bomb ridge, just airfield; they were out of their holes
watching raid! Bomb fragments do ghastly damage to
flesh and bone. Two amputations, one by Doc Goldman, a
leg—and one arm cleanly severed by Jap metal and left on
the ridge. One boy, a tough raider, hit in shoulder, was qui-
etly cursing over and over as Ian worked on him. Ian did
a great job and we got him quickly to the beach. Think he'll
make it. Worst day at hospital since the Tenaru, but I must
regret, it's good practice for tomorrow. Tomorrow night is
first night of Edson's Ridge battle. Marine raiders under
command of Col. Merritt Edson hold on heroically. Have
alerted Ian about battle and estimated casualties as best
as I can recall. He's made sure everything is ready. Has
adjusted shift schedules to maximize sleep for crews. I
took supplies from Palace and tarped them just outside
hospital. Lots of morphine, dressings, splints, etc.

Would like to go to ridge to help and see, but will not. This battle really scares me—much more than the Tenaru. Also, will be needed at hospital. Would love to see Edson and his red hair though. Tregaskis wrote that when he smiled, his eyes didn't. Tough guy, but killed himself in Vermont in 1956. Question: Was it the war and his responsibilities for the young men, or did those eyes belie something in his past? Edson's Ridge, or Bloody Ridge as the media will dramatically baptize it, was a horror. Thank god Tom's unit is out of harm's way . . .

. . . Ian is mostly incredulous when I describe my life back in the world. He doesn't get it at all, and it's funny because I don't know if I get it either! Told him how one of favorite hobbies of mine and my pals at the club was to go to the pool after golf to see if any young housewives had trotted out a re- engineered set of boobs. We were often successful. Described process and how boobs looked afterward. Thought he was going to bust a gut. I don't think he holds it against me at all. In his opinion I'm a good man who lost the plot. Love that one—'lost the plot'.

Why did I have to wait so many years and travel so far to learn all that I have here on the island?

Tomorrow—sleep as much as I can during day. Then, get ready. God Bless the Marines on the ridge and the families of those who are going to die.

31

The next day passed quickly. Nerves weren't helped any by a large Japanese air raid that thundered at noon. The raid destroyed the main radio station and three Dauntlesses on the ground. Thirty-two Wildcats, many of them newly arrived Navy fighters, rose to meet the 38 attackers. Marines cheered as they watched six enemy planes spin into the jungle and sea. When the air battle was over, Jack watched the planes land from outside the Cave. He saw one Wildcat make a rapid, wobbly approach, slowly realizing the plane wasn't making any noise. He looked closer and saw that the propeller was locked up, the engine dead. Jack watched in horror as the plane slammed onto the runway, bounced, then rocked to the right, its wing-tip catching the ground. The plane cartwheeled off the runway in clouds of dust and smoke, came to a rest and burst into flames. He watched the young aviator's funeral pyre for several moments, then turned away heavyhearted.

Jack went back inside the Cave and laid down on his bedroll. He put his hands behind his head and stared at the ceiling, thinking about the death of the pilot and the hundreds that would die on both sides in the next thirty-six hours. He closed his eyes and muttered, "Crazy . . . it's goddamn insane." As he thought of the rapidly approaching battle, he recalled that Louie the Louse would drop a green flare over the ridge sometime after 2100, illuminating it for several Japanese warships standing off shore. The naval shelling would mark the beginning of the battle.

At 1800, Jack, though he'd already completed his shift for the day, went to the hospital, looking for something, anything to do. Frank had also come to the hospital, and they chatted nervously about what may be to come. "You think they'll attack tonight?" Frank asked. "I had a Marine in here earlier with a broken finger and he told me there're Japs all around us."

"I don't know," Jack lied. "But I think we'll be okay if they do. The Marines know what they're doing."

"Sure they do, but what if there's, I don't know, a hundred-thousand Japs out there?"

Jack chuckled, "There aren't a hundred-thousand Japs out there Frank. How the heck would they get that many people here?"

"Well," Frank said with a sigh, "I sure hope you're right."

"I'm right, Frank; I'm always right. Now let's go over the new triage procedure Dr. Goldman taught us. If there's going to be a big fight, I want to be ready." Dr. Goldman, expecting more casualties than they had handled previously, had changed the triage procedure to ensure adequate space in the hospital for the most seriously wounded. Primary triage was to be conducted outside the tent on the ground. Earlier, Frank and Turk had taken a large canvas tarp and tied it to the edge of the tent roof, staking the opposite corners into the ground. The crude lean-to would provide adequate shelter for those lying outside. If it were dark, the corpsmen would use pen lights to analyze the nature of wounds. Only those in very serious condition would be immediately taken inside to be cared for by Ian or Dr. Goldman. The rest would wait outside until things quieted down, or would simply be treated there until they were either sent offshore or, most likely, back to their units.

At dusk, Jack stepped outside for a cigarette. He gazed out toward Edson's Ridge, still visible in the fading light, and felt a shiver. The ridge reminded him of gunfighters' makeshift graves as depicted in old western pictures. He imagined a giant cross jutting skyward at the southern tip of the ridge, the very top of a dusty boot protruding from the other. He shuddered involuntarily. He pictured the men on the ridge making last second preparations, stringing wire and clawing soil with their entrenching tools. Officers would be changing troop positions and barking orders. He imagined Colonel Edson in his CP, poring over maps, trying to anticipate the main routes of attack, deciding on how best to defend the ridge. Then he thought of the dozens of young men working feverishly on the ridge who would be dead in just hours: young, brave, and so alive. In the morning they would simply be cold, shredded corpses, nothing more. It seemed so senseless, so outrageous that it was difficult for Jack to conceive. But intellectually he knew it would happen, and steeled himself. He flicked his cigarette away, stared at the ridge for several more moments, then said quietly, "Good luck, guys."

A couple hours later, just before 2130, Jack was moving some supplies inside the tent in preparation for what was to come. As he bent over a case of iodine, he heard a coughing aircraft engine approaching from out to sea. He froze as the sound grew louder. "Flare plane," he muttered out loud. He gazed skyward, seeing nothing, but clearly hearing it pass in front of him, along the length of the airfield. Jack waited for the parachute flare to explode and illuminate the ridge. Moments later it did, and in seconds the Japanese warships, cruising unmolested in the sound, opened up. Frank and several others burst out of the hospital and stood with him, watching as the ships' shells exploded along the ridge, sending what appeared at a mile's distance to be little puff-balls of dirt into the air. They all knew though, that up close the explosions were a terror of concussion and flesh tearing, limb shattering, shards of metal.

"Should we take shelter?" Frank asked.

"No," Jack said somberly. "They're just targeting the ridge."

"You think this is it?"

"Yeah, I think it is," Jack said softly. The calmness in his own voice surprised him; he was pleased. "Let's get back inside and make sure everything's ready. We're not doing any good standing out here watching." Unlike his first night on the island watching the deadly sea battle, he had accepted the inevitability of the fighting and his inability to do anything about it. But he couldn't stand by helplessly and watch as the Marines, his Marines, got shelled. Back at work in the hospital, they soon heard the sharp crackle of rifle and machine gun fire, grenades and mortars exploding with hollow booms. Shortly after, the sounds of Marine artillery joined in; the discharge of the guns and the jarring crash of the shells echoed in Jack's chest. Though he knew the outcome, he said a silent prayer for the men; hell on earth had been visited upon them.

The sound of the fighting had brought the entire staff to the hospital. Ian's adjusted shift schedule had worked, Jack noted. All of the men appeared well rested. Jack found Ian and they locked eyes for several moments, then, unsmiling, Ian flashed Jack a thumbs-up. Jack returned it, then went to work. For an hour, he and the others nervously checked and re-checked equipment and medicines, as the sounds of the raging battle thundered outside. Jack spent much of the time lining up surgical instruments in perfect, evenly spaced lines. As soon as the first casualties arrived, of course, his careful work would be jostled and strewn about, while he worked furiously wiping sprays and smears of blood off the instruments. For now though, it gave him the sense of doing something, of preparing. The usual banter was muted. Most of the anxious staff were lost in their own thoughts and fears. They wondered how many men they would treat tonight, how many would die. They wondered if they themselves would be alive when the sun rose. All their concerns evaporated, however, when the first casualties arrived just over an hour after the green flare had blossomed like an evil ray over the ridge. A captured Japanese Chevy truck whined up to the hospital and came to a slow halt. The driver shouted, "I got wounded!" Corpsmen rushed from the hospital and began to unload the men on litters and lay them on the ground under the lean-to. Several medics ran to the Cave and gathered up all the bedrolls and spread them on the ground. Dr. Goldman had appointed Turk head of triage. It was a good choice. Jack watched as he quickly assessed each man's injury, a look of urgent determination on his face. After checking each one, Turk would bark a command to the waiting cluster of corpsmen.

"Zimmer, change this guy's dressing and uh . . ." Jack saw him check for morphine syrettes pinned to the Marine's shirt, "no more morphine; he's had enough."

He moved to the next man, looked him over quickly, then urgently ordered, "Sucking chest wound! Get him inside, now!"

"Flesh wound, upper arm," Turk said of the next man after peeking under his dressing. "You sure you ain't hurt nowhere else, bub?"

"I'm sure," the Marine grunted.

Turk turned to Jack, "Give this man a clean dressing." Jack leaned down, unwrapped the dirty dressing a corpsman had applied on the ridge, and inspected the boy's injury. The wound was not serious, and though the boy seemed a bit dazed, on the whole he was remarkably calm.

Suddenly, they heard Turk bark, "This man's dead goddamn it, and it ain't just happened!" He shouted to the corpsman unloading litters from the trucks, "Hey dumb shits! Check 'em before you bring 'em over, will ya?" After Turk spoke, the Marine Jack was treating stiffened, then slowly set his gaze on the dead soldier. His face fell and a low groan rose from deep in the boy's chest.

"Oh, Jesus," he cried quietly. "Not Tzakis. Oh, Jesus . . . I . . . I can't believe it." Jack gently lifted the young man's arm, preparing to clean and redress it. Stunned, the Marine kept repeating in a monotone, "I can't believe it." Jack turned on his penlight and clenched the unlit end in his teeth. Other penlights jittered and danced like giant fireflies in the blackness. He swabbed the wound.

He wanted very much to offer the boy some comfort, but he couldn't think of what to say, so he simply asked, "What's your name, son?"

"Uh . . . What?" the boy stammered. "Oh . . . um, Warren."

"I'm Jack. Good to meet you Warren, but sorry it's under these circumstances." The young man seemed not to hear, and after a pause Jack asked softly, "Were you and he good friends?"

The boy slowly turned toward Jack, stared at him for a moment then said, "Yeah. We were talking just before the Jap ships opened up, about what we'd do the minute we got home." The boy was calm, but clearly still dazed by his friend's death. "Meat was gonna . . . Meat's his nickname . . . his first name is Demetrious. Meat said he was gonna ask his mom to cook him up a plate of her special eggs and sausage. Then he was gonna go upstairs and, no matter what time of day it was, take a bath in his own tub and then get into his own bed and stay there for twenty-four hours. That's what Meat was gonna do. Jesus . . . I just can't believe it."

"I'm sorry, son," Jack said.

"Oh god," the boy groaned. "This is going to kill his ma. They're real close. I mean really close. This is gonna kill her." When Jack finished wrapping the new dressing on the boy's arm, he couldn't think of any words to say to him about his dead friend. It seemed the death had happened too quickly, was too fresh to render any real substance to words of comfort. He wasn't as much grieving as shocked, utterly stunned at the violent, sudden end to his young friend's life. Jack felt sympathy for the boy, but largely he was left numb by the first fatality. It was not the first time he'd seen a dead young Marine and he knew it wouldn't be the last. Others would come tonight, more tomorrow night, torn apart and broken on the ridge. As well, to get through it he'd forced himself into a sort of mild trance, his emotions chilled and hidden. Jack looked at Warren still trying to think of a way to comfort him.

"You hurting?" he asked.

"Huh?"

"Your arm . . . are you having pain?"

"No . . . yeah, fuck I don't know. I just . . . oh goddamn!" Tears welled in the boy's eyes as the finality of his buddy's death settled in. Jack checked his shirt for used morphine syrettes, found none, then reached into his kit for a dose of the narcotic. He took off the protective cover, then jabbed the needle into the boy's thigh. The drug would ease his pain, but more importantly, it would help assuage his grief.

"You're going to be fine here and I'll check on you from time to time," Jack assured him.

416

"Okay," the boy muttered. Jack turned and looked toward the ridge, noticing that the firing had died down considerably. Occasional streaks of red and green tracer rounds could be seen, and every now and then the muffled sound of a grenade would crump. It helped him recall that the first night of fighting, though sharp and deadly for some units, ended relatively quickly after the initial Japanese assault had been blunted. The Japanese would regroup during the day and try once again the next night to breech the Marine lines with a larger force, resulting in an even more desperate and deadly fight. For now he felt relieved though, that the fighting, other than minor skirmishing, was done for the night. His relief was shattered seconds later by the sound of another truck hurtling down the road toward the hospital. Jack took up station near Turk, where they waited for the litter bearers to deliver the next batch. Then, to his dismay, he heard another truck pull up behind the first.

The next several hours went by in a chaotic, bloody blur. Several jeeps had followed the trucks, and every member of E Company was working feverishly. Turk's urgent commands and loud requests by the two doctors mingled with moans from some of the injured. Triage essentially ceased operations shortly after the last jeep had delivered its load. The hospital was full with medical staff and badly injured men. A dozen or more remained outside with Warren. Jack, as Ian had instructed weeks ago, was relegated to changing field dressings, cleaning wounds, and fetching supplies. He saw, it seemed, every conceivable injury a man could suffer. Shattered limbs, shrapnel laced eyeballs, a jaw shot away, and perhaps the most horrible, a man's penis and testicles gouged out as if by some ghastly ice cream scoop. The smell of feces and open wounds hung in the air. Ian was operating on a Marine who had suffered a freakish injury. An enemy soldier had surprised him in his foxhole and plunged his bayonet into the boy's ribcage. An instant later, one of the Marine's buddies shot the enemy soldier dead with a burst from his Tommy gun. The bayonet, still in the young man's chest, was struck by one of the bullets and snapped off right at the point where it had entered. Miraculously, it had not harmed any internal organs. Jack, while changing a dressing, watched in admiration as Ian quickly and deftly made incisions around the knife's entry point, then, using forceps, carefully slid it out of the boy's chest. Minutes later, Ian was working on another patient, the bayonet victim having been moved to a cot where Frank was expertly suturing the wound.

Another Marine lay on Dr. Goldman's litter, his entrails spilling out of his stomach and over the edge of the makeshift operating table. Jack delivered clean surgical gear to the surgeon and noticed that a loop of the boy's yellow/gold intestine was resting on the dirty, matted floor. Alarmed, he bent over and gently gathered up the long organ. He quickly cleansed the area that had touched the ground and laid it in a basin he set in the wounded man's lap. Dr. Goldman curtly nodded thanks. Moments later, the gutted Marine began to gasp and wheeze loudly; his body jerked and shuddered. Dr. Goldman pumped the blood pressure cuff, then grunted, "Pressure's dropping!" Jack looked at the boy closely. Though his pallor was gray, he reminded Jack a great deal of Tom. He had the same eyes, hair, and similar build. Spooked, he turned away just as Dr. Goldman declared him dead. Once again, the uncomfortable, gnawing sensation at the base of his spine began to rise. It was more difficult than past assaults, but he successfully smothered the threatening emotion. He worked on; he would never quit . . . he could never quit again.

An hour after the first truck had arrived at the hospital, jeeps began carrying loads of patched and partially mended men to the beach for transport offshore. At dawn, a dozen or so boys, some limping, others sporting bandages, were hauled back up the ridge to rejoin their comrades. The grieving boy named Warren was among them. Only half the cots were full, and only a few men still sat or lay outside, all the badly wounded were gone, and the hospital was relatively quiet. Thanks to Jack, Ian knew that the next night would be longer, with more wounded. He told half the staff to get some rest. He motioned Jack over and asked him if he wanted to join him for a cigarette. Jack eagerly agreed, wanting to escape the misery of the hospital as well as talk to Ian about the strange emotions Dr. Goldman's dead Marine had unleashed in him.

Ian fetched his cigarettes and they ducked into one of the bomb shelters. First, they talked about the lives they saved and those that had been lost. They talked about what kind of lives the blind man and the man whose genitals had been torn away would have. They talked about the second night of the battle and what that would likely bring to the hospital. Then, Jack told Ian about the boy who had died on Dr. Goldman's operating table and how he hauntingly reminded him of his father.

"He looked a lot like him," Jack said, shaking his head. "For some reason it made me think of when he died . . . when he was dead."

"Go on, mate," Ian quietly urged.

Jack sighed and said, "Something about my old man, something about me and him . . . our lives, his death and . . . Christ! I don't know. I can't put my finger on it."

They sat quietly for a minute, Ian reflecting on Jack's comments. Then Ian said, "Listen mate, you're tired and upset. Don't you think you should get some rest?"

Ignoring the doctor's advice, Jack blurted, "It didn't bother me at the time, but now I can clearly see the look on his face when I told him that I was selling the company. You see, there's just one difference between my guilt and my father's. Tom's is associated with the carelessness of an innocent ten-year-old boy and the inexperience of a teenage corpsman. Mine is caused by the reckless greed of a forty-year-old son."

Ian sighed and after several moments said, "Listen mate, I can't really know what went on back in your world, but I do know that there's nothing you can do to change it here. Let it go; focus on here . . . right bloody now."

"Yeah," Jack whispered. He smiled wanly and clapped his friend on the shoulder. "Let's go get some sleep. We've got another shift tonight." All of the bedrolls were still at the hospital, so they laid down on their normal spots in the dirt. Jack said goodnight to Ian, then removed his journal from his rucksack and wearily began to write.

September 13, 1942

First night of Edson's Ridge over. Horrible; wounded broke my heart. It's so awful, so senseless and brutal, god-damned medieval. Word 'absurd' keeps coming to mind. The word seems too whimsical or whatever to really fit something so violent and gruesome, but it does for some reason. It is absurd, absolutely absurd.

Before battle I looked at ridge and worried about Marines. Strangely, I never once, not once thought or worried about the Japanese boys being led to slaughter by their incompetent leaders. I do not even feel badly about the fact that I'm unable to feel sadness for the tragedy that befalls our enemy. Question: is this another reason it is much too easy for us to do this? That in reality, we, not just as Americans, but the whole family of man even, don't have much empathy for those not of us, that all we really do is give this sort of thing lip service? Jesus, enough philosophizing . . .

. . . Hated to see Marine pilot crack-up trying to dead-stick at Henderson. Seems like if you have to die in a war, it should be that the enemy killed you, not a stalled engine. Any other way, an accident or disease or something, seems more of a waste for some reason. It should be the reverse of that, shouldn't it? But its not, not for me—not for most people I'd guess. Another question: is this another fucked up way we look at war? That if you die in battle it's somehow justifiable and honorable; but if you die in an accident it is an unfortunate tragedy. I don't know; getting killed by another human seems more tragic and wasteful

420

to me than hitting an oak tree in the family sedan or a crash landing.

Tomorrow night will be worse. More wounded than tonight. Have decided we have enough supplies, so instead of going to depot, will go visit Tom for a bit. Fighting starts again around six in the evening if I recall. Will make sure I'm back well before then.

Tomorrow (actually today)—Shift at 9 a.m. After that to Tom, then come back and get ready for second night of the ridge.

32

By the time Jack started his shift the following morning, there were very few patients left in the hospital; those being the men who were to be sent back to their units after a brief recuperation. Since the battle on the ridge had commenced, Jack's feelings of dread and anxiety had largely dissipated. He knew the coming night would be long and bloody, but he was eager to have it over with.

When his shift ended, Jack asked Ian if he could borrow the jeep to deliver some beer to Tom and his mates. Ian agreed, but told Jack to come straight back and make preparations for that night. Jack had told Turk earlier in the day that he would be going to the creek. He was delighted when he found that Turk had stacked two cases of beer in the jeep, covered by a poncho.

As Jack pulled away, he noticed Turk walking from the Palace to the hospital with a crate of blood plasma. He pulled up beside him, "Hey, thanks for the beer, buddy."

"Don't fuckin' mention it, Jacko."

"Would you please tell me where you're getting this stuff . . . it's killing me."

Turk smiled slowly, then leaned toward Jack, preparing to whisper the secret in his ear. After a dramatic pause, Turk whispered, "You know that old guy up at D Company sick bay, that fat, ugly fucker with hair growin' out his nose and ears and shit?"

Caught up in the moment, Jack whispered in response, "Oh . . . yeah . . . yeah, I know who you're talking about. He's got real red skin, right?"

"That's him."

"Yeah?"

After another pause, Turk continued, "Well, me and that fucker have gotten kinda close, in spite of all his ugliness and shit; his name's Sturgeon for some reason. I figure it's on account that he's so goddamn ugly. Anyhow, I go up there nearly every day to see ole Sturgeon, right?

"Uh-huh." Jack said, his tone rising in anticipation.

"Well, I get as much fuckin' spaghetti from the C's as I can and I let him eat that shit, then I pour water and 'bout half a bottle of fuckin' *sake* down his pipe, you know?"

"Yeah?" Jack muttered, his eyes narrowing suspiciously.

"Well, then I get Sturgeon to trot around the hospital several fuckin' times, you know, to mix things up good."

"What?"

"Hang on, Jacko . . . it'll all make sense."

"Okay," Jack said warily.

"Anyhow, then Sturgeon sits still for three or four hours 'til they're ready."

"'Til what are ready?" Jack asked, exasperated.

"The fuckin' beers, Jack . . . the beers!"

"What beers?"

Turk rolled his eyes in mock frustration and said, "The fuckin' beers ol' Sturgeon shits out his ass, Jack . . . Jesus, you dumbshit!"

A wry smile slowly spread across Jack's face, "You're an asshole, Turk."

Turk laughed mockingly and taunted, "You ain't never gonna know where I'm gettin' those beers, Jack . . . never."

Jack pulled away chuckling, then shouted over his shoulder, "You're a jerk, Turk."

"Oh ain't that fuckin' nice," Turk shouted back, "he made himself a cute little rhyme."

As Jack rounded the southern tip of the runway, he could see trucks heading out toward the ridge, augmenting and replenishing the Raiders and 'Chutes supplies. Minutes later he was at the creek, parked behind Tom's platoon.

"Thy beer hast arriveth, motherfuckers!" Jack shouted. Scooz, Danny, Louie, and Big Mikey walked up to the jeep excitedly. "Two cases today, boys."

"Ahh yes," Big Mikey purred.

"Hey, Jack," Scooz said, "what'd you hear about the fight the Raiders had last night?"

Jack told him everything he knew and the boys nodded with satisfaction when he said the attack had been broken up relatively quickly. He didn't mention the bloody horror of the hospital. Jack looked around the squad area searching for his father.

"You lookin' for Tom?" Big Mikey asked.

"Yeah."

"He ain't here." The boy pointed a meaty finger in the direction of the ridge and said, "He's with the Raiders on the ridge."

"What?" Jack gasped.

"Yeah," Scooz said. "They came looking for corpsmen to beef up the medical teams up there. Tom volunteered right away."

"Shit," Jack growled. He thought for a moment, his brow creased with a deep frown. "Did he say what unit he was attached to?"

"Yeah, he did . . . B Company, Raiders." replied Scooz.

"I've got to get back to the hospital, guys," Jack said impatiently. "Take care." With that he roared off, glancing at his watch. It was 1530 hours. The second phase of the fighting wouldn't start for three hours. There was plenty of time to get the jeep back to the hospital and walk, or hitch a ride, to the ridge. He had to be with his father through the long, awful night. He couldn't let him down, not again.

As he sped back to the hospital he gripped the wheel so tightly his knuckles turned snow white. He felt no fear, just a desperation to get to the ridge and find his father. After he arrived back at the hospital, he found Ian, pulled him aside and told him the situation. "I gotta go, Doc," Jack said.

"I know, mate" Ian replied. "We sure could use you're help here, but I understand and we'll make do. I'd give you a lift, but Frank needs the jeep to deliver some plasma to D Company."

"That's alright, Doc, it's only about a mile." Jack began stuffing his medical pouch with as much sulfa, morphine, and dressings as it could hold. Then, following his father's lead, he filled a rucksack with several bottles of plasma, water, and piping. When he was done, he filled his canteen from a barrel in the tent, then bade Ian farewell.

"See you in the morning, Doc."

"Be careful, Jack." The two men shook hands firmly. As Jack made his way toward the door he heard Ian's voice, "Oh and one more thing." Jack turned back toward the doctor. "Do your job well, okay, mate?"

"I'll do my best, Doc, I promise." He walked out the door and was 20 yards down the road when he heard a familiar voice bellowing.

"Hey, Jack! Where you going?" It was Turk.

Jack closed his eyes, hesitated a moment, then said, "I'm headed up to the ridge."

"What? I heard the fightin' ain't over yet."

"They're looking for corpsmen to volunteer."

"Volun-fuckin'-teers?" Turk sputtered. "No one asked me to volunteer. You wait here, Jack, I'm gonna go get my pouch and canteen."

"No, Turk," Jack replied firmly. "You can't come."

Turk's face twisted with anger. "Goddamn it, Macmillan! You promised to take me along if you were going into a combat situation! You break your fuckin' promise and I swear I'll break your fuckin' face and we won't be friends no more! I let you get away with leaving me behind the first time, but not again! Not this time, you fucker!" Turk made a menacing move toward Jack.

"You're right Turk," Jack said with a slight smile. "I did promise you, bud. But you have to clear it with one of the docs. If they say it's okay, get your gear." In an instant Turk's face went from a look of rage to one of joy.

"Okay, it'll take two fuckin' seconds!" Jack was fairly certain the doctors would want Turk to stay, so he was somewhat surprised when the boy exited the hospital a minute later, geared up and beaming. Ian or Dr. Goldman must have decided Turk could do more good on the line than back at the hospital. Jack thought they were probably right and was actually glad to have the company and help. They tramped up the road toward the ridge. As they walked around the southern end of Henderson's runway, a flight of Wildcats approached, looking as if they would land right on top of them. Paranoid after the C-47 incident, they jogged quickly out of the flight path. Jack looked at his watch, 1615 hours. The Japanese were moving into position, preparing to strike.

As they continued walking, Jack casually asked Turk, "You did clear your trip to the ridge with the docs, didn't you?"

Turk wiped his nose on his sleeve, looked at his boots and mumbled, "Um . . . yeah, sure."

"Oh god," Jack groaned. "Tell me you didn't sneak away, Turk. They're going to have your head, and mine. What are you thinking?"

"They'll be fuckin' pissed alright, but what are they gonna do? Send me to the front lines?" Turk cackled merrily as Jack slowly shook his head. In spite of his concern for the trouble he might be in, he was still pleased to have Turk along. There was an invincibility about Turk. He remembered with dread, though, that he had felt the same about Lt. Grimes.

"Don't do anything stupid," Jack said. "We're not heroes, and the last thing I need on my conscience is you being hurt . . . or worse."

"I volunteered, Jack. You didn't force me, so what're you fuckin' whinin' about?"

"You volunteered . . . yeah right. Who did you volunteer to, then?"

"Frankie!" Turk chirped happily. "I said, Frankie boy, I volunteer to go to that fuckin' ridge and help smote them nasty Japs. Ol'

Frankie clapped me on my fuckin' shoulder and said, 'go forward my faithful son and make us proud.'"

Jack rubbed his eyes and muttered, "Jesus Christ." Moments later they heard the thrumming drone of Betty bombers and the higher pitched chug of their Zero escorts approaching the airfield. Jack and Turk took cover in a shell crater and watched as a dozen Wildcats pounced on the flight, sending several bombers and fighters spinning to earth in flames. Though the fight was well over a mile above their heads, the rattle of machine guns could clearly be heard. Having become accustomed to the air and sea bombardments, Jack was actually more relieved for the break than he was cowed by the enemy planes. When the fight was over they pulled themselves out of the crater and continued their trek to the ridge.

Turk talked excitedly the rest of the way about his opportunity to serve with Marines, Raiders no less, in combat. At one point Jack told him that by the next morning his dream may have become his greatest nightmare. Though Jack's comment was more accurate than he could possibly know, Turk happily ignored him.

By the time they crested the ridge, Jack was exhausted and soaked in sweat. After taking a long pull from his canteen, he asked a passing Marine for directions to B Company's position, and they immediately set out. Jack recalled that Edson's command team had planned a surprise if the Japanese attacked again. He'd withdrawn his front line 200 yards up the forward slope of the ridge, hoping to confuse the attackers as well as give the Marines more open ground to bring down fire on the enemy. The ridge ran roughly on a line north and south and was 2000 yards long by 500 yards wide at its widest point. The Marine line was set 500 yards back from the southern tip, or front of the ridge, and ran directly perpendicular to its length. The line formed the cross of a lower case 't' with the ridge itself forming the stem. Jack and Turk found B Company dug in at the right-center of the Marine line. They were flanked on the left by D Company, 1st Engineer Battalion, and on the right by B Company, 1st Parachute Battalion. Farther to the right, at the bottom of the ridge, sat Company A, Raiders. Col. Edson had quickly cobbled the mixed battalion together in the previous few days. The ragged force totaled nearly 900 men; arrayed against an overwhelming several thousand of Japan's finest troops. They passed through C Company, Raiders, approximately 300 yards behind the lines, in reserve. When they were just yards behind B Company's lines, Jack noticed a group of men huddled together, some kneeling, some sitting on crates. One man immediately caught Jack's eye. He was talking slowly to the group, pointing toward the base of the ridge to the south. He was a stocky man with close-cropped orange hair. The other men were raptly listening to his instructions. "Un-real," Jack said under his breath. "Lieutenant Colonel Merritt Twining Edson . . . Red Mike." Jack was briefly mesmerized by the sight of the Medal of Honor winner.

Turk looked at Jack quizzically and said, "What the fuck you mumblin' about, Jack? And why are you staring at that red-haired guy." Edson was an officer, but he was also as much a combat Marine as the men he commanded. His bravery and penchant for commanding from the front was already becoming legend. Jack couldn't resist the temptation to meet the man who had killed himself a year before Jack was born.

"Uh . . . what, Turk?" Jack muttered.

"What is it with that guy?"

"I think I might know him . . . from home or something. I'm uh . . . I'm going to go see. You wait here."

"Okay, Jack. You're fuckin' scaring me though. Don't you go givin' that guy a kiss or nothin'."

Jack ignored Turk's comment and slowly walked toward Edson, perched on an ammo crate. He stood in front of him for several seconds, trying to find his voice. Finally, the colonel looked up and asked, "What do you need, mister?" For a moment Jack was frozen by Edson's eyes. They were just like the history books described; pale blue and showing nothing of what the man might be thinking or feeling. After a moment Jack, bent over, extended his hand and replied, "I'm sorry, sir. I'm just a corpsman who volunteered to come up here and help you guys out. I've heard good things about

428

you, Colonel, and I just want to wish you luck." Red Mike Edson fixed Jack's hand with a firm grip. The historians were right, Jack thought as they shook hands. The colonel was smiling, but his eyes weren't. They were completely devoid of emotion. He almost shuddered at their visage. Did those eyes represent a cold, unfeeling man who could send young men to their deaths without remorse? Or were they the eyes of a tortured soul who had seen and been a part of too much death and suffering? Jack's thoughts were interrupted by Edson's gruff voice.

"Thank you, sailor. And thanks for coming up; we're going to need all the help we can get. Good luck to you."

"Thank you; take care, sir," Jack replied. He nodded to the colonel, then turned and walked back to Turk.

"Did you know him?" Turk asked.

"Naw. He just looked like a guy I knew back in Chicago."

Turk chuckled, "Oh, my silly little friend. If I didn't know you was crazy and can't help yourself, it would just be too fuckin' embarrassing hanging around with you."

Jack smiled, "Fuck you, you Portuguese ape." Turk gave Jack a playful shove and they set off. When they entered B Company's area, Jack walked from hole to hole, asking the occupants if they knew where he could find a corpsman by the name of Macmillan. Finally, he heard a shout.

"Hey, Jack, Turk!" Tom hollered. "What the hell are you two slackers doing up here?" Jack looked up and saw Tom digging a foxhole with his entrenching tool. He was shirtless and sweat glistened off his young body. They walked over, and he and Turk shook Tom's hand.

"I thought I'd just mosey on up here and see what's going on," Jack replied. "Maybe rough up a few Japs; you know, slap 'em and kick 'em in the balls and such."

Tom grinned. It was not the same smile of two weeks ago; it was shallower, more forced. "Did you guys volunteer?" he asked.

"Uh . . . yeah," Jack replied. "You mind if we hole up with you? They, uh . . . they told us to attach ourselves to B Company."

"Raiders or 'Chutes?"

"Raiders."

"That's us," Tom said eagerly. "Of course you guys can hole up with me. We'll make this hole into one big one, okay? A way, way forward aid station of sorts. Why don't you start digging while I give you the dope?"

Jack took off his rucksack, proudly patted it, and declared his haul of plasma. "Well done, pal!" Tom said. "Can't get enough of that stuff up front. I wonder when the brass is going to figure it out."

Jack and Turk borrowed entrenching tools from some nearby Marines and began to dig the heavy soil of the ridge. Tom had set up shop just 50 yards behind the main line of resistance. They were at the extreme right of B Company's lines, with elements of D Company Engineers yards to their right. All around, men were digging and stringing wires. Others were cleaning weapons, sighting machine guns, and carefully stacking grenades in their holes. Some of the men wore bloody, mud-stained bandages, and all the Raiders looked tense and exhausted. The mood of the men on the whole was grim and reserved. Still, at times, false bravado induced humor, much of it dark, abounded as the officers continually exhorted and encouraged their charges, lending a sort of perverse pre-football game atmosphere to the ridge. To Jack though, it was haunting and surreal. He had seen similar scenes in movies and history book photos. Young men preparing to fight other young men to the death with modern weaponry that not just kills, but butchers. Anticipating the carnage firsthand, being a part of it, was very different than seeing it in a picture or on the TV screen. Jack was tense but not scared. Mostly, he felt a deep sadness that many of the young men working around him would be dead or mutilated by morning. Most, if not all of them, still had a youthful sense of immortality and believed they wouldn't be one of those maimed or killed. But many of them would be, their lives prematurely snuffed out or grotesquely altered, on a rotting, primitive island so far from home. Jack looked at the men and knew that some of them were still alive back in the world, old men grateful for the gift of a long life, but memories of the next hours still haunting their dreams. Others though, were living the last hours of their lives. Suddenly, the horror of what was about to happen nearly overwhelmed him.

"Go . . . just go!" he screamed to himself. "You're going to lose six decades . . . six goddamn decades! It's not worth it! Run goddamn it!" He didn't scream out loud, though, for he knew it was a battle that *had* to be fought; that *would* be fought no matter what he did. He wished someone else could do the dying; someone other than these young men he'd come to love. They were human to him now, just boys; not pictures in a book or wrinkled, larger-than-life old men standing on a peaceful ridge back in the world. He looked west toward Skyline Ridge, wondering for a moment if survivor's guilt would be yet another blow to his father's damaged psyche, a psyche already pressed to the limit. Suddenly, his head whipped back toward his father. Jack wondered desperately if he'd volunteered for the Ridge in hopes of catching a bullet. His thoughts were interrupted by Tom.

"This company is under strength a bit; it has about ninety to a hundred who are fit for combat, and some of those are a stretch," he told them. "They lost some guys last night and they've been raiding, fighting, marching, and digging for nearly a week, so they're all but spent. Some of the guys are even glassy eyed and act dazed, so keep an eye out for any sort of breakdown or something. These boys are damn tough though, so are the 'Chutes. I think they still have some fight in them."

"Are they saying for sure the little fuckers are going to attack again tonight?" Turk asked.

"Captain Sweeney, the company commander, told us a couple hours ago they were almost certain of it, and that we could expect to take the first hit."

"Lovely," Jack muttered. He had only dug a couple feet into the ground but was already fatigued. Sweat stung his eyes and dirt encrusted his bare arms and chest. Every ten seconds or so he had to pause digging to swipe at a fat mosquito feeding on him. They, along with the rats, lizards, and other vermin, would eat well tonight, he grimly thought to himself.

Tom continued, "Some of the guys told me that last night when the Japs attacked they all were screaming *'Totsugeki!'* which means charge, I guess, and *'Banzai'* . . . I don't know what that means. They said it was pretty damn creepy, so be ready for that."

Jack looked down at the ridge sloping away to the south. A stiff wind roiled the jungle that crept several hundred yards up the hill. To Jack though, it seemed to be seething and boiling . . . thousands of determined enemy soldiers crabbing about beneath its canopy. They're down there he thought, down there in the trees; waiting to charge up the slope not just at the Marine lines, but at him. He whispered to himself, suddenly aware of a simple truth, "They're coming and they want to kill me. Kill me, Tom, Turk and all the others." His throat muscles tensed and his stomach churned. He looked at Turk and was somewhat surprised to see his jaw muscles taut, frowning slightly. Jack prayed that he would be alright.

"We patch 'em up as quick as we can and get 'em to the rear," he heard Tom say. "If a guy can walk, he walks back to the forward aid station several hundred yards rear. There are some very good surgeons there who'll take the next step. So, fix 'em up as fast as possible, no time for art work. If you're certain a guy's gonna die before he can get back due to loss of blood, tourniquet or not, hook up the plasma. But only if you're sure; we don't want to waste the plasma or the time." Jack, his anxiety spiking, needed to get his mind off the upcoming nightmare. He glanced at his watch. 1730 hours, an hour left. At that moment, Red Mike Edson strolled by with, Jack assumed, Captain Sweeney. Edson told the men that he'd stay just behind them and that they would be fine if they remembered their training, stood fast, and followed orders. He also told them he was the only one who could issue orders to fall back. For some reason the visage and voice of the stocky colonel gave Jack confidence and he relaxed considerably. When Edson walked away Jack turned to his father.

"Tom," Jack asked quietly. "How come you volunteered to come up here?"

"Oh, I don't know," he replied. "I guess when they said they were short corpsmen I felt a responsibility to go. I feel like I owe it or something." Jack noticed a distinct flash of pain cross Tom's face.

"You worried about getting killed?" Jack asked.

Tom looked at Jack for a long moment then said, "Naw. If it happens, it happens. I won't know it . . . I'll be dead, right?" Tom chuckled lightly then his face went flat and he added, "Besides, if it does happen, perhaps Hank and I can go fishing together every day in the Lord's trout streams. That wouldn't be so bad, would it?"

Jack, struggling to contain his emotions, replied, "Uh . . . no, well yeah. I mean who wants to die, right? I mean it would be great to see your brother again, I'm sure but . . ."

Tom raised his hand and smiled, "I know what you mean. I'm just saying I'm not going to worry about something I can't control is all. There's no point."

"I guess you're right, but most people can't do that."

"Well I can, pal." Tom said confidently.

Jack knew his father would survive the ridge, but he firmly believed Tom was, at best, ambivalent about his own survival, and at worst, willfully preparing to sacrifice himself. It unsettled him. His thoughts drifted back to the world and Tom's death. The old gnawing sensation in Jack's spine suddenly reared up, creating a burst of anxiety. His hands trembled. He whispered to himself, "Calm down, bud; just calm down."

He forced himself to focus on the present. It helped when his father asked, "Why'd you volunteer?"

After a pause, Jack answered, "I guess I feel like I owe it too."

For the next 30 minutes, they chatted, though sporadically, until they'd finished the hole. The light was fading and Raiders began climbing into their foxholes, slapping their helmets down on their heads and readying their weapons. As the time drew nearer for the attack, Jack tried to calm his nerves with humor.

"Hey, Turk," he chided, "have you shit your pants yet?"

"Why, you smell fuckin' roses or somethin'?" Turk replied without missing a beat.

The banter loosened them up. While Tom chuckled lightly, Jack and Turk continued trading insults as night rapidly fell. They stopped though, when they clearly heard the enemy yelling shrilly in the jungle below. Jack knew the battle would ebb and flow until dawn: mind-bending spasms of violence giving way to periods of relative calm as the attackers regrouped for the next assault. The impending fight became more unnervingly personal when the combatants began to exchange individual threats and insults.

A heavily accented voice screamed, "You die tonight, Maline!"

Another screamed, "Maline, die! Maline, eat Babe Luth's shit!"

"Come get us, you fucking monkeys!" a Raider bellowed back before firing a single shot into the jungle. The insults and bullets flew back and forth for several minutes. Then, at 1830, it started in earnest.

Jack heard countless, high pitched screams from the jungle below as the Japanese worked themselves into a frenzy. The hysterical, violent screams made the voices seem inhuman, ghoulish. Jack shuddered and clenched his jaw. Then the voices, screaming in unison, sounded strangely close. *"Totsugeki! Totsugeki!"*

"Here the bastards come!" Jack heard Captain Sweeney scream. "Give the fuckers hell!"

Green flares, shot skyward with dull thuds, lit up the night. Jack gasped and recoiled to the back of the hole when he saw the boiling mass of charging Japanese soldiers. To his left, and only 75 yards in front of the Marine line, were several hundred crouching, running Japanese soldiers clotted in small groups. Some waved swords, all of them were screaming incoherently. The Marines opened fire with Springfields, BAR's, .30 caliber machine guns, and even Colt pistols . . . scything down clumps of the attackers. The attacking force was overwhelming though, and soon sliced through the line at the gap junction of D and B Companies. The Japanese force managed to pierce B Company's line at a point that completely isolated the platoon Jack, Turk, and Tom were attached to. They watched in stunned awe as the fanatical enemy surrounded them.

In an instant it seemed, the Japanese were among them, bayoneting and shooting. The Marines picked them off, but not fast enough, all around hand-to-hand struggles ensued. Jack was shocked and confused. He looked on numbly as the battle swirled around him in slow motion, just as it had when he'd made his mad dash for Schmid's position at the Tenaru. He saw a Raider get spliced by a Japanese sword. Another Raider plunged his bayonet into the throat of a Japanese soldier, turning a scream into a horrible, gurgling gag. The sounds of the battle were hellish, otherworldly: screams, howls of pain, curses, gunshots, the crump of grenades and mortars, rifles clashing together, shots . . . the sounds of unimaginable violence. Jack was momentarily paralyzed by fear and shock. It was worse, far worse, than he'd imagined, and far worse than the Tenaru. This time he was in the middle of the fight. In fact, it was impossible for any human who has not experienced it, no matter how much they've studied it, to even begin to know or understand the monstrous horror. He felt an urge to curl up in the fetal position at the bottom of the hole and cover his ears. Then, out of the corner of his eye, he saw Turk rush out of the hole and pick up a rifle from a wounded Marine, raise it and shoot dead two enemy soldiers who'd been advancing on them. After that, he picked up the Marine's ammo pouch and reloaded the gun, then dragged the wounded man to the hole. Tom bent over the injured Marine while Turk leaned forward in the hole, guarding them with the rifle. Tom, Jack noticed, had placed his body between the injured man and the Japanese attack. Suddenly, Jack felt a deep sense of pride and love. They were doing their jobs bravely, loyally, protecting each other and the others. The feelings woke something in him and finally he moved, springing out of the hole as he saw a Marine staggering back from his position, his face bloodied and his right thigh a pulpy mess. He pulled the man's arm around his shoulders and guided him to the hole. He laid him down next to Tom's casualty and immediately began inspecting his wounds.

Tom glanced at Jack and his patient and calmly said, "His lower jaw is mostly shot away. I gotta get some plasma going. What've you got?"

Jack took a deep breath and huffed, "Mid thigh's pretty torn up by shrapnel, but with a tourniquet and some morphine I think he can make it back to the aid station on his own."

"Okay," Tom said. "Do it quick." Jack sprinkled sulfa on the wound, applied a tourniquet to the Marine's upper thigh, then jabbed a morphine syrette into the other leg. In the meantime, Turk had dropped the rifle, even though the battle was still raging around them, and was assisting Tom in getting plasma flowing into the jawless man. They all knew that at any moment a swarm of Japanese soldiers could roll over them, but they worked on.

Jack finished with his patient and quickly shooed him toward the forward aid station. The man muttered, "Thanks, doc," and limped off.

Moments later they heard Captain Sweeney bellow, "1st Platoon, fight your way to the top of the ridge! Pull back 1st Platoon!" He was urging the men to break from their encirclement for the safety of higher ground. Immediately, the platoon's Raiders rose from their holes and began attacking backwards, successfully overrunning the enemy trying to cut them off. Tom though, didn't move. He was applying a bandage to the lower portion of his patient's face.

"C'mon, we gotta move!" Turk yelled.

"Give me a minute. I've got to finish this before we move him." Jack and Turk glanced uneasily at each other. Turk picked up the rifle and once again stood guard. After what seemed an eternity, Tom said calmly, "Okay, let's go." Turk slung his rifle and grabbed the horribly injured Raider by his ankles, while Tom looped his hands under his armpits. They slowly rose out of the hole, Jack holding the plasma bottle above his head. They had gone only a few steps when Jack suddenly spotted a diminutive figure rising out of the dark, brandishing a sword. He was charging directly at Turk, whose back was turned to the attack. Jack froze momentarily, then

436

dropped the plasma bottle and screamed as he moved to intercept the killer. His animal-like warning blended with that of the attacker's fierce cry as the two men closed on each other. Jack ducked, hurling his body at the man's waist, sending him crashing to the ground. The blow had knocked the soldier's sword loose, and a desperate sense of panic swept over Jack as he saw him scrabbling to retrieve it. Jack clawed at the man's trousers trying to keep him from reaching the sword. Several deafening cracks, each briefly interrupted by the metallic crunch of a Springfield bolt being rammed to and fro, roared, and he watched as the enemy's body jerked from the impact of bullets slamming into his chest. Jack, wild eyed, looked back to see Turk lower his rifle, a wan smile on his face.

"Guess that makes us all even in just a few fuckin' seconds, eh?" Jack, speechless and stunned, staggered to his feet, patted Turk on the shoulder and picked up the plasma bottle. Together, the three corpsmen and their patient continued their slow climb to the top of the ridge, following the path swept clear by the Raiders.

Once there, things seemed to quiet down a bit as the Japanese regrouped, though Marine 105mm artillery was now fully in the fight and doing considerable damage to the Japanese. As soon as they'd arrived at their new position, Tom had applied a dose of morphine to his patient and then hollered, "Litter bearers, now!" Within moments, several Marines appeared and hauled the wounded man to the rear.

They collapsed in a previously dug foxhole, checked their medical equipment, and took long pulls off their canteens. Jack couldn't be sure how long it was before any of them spoke, but it was considerable. He looked at his watch and was shocked to see that over two hours had passed since the first wave of attackers had come. At some point during the lull, the rest of B Company joined them. Jack heard Captain Sweeney tell a runner to inform Colonel Edson that the company's fighting strength was down to only 60 men; roughly 10 dead or missing and the rest wounded.

It was Turk who spoke first, "Thanks for stoppin' that fucker from shish-kaboobing me back there, Jacko."

"Don't mention it," Jack replied wearily. "If you hadn't moved so quickly, that son of a bitch would've separated my head from my shoulders . . . would a hurt some, I suspect. Like you said, we're even."

"Both you guys did good," Tom said, "but this thing's far from over." As if on cue, they heard a new attack boiling up the ridge. Red Mike had moved his CP forward to a knoll on the ridge just yards from where the three corpsmen were resting. A loud voice bellowed from in front of Edson's CP.

"Red Mike says it's okay to fall back!"

They heard a nearby forward artillery observer shouting instructions into a radio, "Add 60 and walk it back and forth across the west and center ridge." Shells rained down on the southern slope of the ridge, and fifteen minutes later, delivered by the furious bombardment, the rest of C Company, along with several parachute companies, successfully fell back to the knoll and formed a horseshoe around it; essentially the last significant force standing between the Japanese and Henderson. Jack recalled that the force, numbering just 300 men, was defending against nothing less than a battalion of Japanese soldiers. He observed with much sympathy small clusters of young Marines continuing their withdrawal past the knoll. They were quickly brought back into line by an agitated, acid tongued officer. "Shit," Jack muttered to himself. "Must be Major Bailey. Guy's got balls but you can't hardly blame the boys."

The artillery barrage had decimated the Japanese and had forced them to once again fall back and regroup. Jack, Turk, and Tom took advantage of the lull and moved amongst the men, applying sulfa and bandages to a myriad of shrapnel and bullet flesh wounds. Jack treated a boy who had taken some sort of small explosive blast to his face, pock marking it as though he'd contracted some form of monstrous acne. Miraculously, the boy's eyes had been spared and he stayed in the line. If a Marine could sit or lay and fire a rifle, he stayed in the horseshoe. Only the most grievously injured were evacuated.

After a half hour or so, the continuous, deadly Marine barrage impelled a courageous Japanese officer whose unit was being held in reserve, to ignore orders and assault the ridge. The attack by two Japanese companies fell squarely upon the remnants of B Company, Raiders. The three corpsmen's position was just 15 yards behind the main line. Colonel Edson had ordered the artillery to walk slowly back toward the Marine lines, dangerously close. But this decision severely weakened the enemy attack. Still Jack, his eyes peering just above the rim of the foxhole, was transfixed by the latest horror. He saw the leader of the attack, screaming, his face twisted in rage, racing toward the Marine lines swinging his Samurai sword in wild loops above his head. Marines rolled grenades down the slope into the attackers, blowing small gaps in the phalanx. The 105s were taking a horrible toll, but still the enemy came. Then, the first call came. "Corpsman! Corpsman up goddamn it!"

Tom turned to Turk and ordered, "Cover us, Turk, c'mon, Jack!" Father and son scrambled from the relative safety of their hole and sprinted, crouching, toward the call for help. They followed the shouts and found an impossibly young-looking Raider lying behind a clump of sandbags, moaning softly. His foxhole mate exhorted them to help his buddy, as all the while he fired into the Japanese and intermittently rolled or tossed grenades in their direction.

Jack and Tom crammed on either side of the boy. A moment later Tom declared urgently, "Femoral artery! Get a tourniquet on him fast, Jack! I'm gonna' hook up the plasma." By the light of the flares, Jack quickly tied a tourniquet around the boy's upper thigh; for the first time oblivious to the hell swirling around him. After applying the tourniquet, he could see that the boy was beginning to suffer the effects of massive loss of blood. His eyes were glassy and he wasn't moving; his breathing shallow. It appeared he would lose consciousness any moment.

Jack continually checked the wound to make sure the tourniquet was holding, while Tom completed the initial phase of infusing the boy with plasma. Then he placed a bandage on the wound and compressed it firmly. A rattle of Japanese fire off to their right was followed by curses and screams of pain. It brought Jack back to the battle and he looked up and saw a group of seven or eight Japanese soldiers, just 20 yards away, penetrate the Marine line. Some jumped into foxholes, and Jack could see that invariably, the smaller Japanese were shortly flung back out, shot or stabbed to death. He felt no pity for them, none. He only felt a deep hatred for the enemy soldiers and a sort of disbelief. It seemed bizarrely audacious, these were his boys. What right had they?

Jack turned back to his patient and was relieved to see that the plasma was already taking affect. The boy's eyes were alert and his breaths were deeper. Jack forced a smiled and said, "It's your lucky day, son. We got to you just in time."

"Thanks, doc," the boy grunted.

Tom looked at his son and said quietly, "Congratulations, buddy, you did good." Jack looked down at his young patient, smiling with satisfaction. Just as he did, he heard a crack and the boy's head jerked. He watched in horror as a small geyser of blood shot out of a small hole above the boy's right ear. Dazed, he stared at the dead soldier for several moments.

"Oh, Jesus . . . oh god!" he yelled, his voice choked with anger and grief. "They shot him. One of the fucking bastards shot him!"

"What?" Tom yelled.

"The goddamn motherfuckers killed him! His fight was over and the bastards killed him anyway!" A deep, uncontrollable rage overwhelmed him. He lunged for the dead boy's Tommy gun and rose. Turning toward the Japanese attack, he screamed, "I saved him you fucking animals!" He fired off several bursts, the submachine gun slugging his shoulder repeatedly. He barely felt the hand that dragged him back down behind the sand bags. In a fog he heard a firm voice.

"Jack," Tom said. "Get rid of it. We have more work to do. Just get rid of it. He's dead . . . there's nothing you can do about it!" Jack turned and looked at his father for a moment. He was looking at Jack intensely, no sign of sympathy in his eyes.

"Yeah," Jack said slowly. "They need us don't they?"

"Yes! Now you ready to get back to work?"

"Yeah, I'm ready."

They dashed back to their hole, waiting for the next call for help.

The latest attack had spent itself, but Jack knew it was not the end. The Japanese graciously announced each renewed assault with a cluster of red flares flung skyward. Several attacks were again repulsed with the aid of the supporting artillery. After each assault, Jack, Tom, and Turk would respond to the calls for a corpsman, treat the injured as best they could, and send them to the rear. Several times, their response to cries for a corpsman had them finding only a corpse, a shocked and grieving buddy asking them to perform what could only be a miracle. Jack carried on only by the aid of bursts of adrenalin and a numbed shock that had settled his senses.

During a lull he looked at his watch and was stunned to see it was 0130. Though the actual events and movements of the battle seemed to proceed in slow motion, time itself seemed to accelerate. He rubbed his eyes and shook his head, trying his best to remain alert. The Japanese assault seemed to be ebbing along much of the front; the intensity and regularity of the attacks were less frequent and aggressive. Jack prayed that for him, Turk and his father, the battle was over. His prayer went unanswered for moments later a mortar shell exploded some 30 yards to their right, followed by several agonized screams for a corpsman.

"C'mon guys, let's go!" Tom barked. Crouching, they scurried forward. They quickly came upon a cluster of four men hiding behind a two-foot-high rocky crag. Jack was briefly taken aback, recognizing it as the same miniature Gibraltar he'd observed on his jeep excursion to the ridge weeks before. If it was an omen, he had no way of knowing if it was good or bad. One of the men had been hit in the buttocks with grenade fragments and was not seriously wounded. The other though, had been hit in the lower arm, shattering his wrist. He was rapidly losing blood. Tom immediately went to work wrapping a tourniquet around his arm, then cleaning and dressing the wound. At the same time, Turk was administering plasma. Jack meanwhile, had pulled the trousers off the other man and was picking out jagged metal fragments from his buttocks with a forceps. When he was done, he wiped the wounds, applied sulfa, and taped a large dressing over the man's speckled rear end. Amidst the carnage, he heard an unexpected chuckle.

He looked over at Tom, who had finished with his patient, and saw him grinning. It provided Jack with some much needed comfort. "Nice work, pal. You handled that fat ass like a pro."

"Very funny," Jack responded dully. "Hey . . . is your guy okay?"

"He is now. He wouldn't have lasted too long if he kept spilling blood like he was."

"Good job, bud . . . you saved his life." Tom ignored the comment, but Jack hoped all the work he'd done on the ridge would restore some of his father's confidence.

Tom rose to his feet, "Okay, let's get these guys back." Just as he finished speaking, a nearby rifle barked. Tom jerked back a step and clamped a hand over his lower left side; then crumpled slowly to the ground.

"Christ!" Jack grunted. He quickly scrambled over to his father's side; Tom's face was twisted in pain. Jack carefully examined the wound. He'd been shot where the upper thigh joins the torso, just an inch or so from his penis. Blood flowed steadily from the wound, but not in the gushing pulses he'd seen from other casualties. Jack shouted back to the two unhurt Marines to take their comrades to the rear. Then he yelled for Turk, who'd been crouching several yards away on the look out for other casualties or enemy soldiers.

"Turk, Tom's hit! Give me a hand!" Jack turned to his father and asked, "How you feeling, buddy?"

Tom forced a tortured smile and said, "It stings a bit. How bad does it look?"

"It's real clean, but it's bleeding pretty badly." Jack was surprised at his own sense of calm and confidence.

"Is it a steady flow?" Tom asked weakly.

"Yeah, real steady."

"Nothing real important was hit then. Just compress it a bit, clean it, bandage me up and get on to the other guys."

Jack quickly went to work on his father. The main Japanese attack had once again been blunted by the outnumbered Marines, and the battle had largely died down. Sporadic volleys of gunfire still erupted and Marine artillery continued to hammer the Japanese on the south slope of the ridge. As he compressed his father's wound, he marveled at the man. He'd never had the slightest inkling that his father had been seriously wounded; the scar being in a perfect spot for concealment if one wished it to be concealed. He briefly wondered why his mother had never told him, even after his father had died. After a minute, Jack raised his hand off the wound.

"Oh, thank god," he sighed. "The bleeding's subsided." Jack cleaned the wound, poured sulfa on it, and applied a field dressing. While he was doing this, Turk inserted a plasma needle into Tom's arm and looped the bottle around the low branch of small tree. Moments later, a wounded marine, his dungarees soaked in blood, staggered toward them, then collapsed 10 yards away. Turk rushed toward the boy, while Jack hesitated, hovering over his father.

"I'm fine," Tom said. "Go give Turk a hand. I can already feel the plasma lighting things up."

"You sure?" Jack asked.

"Go!" his father ordered. Jack rose and scurried toward Turk who was already working on the Raider's shattered shoulder. But, moments after he arrived, he heard a banshee-like scream and the scuffle of running feet. He looked back toward his father, and to his horror saw a Japanese soldier rushing at him with a raised bayonet, screaming, *"You die!"* The soldier was larger than an average Japanese and his face was made ugly, monstrous, by a look of hatred and rage.

"God!" Jack screamed. He leapt up and sprinted toward his father, positioning himself between him and his executioner. The Japanese soldier lifted the bayonet-tipped rifle above his head and prepared to bring it down on Tom. Just as it started its downward arc, Jack reached up and grabbed the end of the rifle with both hands. For a second, though it seemed like an eternity, Jack struggled with the soldier, pushing the bayonet away, gazing into his raging eyes. The Japanese boy was too strong though, too young. After several seconds Jack's arms slipped off the stock and the bayonet ran through him just below the sternum. He heard an animal like scream as the blade penetrated his body. As in an echo chamber, the scream seemed distant; otherworldly. The burning pain though, radiating to all points of his body, caused him to realize the agonized scream was his own. In ethereal slow motion once again, he sensed the Japanese soldier attempting to pull the blade out. But now, instead of pushing against the rifle stock, he grimly held the blade in place. Out of the corner of his eye he could see Turk struggling to un-shoulder his weapon. He couldn't allow the bayonet to be freed as his father was lying helpless at his feet. He watched as the Japanese boy's eyes grew wide in shock and confusion. The Japanese soldier noticed Jack glance pleadingly toward Turk; he quickly followed Jack's gaze and howled just as Turk pulled the trigger and sent a bullet into his brain. Jack imagined he could actually see the slug enter the soldier's skull. A squirt of blood flew from the enemy's head, his arms violently releasing the rifle. He fell heavily to the ground, dead before he landed. Jack didn't have the strength to hold the rifle up, as the majority of the weight was in the butt end. The bayonet twisted up, ripping through his body. He screamed in agony again and slowly dropped to his knees. Then, he fell backward, his head and shoulders lying on his father's chest, his legs contorted and tucked behind his back. As if in a dream, he heard Turk curse, then vaguely sensed him kneel alongside, ripping open his shirt.

"Don't worry, Jacko," Turk said. "Ol' Turk's on the job. You're gonna be just fine, pal. It's not too bad. Not for a fuckin' tough old nut like you." Jack felt Tom reach down to his wound and probe it with his fingers. After a few seconds, he suddenly pulled his hand away and let out a deep, tortured sigh. Jack slowly twisted his head up and looked at his father. Illuminated by flares, and for the third time in his life, Jack saw tears well in his eyes.

444

Turk was working furiously, compressing the wound and sprinkling sulfa all at once. He handed Tom a morphine syrette which he immediately jabbed into Jack's arm. The morphine brought quick relief from the searing pain, but Jack began to feel an indescribable weariness. He grabbed his father's hand. Then his father, grimacing in pain, removed the plasma needle from his own arm and inserted it into his son's. Tom gently stroked his son's hair. "You saved my life," he said. "You're a good man, bud, and you're a great medic."

Jack smiled, then started to cough; his breathing labored. "C'mon, Jack," Turk urged softly. "Hang in there, pal." Jack could hear Turk, but his voice was rising and falling, as if he were shouting through a gale . . . near at once, then far. He felt increasingly light headed and tired.

Jack looked up at his friend and managed a weak smile, softly saying, "It's okay, buddy." The irresistible weariness gripped tighter and he closed his eyes. Again, as if in a dream, he felt Turk lightly slapping his face and shouting.

"Hey, you know what buddy?" Turk asked. "I'm gonna tell you where all them fuckin' beers been comin' from as long as you agree to fight this little nick you got. You ready to listen up?"

"Yeah, okay," Jack whispered.

"Well that ugly fucker Sturgeon I told you about, remember?" Jack nodded slowly. "Well he ain't made up and he's from South Philly just like me. You see, Sturgeon, he was a hell of a bookie before the war and after he shipped out he had all kinds of bastards holdin' IOU's. Well, he and I cut a deal. When the war's over, I, along with a few of my pals, will lay the muscle down on anyone who owes ol' Sturgeon a dime. His part of the bargain is to supply me with the Jap beer I been givin' ya and the boys. Don't know where the fucker has it stashed, but him being an old WWI gunny seems to have given him some sort of special rights."

Jack smiled, "That's great, Turk. But after the war, stick to your singing, okay? It's a gift, son. Not many get one . . . most of us are just schlubs . . . not you though; you got it. Sturgeon will do just fine without you."

445

"Okay, Jack, whatever you say," Turk said sincerely.

Jack thought of Laura and the kids, praying he would journey back to them along the same metaphysical path that had brought him here, though somehow he was quite certain he wouldn't. "Ian . . ." he whispered. "Ian will take care of everything, buddy. Ian will make sure everything's okay." As Turk continued compressing the deep gash in his midsection, Jack suddenly vomited a gob of scarlet blood. It splashed onto his cheeks and rolled onto his father's neck and chest.

"Christ!" Turk gasped. "Hang on, pal." With great effort, Jack opened his eyes and offered Turk a small grin.

"It's okay, bud," Jack said calmly. He slowly reached up and stroked the boy's stubbly cheek, then let his hand fall away. It landed on top of a small, coral rock. With great effort, Jack lifted it from the soil of the ridge. He reached for his father's hand and opened it wide. He planted the rock firmly in Tom's hand, then tightly wrapped his palm and fingers around it. "Remember me, Tom," Jack said, barely above a whisper. "Remember my faith in you."

Jack saw his father's knuckles turn white, as he clutched the rock tightly. Tom was softly weeping. "Okay," he choked. "I'll remember . . . I'll do my best . . . I love you, buddy."

Jack smiled and a calm sense of peace enveloped him, "I love you, too," he weakly replied.

At that moment the skies opened and a warm tropical rain washed over them, mixing their blood together as it ran into the torn soil of the ridge. Jack pleasingly believed it to be a divine symbol of the immortal words between father and son that had finally been spoken. Turk leaned away, his own tears adding to the deluge. Jack, the son whose father once told him he'd regretted the name he bestowed upon him, clutched Tom tighter. For the first time since his father died back in the world, he felt completely at peace and his smile widened, deeply grateful at the divine opportunity to save the life he'd taken. As his heart fluttered, then took its last beat, the peaceful smile remained, undisturbed.

EPILOGUE

August 10, 2002—Grand Rapids, Michigan

The old man, still attired in the musty brown linen suit he'd worn at the Point Cruz Yacht Club on Guadalcanal days earlier, crawled into the taxi parked curbside at the airport. In spite of his son's urgings to check into their hotel and get some rest, he insisted on having the taxi take them directly to their prime destination. The tropical flower that had adorned his lapel on Guadalcanal had been replaced with a white carnation he'd purchased from a floral vendor at O'Hare, just before they'd boarded the small plane that would take them on the brief flight across Lake Michigan; the last leg of their long journey. The taxi pulled away from the curb and was soon gliding past the strip malls and cookie cutter developments of the Midwest American city.

Minutes later, they were slowly cruising past manicured lawns and impeccably kept homes. The old man's watery eyes looked upon the pristine landscapes of the suburban community and children frolicking, not on dusty roads as he was accustomed, but in backyard pools and cedar play structures as mothers or other minders watched over their broods in the sublime comfort of their cozy environs. It was much as the old man expected; his dear friend had described it well. The vast majority were not rich, and most homes were unpretentious, though on the whole it was a sort of paradise for those souls who could truly appreciate it for what it held, without ensnaring themselves in its false promises. The taxi finally

447

pulled into the driveway of a home in one of the old money neighborhoods of the community. The house they'd arrived at was a beautiful Victorian structure, containing several recently added wings and immaculate gardens. The old man thrust the cab fare over the seatback into the face of the driver who gently removed the cash from his trembling, caramel colored hands. Then, he struggled slowly out of the car, tersely rejecting any assistance from his son. As he had on Guadalcanal several days earlier, he tightly clutched the battered British medical journal; its contents yellowed by time, but still easily decipherable. He checked once again for the wedding ring in his suit pocket. From his breast pocket he pulled two photographs and tucked them inside the front cover of the journal. One, a grainy black and white photo yellowed by time, depicted a crude wooden cross aligned in sandy soil with other crosses, a dark, ominous jungle as a backdrop. The cross had a metal tag and small palm frond nailed to it, its words indiscernible. The other also pictured a cross, but much different from the first. The brightly colored Polaroid depicted a gleaming white marble cross surrounded by the manicured green grass of the vast U.S. military cemetery in Manila. The words on this cross were easily read. The old man, looped his arm through his son's, and walked slowly to the front door.

"You okay, father?" the son asked.

"I'm bloody fine!" the old man grunted indignantly. "Ring the bell, will you?" The son complied, though not loosening the grip on his father's arm. A dog yapped and they heard a young girl cry out. "Little Grace," the old man said out loud, a knowing, affectionate grin creasing his face. Moments passed, but soon they heard a lock being released and the heavy front door swung open, leaving only a screened door between them and the interior. Standing before them was an attractive, though harried looking young woman. The trio stared at each other for several moments, then the old man, tears spilling as they had several days before, spoke.

"Laura?"

"Yes," the woman replied uncertainly. "May I help you?"

448

The old man bowed slightly and said, "Mrs. Macmillan, my name is Ian Smith. I am an old and dear friend of your husband. I have been waiting many years to have the honor of calling on you. My son and I have traveled a great distance to meet with you." He held up the journal and said quietly, "There is much we have to talk about."

After hesitating briefly, Laura opened the screened door and welcomed them inside.

THE END